"Monsieur Belmont ~~Reme~~, ~~........~~ ~~........~~ my pleasure to introduce Monsieur Sam Clemens."

Clemens—later to be known as Mark Twain—caught his glass with his left hand and extended his right for me to shake. I seized it, trying not to let my fingers tremble. His hand was surprisingly delicate, and I realized that his oversized head made one forget his slight frame.

"I was sired by the Great American Eagle and foaled by a continental dam . . .!" And so he launched into his burlesque of a Fourth of July oration. My head was too busy for me to follow along. Discreetly if I could, baldly if I must, I had to discover his plans—if such a careless young raconteur was capable of them. Then and only then would I be free to pursue my own ends. . . .

Ace books by Kirk Mitchell

PROCURATOR
NEW BARBARIANS
NEVER THE TWAIN

KIRK MITCHELL

NEVER *the* TWAIN

ACE BOOKS, NEW YORK

This book is an Ace original edition,
and has never been previously published.

NEVER THE TWAIN

An Ace Book/published by arrangement with
the author

PRINTING HISTORY
Ace edition/November 1987

ISBN: 0-441-56973-0

Ace Books are published by
The Berkley Publishing Group,
200 Madison Avenue, New York, New York 10016.
The name "Ace" and the "A" logo are
trademarks belonging to Charter Communications, Inc.
PRINTED IN THE UNITED STATES OF AMERICA

10 9 8 7 6 5 4 3 2 1

Acknowledgments

I wish to thank Bernard Deitchman, who—now in his eighth decade of intellectual prowess—remains a tireless defender of what the Bancroft Library persists in cataloguing as *The Rettie Apocrypha*. Certain details in the original handwritten text required elucidation beyond Belmont Rettie's passing references; desiring nothing as obtrusive as footnotes, I wedged these slivers of information into the body of his narrative. For many of these clarifications I offer my appreciation to the staffs of the Nevada State Library in Carson City, the Chollar Mine in Virginia City, and the Pioneer Memorial Museum in Salt Lake City. The latter displayed to an inveterate Roman Catholic the patience and warmth long associated with the followers of the Mormon faith. And, of course, my editing of the Rettie papers could never have been attempted without making use of Dan De Quille's *The Big Bonanza* (1876), which Rettie himself borrowed from in describing Nevada-style legalese in Chapter 23 of this work, and A.M. Phillips's "Time Travel Happens!" in *Unknown* magazine (1939). I thank G.P. Putnam's Sons for permission to reprint the final chapter from *The Vanishing Gedankist*; and my archbishop and my dean of faculty for allowing me the time and resources with which to complete this project—they, as I, immediately glimpsed how these papers chronicle a spiritual odyssey, despite the *via vulgata* Rettie most often traveled. Lastly, I must express my gratitude to Susan Allison, who saved me from the purgatory of my own good intentions and suggested how this tale might be presented to a world that questions all its miracles.

Fr. Kirk Mitchell, SJ
University of San Francisco
2226 Anno Domini

THE TRIBULATIONS

1

"HOWARD, COME OUT here," Marguerite said. Her ordinarily sweet and sexy voice, that of a very fat woman, was strained. "Something's terribly wrong with the mail."

I refused to get up and hurry through the open door to the outer office. I was on the phone, three hundred dollar Italian shoes propped up on my oaken rolltop desk as I watched the Golden Gate Bridge skim through shards of fog.

"Howard, please—the mailman was just here . . . it's *weird*."

"I'm on the line with Amtrak, for Chrissake!" I hissed, palming the mouthpiece. Then I smiled, hoping it would not be attenuated to a snarl by the glass fiber that linked me to the bureaucrat across town. "So you're still feeling a little rough this morning, Bruce?"

He groaned. "When did we quit, Mr. Hart?"

"I dunno—three, four. Who counts when you're having fun? And what's this Mr. Hart crap? You're talking to *Howie*, Bruce ol' buddy."

He chuckled, then sucked air over his back teeth like he'd been cut. "Ouch—my head. I guess we got a bit tight."

"Tight? We got *ripped*. And I intend to postpone the hangover

3

until medical science comes up with a way to cure the bastards. Want to join me? How about the bar at your hotel in half an hour for Bloody Marys?"

"Mr. Hart, last night was really fun. I didn't want to spoil it with Amtrak business, but . . ."

I didn't have to listen to his words to know that my dreams were breaking up on the shoals of his explanations. Eyes bleared, I stared out the curved bay windows of my office, the third floor of a converted Queen Anne Victorian. After an investment that included everything I could lay claim to—and some things I probably shouldn't have, my plan to connect San Francisco to a Sierra Nevada ski resort with weekend rail service was foundering in the undulant sound waves issuing from the receiver.

"So the bottom line is this," Bruce from Amtrak concluded, "a national park is really inviolate, even for an administration friendly to business, like this one."

"God, I really appreciate that," I heard myself saying, self-preservation overriding the sudden urge to tell him off. The yet uncombusted brandy was sloshing around in my stomach like carbolic. "Did I mention last night that my corporation contributed ten thousand to the Sierra Club in tax year 1985?"

"I think so," he said vaguely. "But that changes nothing. Your spur would still have to cross one mile of lands inside Yosemite."

"On an *existing* rail bed. Didn't we go into this?"

"Yes," he said more definitely. "But that logging line was abandoned in 1902 and allowed to revert to forest."

"Forest? Bruce, old man, let's hop in my Mercedes and run up there today—"

"Oh . . . no driving . . . no motion . . ."

"Then trust me, that line still cuts through the park like a freeway. I could clear it with a lawn mower."

"Mr. Hart . . ." He began swallowing—loudly, rhythmically.

"Promise me this, buddy—let me come back to Washington and talk to your people. I put on one hell of a dog and pony show."

"We'll see." He gagged. "I'll phone . . ." Then, clumsily, he hung up, cutting short some sounds that, had they continued, might have persuaded me to gallop for the washroom down the hall.

"Howard?" Marguerite called from the outer office again. "Are you finished? I want you to—" Her phone rang. Except that it didn't really ring—it chirped like crickets, the option she had taken over Big Ben chimes. "Good morning, Hart Enterprises, Incorp— Oh, hello, Louie. He's not in yet. May I take a message?"

"Wait," I said, "let me talk to the son of a bitch."

"Oh, hang on, Louie—here he comes through the front door right now."

I clenched the receiver as if it were a sap. "Louie?!"

"Howie?!" he mimicked my anger.

"You tell Cletus I know he's pulling strings with Amtrak back in D.C. If he sinks this project, I'm going to slit his throat on both sides!"

"Can I tape this?"

"Yet bet!" However, the beeping in the background brought me back to my senses, as Louie had known it would. He was one of my ex-father-in-law's second-string attorneys, and we'd been drinking buddies in better days. But now that the Cavanaughs had tasked him with needling me over trivial matters, usually related to the boilerplate of the divorce agreement, we'd parted company. Still, in remembrance of our former friendship, we both cultivated a sense of proportion during these dealings.

"Please give my regards to Cletus and Eleanor," I said pleasantly, knowing that they would be listening to this cassette later in the day at their penthouse atop the fifty-six stories of the Cavanaugh Industries Towers on Rincon Hill. "How are the dear Cavanaughs?"

"Where's the brooch, Howie?"

"What brooch?"

He sighed. "Let me describe it to you. We are discussing an heirloom of the Beauchamp-Cavanaugh family—"

"Beauchamp . . . Beauchamp—are these the same illiterates who pillaged nineteenth century Nevada?"

Louie ignored the barb. "The piece of jewelry at issue is made of solid silver, so be wary of its softness. Don't scratch it."

I took a swig of disgustingly cold coffee. "It must be valuable."

"No, it's of modest value—but has great familial significance to your former wife. It was fashioned from bullion smelted from the first ore extracted from the Madonna Consolidated Mine in Virginia City, Nevada—"

"—in 1859," I finished for him. "It was presented to Eleanor

Louise Beauchamp, my former wife's namesake and great-great-great grandmother, by her uncle, one of five grubby conspirators who finagled Henry Comstock out of his claim and went on to make millions while poor old Henry drifted away to eventually put a bullet in his brain."

I must have said this more severely than I'd thought, for Louie asked with what sounded like genuine concern: "You doing okay?"

"Yes," I lied, visualizing Eleanor and Cletus sipping toddies and smiling askance at each other as they listened to the tape. "I'm a survivor. A fighter. Orphans are tough. And I don't know where Eleanor's goddamned brooch is. . . ." Meanwhile, I had removed it from a pigeonhole in my rolltop desk and was slowly turning the tarnished, heart-shaped piece between my fingers. The work was anything but delicate, and the motif was oversentimentalized by calla lilies in full droop. Still, the brooch had been an object of fascination to me ever since I had first glimpsed it at the apex of Eleanor's cleavage during the Stanford Young Republicans mixer at which we'd met. "So, let's move right along to the next indignity, Louie."

"Okay, sure. Just between us," he said, as if he were leaning across our old corner table in the bar at the Top of the Mark, "why'd you marry her?"

"The truth?"

"If you're capable."

I could picture Eleanor and Cletus holding their tumblers still so the ice wouldn't clink, locking those identical, predacious stares as they waited for my answer. "Well, when I was still an economics undergrad, I went to a seminar at the Palo Alto Holiday Inn—How to Be a Millionaire Before You're Thirty. There must have been twelve of them—"

"Twelve what?" he prompted, ever the attorney under that desultory affability.

"Young millionaires—are you listening? One right after the other—telling us hopefuls in three-piece suits how, with intelligence, unmitigated drive, and faith in the American Way, they had pulled it off. They all spewed the same party line—except the last one. He staggered to the podium, eyes red, and said—"

"You mean he was drunk?"

"*Bombed*. And he said, 'Everything you've heard up to now's been bullshit. . . .' Needless to say, the pep rally got real quiet all of a sudden. 'You Horatio Algers want to know how we did it?' Everybody just stared at the poor bastard, waiting for someone to drag him off by the tie. 'Sure you want to know. You all paid a hundred bucks a head to get in the door, didn't you? You jerks all want to be millionaires, don't you? Well, forget everything you've heard today—the crock about us winning our fortunes on the bloodied sands of free enterprise. A spoonful of pap for wanna-be's. Know why? Because not one son of a bitch up here earned a dollar of it! Here's the one hundred dollar secret—ready? We all *married* it!'"

Louie was silent for a long moment. "The Cavanaughs want the brooch, Howie—bad."

"I don't have it."

"Like the Frederic Remington you didn't have—then auctioned off last year?"

Marguerite's ample face appeared through the partially opened door, her lovely green eyes frantic. Occasionally, in a fleeting moment like this, I was reminded of what a breathtaking Irish-Spanish beauty she had once been.

"Hang on a moment, Louie." I cupped my hand over the phone. "Give me the mail, Marguerite."

"There isn't any."

"What do you mean? We get mail every morning."

"The postman said he can't deliver it anymore."

"You mean he's on strike or something?"

"I don't know. He said to phone the postmaster if we have any questions."

"*What?*" I took my shoes off the desk. "Hey, Louie, I got to run."

"Where you going to be this afternoon?"

"Why?"

"I thought we might get togther for a drink at the Mark."

This made me pause. Ever since the divorce, Louie had let me know in no uncertain terms that, his affection for me notwith-standing, I now belonged on Molokai with Father Damien and the rest of the lepers. "You still working for Cletus?"

"Of course I'm still working for the Cavanaughs."

"Then *why* do you suddenly want to get together, Louie? This is Howard Hart speaking—the friend you dropped like a hot potato. Level with me, dammit."

"All right." He chuckled. "I wanted to lay some papers on

you. Now you can plan on dodging our process server for the next few weeks."

"No, there's something more to this than harassing me with another chickenshit lawsuit."

"You still sleeping with that librarian in Sausalito?"

"No, she got married."

"Damn—that means I got some legwork to do. How about giving me a hint about the latest one?"

"Sure. She's bigger than a bread box but smaller than the national debt. Bye." I hung up and sat thinking about what the Cavanaughs might be up to—as Marguerite stood glaring at me. Finally she gave up and went back to her desk, probably to scratch out more calligraphy, one of a dozen nervous habits she had acquired in the last twelve years.

I had fibbed to Louie: There was no woman at the moment. And, I admitted to myself as I put away the brooch, I'd married Eleanor because, of all the eligible young heiresses I had been stalking, she was the one I'd fallen in love with. I was probably still in love with her. Then why had I stolen the brooch from her black enameled jewelry box? I'm really not sure, although I've always stolen small things. Brother Tom and a regiment of Franciscan disciplinarians at Our Lady Clare Orphanage had never been able to break me of it, and the shrink the Cavanaughs had sent me to when they began suspecting my infidelity had grunted softly when I confessed this blatantly impulsive behavior. That was his only editorial on my then thirty-two years, other than: "Your time is up, Mr. Hart. . . ."

I strolled into the outer office to make amends for ignoring Marguerite. "Okay . . . what's this mail thing about?"

"I don't know!" she said, chins trembling. "The postman—he dropped by and said he was sorry but he couldn't deliver our mail. That's all he—"

More chirping. Two telephone lines had lit up within an instant of each other. She answered both, putting them on hold. "Mr. Ashkenazy on one . . . the landlord on two."

"Tell the landlord I'm gone for the day. I'll take Ashkenazy's call in my office." I shut the door and put on my velvet voice, careful once again to project a smile into the transmitter. "Walt, how are—"

"Confused."

"How's that?"

"Well, you know the check I was going to send you?"

"Sure—I forget the amount right now."

"Fifteen thousand."

"Of course."

"Well, the letter got sent back to me."

"I don't understand."

"That makes two of us, Hart. It's stamped: Return to Sender—Order Issued against Addressee for Violation of False Representation Law."

I could feel my smile twist into a sickened grin.

"You still there, Hart?"

"Yes, although I'm utterly dismayed—"

"Yeah, sure. Well, I had my doubts about this thing all along. In case you've forgotten, I've already entrusted you with ten grand. If you're being investigated by the feds, I want it back—now, Hart. Today. Otherwise I'm turning this over to my attorney. Today."

"Walt, there's been some kind of ridiculous mistake. You know the post office—"

Mr. Ashkenazy had hung up on me.

Slowly, I replaced the receiver in its cradle. Then I picked it up again with my left hand while my right riffled through the phone book for the postmaster's number. The line was ringing when I decided to disconnect. I dialed the intercom instead: "Marguerite, didn't Rodrigo do some work for the Postal Service recently?"

There followed a long, miserable pause—her usual martyrdom in response to mention of his name. "I think so."

"Good—that could help clear this up."

"A Mr. Treacher is waiting to see you."

"Client?"

"No."

"Prospective?"

"Not likely."

"Does he look like a cop, for Chrissake?"

"I don't think so."

I took a deep breath, held it, then exhaled. "Okay, send him in."

An enormous man minced through the door, crossing my office with arms held closely against his sides, as if he were fearful of breaking things. "Howard Coolbrith-Hart, I presume?"

I said nothing at first. Only a seventy-year-old Franciscan monk and Rodrigo Estrada, my de facto brother, knew that I had a hyphenated name. And, clearly, I could hear the hyphen—that illicit link between two famous names—in the stranger's precise enunciation.

He smiled. Then he looked right through me as if Bret Harte and Ina Coolbrith waited somewhere beyond my eyes.

2

HE HAD THE ruddy but unvaricosed complexion of an Irish soccer player who still has his drinking under control. Yet there was no bluster to the man, and his speech was as neatly clipped as his chestnut-colored beard. "Mr. Hart, my name is Geoffrey Treacher. May I call you Howard?"

I nodded, trying to figure out what kind of enforcement agency would hire a man whose corduroy coat and piebald chukka boots had Salvation Army written all over them.

He broke off his watery stare to admire the Victorian Gothic furniture and apointments of my office, beginning with the button-tufted wing chair in which he slouched. "This is all so very nice . . . so *epochal*." He smiled at the heavy velvet curtains, the gold-scrolled wallpaper, the rolltop inlaid with mother-of-pearl—before his eyes lit on the gilt-framed lithograph over my desk. "Ah, the Beauchamp mansion in Virginia City."

"Yes, my former wife is a Beauchamp-Cavanaugh."

"I know," he said, then offered nothing more.

I decided to hold my ground and force him to divulge his purposes. I sat back and admired the fine old house. Owing to the mountain slope on which Virginia City had been erected, the ancestral estate of my ex-in-laws had been reached by climbing a steep staircase that cleaved a twelve-foot high granite parapet. Now, waiting for Treacher to explain himself, I surmounted those stone steps and peered up at the donjonlike tower.

"It's a shame the place was lost in the great fire of 1875," he murmured.

"Yes."

"And you must have a feeling for that era—to so charmingly reproduce it in your surroundings."

"My former wife and I made a hobby of collecting Victorian antiques." I made sure he noticed me checking my wristwatch. "You're not from the U.S. Postal Service, by chance?"

He laughed at the suggestion. "Oh, forgive me, Mr. Hart. Let me tell you why I've intruded on you. Through a friend, I was able to use the genealogical library of the Church of Jesus Christ of Latter-day Saints." He paused, smiling.

I suppose he was waiting for me to volunteer that I was a Mormon. On occasion I had pretended to be one, if only to take advantage of the assumption by Gentiles, as Saints call nonbelievers, that Mormon businesses are as well-run as Mormon households. But in truth I was Roman Catholic down to the beads. My father, a lapsed Saint, had fallen prey to Vatican-style evangelism: My mother had said no until he said yes to the Bishop of Rome. But for the moment I decided to remain noncommittal. "Does this have something to do with Ina Coolbrith?"

"It does." He hesitated briefly. "Do you mind discussing that branch of your family history?"

I hiked a shoulder. "Why would this interest you?"

"Oh, please forgive me. . . ." Treacher began frisking himself for a business card, I assumed, but finally gave up. "I'm an associate professor at Berkeley, American literature, and—"

"You're doing a doctoral thesis on my great-great-great-grandfather, Bret Harte."

Treacher's eyes began glistening, and he had to compose himself before he could ask, "Good Lord, has someone else approached you about this?"

"No, I was simply putting two and two together."

"I see," he sighed, then chuckled. "Well, to be completely up-front with you, my project deals with the famous literary rivalry between Harte and Mark Twain."

"Who won?"

"I'm afraid your ancestor came up with the short end of the stick."

"Figures."

"What I'm begging of you, Mr. Hart, is just few minutes of your time. . . ."

I was tempted to send him away—after all, my corporate ship had been torpedoed by the federal bureaucracy this morning and was now threatening to capsize in a sea of red ink. Yet, perhaps for this very reason, I heard myself inviting him to stay. And maybe I felt like gloating a little: In a backdoor way, I was as much San Francisco aristocracy as the Cavanaughs, although I had not used this fact to mitigate my prenuptial with Eleanor, which contained only slightly fewer codicils than the Duke of Windsor's when he took his commoner for better or for worse. I had hidden something from my future in-laws: Bret Harte had been a quarter Jewish—and the Cavanaughs associated Jews with trade unions, covens of Democrats, and other forms of populist revolt. Even a whisper of Semitism this faint would have been enough to land me on their veranda atop my luggage.

Yet now that I had been cut off forever from the Cavanaughs and their mind-boggling fortune, I found myself feeling proud of this bastardized lineage I had once concealed—and would have buzzed Marguerite for more coffee. But after she had joined a Catholic feminist group, we'd struck a deal that she would make the morning's first pot if I made all the others.

"Fire away, Mr. Treacher."

"Oh, thank you, Mr. Hart, I know how busy you must be."

"Please call me Howard."

"Of course. I want to know *everything*." He eased back in the winged chair, stroking his beard as he waited for me to find some place to begin.

"Well, if this is the subject of your thesis, you know ten times what I do."

"Perhaps. But so far I've had no access to an oral history from your side of the family. And it seems that you are Bret Harte's sole surviving descendant."

That was news. "I am? What about the *respectable* Hartes?"

"The last one died childless some years ago."

I sat a little taller. "Well, let's see . . . Ina Donna Coolbrith . . ." Haltingly at first, but then with rising confidence as Treacher leaned forward and planted his elbows on his knees, I told how my great-great-great-grandmother on my father's side had been born a niece of Joseph Smith, the martyred Mormon prophet. Married at an early age—but to no *Saint* in any sense of the word—she'd followed her drunken husband to Los Angeles. Pathologically jealous, he was a wife beater; and in an age when corporal punishment for wives, children, and servants was upheld by the law, she could find safety only in flight. Escape to the fledgling city of San Francisco led to other forms of rebellion, and Ina fell in with a coterie of self-styled Bohemians, young poets and writers who aspired to capture the woolly spirit of the burgeoning West. Among them was the rather reserved private secretary to the surveyor general—known to his friends as Frank B. Harte; and a shabby twenty-eight-year-old journalist newly arrived from Virginia City, who hid his rapacious literary ambitions behind a slouch and a careless Missouri drawl.

Rumor had it that my lovely, gray-eyed poetess of a great-great-great-grandmother had taken both Frank Harte and Sam Clemens as her lovers, and Treacher now confirmed his knowledge of this with an unconscious nod. I hesitated at this juncture, uncertain how to proceed. My instincts for profit were chittering inside my head, for I now suspected that I possessed something Treacher needed—badly. "Pardon my asking something, Geoff . . ."

"No, no, please, Howard—go right ahead. Anything."

"Are you doing this project . . . unaided?" I tried to keep my gaze from commenting on his tawdry appearance.

"Oh, no!" he blurted proudly. "I won a very generous grant from the John W. Mackay Foundation!"

"Congratulations."

Probably unbeknown to Treacher, none other than Cletus Beauchamp-Cavanaugh sat on the Mackay Foundation's board of trustees, and Cavanaugh Industries played tax games by donating hundreds of thousands to this Comstock-born philanthropy each year. Now I knew exactly how to proceed. "Well, accident or not, Ina carried Harte's child . . ." I purposely avoided corroborating the paternity of this child with any evidence, and prattled on about how she had become aware of her pregnancy at the same time Harte's wife, a soprano in the choir at the church he attended, had, to the chagrin of his Bohemian friends, finally succeeded in transforming him into the quintessence of a proper Victorian husband. Ina swallowed her pride and returned to Salt Lake City to bear her natural child. There in the heart of Deseret—the Mormon empire so ably administrated by Brigham Young—she perhaps felt that the issue of sanguinity might be confused by polygamy, since some fathers required lists to distinguish their children from their legion nieces and nephews, according to unfriendly accounts of the practice of "spiritual wifery." The boy, my great-great-grandfather, was raised by one of Ina's male cousins, a Smith, and lived his entire life in Utah.

"Excuse me, Howard," Treacher interrupted, "but for the sake of historical accuracy, I must ask something."

"Very well . . ."

"This must sound terribly indelicate—but what proof is there that your great-great-grandfather was Bret Harte's illegitimate son?"

I glared at him. "Surely you know that a few months after Bret Harte's death in 1902 Ina revealed that she had a son in Utah—and that he was Harte's child."

"Yes, yes, and persuaded him to change his name from Heber Joseph Smith to Heber Coolbrith-Harte. But I'm afraid the reason behind Ina's public confession makes it suspect. At that time she was having a September-May romance with Jack London—who was trying to come to grips with his own illegitimacy." Treacher's fingers were quivering. "No, I'm looking for something else—the smoking gun to this affair, so to speak."

"Like what?"

"A baptismal certificate. Correspondence."

"Oh, Christ!" I slapped my hand to my forehead.

"Howard, what is it?"

"Oh, Jesus . . . no . . . no."

"Please—tell me. Are you feeling all right?"

I replaced my look of anguish with a sheepish grin. "Geoff, as you probably know, I was orphaned at age five—"

"I surmised, because the deaths of your parents fell on the same day."

"And I was raised by the Franciscan Brothers here in town, who were the executors of my parents' estate as well. At twenty-one I was remanded a whole batch of family memorabilia . . ." This much was the truth: Brother Tom had hesitated before handing over the worn leather portfolio, explaining that the only guilt we inherit is that from the first man and woman to sin, otherwise we're blameless for the past. Of course, despite my dissembling, the Cavanaughs had always suspected that I'd sprung from a long line of bastards.

But enough of the truth. What I said next was strictly business: "Geoff, you're going to kill me—but you have to understand that I had to put myself through Stanford. My parents died heavily in debt. The memorabilia was the only thing of worth I inherited. I sold the entire collection to a private party in Marin County."

"*Sold?*" he gasped. "What . . . what did it include?"

"Love letters."

"*From Bret Harte to Ina Coolbrith?*"

I shook my head yes, morosely. "I believe one of them contained exactly what you're looking for . . ." I was positive it did, as I had gradually memorized the passage after years of visiting the portfolio in its home at my safety deposit box in the downtown Wells Fargo Bank: ". . . I believe with all my heart," the then celebrated author had written her in 1873 from his New Jersey home, "that you had abrogated all other relationships at the time of our most intimate friendship. The knowledge you have wisely shared with me enables me to read *The Luck of Roaring Camp* as if it had been composed by another, and pine anew for its unfortunate infant. My dearest Ina, my first love, let me manifest my secret delight in this way . . ." He had included a bank draft for five hundred dollars, the first of several sent to her over a period of fifteen years—until he hit upon the hard economic times that dogged him until his death by throat cancer.

Treacher tried to clear the growing hoarseness out of his voice. "Did Harte happen to confess paternity?"

"He didn't happen to, Geoff—that was the purpose of his letter. He even included a draft for child support—although Ina never cashed the first one. Maybe she had a lawsuit in mind. Or didn't want his help. I don't really know why she held on to it."

"You actually had a draft from Harte to Coolbrith?!"

I shrugged with the same apologetic smile.

Now his mind was jamming into gear. "I always knew she was the source of the rivalry between Twain and Harte. I was absolutely positive it was psychosexual—the literary disputes were only symptomatic." He glanced up from these mutterings at me. "Please, Howard, *who* did you sell the collection to?!"

"Sorry, it was a condition of the sale that I never divulge his identity. This party didn't want to be bothered by—"

"Researchers like me," Treacher said pathetically. "Would he consider giving me photocopies?"

"Geoff, if you owned the first Gutenberg Bible, would you hand out facsimiles of it to anybody who asked?"

"No, I suppose not. God, I'd give anything to have those materials!"

I paused a beat. "Anything?"

"Is there a possibility you can buy the portfolio back from this collector?"

"Oh, I suppose—if I could meet his price."

"What are we talking about? In cold cash, mind you."

"I really have no idea."

"The Foundation budgeted me ten thousand for research materials. What do you think? This is outside my expertise. Would ten thousand cover it?"

"We can try."

"*We?*" Treacher grinned. "Oh, thank you, Howard! I could never do this by myself."

"Now, it's been my experience that the negotiations are opened by the prospective buyer fronting some earnest money."

"Of course."

I fought down a smile as I watched his large hand dart inside his corduroy coat and emerge again clutching a checkbook.

"How much do you think, Howard?"

"Not too much—it'll only induce the seller to raise his price. Let's open the discussions with five thousand." I expected him to wince, but Treacher penned out the moment, recounted the zeros to make sure he hadn't errored, then split the silence with the pleasant sound of a check being ripped free of its perforations. He even banked where I did—Wells Fargo—so cashing it would be a snap.

"Yes," I reassured him, "this should do nicely—" Then I noticed that he had misspelled my last name. "Whoops—how about crossing out the *e* on Harte? And initial it, please."

"Oh, terribly sorry—habit after ten years of research. I was going to ask you about that."

"My grandfather was responsible. A no-nonsense farmer in southern Utah. Obsessively frugal. He decided not to use up five good letters when four could do the job just as well." The check quickly disappeared inside my own inner pocket. Now, having closed this unexpected sale, I moved to rid myself of Treacher as affably as possible—before second thoughts curled up through his enthusiasm like sulphur fumes. "Well, Geoff, it looks like I've got to make an important call to Marin County."

After a moment he realized that I had come to my feet. He slowly did the same. "You know, it's a shame you ever had to sell the portfolio."

"Well, we all must accept what life hands us."

"Yes," he said brightly, although I was leading him by the elbow toward the door. "And the real irony is that, but for a minor happenstance event in territorial Nevada, you, Howard Hart, might be one of the wealthiest men in the world today."

3

I SWUNG ASSOCIATE Professor Treacher back into his chair. "How about some coffee, Geoff?" This was an order, not a question, and then I snapped through a crack in the door, "Marguerite—two cups *pronto*, please."

She shot me a look no one has seen on a Catholic face since the Inquisition, which I ignored as I sat down opposite Treacher again. "What do you mean I might have been one of the wealthiest men in the world?"

"It's really only my theory. . . ."

"That's all right."

"Well, Howard, the Clemens are in no better shape than the Hartes. Some years ago, with no surviving heirs to lay claim to it, the estate of Mart Twain reverted to the State of Connecticut."

"What was it worth?"

"Seventy-five million dollars."

I asked him to repeat the figure because my ears had started ringing. He did, then continued: "That fortune might have been yours—had history zigged when it zagged."

"You've lost me already. Are you saying I'm Sam Clemens's heir, and not Bret Harte's? You know, I've wondered about that myself. And there was a rumor—"

"No, no, Howard—I never believed that old piece of gossip. As your evidence now confirms, your great-great-grandfather was indeed Harte's son. No, this involves something entirely different." Not understanding that greed was the reason for my rapt attention, Treacher beamed with scholarly fellowship as he leaned forward and laid his heavy hands on my shoulders. "No one who knew Samuel Langhorne Clemens in the early 1860's ever dreamed he'd wind up the American literary lion of the nineteenth century—least of all his mentor and friendly rival for Ina Coolbrith's affections, Francis B. Harte. Privately, Harte said Clemens wrote like a hayseed. Yet inexorably, Twain's robust talent eclipsed your great-great-great-grandfather's. And *The Adventures of Huckleberry Finn*, the first truly American novel, put the final nail in the coffin of Harte's career. He was compelled in later years to take up government service again—this time as a consul in Germany." Treacher's smile faded. "But I must be telling you nothing you don't already know."

"What possibly could have happened in the Territory of Nevada that would make me rich today?"

"Consider this—a writer's work is inevitably compared to that produced by his contemporaries. In fact, nineteenth century authors are compared more than read. But regardless, even good work pales when held up to the output of a towering genius. Imagine for a moment Eugene O'Neill's misfortune had he been born in Elizabethan England. We wouldn't even know about him today—Shakespeare's shadow is that smothering." Treacher must have seen me chafing: "But back to Clemens—"

"Right."

"He had a rather ignoble reason for writing. He wanted to be rich."

"What's wrong with that?"

"Well . . ." Treacher, appearing to size me up for the first time, decided not to argue. "The point is that he turned to writing for his livelihood only after failing at a number of other endeavors. Even later in life he considered writing to be about as serious a pursuit as playing billiards. Bravado perhaps, but perhaps not. An insecure man, especially in the company of women, and of humble origins—I think his statement is insightful."

"Yes, but what does this—"

"What do you know about Aurora in western Nevada?"

"Only that's it's a ghost town. I've never been there."

"Well, it's not even much of a ghost town, believe me. Most of the surviving buildings were demolished in the 1950's for their used brick. But that's where young Sam Clemens experienced what he later considered to have been the most 'curious time' in his life—he became a millionaire for ten days, then bungled the ownership of a mine that ultimately produced millions in silver."

"How the hell did he do that?" I asked incredulously.

"The entire story of the Wide West Mine affair is in Twain's account of his western years, *Roughing It*. In a nutshell, he and his partner failed to do some work on the claim required by the district mining laws. Pure sloth partly excused by misadventure. And here's my point—had Clemens become a silver baron, he would have been content to lay down his pen for as long as he lived."

"I still have no idea what this has to do with me."

Treacher withdrew his hands from his shoulders. "Permit me to speak crassly for a moment—"

"By all means."

"Mark Twain fulfilled a need in the literary marketplace. Had he never become a writer, someone else would have stepped into the commercial breech, you see. That person, undoubtedly, would have been Bret Harte. He was already the darling of western fictionalists when Twain supplanted him. And there's a sporting chance the estate of seventy-five million I just mentioned would have ultimately found its way into your hands, Howard Coolbrith-Hart."

For the first time in weeks I was reminded that I owned a grandfather clock and that it was understating the passage of time, the injustices of this world, with soft tick-tocks from the corner. I checked its tarnished brass hands against my digital wristwatch: It was forty-seven minutes slow. Crossing my office, I opened the case and brought the antique face into agreement with the present—but its gearing resisted the pressure of my fingers, and I knew it would fall behind as soon as its noise turned white once again.

In those steps, I resolved to rid myself of the associate professor as quickly as possible.

"Wouldn't it be grand. . . ?" he asked wistfully, not finishing his thought as he accepted a cup of coffee from a flint-eyed Marguerite, who withdrew across the parquetry hard on her high heels. She had refused to serve me.

"What'd be grand, Geoff?"

"To manipulate time as easily as you just did there—to go back or forward by nudging the hands of the old clock?!"

I came close to mentioning Rodrigo's obsession with this very subject, but then decided against it.

"Howard, I hate to ask this . . ."

Silently, I prayed to the handiest saint that he didn't want his check back. All at once his brow was a latticework of second thoughts.

"May I have a receipt? One can't be too careful when it comes to money."

"Absolutely." I raised Marguerite on the intercom: "Please furnish Mr. Treacher with a check receipt for five thousand dollars. Reference: investment in historical documents." I glanced back at him. "Will that do?"

"Oh, thank you, Howard. This has been the most productive morning I've had in ten years. You'll never know what it might eventually mean to me."

Then I pretended to listen attentively to my secretary, and although she only tried to scathe my ears with a hiss of Spanish like live steam, said, "Okay . . . tell the senator I'll phone him back in a few minutes."

This did the trick. Setting his coffee cup on the floor, Treacher unfolded himself to his full height. "I shouldn't keep you any longer from your business affairs. Again, thank you ever so much."

"My pleasure. Give your telephone number to Marguerite, and I'll get word to you when I hear back from Marin County. . . ."

As soon as he was gone, I intertwined my fingers behind my head and sighed with satisfaction. Now I had some operating revenue until I could clear up this little misunderstanding with the U.S. Postal Service. In a few weeks Treacher would get his money back, and perhaps photocopies of my Coolbrith-Harte documents as well, if he turned out to be as on the level as he seemed at first meeting. It had crossed my mind that the Cavanaughs might have sent him to ensnare me in one of their Borgian machinations; however, while my former wife and father-in-law were undeniably devious, using Treacher would have been predicated on their knowing the truth about my past—something Cletus's thorough investigation of my background had failed to uncover prior to the wedding. Besides, I honestly had some materials that would be of value to the professor, if he were indeed slaving away at a doctoral thesis. And I could produce those documents in court. So I almost hoped that Eleanor and Cletus were behind Treacher's appearance:

Unwittingly, they were keeping me solvent until a few annoying matters could be tidied up.

On an impulse I slipped their precious brooch in my coat pocket. It felt like owning a piece of them.

The red intercom button was throbbing. "Yes, Marguerite?"

"Howard, I've got two more clients on hold." She sounded close to tears. "It's all about the mail. They want their money back. They're saying awful things to me. What can I do?"

"Tell them it's a mistake on the part of the Postal Service."

"Is that true?"

"Kind of. Meanwhile, I'll have Rodrigo put some heat on the bigwigs to quit harassing me. How about phoning him? Tell him that after a few errands I'm on my way."

This morning's trials, now coupled with mention of Rodrigo, proved too much for her. Marguerite began sobbing.

"Hang on . . ."

I went to the outer office and embraced her. She threw her hammy arms around my neck, and her body shook with a grief for which I had no solution. She was enormously gentle and sensitive—the twin culprits at work in most sad people.

"I know . . . I know . . ." I murmured.

"Tell him . . . tell him . . ."

"Yes, I'll give him your love."

"*Why?*" she snuffled, then clung to me all the more fiercely. "Will someone just tell me *why*?"

"He's working things out for himself. It just takes him longer than most."

"*Twelve years?*"

"Well, he's smarter than the rest of us," I said inanely.

She nodded, pretending to understand, then completed the ritual by snapping a carnation off the small bouquet she bought for herself at the florist down the street each morning to brighten her desk, her life.

As fate would have it, Rodrigo Alejandro Estrada y Aguilar and I, who'd been leading the ordinary lives of five-year-olds, had passed through the maw of sudden death and loss on the same day. My parents, the artistic directors of the San Francisco Opera Company, had vanished forever on a foggy curve on Highway 101 while en route to a consultation for an amateur Gilbert and Sullivan production in Santa Cruz; and perhaps at the very instant their new 1957 Ford Comet was disintegrating into a coma of glass and chrome and torn librettos, Rodrigo's father, the Panamanian consul-general in San Francisco, had fired his last bullet into the body of his Mexican-American wife—and was turning the muzzle of the revolver back on himself, closing his lips around the sharp tastes of gunmetal and spent powder.

Rodrigo and I had arrived at Our Lady Clare Orphanage on Russian Hill at the same hour, I clutching the hand of a neighbor woman, and he that of a Panamanian diplomat with a goatee like a spike. We traded hostile glances across the tile-floored vestibule, then tried to ignore each other by studying the marble statue of Saint Clare. Her expression was tender and loving, her arms opened wide to us. I had never seen anything more achingly beautiful. The starkly handsome Hispanic boy must have felt the same about the statue, for quite clearly, a whimper escaped him. His dark eyes snapped toward mine to check if I'd overheard. He saw that I had, and his light brown face hardened. He neither whimpered nor cried ever again—even in the throes of Franciscan discipline.

I discovered my own resolve in that vestibule, echoing with the clatter of the receptionist's typewriter. In the weeks since the funeral I had keenly sensed that I was a bother to the neighbor woman, who was unused to children; and now the first person I encountered at the orphanage seemed no more eager than Mrs. Fermi to take possession of me. The receptionist offered me a brief smile, but it quickly dimmed, as if a fuse had blown somewhere in her heart.

Never again would I be so powerless. It was as close to a vow as a five-year-old can make, although then it was a feeling only half-formed in words.

Mrs. Fermi mentioned something about the "Harts' lawyer," and the receptionist responded that, yes, a leather satchel had been delivered this morning.

Then a mountain of brown wool loomed forth from the shadows. Brother Tom, I was told by the receptionist. The folds of his coarse robe were as expansive as those of the proscenium curtain at the opera house, where my mother had recently made me suffer through *Aida*. The monk's expression was lost far above me: All I could glimpse were two nostrils, as large and round as portholes.

I once fancied that I could recall my own birth. But a later reflection convinced me that I had confused that irreclaimable event with my entry into Our Lady Clare's. Brother Tom seized our tiny hands, and giving us no chance to make appeals to our temporary custodians, led us down a long, dark catacomb of a corridor whose far end was aglow with a milky effulgence which grew brighter with each halting step. Rodrigo and I peeked at each other behind the monk's habit. The boy's pupils were hard glints of suspicion, and I'm sure mine were no less severe. Suddenly both of us dug in our heels when we saw that the passageway opened onto a bright chamber reverberating with the brassy voices of boys. The monk barked at us to stop squirming, then yanked us forward with a snap of his wrists. After that we were beyond the sanctuary of the dark tunnel, and the chamber fell silent before us, the harrowing silence of examination. "Lads," Brother Tom said in a funny, lilting voice which I learned only in adolescence was a County Wexford accent, "I want you to meet your new brothers— Rodrigo and Howard. . . ." And from that moment on it was never questioned that he and I were a set, a pair, two brothers despite obvious differences in ethnicity. We had been expunged from the womb of a safe and loving past at the same moment and born into a new world we must have known, even then, we could never fully escape. "I want to go back!" I then burst into tears, an infraction for which I would later get my nose bloused by a boy called Cannonball. And mysteriously, as awe-inducing as the tales of Lourdes we heard that evening from a nameless friar who died soon after of coughs, Rodrigo flew out of the shrieking throng of sky-blue pajamas and knocked Cannonball flat on his ass.

Now, as I skirted the quasi-Roman ruin of the Palace of Fine Arts—the only surviving structure of the Panama-Pacific International Exposition—I smiled in recollection of Cannonball nursing his pudgy lower jaw.

The traffic slowed before I could reach the main thoroughfare of Richardson Avenue, and my "Yuppie-gray" Mercedes—as Rodrigo called it—was locked in fore and aft by other cars, preventing me from veering out into the oncoming lane and bypassing the stalled traffic. I checked my rearview mirror. As I had pulled away from the curb in front of my office, a white Dodge Monaco had signaled title to the vacated parking place. My last glimpse had been of two men in business suits alighting from the car, and I had wondered if Louie had consigned the Cavanaugh's account to a new pair of process servers. Now, annoyingly, the same Monaco was a dozen or so vehicles behind me.

Then, as I drummed the padded steering wheel with my fingertips, it came to me: I had never seen processor servers work in pairs. Like eagles, they hunted alone.

Five minutes passed, and the traffic didn't budge.

Auto repossessors *do* work in pairs, I reminded myself, unable to recall if I was presently two or three payments behind on my gleaming gray beauty. But these types had not looked grungy enough to be repo men.

I got out to glimpse the reason for the delay. Ahead, the emergency lights of cop cruisers and ambulances were freckling the faces of the onlookers red. The sidewalks were jammed with people, and I wondered if it was some kind of political demonstration, because I could see no damaged cars. I didn't steal a glance at the Monaco for fear of drawing attention to myself.

Then I got back inside and battened down all hatches, locking the doors, even raising my side window the inch it had been lowered so a summons couldn't be slipped through the crack into my lap.

I remembered something about a developer hoping to erect a fifty-story apartment complex in this neighborhood, and that his plans were being challenged by the Bay View Preservation Society, whose latest tactic was an injunction based on a threat to a potential historical treasure. It seemed that at the close of the 1915 Pan-Pacific Expo, when Americans felt supremely confident that they had something worthwhile to share with the future, a time capsule had been lowered into the ground with the hopes it would be dug up in the year 2015. Unfortunately, when the fair was dismantled, the capsule's exact location was lost. The Bay View Preservationists were now using this gambit to delay the developer until they could mobilize their allies in city hall against the apartment project.

The cars ahead of me began inching forward. I joined the laborious procession.

A gay yellow ribbon, marked boldly in black, POLICE LINE—DO NOT CROSS, glided into view, looping gracefully from lamppost to lamppost, cordoning off one side of the street. A gurney was being wheeled toward a San Francisco County Coroner's van by a tapioca-faced man in plainclothes and a blue-suited cop, who moved without urgency; a blanket was pulled completely over the unmoving human form. Farther down the street a young woman was being loaded into an ambulance. Her dazed eyes caught mine, and she smiled with the faint, mindless amusement of someone in deep shock.

Tuning in one of those radio stations that constantly pours forth news like some existential stream of consciousness, I tried to find out what had happened, but the commentators prattled about things that seemed far away and unimportant. Lunch hour traffic forced me to avoid downtown surface streets, and by the time I had turned off the pier-studded Embarcadero and was wending my way toward the Wells Fargo Bank at Montgomery and California streets, I had largely forgotten the grisly scene outside the Palace of Fine Arts. Once again, with the Dodge Monaco no longer behind me, I was free to recall the thirteen years Rodrigo and I had shared together at Our Lady Clare's. I also warned myself about ruminating like this: It's far too easy for an orphan to become obsessed by the past. This is what had slowly happened to Rodrigo Estrada . . .

Although he denied it with reflexive modesty, Rodrigo had been won over by the Franciscans on all counts: poverty, chastity, and obedience. As for me—well, Brother Tom always espoused good sportsmanship, even in lopsided losses to Satan. Our monk, in addition to warding off deviltry, taught composition and literature at the twelve-grade parochial school that, with its roof of red terra-cotta tile and white plaster walls, was indistinguishable from the orphanage that abutted against it on the cluttered flank of Russian Hill. And, if the friar acquainted us with the works of an inveterate agnostic like Mark Twain, it was done under a dense miasma of Catholicism:

"'What is the chief end of man?'" he had once read to us, his voice cudgeling our obedient stillness with his blunt Celtic irony. "'To get rich. In what way? Dishonestly if he can, honestly if he must. Who is God, the one and only true? Money is God!'" He must have seen me rocking my head in agreement, for he snapped, "Howard, do you concur with these ideas?"

Rodrigo shot me a glance of warning then looked away, his fingers gravitating toward a large, ripe pimple on his chin.

I stood, as was the custom. "It's not that I agree or don't agree, Brother Tom. What we're talking about is the way of the world. Money is to man what water is to fish. One learns to swim in it or—"

"Rubbish—sit down!" the monk exploded. Then, while trying to calm himself, he scowled at me, letting me know he was thinking of my father's Mormon antecedents—"that mercenary cult of polygamists!" as he had once denounced them to my face—having returned from a Knights of Columbus meeting with Madeira on his breath.

"Let us learn from the example of the anonymous benefactor of this holy institution," he went on to the class, the end of his waist sash trembling in his fist. "A man who, having made his fortune in the silver mines of Nevada, realized the great emptiness in wealth. For did our Lord not say 'twas easier for a camel to pass through the eye of a needle than a rich man to enter in to heaven'? Yes, lads, our benefactor—whose face was known but to God—"

"And the most reverend archbishop," I whispered, so only Rodrigo could hear, "who palmed the checks under the table."

"—laid down his overburden of manna so he might pass into timeless glory!"

Rodrigo played the Trappist with me for three days after this indiscretion, and during that lonely time I sincerely believed that I would have gotten along much better in a Jesuit home—at least the Jebbies appreciated the incalculable good money can do in a world crawling with wicked, manna-grubbing WASPs. God knows what Rodrigo would have done had he found out that during this same crisis in my spiritual development, I was undressing an Italian girl from our tenth-grade class in the sacristy, while within echoing earshot, the rest of our cell of the Catholic Youth Organization was having a fascinating debate about the probable outcome of Vatican II. My scorn for Brother Tom's naiveté about finance was nothing compared to what I discovered during the epiphany of my first nonsolo orgasm: Once again, the good monk was dead wrong—there was no such thing as "inappropriate sex." Like an act of charity, it instantly evoked a state of grace, then slowly raised a fresh longing for such bliss. And if that isn't religion, I don't know what the hell is.

Never once did I catch Rodrigo even masturbating—while, on the other hand, he interrupted me so frequently we finally had to arrange a signal, and I hung my catcher's mitt on the outer doorknob of our room when I wished not to be disturbed. But there were ways in which I reciprocated his discretion: I told no one about his night terrors in which his haunted murmurings rose to a single gasped word that finally awoke him. It was always his mother's name—not *Mother*, but her Christian name. Nor did I tell anyone about the copy of Mendel's paper, "Experiments on

Plant Hybrids,'' he hid under his mattress as if it were a copy of
Playboy.

Recognizing a fledgling cardinal, the Franciscans monitored
Rodrigo's development with fond eyes until a complication
became apparent: Rodrigo was a genius, his gifts so beyond the
teaching capabilities of the brothers, he was shipped every
weekday afternoon across town to the University of San Francisco, although it was feared that the Jesuits there might try to snatch
his soul for the sake of their own order. His only act that could be
construed as disobedience was motivated not by obduration but, I
think, by an unwillingness to part company with me. Both of us
had been granted the obligatory scholarships to Saint Bonaventure
University in New York when I balked and applied to Stanford, a
paradise for young fortune hunters. Brother Tom was more
concerned about the effect of my rebellion on Rodrigo than my
loss to Catholic scholarship, which everyone in the archdiocese
agreed would not put a ripple in Thomas Aquinas's eternal
slumber. The monk reported us to the guardian, and he to the
archbishop, whose personal secretary picked Rodrigo and me up
in a black Cadillac as long as the Shroud of Turin.

Rodrigo was called on the carpet first, and as the mahogany
door noiselessly swung shut, I glimpsed him kneeling to kiss the
proffered ring. He emerged a half hour late, pale to the lips. Yet as
he joined me in the foyer, he whispered fervently, "I'm *going* with
you to Stanford."

I had no chance to pump him for a clue as what to say in his
behalf, for then it was my turn.

The expression on the archbishop's face looked like it had been
set there by an embalmer.

When he finally spoke after scrutinizing me with his foggily
bespectacled eyes, his vowels were as round and smooth as pears:
"A young man like your friend Rodrigo comes along once or
perhaps twice in a generation. Sometimes not at all. Even had the
guardian told me nothing about him, I would have seen for myself
that Rodrigo has that remarkable blend of intelligence and piety
the Church so desperately needs in this modernistic age. I like to
think that *my* bishop recognized these qualities in me." Leaning
forward slightly, he smiled at me for the first time. "Now, we must
discuss your future in different terms than Rodrigo's. Do you
know why?"

"No, Your Grace," I said huskily.

"Because you, Howard Hart, are a craphead."

I blinked several times, but betrayed no resentment: In those days even an archbishop wasn't above boxing your ears and then turning you over to a priest who had mauled Protestants on the gridiron for the glory of Notre Dame.

"This doesn't mean I find you utterly lacking in qualities, my boy. The guardian informs me you have a keen eye for detail and can turn a good phrase when the Muses give you a nod. He believes that supple convictions and an abrasive curiosity come naturally to you. Have you ever considered a career as a journalist?"

"No, Your Grace."

"Have you ever wanted to see Rome?"

"Of course, Your Grace."

"Soon I will make my *Ad Limina*. . . ." He was referring to the periodic junket a bishop must make to the Holy See. "I want you to go with me. I believe I can find you a position with the English edition of *L'Osservatore Romano*. What do you say to that, my boy?"

"No thank you, Your Grace."

A purplish blood vessel bulged on his forehead. "Get the hell out of here, you son of a bitch. . . ."

Rodrigo followed me down the peninsula to Stanford, where we worked on the maintenance crew and took out federally guaranteed loans to make our own way (he repaid his in full; I've got a court date on mine in September). For this, Brother Tom promised never to forgive me. Perhaps to assuage him—for reasons I myself don't fully understand—I began tithing to the orphanage as soon as I was graduated. Even, as in the past few months, with a cabal of creditors screaming for my blood, my first check of the month goes to Our Lady Clare Orphan Asylum, as it is legally called. The only thanks I get from Brother Tom for this is an Alzheimerish admonition: "Do not be the kind of man who keeps faith only with his resentments."

Yet I can't forget that when no one in the world wanted me, he did.

Rodrigo tithes as well, but not to the orphanage. He helps support a woman he slept with once, if at all.

4

A TANKER TRUCK had jackknifed and exploded on the Bayshore Freeway, resmudging a sky that had just been cleansed of fog. Forewarned by the radio, I had found an exit a half mile before all four lanes clotted into a red Milky Way of brake lights. I was winding through the sylvan residential streets of San Bruno toward the Junipero Serra Freeway, which I probaby should have taken in the first place to avoid mid-afternoon snarls, when I saw that the Dodge Monaco was once again vibrating in my rearview mirror.

Purposely slowing, I waited for the vehicle to catch up with me. But the driver kept a cautious distance—not exactly typical behavior for a process server, who got paid for handing his victim a sheaf of civil papers, not for shadowing him. I sped up as soon as I was past a school zone, then glimpsed an opportunity to shake my pursuers in the form of a patrol car parked below the crown of the hill I had just sped over.

"Officer—"

The cop lowered his hand-held radar gun. "Do you realize this is a twenty-five-mile-an-hour zone?"

"Right, thank you. There are two guys in a white Dodge

31

Monaco back there. They were stopped at the school, talking to a little girl through the chain-link fence."

"You're kidding."

"No, sir—"

But he had already roared off to intercede.

Settling back, I began to feel better for a number of reasons: My hangover, reaching its half-life after last night's revels, had decayed into a mellow weariness; my wallet was bulging with fifty one hundred dollar bills of Mackay Foundation money; and after clearing up this slight misunderstanding with the Postal Service, Rodrigo and I would be spending a pleasant evening knocking back Cuba Libres.

I turned up the radio volume as the announcer said: ". . . going back to our reporter on the scene near the Palace of Fine Arts . . ." At that moment I passed under high-tension line, and only gradually did a voice sift out of the static: ". . . a police spokesperson said that a fifty-nine year old Pacifica woman veered her station wagon onto the crowded sidewalk near the Palace, killing one man and injuring two women. Prior to plowing her vehicle into the pedestrians, she had been reportedly screaming obscenities out her open window at passersby—"

"Give me simpler times." I reached for the tuner and found some Muzak that would sedate me all the way to the Sunnyvale-Silicon Valley exit. Then, suddenly aware of a blithe scent, I dug Marguerite's now crushed carnation out of my coat pocket and sniffed deeply. . . .

Our senior year at Stanford, Rodrigo had started dating one of the secretaries at the physics department, a gorgeous twenty-year-old from a bona fide *Californio* family, original Spanish colonists who had often intermarried with Irish adventurers of the early nineteenth century. Their wedding that June at Old St. Mary's Cathedral was a riot of orange blossoms, mariachi music, lovely Hispanic girls with faint wisps of down being teased by the air at the base of their upturned coiffures—and quite literally, a riot: The father of the prettiest of the bridesmaids found me compromised with her in the baptistery and let his Latin temper get the better of him. I missed the remainder of the reception while hiding in nearby Chinatown from a well-coordinated search conducted by her legion brothers and male cousins.

That night I opened my apartment door to the bride herself. Weeping, she tumbled into my arms.

"What is it?"

"Rodrigo—" She was too choked up to finish.

"Yes?" He'd been killed in some hideous accident, I just knew it. "Tell me, dammit!"

"He's . . . he is going to apply to the church for an annulment!"

"What?"

"He doesn't want to be married to me . . . to anyone, he says."

"Why?"

"I don't know . . . I don't understand." She sniffled into a hankie. "He shot up in bed out of a dead sleep—like from a nightmare. It was awful. He couldn't catch his breath. But when he finally did, he started talking about an annulment. And ghosts. He said there were ghosts to face before I will be *safe*. What can he mean, Howard? You know him better than anyone."

I could only shake my head, but I promised to talk to him. It proved easier said than done.

For more than three months Rodrigo vanished, and only by staking out his mother's grave on weekends was I eventually able to collar him. One autumn afternoon, the wind brawling with the clouds high above the bay, he came strolling up the lawn beneath the Monterey pines. My ex-wife had always referred to him as "Howie's little Mexican friend," but I remember thinking then how tall and lank he was, how hugely agonized-looking. There was nothing little about him.

He showed no surprise when I stepped up to him from behind a guano-splattered obelisk, but his eyes were evasive.

"How is she?" he asked.

"Brokenhearted."

He accepted this news with a slight nod. "Take care of her."

"Me take care of her?"

"Yes, I want you to give her a job."

"As what?"

"Your secretary."

"Rodrigo, Hart Enterprises is all of four months old. *I'm* my own secretary."

"We'll come to an arrangement. I'll give you the funds to pay her."

"Where are you going to get that kind of money?"

"I'm working now—down at Sunnyvale. Exciting things are happening there." His thin smile ran off his face. "I'll contribute on a sliding scale as your firm grows and prospers, but never less than fifty percent of her salary."

"I'll do it—"

"Thank you."

"—only if you tell me why you're tossing her away like this. Don't you love her?"

"Of course I do. I'm doing it because I love her." Inadvertently the toe of my shoe had come to rest on his mother's oxidized brass plate, and he gently nudged me back a pace. "I was too hasty. I married against my better judgment."

"Why? You seemed so happy before the wedding."

"There are things I must find out about myself. That's all. I don't want to talk about it."

"Jesus," I blurted before I could think better of it, "you're not gay, are you?"

"Howard, I'm a *Catholic*. I insist we change the subject at once."

"You mean you're going to let everything just lie?"

"No . . ." He turned directly into the brisk westerly, which raised the moisture in his eyes. "I'm doing something about it. Something extraordinary. But you wouldn't understand."

"Thanks."

"I don't mean to offend you, Howard. You're very bright, and I love you." A cunning smile cricked a corner of his mouth, disquieting me: I'd never seen it before. "'There are more things in heaven and earth . . . than are dreamt of in your philosophy.'" There was nothing hokey about the way he said this; it came close to giving me chills. Then he clasped me around the shoulders and steered me away from the grave as if he didn't like me being there. "There's an evening mass at the mission. In Latin. Will you come with me?" He must have noticed my wince. "Howard?"

"I'm afraid I'm not a Catholic anymore."

"Nonsense, you may have lapsed a bit but—" He jerked me to a halt by the arm. "You've converted for Eleanor Beauchamp-Cavanaugh, haven't you?! You've done it to marry her!"

"It's not so bad being an Episcopalian. The ritual's much the same, and I like Grace Cathedral. Besides, I'm in good company—"

"Yes, you and Henry the Eighth!" he said, ruining the little joke I'd intended to use to buffer the news.

Then, going on alone, he melted into the shadows beneath the pines.

Rodrigo's annulled wife, of course, became my secretary, who was being paid half again the going rate for secretaries in San Francisco but still pestered me the first of every month for a raise. Over twelve years I had watched Marguerite transformed from a lithe Irish-Spanish beauty into two hundred pounds of confirmed spinsterhood. Rather than date—and risk offending the strange young man she still loved—Marguerite took up calligraphy and chocolate. With her senses thus occupied, she dreamed of the miracle that might one day give her back her husband.

As usual, Rodrigo seemed annoyed at seeing me, almost pouty—as if I had neglected him so long, he wasn't about to reveal any pleasure at my arrival. He accepted Marguerite's carnation without a word and took it inside his bedroom, where he probably had a steamer trunk full of them by now.

If I had any doubt that the Franciscans had done a thorough job on him, it was quickly dispelled by the appearance of his latest condominium: The place was as barren as a mendicant's cell. His sum total of furniture consisted of a pallet-thin mattress thrown down on the bedroom carpet, two beanbag chairs in the living room, and an assemblage of personal computer equipment looming against the blank wall of the dining alcove like an altar. While my appetite for privacy had been honed to a decadently keen edge by thirteen years in an orphanage, his had been eradicated—and to prove it, there wasn't a drape or curtain on any of the windows; the one I was looking through was raucous green from a hillside wearing the first grass of the moist California spring. I sank into one of beanbags with the suspicion that it was actually a gigantic sea urchin, which given enough time, would digest my rump out from under me.

"Do you want a drink?" he asked.

"Do I want a drink?" I echoed ironically—it was one of our little rituals of which we were inordinately fond. "Would *you* want a drink if you were me?"

"I'd never want to stop drinking."

Then, while he fiddled with the ice and glasses, I filled him in on the day's events: the snafu with Amtrak over the Yosemite right-of-way; the five thousand dollar windfall that had arrived on the wings of Treacher's visitation; and the associate professor's curious but entertaining hypothesis that a twist of history had deprived me of a fortune—which made Rodrigo stare at me for a moment before he eased into one of the chairs. I saved the news about the curtailment of my mail for last, asking him if he knew any muckamucks in the Postal Service who might be able to help me out.

"Perhaps . . . I've got a few names."

"All right!" I smacked my palms together.

"But don't get too excited."

"Why? You've got what I need—some leverage with these bastards."

"No, I don't. I lost the contract."

I could feel my grin collapse. "What are you saying?"

"I got canned. They're suing me for nonperformance."

"*You*—accused of nonperformance? Why? Did you forget to include something minor?"

"Oh, I the completed the project. . . ." And to prove it, he hurled himself up out of his beanbag and retrieved a foot-high stack of black cardboard-bound tomes from the bedroom, dumping them at my shoes. "Here it is . . . *in totum.*"

I picked up the topmost volume and grimaced at the title: *Unaccountable Mail Outside the Context of Dysfunctional Cybernation.* I had to go no further than the title to realize that the rest would be Greek to me. "Well, what's the problem? This looks like one hell of a job."

"It is," he said, gazing out the window. His light brown cheeks now had an underlying rum flush. "The fundamental problem is that I must seek patrons so I can afford to do the work I must do—and these patrons never have the capacity to understand what I'm doing. The postmaster general proved no different."

"Would it help if you landed a position with a university?"

He patronized me with a smile. "Howard, a university has as many vested interests as any other business entity." He had not sat again. "How about an early dinner?"

"Fine, I haven't eaten since yesterday—I think."

"There's a new restaurant across the barranca. I'm sure you'll like it. It'll take me just a minute to change."

I began leafing through his work. The language was teasingly like English, but in reading it, I felt like Geoffrey Chaucer trying to make sense of Harold Robbins. Giving up, I skimmed through the dense-looking pages of two volumes, then paused at the third, which was nothing but a sheaf of nearly identical maps—of France. The difference of one from the next involved only the

placement of black squares and amoebalike blobs of blue shading.
"I thought you did this for the *U.S.* Postal Service," I called out
to Rodrigo.

"I did."

I turned the volume sideways, even bleared my eyes to alter my
perspective. Yes, definitely France. Yet even more baffling was
what was zipped inside a clear plastic pouch at the front of the
next tome: the January 1925 issue of *National Geographic*.
Without really thinking, I removed the magazine and began
thumbing through its dusty-feeling pages. *Governor Baxter of
Maine keeps to a schedule with a Hamilton*, an advertisement
declared. *Pictured here is Governor Percival P. Baxter of Maine.
With him is his dog "Garry." They are inseparable, as anyone
around the State House can tell you. . . .*

But did any of this have to do with dysfunctional cybernation? I
turned back to the contents framed in oak leafs and acorns on the
front cover:

Seeing America from the "Shenandoah"
   With 41 Illustrations   *Junius B. Wood*

The Palace of Versailles, Its Park, and the Trianons
   With 4 Illustrations   *Franklin L. Fisher*

Versailles, the Magnificent
   14 Autochromes Lumière   *Gervais Courtellemont*

Then the connection was formed along some brandy-damaged
synapse of my brain: of course, *France*. I turned to Fisher's
Versailles article (although Courtellemont's turned out to be a
photoessay inserted in Fisher's) and quickly scanned the text,
trying to glimpse some relevance to Rodrigo's project. Finally,
after several long minutes made all the more annoying because
Rodrigo could be heard meticulously brushing his teeth, I gave up
and concentrated on Monsieur Courtellemont's *autochromes
lumière*:

The first plate showed a man in white wig and green waistcoat
stalking three gowned ladies of the court in a game of blindman's
buff around the base of a chestnut tree—costumed players, the
caption explained, commissioned to reenact *le grand siècle* of
Louis XVI. Perhaps it was the dreary day on which the picture had
been taken, the slightly bleared human figures, or the tint of the
primitive color process itself—whatever the cause of the effect,

the wooded scene was vaguely haunted, its handsomely attired subjects ghostly despite their outward merriment. Several of the plates—especially that of Marie Antoinette's vine-clad house in the Petit Trianon, where the queen "found pleasure and recreation in watching the simple lives of rustic households which here carried on real farming as a sort of performance for royalty"— were powerfully imbued with this quality. It was a few minutes before I could put my finger on it: There was a nebulous demarcation between light and shadow; Courtellemont had either captured or created a netherworld that was viscerally unsettling, especially for a man on the mend from a hard night.

"Ready?" Rodrigo had changed into his idea of formal wear: A short-sleeved white shirt, its pocket indelibly smirched by leaky ballpoint pens; a skinny tie so lackluster I had to look closely to make sure it hadn't been drawn down his shirt front with a lump of coal; and cords that had passed out of fashion even at parochial schools.

I fought down a smirk. "Say," I asked, holding up the *National Geographic*, "what's this French stuff all about?"

"I'll explain during dinner."

5

RODRIGO NO LONGER operated automobiles.

Three years before, the State of California had finally declared him a negligent driver and revoked his license—after he had achieved the Santa Clara County record for noninjury accidents. In each instance drugs, alcohol, or a combination thereof were suspected by the cops to be the cause, but Rodrigo breezed through all breath, urine, and blood tests under the dull gray banner of sobriety. He spent more time in driver's education than he had in quantum theory physics, and his insurance premiums for a used Plymouth Valiant, his preferred chariot of destruction, were only slightly less than what Lloyd's of London charges to underwrite a Cunard liner.

I alone knew the true reason for his abominable driving habits: Rodrigo found operating a car such a ponderous bore, he read while at the wheel. Reducing his speed to a crawl, hugging the right side of the pavement, he would putter forward on a fairly straight tack until, all at once, the subject matter so engrossed him he would stop glancing up with metronomic regularity—and veer off toward another appointment with Ernesto's Body Shop, whose owner was so grateful for the business, he made Rodrigo godfather to his fifth child.

I never ribbed Rodrigo about losing his license, for it was such a canker of humiliation to him, he rarely entered a car—even as a passenger—and did all of his distance traveling by bus or commuter train. Around Sunnyvale he hoofed it, having ensconced himself in a neighborhood where all his necessities and most of his amenities were within walking distance—a rare find in the suburban sprawl of the south Bay. When he changed addresses, which he did regularly and as if progressing along the Stations of the Cross, he remained within the same general pueblo of condominiums.

We now set out on foot from his latest cubistic rental, cutting across the grassy mounds of a small park, breaking into a trot as a rainbird sprinkler unexpectedly thick-thicka-thicked to life and speckled our trousers. Rodrigo's smile turned mischievous as he led me down a narrow path worn smooth by bicycle tires and into a barranca shaded by oaks. He stripped the spindly stems off an anise plant with a swipe of his hand, and all at once the ravine was filled with a licorice pungency, the perfume of a coastal California rapidly being conquered by house framers and cement finishers. My urge to linger in the barranca was so persuasive, I fell behind Rodrigo, and he stood waiting above me, waist deep in mustard plant—a frenzy of tiny yellow flowers that were luminous in the fading light. I could see by his grin that he had no difficulty reading my thoughts: He had always recognized the onset of the Affinity. But I also saw something else in his face—a reluctance to broach some unpleasantness, I suspected.

We emerged from the barranca onto the backside of a Kmart, whose cinder-block battlements extended out in an L shape to embrace a host of lesser stores. As we marched in step down the littered alley, Rodrigo bent over, scooped up an envelope, read its face, discarded it, and broke stride to catch up with me, only to reach down again several yards later to seize another letter that had obviously blown out of one of the dumpsters. "Helluva cheap way to collect stamps," I said.

He chuckled, but didn't explain.

The restaurant he had chosen was meant to please me: Its exterior was typical late twentieth century shopping mall, but once past the door, we were bumping half blind into other patrons lined up at the reservation desk, waiting to be admitted into a gas-lit ambiance of nineteenth century opulence. It was all ersatz, of course, down to the amber electric bulbs guttering in the Tiffany lamps. The college coed, decked out in a taffetized gown only

Mary Todd Lincoln would have looked comfortable wearing, led us toward our table, her skirts rustling.

I feigned delight with the place, of course, because Rodrigo would have slipped into a funk if I hadn't. But the truth was that this kind of replication did not assuage the Affinity—it intensified it with a peculiar loneliness I can only explain as the feeling of being absent from a place where I'm direly needed by those who love me. Often it makes me want to drop whatever I'm doing at the moment and *go there*. But where?

Rodrigo, also an orphan, understood it perfectly, I suppose.

"Well," I said, lifting the first glass of the evening in his direction, "how'd Versailles get you in hot water with the Postal Service?"

His forefinger darted to his lips. He glanced over his shoulder at a middle-aged couple across the aisle from us, who, having spent all their conversation decades before, were eating in grumpy silence. He refused to discuss anything except the bad news about my railroad project—until the pair was supplanted at their table by another forty years younger, who had everything from suntans to herpes infections to talk about in loud voices.

Only then did Rodrigo begin in a whisper: "In the garden of Versailles is a small villa—"

"Right, the Petit Trianon. I read the article while you were getting into your . . . duds." This word to describe clothing had never seemed appropriate until now. "Kind of a spooky looking place."

Rodrigo tilted his head in bewilderment, as if I had stumbled on something. "Yes . . . quite." He hesitated, then decided to plunge ahead: "On the tenth of August, 1901, two Englishwomen of good character and superior intellect, the principal and vice principal of an Oxford college on holiday in France, decided to visit Versailles—despite an oppressive sky and a wind promising rain. . . ." Noisily, he took a sip of wine, his eyes hard on mine over the silvered lip of his glass. "On that date all of central Europe was covered by an immense electrical storm. . . ."

"And?"

"Exiting the palace, they strolled past the Grand Trianon and onto a garden path they believed would take them to the Petit Trianon. But their guide book began to confuse them. It didn't jibe with what they saw before their eyes. Both spoke French—with British accents, of course—and they asked two guards the way to the Petit Trianon. These men, who wore green uniforms and tricornered hats, seemed to be amused by the women—remember that. They pointed at a path straight ahead, one that took the women past a plow resting against an outbuilding. . . ." Rodrigo paused as our plates arrived, expressionless until the waitress left us alone again. "As Miss Moberly and Miss Jourdain continued toward the Petit Trianon their good spirits were gradually replaced by feelings of depression. Of loneliness. They might have dismissed this as travel weariness except that the landscape itself had grown remarkably eerie. Windless. Shadowless. Deeply silent."

I was about to remark that I had gleaned that quality from Monsieur Courtellemont's *autochromes lumière*, but Rodrigo held up a palm for me to keep quiet. "They walked into a gloomy stand of woods," he went on, the steam of his shellfish dinner curling up around his face unnoticed. "And in a small open structure Miss Moberly described as a garden kiosk, they saw seated a man who greatly disturbed them. Why? Well, it wasn't just his repulsively pockmarked face, his leer, his somber cloak and slouch hat. It was the overwhelming *veracity of epoch* that attended him. He was an aggregate of minutiae that cannot be duplicated in this age. He overloaded their senses with the shattering truth he *represented*."

I lowered my fork. "Which was?"

He ignored my question. "At that moment the women were relieved to hear someone running toward them. But it was another man in a dark cloak and slouch hat, although he was younger and seemed less threatening. Breathlessly, he rattled off a long, urgent phrase, but they caught only *'cherchez la maison'* before he insistently told them to bear to the right along the web of paths. They did so, and crossed a footbridge by a waterfall, a meadow, and at last came within sight of the Petit Trianon. At this juncture Miss Moberly—but not Miss Jourdain—saw a woman in late eighteenth century dress. She was perched on a stool, sketching some trees, and modestly turned her paper as the two strangers passed. They walked onto the terrace surrounding the house and were confronted by a man who told them they must enter the Petit Trianon from the front. He led them around the west side of the house through a garden. He, like the guards, kept looking back at them with amusement—as if he found their appearance peculiar. At last he delivered them onto the path by which they had entered the grounds. Their melancholy lifted. And they knew they had returned. At last, as inexplicably as everything else that had happened, they had *returned*." For the first time Rodrigo looked down at his pile of clams and oysters, which was no longer issuing warm vapors.

I found myself unable to stop staring at him.

He shucked an oyster out of its shell with a miniscule fork. "Comments?"

"Yeah, what's this have to do with unaccountable mail?"

"Everything."

I sighed. "Come on, the bottom line so I understand."

"The bottom line is that, quite adventitiously, these ladies took a promenade through the Gardens of the Trianon of 1789—a physical environment that had radically changed by 1901." He clenched an oyster between his front teeth and chewed—but carefully—as he studied me for a reaction.

After a long moment, with the background noise of the restaurant swelling to prominence once again, I laughed, helplessly, stupidly. Somehow I hoped that he might join me. He didn't, of course.

"I thought so," he said in disgust.

"Look, I'll never have the intellectual ammunition to shoot down anything you say. But okay if I play the devil's advocate for a minute?"

"By all means. Lord Kitchener did the same some eighty years ago when, as a trustee of the college, he asked Miss Jourdain to recant—or resign her position."

I pushed back my plate. "Where in hell did you come across this story?"

"J. W. Dunne, the English physicist, mentions it in his treatise on serialism and fourth-dimensional time. The original statements made by Miss Jourdain and Miss Moberly are preserved in the Bodleian Library at Oxford and—"

"Okay, okay." I waved two fingers at the cocktail waitress. "Rodrigo, the *Geographic* article shows players in period costume cavorting around the gardens in the 1920s—"

"That's true. And your question is—had the women seen actors or docents in late eighteenth century clothes assembled for a fete, a photographic study, or a motion picture? These possibilities were eliminated by checking with the coadjutator at Versailles, who consulted his daybook of permissions . . . and by checking with all the Parisian photographic studios, *and* with pioneer filmmaker Charles Pathé, who'd shot work at Versailles previously." Rodrigo smiled. "This brings me to the first of seventy minute historical specificities that helped corroborate the testimony of the women. The green uniforms were the livery worn by Louis XVI's guards. That fact had largely vanished with archives destroyed during the Revolution. And what astounded a French colonel, *the* authority on the history of his country's military uniforms, was the detail the Englishwomen could provide about them. This arcane information was difficult for even him to access, an officer in service."

"Which brings me to my next question," I tried to say sympathetically, for his voice was gradually becoming shrill with defensiveness. "These women were probably avid readers of French history—"

"Yes, yes—abject Francophiles, I'm sure."

"Perhaps they'd read old documents, seen old maps that persuaded them to imagine . . ." My words trailed off: I could see by Rodrigo's smug expression that I had stumbled into one of his traps.

"Exactly. But even their detractors had dismissed this notion. And why? Because the only known map of the Trianon of 1789 was a copy of Mique's original by a fellow named La Motte. Mique was Marie Attoinette's landscape gardener—guillotined in 1794. Everyone was laughing behind their hands at the crazy English ladies because La Motte's copy did not show features where the women said they'd seen them. The laughing stopped in 1903, when Mique's original was found in the bricked-up chimney of an old house in Montmorency. It placed each of the heretofore unknown features—the footbridge at the waterfall, the kiosk, the covered terrace at the Petit Trianon which was later razed— *precisely* where Miss Jourdain and Miss Moberly had seen them in 1901. Even the plow, which had been forgotten by history, was later discovered to have been purchased by Louis XV, who'd ordered plowing lessons given to his grandson, the dauphin."

"Still—"

"Howard, a barrage of facts leads to one irrefutable conclusion: These women partook of a human experience that is less rare than one might think. Indeed, they made a similiar tour some years later—again adventitiously. We are only fortunate that they, of thousands before and after them, were articulate, intellectually courageous, and not encumbered by superstition. What poor fools witnessed the assassination of Julius Caesar or William Shakespeare performing William Shakespeare, or Francisco Coronado riding across medieval Arizona—only to die muttering to themselves in skid-row gutters of our own *enlightened* age?"

I knew the irritation in my face was paining for him, but I could

no longer hide it. Rodrigo had been working too hard again.
"Then tell me—in terms I'll understand—how something like this
is possible."

"Very well, I think you're prepared to grasp the postulate in my
study for the Postal Service."

Then, while I still sat there with my chin resting on my fist, he
rose and walked resolutely for the front door, leaving me to
hurriedly square the bill.

Outside, a bank of champagne-colored fog was bumping along
the tops of the parking lot light poles. The barranca was now too
dark to safely cross, so we marched along the surface streets,
dodging traffic, jumping back to a curb once when a police car,
spangling the night with its bubblegum machine, its siren yelping,
rounded the corner in four-wheel drift, one of its stern-faced
occupants mouthing into a microphone and his partner removing
the shotgun from its dashboard rack in the arrested split second
before they were gone around yet another corner to a second
screak of locked tires.

My heart was still pounding when Rodrigo calmly bent over to
inspect a discarded envelope.

"Have you gone off the deep end?"

When he looked up at me, his eyes were shining. "Of course
not."

"Then why do you keep doing that?"

He planted me in a beanbag chair, then raced into his bedroom
for yet another stack of oversized tomes, particularizing all the
while about quantum waves; and the magnetosphere, which
sounded like where the high tension wires cross heaven; and
phantoms that go faster than light, called tachyons, which in
Greek, he explained in the same tapering breath, meant cherubim
that soar faster than greased lightning—or something like that; and
how Albert and the Faithful had held that anything propagating
faster than light can be observed, perhaps even experienced, in
contrary time sequences, or something like that. Rodrigo snapped
his fingers mid-Einstein and hurried back into the bedroom for yet
another volume, which he dumped at my feet with the glorious
riddle that a quantum wave tells us where and when something is
likely to happen, a kind of yardstick for a probability, although
this apprehension not only exists in our minds but actually moves
through time and space, or dances on the head of a pin, or does
most anything imaginable—science coming around full circle to

religion again, I suspected, but didn't say. On the brink of a fatal
hyperventilation, he asked, "Do you understand so far?"

"Nope."

He stared through my eyes and out the back of my head, then
patted my shoulder. "Well, this is all background—none of it
really applies." Just like a physicist to spend a half hour building
an elaborate house of cards, only to knock it down in an instant of
impulsive delight. When he continued, it was at a much slower
tempo: "Simply try to get a *sense* of the dynamics of adventitious
time travel."

"Adventitious?"

"You know, accidental. What Miss Jourdain and Miss Moberly
experienced." He began thumbing through the maps of France.
Pausing at the final one in the sequence, he asked, "You know
how a cartoon works, don't you?"

"Maybe."

"The animator draws a slightly altered figure on each frame to
give the illusion of motion."

"Oh, like drawing Goofy on each page of a pad, then fanning
the pages to make him walk?"

He patted my shoulder again. "Exactly. Now, that's what I've
done in *Unaccountable Mail Outside the Context of Dysfunctional
Cybernation*—but it isn't Goofy I show walking—it's magnetic
fields and electrical storms." He blew air out of his cheeks.
"All right—the very existense of tachyons was hypothetical until
a friend of mine at Berkeley . . . do you remember Ghan
Thapar?"

"The geek with the paisley turban?"

"Yes, yes, the particle physicist," he muttered, not really
having heard me. "He was doing work on how the earth's
magnetic quality changes with sunspot cycles, something that had
been largely a mystery. The answer, quite unexpectedly, might be
particles faster than the speed of light—"

"Tachyons," I interrupted, feeling juvenile that I could find
pleasure in his approval. "Which are what make time travel
possible."

"No—not solely, at least. No more than they solely cause the
fluctuations in the speed of solar wind. But let's not get into proton
acceleration. Now watch something fascinating. . . ." His forefinger tapped a black square situated somewhere over the English
Channel. "This is a magnetic field, vectoring to the southeast, as
you'll see." He raised a sheaf of pages and began letting them slip

out from under his thumb: The square began sliding across the
waters toward the Cherbourg peninsula. But then he pinched off
the flow of tumbling pages and indicated a number, 310701, in the
lower right-hand corner: "The date—the thirty-first of July, 1901.
And now, plotted from the meteorological records of the Royal
Navy, the emergence of a huge electrical storm on the European
scene. . . ." He began flipping again, and all at once the shaded
blue area I had noticed before drifted over the Bay of Biscay, spun
all the way north to the Irish Sea, and idled briefly over Belgium
before converging with the magnetic field right smack dab on a
small red dot labeled VER, which I had ignored during my first
perusal, not realizing until now that it meant *Versailles*. Rodrigo
had reached the last page: It was numbered 100801—10 August
1901, the date on which the two Englishwomen had embarked on
their stroll under threatening skies.

After what I hoped would pass for a sufficiently thoughtful
silence, I asked, "How, then, does this overlapping of a magnetic
field and an electrical storm make time travel possible?"

"Beats me." Laughing, he slapped me on the back. "But I was
first to recognize the periodic tendency in the data. And now I'm
sure I can make use of it."

"No offense, Rodrigo, but I can see why the Postal Service got
pissed."

He looked genuinely bewildered. "Why?"

"Well, Christ, you handed in a bunch of cartoons of turn-of-
the-century France, and it's my guess they wanted to find out what
happens to mail that can't be accounted for."

"And that's just what I did for them! So sue me!" As we
remained frozen, glaring at each other with unaccustomed
ferocity, someone in the condominium below tapped his ceiling
with what sounded like a shillelagh. Were these outbursts more
common of late than I might have thought? Rodrigo's was the
most compartmentalized mind I'd ever known (how else could a
physicist belong to the Church that had persecuted Galileo?), and
now I watched with unease as he turned out the lights on his
patience with me. Is this how it had begun when he'd exiled poor
Marguerite to the frontier of his affections?

"Wait—I think I get it."

"Yes?" he asked hopefully.

"The postal bureaucracy is so slow, a person can actually *mail*
himself into the past!"

"No, no, no," he whined, batting volumes off the stack until

reaching the one he wanted. "Look here!" This series of maps
was of California and Nevada, and the small red dot was labeled
ORO. "On the fifth of September last year, an estimated two
metric tons of mail were put on a conveyer belt at the postal
sectional center in Oroville, California . . ." Pages began
zipping past his thumb, and as I now might anticipate, the black
square and the shaded blue amoeba converged on Oroville.
". . . . the supervisor at the end of the belt swore in an affidavit
on penalty of perjury that the two missing tons of mail never
arrived in his section."

"Where'd it go, Rodrigo?" I asked, trying not to sound like the
night orderly in a mental ward.

"Gone. Dumped into the past . . . or the future."

"Okay, then why doesn't anyone come across letters with some
pretty absurd cancellation dates on them?"

"Because no one is looking—except me and Ghan Thapar!"
He had me there.

"Please try to appreciate the logarithmetically diminished
probability of a letter postmarked today being remarkable to
someone living in the past. Good God, man, most of the human
race was illiterate until this century. Much of it *still* is. And paper's
highly perishable. It makes excellent tinder—or can even be
eaten!"

"What about somebody living in the future finding that
envelope?"

"Listen—what would you think if you found in the gutter a
message written in a strange language?" He didn't trust me with a
guess: "Why, you'd probably say to yourself—some foreigner's
dropped his mail. Even if you were astute enough to recognize it
as being like modern Hindi, you'd have little inducement to
further investigate and perhaps discover that this piece of rubbish
was actually written in Prakrits, the medieval link of Hindi to
Sanskrit." Sighing, he grabbed another volume. "On the eleventh
of July, 1975, a rural postal carrier out of Genoa, Nevada, started
his sparsely populated route in the foothills of the Sierra
Nevada. . . ." Once more Rodrigo used his trick of animation to
draw a magentic field and electric storm together, this time over
the obtuse angle on the western boundary of the state. "At noon
he phoned in from a ranch house, reporting that his Jeep had
broken down a mile up the road. At first he'd thought that a
hissing sound and a bad vibration were coming from the vehicle.
But when he stepped outside into a mounting thunderstorm, he

realized that these were the very qualities of the morning itself. The old woman at the ranch, whose vision was too poor to permit her to drive, later testified that the rural carrier—still faithfully lugging his mail sack—had set off in his rain slicker to rendezvous with the tow vehicle. He never arrived back at the Jeep. The man was never seen again." Rodrigo seized me by the wrist. "Howard, in 1914, Miss Jourdain and Miss Moberly were visited by a family that had lived and worked at Versailles. They wanted their identity kept secret, but they told the women they'd packed up and quit after a rash of eerie experiences in the Gardens of Trianon. These episodes were invariably preceded by a 'curious hissing sound—and a vibration in the air.'"

At last he released my forearm, his fingers leaving stripes of blush which faded only after several minutes.

"Are you saying this thing recurs in the same places?"

"In the same general areas, yes, within the given cycles. Howard, certainly you've heard of cases in which letters were delivered a half century after they were mailed?"

I nodded remotely.

"Well, that kind of event is rare because it's dependent on a complete circuit of the causal loop, but it explains why the headmistresses *returned* from 1789! Don't you see?! You yourself just mentioned what a mess the mails are in. Everyone all over the world gripes about it. But little do they realize that the postal system is a clue to the greatest mystery of all time!" Turning, he scowled at the telephone, which was ringing in the far corner.

I knew by the sudden stiffening of his spine that Marguerite had called. Trying not to eavesdrop on his self-conscious mutterings to her, I studied the Nevada map. I couldn't help but smile in recollection of Associate Professor Treacher's suggestion that ". . . *but for a minor, happenstance event in territorial Nevada—you, Howard Hart, might be one of the wealthiest men in the world today.* . . ." I was woolgathering along these lines when I realized that Rodrigo was repeating himself for my attention: "Howard—talk to Marguerite. Something terrible has happened." Unconsciously he blessed me with the receiver as if it were a crucifix.

I snatched it away from him. "Yes, what is it?"

"I've been trying to get you since four-thirty—" Her voice cracked. "They came and locked up the office and told me you'd better give yourself up—"

"*Who?*"

"The marshals."

"San Francisco County Marshals Office?"

"Just a minute—they all gave me a card . . . so many cards." She paused; my heart was racing. "No, Howard, it says here he's from the United States Department of Justice . . . and another says U.S. Postal Inspection Service . . . and another—"

"Holy shit." I saw Rodrigo frown: He didn't like coarse language used on Marguerite. "What'd they mean by me turning myself in?"

"They showed me this paper they called an arrest warrant . . . and then somebody—I forget which one—handed me the affidavit."

"Do you still have it?"

"Yes."

"Read it . . . read it."

Rodrigo had brought me another Cuba Libre, which I accepted gratefully.

Quickly, Marguerite susurrated past the preliminaries to the crux of the statement.

". . . to wit, Howard Hart Enterprises, Incorporated, issued and franked a promotional publication for the purpose of soliciting investment, inferring in the said material that the right-of-way for a railroad spur had been approved by the Public Utilities Commission, when in fact only a most preliminary discussion had been held with representatives of Amtrak for the objective of drafting an enviromental impact report to be evaluated at a future date by the commission. An initial investigation by the U.S. Postal Inspection Service revealed that the spur line in question would, of engineering necessity, have to cross 1.3 miles of public lands at the southern extremity of Yosemite National Park . . ."

She paused to catch her breath. "There's lots more, Howard, but it seems to go over and over the same stuff."

"That's okay. I've heard enough."

"The marshals said they contacted your attorney to iron out the details for you to surrender at the federal courthouse—but your attorney said he wasn't your attorney anymore on account of you not paying your fee for other business and—"

"That's fine, Marguerite." I drained the glass. "You say they sealed the office?"

"Yes . . ." Her voice broke again. ". . . and made me open the files."

"The *files*?"

"They brought a nice little man, an auditor from IRS."

I tried to echo *IRS* but nothing came out of my mouth but a gasp.

"Oh, yes, Howard, before I forget—all this had just started when Eleanor phoned. She wants you to call her back."

"My *ex*?"

"Who else?"

"Where?"

"It's Friday," Margerite reminded me. On Friday evenings at precisely 5:45 my former wife and father-in-law were picked up at their downtown penthouse by corporate helicopter and flown twenty miles south along a sunset-gilt south Bay to Menlo Park and what they charmingly referred to as "The Cottage." Outside the family it was known as Linden Towers, the forty-room and sixty-closet Victorian mansion built in 1878 by James Clair Flood, one of the five Comstock bonanza kings, who had gone from saloon keeper to silver millionaire, not by swinging a pick but by manipulating mining stock prices and fleecing legions of small investors. Here, Cletus Cavanaugh spent his weekends bedeviling the illegal aliens who tended the largest rose garden in the Bay Area or feather-dusted one square mile of ornately carved wooden paneling. He was also a trustee of a foundation committed to stemming abuses of the immigration system being foisted on the American people by a Fundy tide of Asians and Hispanics. Eleanor idled away these days lounging around the loggialike veranda in a tennis outfit, although she seldom played, or fine tuning her loin-aching beauty for Sunday's brunch, which was usually attended by the governor or a senator, or in a pinch, an Episcopal bishop with proven conservative credentials.

I now hated to admit it to myself, but I had butterflies that Eleanor had asked me to call.

"Howard, are you still there?"

"Yes, Marguerite, I'm here. . . ." I felt pretty sure that the Cavanaughs didn't know Rodrigo's latest address; he no longer had a driver's license by which the police could conveniently access this information. "Say, listen, you didn't tell anybody where I am, did you?"

"No—" She broke off a whine that threatened to tremble apart into sobbing. "But can I go to jail for lying?"

"Absolutely not, and I have that on good authority from my former in-laws." I held out the receiver to ask Rodrigo if he wanted to say anything more to her, but he turned away dejectedly. "Okay, honey, are you going to be home all weekend?" I asked needlessly.

"Of course."

"Well, I'll let you know how this works out."

"Please be careful, Howard."

"I will. Bye."

After hanging up and pacing aimlessly around Rodrigo's barren living room for a few moments, I sighed and dialed a number I'd never expected to use again. The second ring was promptly answered at Linden Towers by Miss Lee, the Chinese housemaid, who bubbled when she realized that it was me. Yet before we could tease each other as we used to do, Eleanor seized the receiver and said, "Hello, Howie." That should have given me pause to reflect: What was she doing sitting on the telephone in the Carreran marble foyer? But the breathy impatience in my ex-wife's voice dimmed any suspicion I felt.

"I want to see you."

A wince shot down to my toes: No woman is more irresistible than one you have been battling in the courts for eighteen months and who suddenly begs to see you in the night. And perhaps, in that moment of yearning, I was foolish enough to imagine that the Cavanaughs might help me out of my predicament.

"When?"

"Now. Where are you?"

Thank God I didn't toss all caution to the winds: "Knights of Columbus Hall downtown—a small reunion of guys from the orphanage."

"Is your little Mexican friend there?"

"No, Rodrigo's back east somewhere. Society for the Advancement of Science convention, or something."

"Please hurry, Howard. I'll have the front gate watch out for your Mercedes."

"Ellie. . . ?"

"Yes?"

I almost said something I shouldn't have, before whispering: "I'm on my way."

6

I WAS ALMOST to the main gate of Linden Towers when something made me brake and pull over to the curb. Resting my chin on the crown of the steering wheel, I studied the glow radiating up through the misty air from the yet unseen mansion, wondering why I was so feverish to see Eleanor Cavanaugh. In the throes of an impending disaster did I honestly imagine that she might offer some genuine solace? Not likely. "Damn . . ."

On a hunch, I didn't continue up to the gatehouse, but turned off onto the semiprivate drive that girdled the estate's three hundred acres of formal gardens and orange groves. The lights from the main tower windows began flickering through the lush screens of eucalyptus. Midway along this lane, which was flanked by lesser fiefdoms belonging to doctors, lawyers, and other assorted earls of the twentieth century, was an overlook of The Cottage; Eleanor and I had occasionally used it during our Stanford years to make love, although she had always preferred more perilous locales— and was absolutely crestfallen if I refused to get down to business within sound of her father's voice. This quirk and the fact that sometimes her clawing and biting during the act went beyond normal ardor, had caused me no small resentment in the months the Cavanaughs had insisted I see their shrink to determine whether or not I was culpable in causing "our present little vicissitude," as Eleanor referred to my suspected infidelity.

Parking the Mercedes in the shadows, I got out.

And there it was, shining in the night: a great, white wedding cake of a house, tier upon tier of cupolas crowned by the one hundred fifty foot main tower; and every possible surface filagreed, embossed, or otherwise embellished in some manifestation of Victorian Gothic overstatement. European royalty, even Ludwig II of Bavaria at his castle-building maddest, would never have had the nerve to tempt providential lightning with such vaulting opulence. But James Clare Flood, a saloon keeper by trade, born of impoverished Irish immigrants in New York City, had felt no such constraint.

Popping the trunk latch, I fished out my binoculars and trained them on the sea of umbrage surrounding the house, the wide gravel drives now faintly luminous in the starlight. In the midst of the five or six cars the Cavanaughs stabled on the premises, was one more square than sleek in silhouette. Everything they owned was European, and this sedan had Detroit written all over it.

The moon was beginning to bulge over Walpert Ridge across the Bay, and I knew I would have to act fast if I intended to follow through with my suspicions. A luscious whiff of orange blossoms was persuading me to stop dawdling and make full speed for the gate—and Eleanor, who would undoubtedly look breathtaking tonight. She was beautiful in a way that ignited more desperation than affection; still, I needed her more than anything at that moment.

Yet the last time I had set foot in Linden Towers had proved to be the ugliest afternoon of my life.

After brunch that Sunday I had gone to the polo club to exercise the ponies, returning about three to a mansion that was deathly quiet—almost as if the lord of the place were available for final viewing in the Indian teak-wainscotted parlor. I *knew* as soon as I whisked past the Roman busts into the echoing chamber that the game was up: Eleanor and her best friend, Patricia, were perched tandem on the sofa, staring at me, expressionless, although their eyes were bright with expectation. Eleanor rose serenely, clasped her hands together and let them dangle over the faint bulge of her pubic bone. "Who shall it be, Howard? Patricia or myself?"

"What do you mean?"

"You know precisely what I mean. I would like very much for you to go away for a few hours, then return with your reply."

"Okay," I rasped, and drove aimlessly around Menlo Park like a zombie, running stop signs, the saliva in my mouth tainted by bile.

I had never even liked Patricia. Her face had been honed to an exasperated sharpness by long boredom, and what at first had seemed foxy about it soon struck me as being lupine and cruel. I wanted Eleanor, of course, and began composing in my head the most earnest speech of my life. I was so intent on impressing my wife with its sincerity, I decided to practice it first on Marguerite, so I dropped in at her San Carlos apartment. She was still attractive at that time two years ago, having not yet passed beyond the stage of pleasant fleshiness, so I was slightly embarrassed to call on her at home, and she seemed equally confused, distantly suspicious, until the explanation gushed out of me. Naturally, she urged me to test my speech for Eleanor on her.

"Darling, I'm not going to ask for your forgiveness," I began, growing less self-conscious as I went along. "I don't deserve it. But I'm begging you to try to understand. Never once in ten years have you spoken the words *I love you*. You married me, so I assume you do—or did. And I can appreciate how fearful an heiress must be of completely giving her heart to someone, especially to a man of no means. I drifted into this thing with Patricia because I was feeling sorry for myself. The sex really wasn't that pleasurable—the truth is, it made me feel rather sad." I paused: Marguerite's lovely green eyes were glistening back at me. "But I love you . . . and I want you. I want you to love me. I need you to tell me that. I can't remember anybody ever telling me that. I know I'm a long way from earning your love as of today, but if I just had the hope that sometime—"

Then the damndest thing happened—Marguerite and I were hungrily clutching each other, kissing moistly and with more fervor than I'd imagined possible. She moaned with every hunger that had been thwarted in her, and I sprang up from the sofa as if I'd been scalded by her lips. We both shivered—at the enormity of what we had almost done to Rodrigo. We interrupted each other as we hastened to apologize, and I rushed out the front door in a panic when I could think of nothing more to say. We had continued our friendship, but only by pretending that this had never happened.

With mounting despair I wondered if a baby might solve

Eleanor's and my difficulties. But the notion was hopelessly quixotic: My last year at Our Lady Clare's mumps had gone through the orphanage as surely as saltpeter. Because of our advanced youth, Rodrigo and I had suffered the worst cases; and the Cavanaugh's physician had been able to describe my sperm count with the fingers of one hand.

Finally I putted back up to the gatehouse in my Austin-Healy and watched the main tower steam through a wind-scudded fog like the bridge of a huge ship as I waited for Harry, the middle-aged guard, to admit me. But he was nowhere to be seen.

My agnosticism melted under the fear of being abandoned once again, and I shut my eyes in prayer to Saint Clare, whose beatific countenance had smiled down on me all my youth: *Please . . . open the goddamned gate.* After I had choked on my amen, I saw that the wrought-iron barrier was still secured against me, so I laid on the horn. No one came down from the house, even after ten minutes of honking. At last I made a U-turn that so exemplified the moment, I burst into tears—and wept between hiccups all the way back to our silent apartment in San Francisco.

That had been my last experience at The Cottage, I now reminded myself as I backed my Mercedes up to the seven-foot-high brick wall, then used the trunk lid as a platform to gingerly pass over the wicked, arrow-pointed iron spikes into the waiting arms of a deodar cedar. The Cavanaughs, like most folks in this neighborhood, kept savage dogs, but I made it all the way to the moon shadow cast by the carriage house without a bark being sounded. Recalling that beam sensors cross-stitched the walkways and garden paths—waiting invisibly to broken by an intruder—I kept to the pastures of ivy and the thorny copses of rosebushes, to the detriment of my suit, which was snagged and torn in a dozen places.

I crept across the pea gravel of the main drive to what I had glimpsed from the overlook—the nondescript sedan. "Son of a bitch . . ."

It proved to be a white Dodge Monaco. The hood was still warm.

All at once, through the thicket of veranda columns, I watched the Hun in Herringbone himself promenade out through the mahogany and stained-glass front door to loom at the top of the marble steps. I ducked behind the Dodge in the same instant Cletus Beauchamp-Cavanaugh snapped his wristwatch out of his coat sleeve and read it by the light of a window. His chest sank as he exhaled, crossly, and from memory I filled in the glower on his darkened face as he peered down the long, curving drive toward the pinprick of light twinkling from the gatehouse.

"You son of a bitch."

Hands clenched behind him, he strolled the length of the great porch, his impatience obviously allayed by his pleasure with the palatial mansion, which he had bought out from under the California State Historical Society thirty years before. It seemed that James Flood's "last" will contained a codicil that gave Hamilcar Ames Cavanaugh, his closest confederate in Comstock skulduggery, first right of refusal at sale of the estate. Cletus, in one of his rare weak moments, had shared with me that this document was "slightly apocryphal. But that would've suited old Hamilcar to a T. He hoodwinked everybody every chance he got—none more so than the goddamned federal government." Then Cletus had laughed the laugh of a man who believes that because he is very rich, he is also very smart. And I had laughed along, of course: I longed to become rich and smart.

At last Cletus spun on his heels and hurried back inside.

The Edwardian parlor where Cletus and Eleanor ordinarily retired after dinner was on the south side of the house, so I darted from shadow to shadow until I reached a privet hedge by which I could approach one of the floor-to-ceiling windows without being seen. The splayed fans of foliage of a potted palm on the other side of the glass limited my view, unless I squirmed this way and that, but I had a clear shot of Eleanor across the Persian carpet which was probably worth more than everything I had been able to salvage from the divorce. Her lovely long legs, crossed now, were flanked by a brace of male Doberman pinschers, who were squatting obscenely, leering up at her with the expression of mindless adoration I had probably had when in her presence long ago. It was pathetic, but I *ached* at that glimpse of her after so many months, and once again I understood why I had courted her so relentlessly.

On the travertine mantle behind her a five-pointed copper star glimmered in its richly carved wooden frame, a family relic—the badge of some fraternal organization to which old Hamilcar had belonged.

A hand reached across the sofa and patted Eleanor's. She eagerly grasped and held it. It wasn't Cletus's liver-spotted paw, so I changed windows. This gave me a field of vision down the center of the antique furniture arrangement, although I know how to contend with a brass cuspidor brimming with dried straw-flowers. I eased upward—

"Bastards!" I gasped, then dropped to my knees for fear I'd been overheard. But within the parlor the murmur of voices went on without pause.

I had never expected to see Michael again in this lifetime. Yet, slowly rising again, I confirmed that there indeed sat my ex-wife's former fiancé, beaming beside her in full regalia: a three-piece suit, knit tie, and Ivy League haircut. His appearance had the corroborative effect of catching a suspected German spy at his leisure in a spiked helmet, squinting at the Zimmerman telegram through a monocle—for Michael had spent the late 1960's with golden curls dangling down around his then sloped shoulders, disparaging the wealth to which he had been born against his sincerest wishes. I had never been fooled by his affinity for third world causes; beneath that disdain for economic injustice coursed the same hauteur that put the rosy color in Cletus's cheeks: the unassailable assurance that being born disadvantaged has nothing to do with misfortune and everything to do with poor prior planning.

But Michael's presence, his fondling of Eleanor's requiting hand, were not the worst of it.

On the settee beside the organ that had come around the Horn in 1850, were two men, apparently partners—by the way in which they kept looking askance at each other while Michael prattled on about something—obviously cops, by virtue of their bored indifference, most likely *federal* cops because, although their suits were stylish, their shirts were bureaucrat white.

As Cletus swept back into the room to answer a quartet of impatient glances with a wolfish one of his own, I understood at last why a man will hurl a garbage can through a glass storefront and snatch a television set, a stereo, a lamp—anything that can symbolize his rage against the Gross Imperturbability I saw reigning inside that baronial parlor. The brass cuspidor, gleaming within my arm's reach, became such a symbol to me, and I was on the verge of smashing my fist through the thick pane to seize it when, in midst of this insanity, it occurred to me that after so much humiliation at their hands in the past two years, I might not be able to rein in my anger once I got rolling. It would not do to murder the Cavanaughs and their guests, although I couldn't think why during those moments.

As I stole back across the moon's patchwork toward my soon-to-be-repossessed Mercedes—the great bijouterie of a mansion growing smaller over my shoulder, becoming a fairy castle in which a little girl could actually grow up thinking that the Ethiopians should eat cake if they want for bread—I realized why the Cavanaughs labored so incessantly at my destruction: I, with my grubby schemes, reminded them from whence they came, the grubby immigrants who somehow, mystically, had been shown the path to the Money Tree before all the guideposts had been removed and the trace overgrown by a maze of noxious vines.

Eleanor never spoke of her deceased mother, an alcoholic socialite I'm sure Cletus had slowly poisoned with silence. Like Athena, my ex-wife had sprung fully grown and armed from the brow of her god-father.

I arrived back at Rodrigo's condominium in bad shape, having picked up a fifth of Christian Brothers along the way. Trying to sound facetious as I tumbled into a beanbag, I failed and my voice shook apart from rage and hurt. It was several seconds before I could finish saying, "Any chance of sneaking me out of this century . . . tonight?"

Sitting cross-legged in a pile of computer tractor-feed paper, he studied me carefully. "Yes, I think there is. But not tonight. What happened?"

"I'm going to finish this drink, then get on the road."

"Why?"

"It won't take the bastards forever to run down your address. This is the first place they'll come looking."

"Who?"

"The cops the Cavanaughs are siccing on me. Jesus . . ." I shook my head in disbelief. "This time I'm afraid it's federal prison. Nobody skates on mail fraud."

"Are you guilty?"

"What can I say? It's all relative."

Surprisingly, he shook his head as if he understood, then went back to perusing a sheet of computer paper as he said, "I wish you'd never gotten mixed up with the Cavanaughs. Balzac was entirely correct when he suggested that behind every great fortune you'll find a crime. It's something you should think about, Howard."

"*Think about?* Hell, I wouldn't mind that tattooed on my chest."

He frowned. "Please don't talk that way. Especially in light of the opportunity I'm about to offer you."

I closed my heavy eyelids, longing for sleep, oblivion, anything except this catastrophe of a life. "What opportunity?"

"Your chat with that English professor from Berkeley gave me an idea. I surveyed the potentials for nineteeth century Nevada. There's a loop in autumn of 1817—that's too early for you. Don't ask me to explain, but I think the traveler should have some personal interest, some stake in his destination. And Nevada that early is a wilderness inhabited only by Paiute and Shoshone aborigines. Interestingly enough, there's a cluster of loops later in the century, one in spring of 1861 and a second, longer one, from late spring to autumn of 1862—both concurrent with a huge proton flux. These dovetail with some of Mark Twain's and Bret Harte's years in the West, according to my encyclopedia."

Drowsily I asked, "What's a loop?"

"Well, simply put—an event on the order of what Miss Jourdain and Miss Moberly experienced at Versailles. They *went* and they *returned*—a loop. But even more descriptive of the causality—they departed the tenth of August, 1901, and visited the tenth of August, 1789. Conversely, they walked out of that solar day in 1789 and returned to the same day of 1901. Quite unexpectedly, they didn't find themselves knee deep in snow at the end of the *tour*." Rodrigo smiled at his use of this word. "So, in *Unaccountable Mail Outside the Context of Dysfunctional Cybernation*, I referred to this as a Petit Tour—an excursion that involves the obverse and reserve of a single date."

"Is there such a thing as a *Grand* Tour?"

"Certainly, an excursion of several months, or even years. But I'd be loathe to attempt it the first time out."

"*Attempt* it? Are you telling me—in all seriousness—that you've invented time travel?"

"Of course not—"

"Thank God, I've got enough troubles right now without you coming unglued on me."

His eyes had begun smarting. "I was going to say that I've found a way to turn adventitious into *scheduled* time travel, although number of loops in a given century is limited. So, in your lifetime, you will have only one shot at 1861 and one at 1862, just as the English headmistresses had a finite number of opportunities to visit France during the last years of the Bourbons."

"If this shit is possible, why haven't you gone yourself?"

He fisted his hands as he had done long ago to attack Cannonball, and began hollering again. "Because at this stage it'd be impossible! It'd be like anesthetizing myself, then trying to perform surgery on my own heart! Like trying to touch my nose with my elbow! Like—"

"Okay, okay."

He had been prepared to rant on in his way all night, but now restrained himself. His worried eyes softened as it dawned on him that he'd stumbled on the right chord with me: He had shown me his helplessness.

"Does this mean you'll help me?" He refused to blink as he waited for my answer. "Howard?"

THE PETIT TOUR

7

ONLY A WEEK after we had sneaked out of Sunnyvale in the night, I'd had a bellyful of time travel, adventitious *or* scheduled. But failure only redoubled Rodrigo's efforts.

I was lolling against the trunk of a yellow pine. High above me on the canyon wall I could hear traffic whispering over the modern highway between Reno and Carson City, and every so often, the flatulent grousing of a compression brake as a tractor-trailer inched down the grade. But here, in the windlessness at the bottom of the chasm, all was still—except for the creaking of my car's engine as it cooled.

Coated with dust, the Mercedes was parked along the dirt road that one hundred twenty-five years before had wound up from the territorial capital to a sawmill in the Sierra Nevada. In those days these hills had been stripped of timber to shore up the Comstock's mines, and only after all this time was a sparse second growth beginning to dot the dun-colored slopes. Miles down the canyon, across a sagebrush plain that galloped away on the eye, stood Carson City, a misty Oz of casinos and state government buildings shining in the morning's golden light.

I slumped to the ground and dozed.

A big, languid horsefly bumped against my sunburned cheek,

65

then tried to land on my nose before I shooed it away. I unbuttoned the dark blue woollen shirt which had proved far too hot for these past five days of slogging up and down this abandoned track under unseasonably warm spring skies, while Rodrigo carped at my back, "Pick up your pace a little. And if that doesn't work—well, try slowing down. Do you feel depressed yet?"

"Don't ask."

Within the fortnight, I had irrevocably lost the woman I loved— to someone I despised. And Eleanor Beauchamp-Cavanaugh had become the most desirable woman in the world to me, if only because I knew at last I would never have her again; and during my nights of the past week in the overheated Carson City motel room, I had watched in outrage as Michael and she ran wild through my dreams, tussling time and again toward sweaty climaxes, leering at me cheek-to-cheek like naughty children. But not only had I been betrayed in these nightmares, Eleanor and Cletus had in a few effortless strokes demolished the very corporation they had helped me organize on a solid foundation of pro forma "social responsibility" underlaid by chicanery and graft—in essence, a scaled-down replica of their own Cavanaugh Industries; to which, not being of *blood*, I had never been admitted as a corporate officer. But mortally wounding Hart Enterprises was not enough to slake their vengeance. It was also necessary that I lose my freedom; and I was so convinced of this eventuality, I found myself wondering if federal detention centers were air-conditioned (I assumed they were—but I had also assumed that the Cavanaughs would never go this far to get even with me for rutting with Patricia).

So, indeed, I was depressed, although not in the sense Rodrigo was looking for: that sudden and ineffable loss of libido the Englishwoman had experienced at Versailles.

I was also embarrassed:

Yesterday a Jeep load of bosomy girls had bounced past me when I was around a bend from Rodrigo. My slouch hat, red suspenders, and trousers tucked slovenly into my boot tops had drawn catcalls from them. Had they seen that I was ambling away from Rodrigo, they might have thought his magnetometer to be a camera, and then my nineteenth century appearance might have made sense to them. But instead I had to suffer their youthful cruelties in silence. How could I explain that with no place to go, with no options left open to me, I was being blown along by the force of Rodrigo's enthusiasm for a phenomenon I could never understand—one, apparently, that probably didn't exist outside his fitful imagination. But just try to tell a goddamned physicist what does and doesn't exist.

Each morning had dawned clear but with a thin haze clinging to the desert floor. By ten o'clock swatches of cumulus were drifting over the crest of the Sierra; but on none of the hot, humid afternoons had the clouds congregated into the towering thunderhead Rodrigo so desperately wanted to see before the chance glided away. Devoutly he believed that this was the time and place for a Petit Tour. And as we drove away from the Mark Twain Motel at first light each day, I found myself infected by his faith that somehow, by the grace of theoretical physics, I could give the twentieth century the slip.

At the beginning I had been more than willing to trust in the possibility: I had even insisted on taking along some spending money, although Rodrigo, warning me that to dawdle in the past was to risk the unthinkable, allowed me only one double eagle. This 1857 twenty-dollar gold piece was to be used only in the most dire emergency: that is, to keep me moving toward what he referred to as the exit opportunity. With a few momentary exceptions, Miss Jourdain and Miss Moberly had kept *in motion*. Had they done otherwise, they might have found themselves marooned in 1789—so Rodrigo said. I no longer had an opinion on the matter.

Now, as I roused myself to wave away another horsefly, I watched Rodrigo jog to the trunk of the Mercedes and exchange his magnetometer for the very low frequency metal detector he had purchased in Reno. It was mid-afternoon, and my buttocks had gone to sleep under me.

He paused as if to sniff something, perhaps some vagary of solar wind—I had no idea. But it appeared to encourage him. Then he was transfixed by a blaring white cloud that suddenly cleared the walls of the canyon, cooling us with its shadow. Behind its platinum-colored nimbus the rays of the sun fanned out across the sky.

He clambered up a rockfall to a rusty-looking outcropping and began probing it with the dish-shaped head of the metal detector— to an annoying cacophony of blips and squeals. Something caught his attention; he bent down and scooped it up with one hand, then pitched the object across the road to me. "Here!"

It dropped in the sand at my feet—the neck of a broken bottle, the glass a delicate shade of amethyst. There was still a cork in the flared-lip spout, although it was badly dessicated. "Why does it do this?"

"Do what?" He was busy with the metal detector again.

"Turn purple?"

"Old glass contains manganese oxide . . . solar-reactive." His tone of voice told me that he didn't want to be bothered right now.

But I felt like bothering him. Another day spent, and once again we were winding up firmly embedded in the twentieth century. "Any more old bottles up there?"

"Pieces of purple glass all around this knob. Must've been an irresistible target for passing teamsters."

"You mean they drank while they drove?"

"I suppose—don't you?"

"Yeah, but I don't have sixteen mules to think about."

He switched off the detector and packed it over his shoulder as he scurried back and forth down the face of the slide. "Let's tend down the canyon. The rock here has hematite mixed in it."

"What's that?"

"Iron ore—too much interference for me to know if we're well placed within the magnetic field. Start hiking down the road." After a few moments he noticed that I hadn't budged. "Howard. . . ?"

"What?"

"Please start walking while I reset the ground balance calibrations."

"Let's talk."

Standing with arms akimbo, he blinked at me. "Why?"

"There's a pint of brandy in the glove compartment—"

"I don't want you intoxicated during this. I thought we agreed—it'd be dangerous. The first night in the motel room you promised—"

"Yes, dammit—I remember everything I promised." Grunting, I got up and shuffled down the slope, stiff-legged. I put my arm around his shoulders. "Enough, Rodrigo. It was fun in the beginning, but now I'm tired. Sunburned. Windburned. Dehydrated. Fed up."

"Then what do you suggest?"

"Let's go home."

He worked his jaw muscles as he watched me retrieve the brandy from the glove box. "And what about the federal warrant for your arrest?"

"I'm going to turn myself in—after I get roaring drunk and eat everything on the menu at the Top of the Mark. The Cavanaughs win," I said wearily, cracking the seal on the bottle and filing my mouth with cheer. "The Cavanaughs in this world always win. . . ." I was going to let all my self-pity trickle out of a throat now nicely greased by brandy, when Rodrigo screamed as if someone had just run a rapier through his bowels.

"Jesus, what the—"

"Howard!" He touched a glistening spot on his forehead with his fingertips. "I just felt a raindrop!"

"What?!"

"Rain!"

"You know, going to the Mark is second on my list. First I'm going to *commit* you." Drops as big as Thompson grapes began streaking past my eyes and thwacking the dusty road.

"Start walking while I mark barometric millibars!" He tapped the crystal face of the aneroid barometer that was affixed to the magnetometer. "And be ready for the soil level differential. Decomposed granite in an alluvial canyon like this can build at a rate of a foot or more a century." Once again he realized that I hadn't moved. "Howard, go . . . please!"

"*If* I can take the brandy."

"Whatever—just get in motion. I beg you!"

I had gone about twenty listless paces when he called out anxiously, "Do you feel anything?"

"Yes," I answered without turning, "but you don't want to know."

Nursing the brandy, I scuffled down the road in my clunky boots, pestered by a moisture-scented breeze that had risen in the last few seconds and was eddying grit around me. Overhead, a wraith of gray mist was scudding across the face of the huge white cloud that had apparently spawned it and other creamy convulsions now swirling in every which direction across the sky. Thunder cackled then belched in the far distance, and a cottonwood beside the road was caught napping by a sudden gale that lifted the hems of its boughs and shivered the silvery undersides of the leaves.

With four fingers of brandy already downed, I began to enjoy the show: *"Blow, winds, and crack your cheeks! Rage! Blow!"*

A skein of rainfall, looking more like dust than water droplets, plummeted from the belly of the cloud and cloaked the mouth of the canyon a mile below me, although where I walked remained dry but for a rogue pelting that prattled heavily across the road before charging up the slope like a troop of ghost dragoons, trampling the sagebrush as it ran away from me.

Behind me Rodrigo was shouting something. He sounded disappointed.

"What?!"

"Russian thistle!"

"Right," I muttered as I glimpsed a tumbleweed—or Russian thistle, as it was more properly called—go somersaulting down the road far ahead of me. Contrary to hundreds of anachronistic Hollywood oaters, this weed did not make its appearance on the American scene until the turn of the century, when it arrived in a shipment of impure flax seed from Russia. Rodrigo had instructed me to take notice if the ubiquitous plant abruptly vanished from the landscape.

All at once the sky split open along a bright red seam, which then fractured into a web of jagged veins that intersected again before striking a pine snag on the peak above me. Pieces of flaming wood peppered the slope, and I flinched under a paroxysm of thunder.

"Red lightning," I told myself with a chuckle as I stood up out of a fetal crouch. Quickly recovering my dignity, I turned to grin at Rodrigo.

But he was nowhere to be seen.

Nor could I spot any Russian thistle.

And in that instant the *possibility* became a *probability* in my ozone-intoxicated head. My hands, of their own accord, wriggled down into my front trouser pockets, frantically seeking the silver brooch that had belonged to Eleanor's great-great-great-grand-mother. I found nothing but the double eagle.

"Oh, boy . . ." Rodrigo's first postulate to be tested on a Petit Tour, the Naked Englishwomen Postulate: that one travels the loop within the context of self-reference, even down to one's personal accoutrements. Miss Jourdain and Miss Moberly had not tripped into the Gardens of Trianon of 1789 to suddenly find themselves indecent because the cotton of their dresses had unraveled back into the ancestral Egyptian cotton plants from which the fibers of their clothing had been picked, or that their jewelry had converted back into undug mineral ores. Rodrigo admitted the contradiction in all this, for the traveler was supposedly entering an era as it had genuinely been, down to the most minute detail, and to have a ring exist as a ring and also as gold ore confronted the physicist with new vistas of duality—unless, as suspected, the principle of relativity soared beyond light and matter to the most sacrosanct human apprehension of reality as well.

Whatever, Rodrigo was curious to know if the Cavanaugh's brooch would remain in my pocket when I reached the late spring of 1861, or would materialize again on the breast of a young woman of that era named Eleanor Louise Beauchamp, residing in Virginia City with her aunt and uncle. The resolution of this paradox would tell Rodrigo much, although our failure to resolve it might tell him even more—so he said with the unflappable ambivalence of a true man of science. Quite simply, his was a keener ignorance than mine.

Meanwhile, I couldn't find the damned piece of jewelry even after emptying all my pockets and turning them inside out.

I squinted back up the road. The rutted trace seemed more than vacant. It looked forsaken. "Rodrigo!" I shouted against the wind.

Ignoring his warning not to form a cusp in the loop, I began hurrying back the way I had just come, hoping to meet him at the bend in the road. My heart was palpitating. My nervousness began to play tricks on me: I felt sure there had been a smattering of yellow pines along this stretch, but the hillsides were now dotted with knee-high stumps, some of them still oozing sap. After a week of traipsing up and down this canyon, I couldn't recall having seen any sign of recent logging. "Rodrigo!"

The air was buzzing and crackling like it does beneath high-tension wires, giving the atmosphere an irksome frenzy, when I stumbled across a bottle—not mine, which I had snugged in my rear pocket. Cautiously, I bent over and examined it.

A cork was jammed in its slightly off-kilter neck. A plump, fresh cork in a decidedly old fashioned bottle. But the clear glass was yet unblushed by the sun. There was even a trace of amber liquid rolling around inside, and its embossed lettering read:

Jcb. Metzenbaum
Importer
Virginia City, Nev.

Suddenly the bottle glowed vividly, and I laid it back down as if the glass had burned my fingers. It had only been the reflection of another flash of strange, red-tinted lightning; but for an disquieting instant the bottle had seemed to throb with its own surly fire.

I might have panicked at that moment had not a tumbleweed rolled across my path. The hissing and vibration in the air fell away to a faint drone.

Then I saw Rodrigo loping around the bend, hair windmussed, the magnetometer hanging off his shoulder on a strap. He glanced up from the assortment of dials and scowled. "What are you doing? Keep moving! I've got to back off any minute!"

"So back off!" I thrust my hands into my front pockets and tramped down the road. Then I forgot all about the peculiar bottle I had discovered: My fingers had brushed against the brooch. Stunned, I brought the piece out and did everything but bite it to make sure it was real. There was no way I could have overlooked it. I had plumbed each of my pockets down to the lint. Something had *happened*, and all at once I was not so quick to think that some Virginia City tourist trap was bottling bourbon or rye in Old West replicas. I spun around to tell Rodrigo to pick up the bottle and have a look for himself—just as a cloud of dust boiled down off the hillside, obscuring him.

"I know," I reminded myself in his momentary absence, "*keep moving . . .*" But I had taken no more than three strides when I experienced an extraordinary sensation: that of descending a familiar flight of stairs in darkness, stepping off the lowermost step only to realize with a start that it was not the last—and then tumbling blind through space, seemingly forever, but finally hitting the floor with a jolt. My hands flashed open to brace myself as my chest pitched out over my feet. At the same time my shoulder struck the hump in the middle of the road, it occurred to me that I had let go of the brooch.

I sprawled there, catching my breath, congratulating myself on hitting what obviously was rock bottom in life, then began sifting through the coarse sand around me for the brooch.

There was now a deep stillness in this twist of canyon, and I might have considered the unnaturalness of it had I not crawled upon something that made me scuttle back and forth across the road in search of the tire impressions of my Michelin radials. They were not to be found, which given the gale-driven dust, was not surprising; but in their stead was a brace of tracks, the patternless indentations about five inches wide and two inches deep. And within arm's reach lay a scattering of dung—obviously deposited by a horse on the move. Overcoming my revulsion, I pressed a finger against one of the spoors: It was warm, pliant, moist.

Undeniably fresh. Not once in five days had I seen a horse in this canyon.

"Oh, boy . . ." I sat up and clasped my arms around my forelegs. I didn't cry out for Rodrigo—and that in itself was an article of sudden faith.

The sky was beyond overcast; it was dense, nearly unpenetrated by the late afternoon sunlight, and its moist air seemed too heavy to breathe, although I may have thought so only because my chest, particularly the area around my heart, felt thick with loneliness. This, perhaps, at last, was dying.

I needed a drink.

Squatting cross-legged in the road, I was gulping down warm mouthfuls of brandy when a distant, merry sound broke the windless silence. It made me smile.

Bells. Sleigh bells, I was sure. Hundreds of them, defiantly gay in the midst of the deepest blues I'd ever had, tinkling, jingling, chasing off the doom of the world with their brash melee of rhythms.

You better not shout . . . you better not pout . . ." I was hopelessly giddy when the first two mules thundered out of the eerie twilight, digging up divots of sand with the hollows of their hooves.

Hollering, I rolled to the side—but not before, quite absurdly, capping the brandy bottle with my thumb. I cringed against the canyon wall as at least a dozen mules bleared past in tandem, their trace chains rattling in counterpoint to the chiming of the bells affixed to the collar of each lathered animal. I caught no glimpse of a human form, but a small wooden wheel was followed by one six-feet tall, then a slash of yoke before the same sequence of wheels. Only when this apparition was past and consumed by the dusk, leaving an aroma of pine pitch to linger behind, did I realize that it had been two freight wagons hitched together, bearing towering loads of fresh-cut lumber down the grade.

I was on my feet, struggling to make sense of what I had just seen, when the dioramic stillness was jarred by the approach of a second rig, which rounded the bend at a slower clip, giving me time to see that it was comprised of *three* hitched wagons, all as ponderously loaded as the first had been.

A voice cried out—as solemnly as if it had issued from the burning bush. The lead mules began to sidestep and crowhop to a halt. In the absence of shadow I found it impossible to discern any human shape until the front wheel came to rest not ten paces from me and a trim little man in a sombrero thrust the butt of his blacksnake into a whip holster and leaped to the ground. On closer examination, I saw that he also wore white pantaloons. A Sonoran, I thought—and then wondered with a jolt if I might be in Mexico, or if I had arrived in Nevada when it was still a half-forgotten Mexican possession.

The teamster flipped up the wooden bench he had been sitting on and began rummaging in the storage compartment beneath. At first I had believed that I was the reason for his stop, but I grew increasingly alarmed as he went about his business without taking notice of me. He donned an oilskin poncho, which crackled like fire as he moved, and then lit two lanterns off a sputtering match— these he hung under the front axle of the first wagon and the last axle of the third, leaving me all the while to fret that I was diaphanous, or even invisible to him.

But this concern faded when he remounted his bench seat and asked, *"A donde vas?"*

I knew enough Spanish from my years with Rodrigo and Marguerite to answer, but I hesitated to tell him I was bound for Carson City. What if he had never heard of it? Quite naturally, that would give rise to his next question: *"De donde vienes?"* And never it had occurred to me in the past week that I might have to explain where I had come from—the possibility of this conversation had always seemed a bit outlandish, despite Rodrigo's unassailable confidence that a moment such as this would come to pass.

The teamster waited for my answer, his coffee-colored face impassive to the point of seeming brutal, the upturned ends of his mustaches unraveling as if they were wisps of smoke. Like the man the headmistresses had encountered near the kiosk at Versailles, the Sonoran seemed to be of "particularly evil countenance," although I tried to reassure myself that the hostility glinting in his dark, Indian eyes might be less from a hateful nature and more from some bizarre refraction of light that was affecting everything, animate or otherwise.

Propped beside him was a Kentucky rifle, a powder horn tied to its long barrel. Cletus Cavanaugh had one just like it in his extensive firearms collection, and it seemed to me that this muzzle-loading flintlock was manufactured decades before the 1860's. Rodrigo had missed the bull's-eye. I was growing more and more sure of it.

Without thinking, I had rested my left hand on the crown of the iron-banded front wheel, and now, through a desolation of spirits, came a delayed message that my palm was on fire. I reclaimed my hand with a shout, then waved it frantically until the pain became bearable.

The teamster shrilled the darkness with laughter. He sobered himself only when it apparently occurred to him that I might be deaf and dumb. "You English?" he asked, forsaking Spanish.

I nodded stupidly—afraid to admit being an American, especially if Rodrigo had landed me right in the middle of the Mexican War.

"You talk?"

"Yes," I said, sucking on the heel of my hand.

"Do not touch the wheels—never. I chain the wheels to go slow down the steep part of the mountain. They skid then, not roll too fast—you see?"

I accepted his lecture with a meek nod, for it had dawned on me that I was having a conversation with a dead man—at least dead in my own time, and my curiosity was being held within bounds by nausea. I was not sure if I could digest my nostalgia in the present tense.

"Sometime the wheels so hot they smoke—so never touch." He stared at me to the marrow for a few seconds. He sensed that there was something different about me, but couldn't quite put his finger on it. Behind him lightning cracked the sky as if it were a sheet of glass. "You go to Carson?"

Sighing with relief, I dug the double eagle out of my pocket and offered it to him.

"No," he said, with the first hint of affability. "Too much for so little a ride." Licking his lips, he eyed my brandy bottle. "You share a drop?"

"Yes, of course."

"And no talk *a político*?"

I had no idea why he made this demand, but he expressed it so sternly, I agreed not to discuss politics.

He patted the bench for me to sit, and with a flick of the long driving line followed by a lash of whip, goaded the mules into starting down the road again.

To reflect about any of this promised only to overwhelm me, so I decided to make conversation: "Are these good mules?"

"All but the wheelers."

"What are wheelers?"

He closed one eye at me. "Why, *these* . . ." And his greasy boot struck the rumps of the two beasts immediately forward of us. "But my swingers are most excellent. You can see for yourself they are not jar-headed."

I began to appreciate the perils I was courting with my ignorance, so I offered him my bottle and kept silent as I surveyed the peculiar duskscape I can only liken to a sea floor, where light arrives in nebulous pools and slowly fades to shadow again in vague gradations of umber or deep purple. It was grimly beautiful, but it made me want to vomit—which I eventually did, furtively, over the side of the wagon.

When we finally emerged from the canyon, I was awed by the immensity of the electrical storm, a lightning-stitched canopy blackening the entire sky—except for a thin swatch of robin's egg blue in the southwest, the sawtoothed forests of the Sierra looking like they had been cut out of the sunset with a pair of pinking shears. The lanterns of the first rig, guttered by the half mile that now separated us, were swinging across brushy plain toward a cluster of tawny lights I knew, by their location in the darkened valley, to be Carson City, *territorial* capital of Nevada.

The lamplit town awaiting me, the jolting progress of the freight wagon, the tinkling of the bells on the collars of the mules, the popping of an occasional raindrop against the oilskin poncho of the Sonoran teamster—these were not so much the trappings of a new reality but rather the vivid suggestion of an *unreality* I had entered at the bidding of a friend who was yet unborn. The warmly glowing windows of the first house on the road pierced the gloom, reminding me of the faery magic of Linden Towers glittering through the darkness.

Then I winced as I realized that I had lost Eleanor's brooch on the sawmill road which was now completely enveloped by the night.

"*Ciudad de Carson*," the teamster announced, grasping the wooden lever of his brake.

And at that moment, as I sat perched on the brink of the most imponderable adventure a mere mortal could ever experience, all I could think about was Rodrigo trying to get my Mercedes back to the motel in one piece a century and a quarter from now.

I had thought the frightening hissing and vibration had subsided again—when a tongue of flame flashed over the perked ears of the mules and a god-awful roar thumped everything out of my head, supplanting even the last reverberation of a thought with a mindless white dazzle.

8

NEVER BEFORE HAD I been in the mouth of a discharging cannon.

My ears hadn't stopped ringing when the Sonoran teamster thrust the driving line into my hands and leaped down to the road. *"Idiotas!"*

In torchlight the two men beside the road stood gaping at the Mexican, waiting for his hand to go for the hilt of the knife showing from his scarlet waist sash. They wore foppish-looking hats with high peaks and brims that sloped down over their shoulders. The mules were so skittish, braying all the while I tried to hold back, it was several seconds before I recognized the hats to be helmets and the sheepish-looking pair to be firemen.

They told the Sonoran the twelve-pounder had been loaded only with powder and tamp. They had meant no harm. In fact, they claimed to be performing a solemn public service.

"I do not care!" the teamster cried. "If these were horses and not most excellent mules, I would be on the Devil's own ride!"

By now other citizens were trotting out of the darkness.

"God rot the bastard who just broke every windy in my place! Who done it?!" This Nevadan, bare-chested but for suspenders, repeated the question, and when neither of the guilty pair answered, threw a roundhouse that failed to connect with the nose it sought—but nevertheless forced the fireman to stumble backwards, losing his helmet.

"You bloody tosspot!" His partner whooshed a flaming torch back and forth in the face of a second assault by the half-naked man. Such a spirited defense by the cannoneers cut short the complaint of a new arrival that half of his assaying equipment had been rattled off his sideboard by the blast.

Suddenly a revolver thumped against the night.

"Jesus!" I could actually hear the bullet sizzle across the rainy sky. And that was good enough for me: I tied off the driving line on the brake lever and clambered down the dark side of the wagon.

A second gun and then a third opened up against the night. Over my shoulder I could see that the muzzles flashed only skyward— and no man toppled over, although swarms of rounds were being expended. Despite my jangled nerves, I had to admire such uninhibited behavior. And as far as tension relievers went, gunplay beat biofeedback all to hell.

I had not gone far when the clouds loosed a dense tracing of lightning over the main thoroughfare, glistening on the newly painted wooden filigrees and balustrades of a low line of downtown buildings, spangling on the brass hame knobs of horses drafting buggies which, in the absence of any kind of outdoor lighting, I had failed to notice thronging what was decidedly Carson Street. It looked as if the entire populace had turned out; and even before the thunder had resounded, I had decided to investigate—despite Rodrigo's warning to keep moving eastward toward the exit opportunity, which could occur at any instant.

But surely a moment's pause would cause no harm. Hadn't Miss Jourdain and Miss Moberly lingered briefly now and again in the Petit Trianon? So I hurried toward the faintly glowing lanterns hung on the axles of the massed buggies and farm wagons. Without asphalt and concrete, the world seemed so much softer, and the rain-dampened sands of the road crunched nicely underfoot. The night hummed around me, kinetically, but far less ominously than before.

Another spasm of lightning. A short man in a porkpie hat, waiting at the fringe of crowd, startled at my approach—as if I had materialized out of thin air. He appeared to find something unsettling in my face, so I smiled. His cheeks had been cratered by smallpox, but the disfigurement was finally mitigated by a polite nod as I passed him by. My pulse was swishing loudly in my ears, and my nostrils had dilated to admit all kinds of sharp odors—sage, leather, fresh horse dung.

I was fascinated by the brisk, jocular animation of the men around me—there were no women to be seen as of yet—and almost persuaded myself that this quality was normal to them, until I asked myself if something momentous was happening, an unexpected relief from the mundaneness of their lives. But I didn't have the nerve to ask anybody what, for fear that I was the cause of their excitement. Had I arrived like a meteor, blistering down through the clouds? Or had someone seen my doppelganger, or whatever the hell I was in transit between present and past, blearing along the sawmill road like a sixty-second exposure?

This entire thing has too much density for reflection: It rips through the layers of logic as if they were wet tissue papers. Simply go along with it. . . .

Everyone was facing a three-story brick structure. It was the most substantial building on a dirt plaza still knuckled with the charred stumps of brush that had only recently been burned off. Atop a liberty pole a soggy flag unfurled, but only for the strongest gusts: I counted thirty-four stars.

Oblivious to the soft rain, hats raked back off their foreheads, the men looked for all the world like they were waiting for some bigwig to make his entrance onto the balcony. The place was most likely a hotel, its banks of ground-floor windows pulsing in saffron, although there was nothing gimlet about this light. It was silken, bewitching; and it occurred to me that Thomas Edison had stolen the enchantment out of the night.

My boots thumping hollowly along the boardwalk, I threaded my way down a portico to within an arm's reach of the main doors, which were so crammed with bodies, I could go no farther for the moment. While waiting there, I realized that I was the tallest fellow in sight, a Gargantua, in fact—and at six feet, even I had almost considered myself to be of average stature. Heretofore, hats of every description—bowlers, boaters, porkpies, and stovepipes—had given an illusion of parity, but now I estimated that most of the men were six to eight inches shorter than I, while many were a dwarfish five feet in height. For the first time in my life strangers began to make room for me to pass.

The fog of my breath pulsed on and off the bubble-flawed glass of a window as I peered into the lobby. The room seemed slightly shabby, despite the mellow conflagration issuing from its candle chandelier. The worn Brussels carpets were close to being threadbare, and the horsehair sofas were absolutely mangy. But these blemishes on the hotel's respectability seemed to have no effect on the cream of territorial society, Falstaffian nabobs with twisted mustaches, their kettle bellies sagging against quilted velvet vests, right hands confidently grasping the silver heads of ebony canes. In their midst stood a young army officer, clearly pleased to be the center of attention. His uniform confused me: Whereas I might have expected Yankee blue from head to toe, this muttonchopped youth with West Point posture was clad in turquoise trousers with gold piping, a high-collared indigo tunic and a billed cap that was firmly strapped under his somewhat weak chin. No judge of military paraphernalia, I thought that he was decked out for the Mexican War—and once again I wondered in what year Rodrigo had landed me.

By sidestepping to the next window, I could glimpse into a small foyer. And what I saw there came close to making me gasp. There were women within—not as I, a grown man, had come to regard them, but women through the eyes of a small boy: each a matron of comfort and affection with rose-tinted cheeks and white, fleshy, gesticulant hands as fleet as doves. How those hands flew as they spoke to one another! And now the paucity of women outdoors made sense, for here in this second-rate hotel was the entire hoard in the territory, jewel-like in their hoopskirted gowns of glittering metallic sheens; azurite, jade, malachite, and galena. One dowager had trimmed her skirts with peacock feathers, and I imagined in adoring silence that she had plucked them from her mate's tail while he slept. These were the most beautiful women I had ever seen—until I lost this momentary gift of child's sight, and I realized with great disappointment that their faces were plain, altogether too plain.

Quite possibly I had underestimated the strain of the past half hour. For, whatever the cause, I had begun to weep, quietly, feeling no emotion other than vague unease.

"Are you going?" someone said from behind.

Drying my cheeks on the scratchy wool of my sleeve, I turned to face a middle-aged man with an avuncular smile. "I beg your pardon, sir?"

"Are you *going*, my dear fellow?"

I was amazed to think that his words might be some kind of warning for me to get moving again toward the exit opportunity. "Yes," I said with sudden resolve. "I must."

But before I could take a step, he seized my hand and pumped it with both of his. "Agreeably said!"

"Thank you," I mumbled, disengaging myself and rushing across the plaza, giving a wide berth to the storm-distraught horses. Then, making sure no one was following me, I slogged down a muddy alley between a livery barn and a boardinghouse.

I wasn't sure when it had happened, but the ambiance of unnaturalness, the hissing and vibration, had dissipated—or perhaps finally I had come to terms with this incredible reality. It was night in a different time, but nevertheless a night of reassuringly familiar minutiae: of cool wind, of light and shadow clearly defined, of rain softly drumming the ground. My silhouette yawned ahead, then shrank back as the lamplight snatched at me from different angles. An incense of juniper smoke was swirled in the turbulent air, from supper fires I imagined, and I found myself reluctant to continue eastward. I wanted to taste the food cooked by those fires. My Petit Tour seemed to be drawing too swiftly to a close, especially now that my anxiety was wearing off. God, how keenly I found myself wishing that I might remain a little while longer.

At that instant a harsh voice cried, "Halt!"

I halted. Before I could think of another thing to do or say, a torch was lit less than a foot from my face. It flared painfully in my eyes for several seconds, then was backed off. I was surrounded by a dozen or more rough-cut men in woollen shirts and baggy trousers little different from my own. Testicular safety be damned, each ruffian showed the butt of a revolver jutting out of the front of his waistband—apparently, holsters weren't in fashion.

No one spoke, and I tried to smile. The double eagle felt like a hundred-pound ingot in my pocket. Should I hand it over immediately and without complaint? My eyes flitted from face to face, and in none did I recognize the congeniality I so desperately wanted to see. And now that terror had shriveled my sinuses, I could catch a fetid combination of sweat and whiskied breath that promised violence.

The torch brushed past my face again, coming so close I was afraid my eyebrows had been singed off.

"Where you from?!"

"California." I was now already ready to hand over my sole coin and skip these amenities, as charming as they were.

"Nobody canna be from California," an unidentifiable accent

piped up, sneeringly, "save Chumash and Spanishos. And you look like Cousin Jack hisself, lad."

A big panicle of lightning fell down behind them, briefly muting the glow of the torch and bringing them into hideous clarity—God, but they looked like cadavers in that instant.

"You northerner or southern?" the first interrogator asked.

Had I known at that moment what he was genuinely asking I might not have rushed to say "northern." Only later, as I hurried eastward on my way, did I realize that had I hailed from Los Angeles and blindly answered "southern," I might have been dispatched on the spot. Although oblivious to this fact then, I was startled—and relieved—to hear them raise a loud cheer. I was invited to join in three hurrahs for Abe Lincoln and the Union, which I did with gusto, although my knees had become so jellied I could scarcely stand. "What's the most recent news?" I asked hoarsely.

The reports tumbled out of a dozen throats, hindered by interruptions and contradictions; but the gist of it at last became clear: Fort Sumter had been shelled eleven days before by Confederate forces—the account had arrived late this afternoon via Pony Express. The outbreak of the Civil War, not I, was the reason for the excitement in Carson City. So Rodrigo had missed his mark of late spring of 1861 by only a few weeks: It was the last of April.

"God rot Jeff Davis and all copperhead scum!" a youth ballyhooed to laughter and applause.

We parted company on the best of terms. When they learned that I was a registered Republican, bottles were broken out, and I had to decline several hearty offers to take one with me on my way *home*, which not a one of them suspected was a hundred twenty-five years distant. Then they paraded down the alley and rounded the corner to accost some other hapless stranger. Now I understood why the Sonoran teamster had refused to discuss politics.

I had not marched far into the darkness again when a second party, plainly of the same stripe, came trooping down a stockyard lane under the sparking light of a pine-pitch torch. I made no attempt to avoid them, although I saw that our paths would soon converge. In fact, I was so eager to establish my good credentials I strode right up to the goateed stuffed shirt in the van of the procession and declared, "God rot Jefferson Davis and all copperhead scum!"

He said nothing at first, his tremulous eyes riveted on me from under his shaggy brows. It was an intelligent, almost courtly face that was slowly blanching to the color of suet. Touching his hand to the brim of his panama hat, he ventured a wry smile, but it quickly turned sour on his lips. "I take it, suh," he half whispered at last, "you object to the inauguration of freedom recently ushered in by our splendid compatriots in South Carolina?"

Before I could answer something, anything to save my stupid neck, a gaunt-faced towhead elbowed his way to the forefront and leered at me. A thin beard lay on his cheeks like a hoar frost.

I attempted to say hello, but it came out as a weak sigh.

He lifted his upper lip over a pronounced overbite and snarled. "Hang him, Yer Honor?"

That was good enough for me.

I batted the torch out of the hands of the man who held it, and the flame winked out against the ground. Before the first grunt of surprise had been sounded, I was bounding over a corral fence and sprinting for the darkest quarter of the night.

Having once belonged to the Cavanaugh's trap-and-skeet club, I was quite familiar with the throaty bark of a shotgun, but none of those genteel tournaments, toasted afterwards with schnapps at the clubhouse, could have prepared me for the intensely personal experience of hearing an explosion to my back and realizing that the sudden whistling overhead was buckshot. The shooter's aim had been high. Perhaps he had only intended to frighten me with the first shot; but by the time the second boomed out in rolling waves of sound, I was over the last rail fence and thrashing through a line of willows that hid a small stream. Branches clawing at my face, I doubled my efforts when I heard from afar, but not far enough: "You may pursue him, Tyler!"

In that awful moment I had no doubt that Tyler was the cracker with the overbite, and it was now all too easy to visualize him scuttling along on all fours, pimply nose to my trail.

Emerging onto a rain-puddled road, pausing only long enough to get my bearings again, I then ran some distance before I saw that I was headed again for the city plaza—due west, when I needed to go east. And as I agonized there, lungs burning with each breath, it began to hail: big, stinging drops of ice that rattled off the leaves of a nearby cottonwood, which I finally shuffled under.

"Damn!" This little escapade might well have cost me my exit opportunity—and the consequences of that were beyond reckoning for someone who didn't quite believe that he was here in the first place. What was I to do?

East! an echo of Rodrigo's voice exhorted me. I pointed my boots in that direction and began plodding forward again.

The only house along a quarter mile of darkened road was a modest early Victorian with a colonnaded veranda. The white gingerbread glistened like icicles under a flicker of lightning, and as I closed my eyelids, steeling myself for the pang of thunder, my eyes still bore the imprint of a stout woman in a black dress standing on that wraparound porch, snugging her shoulders in a lace shawl as she listened to the hail thudding against the shingles. She lingered in front of bay windows not unlike those of my office in San Francisco, her outline dimly illuminated by a blue-tinted lantern mounted beside the front door. I thought I caught a whiff of perfume in the same instant the wheezy notes of a melodeon were drowned out by the belated roll of thunder.

I glanced westward: A torch bobbed into view across a pasture. And then the figure carrying it reached the road and turned toward me. He halted only long enough for others behind him to catch up. Spinning around, I took three panicky strides before I saw the lantern of a second group of searchers at the opposite end of the road. These men were methodically beating the high brush for me—one of them actually chopping and jabbing at it with a saber.

"Well, do not just stand dere," a husky alto cried above the clatter of the hail, which had begun to whiten the ground. "You tink you got sense enough to come out of de wet?"

It was the woman on the veranda.

I bounded up her boardwalk before she could change her mind. "Thank you . . . thank you so much."

"Ah, a polite one." She chuckled. "Clean and *vite, n'est-ce pas*?" By then I was standing in the light of the blue lantern: "Ah, not so clean—I tink. Leave dem brogans at de treshold, *si'l vous plaît.*" And as I hopped on my left foot while shucking off my right boot, she gushed, "Oh, I am wrong again! Boots—even if dey be pinchy-toed. Where you get such boots? Ah, never you mind. A genleman!"

Decidedly past her fiftieth spring, she filled her floor-length gown with at least three hundred pounds, and the fat of her arms, which shone yellowly through the sheer black lace of her sleeves, was dimpled. Yet she was not unattractive. Her nose was slender, her dark eyes vivid, and her mouth still evocative of a former sensuousness. But beneath it all was the infallible shrewdness of a chess grand master, and she returned my scrutiny with a sly grin. "What you tinking, you sport?!"

My pursuers! I reminded myself with a shot of adrenaline—and checked their progress. For whatever the reason, the copperhead scum had aborted their search down this road and were racing back toward the stockyards. Nevertheless, I concealed my boots under the snowball bush that bloused partly over the porch.

"Ah," she cooed, "I know what you be tinking. . . ."

Obviously the woman was taking my hunted look for something else. But my relief was so great I let her lead me through the front door, down the polished wooden floor of a hallway—the perfume growing stronger with each step—and into the lamplit parlor from which the melodeon music was issuing.

I slowly smiled. The four young women within smiled back at me. One was seated at the spinet-sized instrument; two on a settee, who returned, sniggering, to the book they had been reading before rising to greet me with curtsies; and the fourth, a redhead with alabaster skin, who was standing at the window, savoring the moist evening scents while the chemise curtains billowed back like spinnakers against her pale, bare arms.

You, Howard Coolbrith-Hart, have stumbled into a nineteenth century parlor house!

The setting was quiet, almost familial—and I supposed that the war excitement had dampened tonight's trade.

"I am Madame Richelieu," the big woman said, and it came to me that she might be a Creole mulatto. "I will permit my girls to introduce demselves, I tink. Will monsieur take refreshment?"

The question brought warmth to my cheeks. She sensed my misunderstanding and quickly added, "A cognac perhaps?"

"Yes, please . . . *merci.*" I felt like a hick in my woollen shirt, soiled trousers, and pungent athletic socks; I longed to be smartly attired like the self-satisfied men I had seen through the windows of the hotel lobby. I cleared my throat and again flashed my best smile at the two Irish-looking brunettes on the settee, taking in their ample breasts at the discreet lower periphery of my vision. "What are you reading?"

They snapped shut the volume between them, then hid it under a corner of the crocheted antimacassar.

"Marie! Monique!" In turn, Madame Richelieu scolded each with a jab of her plump finger. "Answer de genleman—as you have been taught!"

"Je vous demande pardon, monsieur," Monique said with an

unconvincing French accent, her R's as flat as potato soup, and handed me the book, her smooth forearm skidding along the back of my hand as she withdrew again.

After accepting the snifter of cognac from the redhead, who then gravitated back to the window with languor, I read aloud from the title page of the book, "*Facts About Boys for Boys*, by Reverend Richard Donkersley, New York, 1859—"

The two young Irishwomen burst into giddy laughter that was cut short when Madame Richelieu clapped her hands together—only once.

"I'm sure it's quite informative," I said, returning the book to the now silently convulsed young women. "But I prefer learning facts about girls."

"*Bon*—dis is a place of leisure. Of companionship. It is expected dat monsieur will remain for breakfast." Madame then stood waiting, smiling at me.

The next move was mine, but I postponed any decision by turning toward the redhead, who was drinking deliciously of the cool air. A thick application of powder had failed to conceal the almost clammy-looking sallowness of her face; and her eyes, when they flickered toward me, were enormous blue vapidities with only pinpricks for pupils. Had she been standing in strong sunlight, I felt sure I could have confirmed what I only suspected—she, like many of her modern sisters, was a junkie.

Almost gaily, she yanked shut the flimsy curtains. I then saw that each panel was a foot longer than it seemingly needed to be; but then the woman bent over and anchored these tails to the floor with two stacks of books, revealing this to be what the household used instead of window screens.

"I am Mimi," she said with what seemed a bona fide accent. Far from pretty, she nevertheless had the effortless chic of a Parisienne, although this stylishness, her vivaciousness, her charms, were obviously in the slow process of being ravaged by her addiction. She noted my lack of immediate attraction with a quiet nod. Given a choice, and I was clearly being given a choice, I would not pick her. Mimi accepted this with neither resentment nor relief; her expression remained distant but gracious.

I turned back to Madame Richelieu. "This is a very nice . . ." I hesitated. *House*, all at once, didn't seem apposite—but neither did *home*. Then it struck me how felicitously French words described the trappings of this business. ". . . *maison*."

"Ah, *merci*," Madame Richelieu rescued me; but then her tone turned defensive: "We would be closer to town but for politics, I tink. Some fools would like to see us gone. Still, we have many fine *amis*—such as yourself."

From this I gathered that her establishment was not yet accepted as state of the art in the local demimonde, although it made my head spin to imagine what the best bagnio in the territory might be like. Probably dandier than Moslem heaven.

The melodeon player now swiveled on her stool toward me, smiling as she fanned the wispy bangs off her forehead with a sheet of music. *"Je m'appelle Michelle,"* she said, as if it were quite naughty of her to reveal her name. She seemed more frolicsome than the others, although I didn't care for the wide space between her front teeth.

"Charmed," I said, finishing the last of my cognac.

A mantel clock struck the hour of seven—and I came to my senses. However fascinating this parlor, I had time to make up—exactly one hundred twenty-five years of it. Springing to my feet, I began to mumble some apology, but Madame Richelieu would have none of it.

"I tink I have misjudged your tastes." And with that she opened a door and called down a dusky corridor that led toward the back: "Musetta!"

"Really, madame, I must be going."

"Pour le moment—remain, *si'l vous plaît."*

A latch could be heard opening then clicking shut again, and soft footfalls approached the parlor.

I noticed her right hand first—small, slight, somewhat bony like a thin child's. It was clutching a strange pair of pelican-billed scissors, and what transpired from that instant onward emerged as the most flustered and hypnotic introduction of my life.

"Oui, madame?" Musetta asked.

"I have dis genleman I wish you to meet. . . ."

Then, I have no idea if it was the imposing Creole woman's smooth insistence (had she actually nudged me toward Musetta, and when precisely had she relieved me of my double eagle?) or my own shock that snuffled me down the polished boards of the hallway, watching Musetta's waspish waist as we turned to go into her room. Farther down the corridor a canvas portmanteau could be seen waiting outside a closed door like a faithful dog.

After the parlor, Musetta's quarters seemed bedimmed, and I saw that only a small candle was burning, catching the highlights of the gold-scrolled fleur-de-lis wallpaper. Her hurricane lamp had been disassembled atop its round table.

"If monsieur will excuse me a moment . . ." And she used the curious-looking scissors to trim the lamp's wick before lighting it with the candle. The glass chimney replaced, she adjusted the flame, and all at once her face glowed ivory-yellow. I must have made a sound, for her dark blue eyes clicked toward me questioningly.

Heretofore I had been alone with only one prostitute in my entire life—and that had been during my salad days at Stanford. I had done this less out of sexual urgency than the notion that on my deathbed I might regret having left some stone of experience unturned. Not only did the poor woman have to endure my pathetic attempt at seeming both world-weary and inexhaustible during the act, she had to entertain the requisite number of questions young men have for their first commercial lover. Did she like what she did? Did she despise her clients? Fear them? Skirting the issue, she said only that an eerie, almost adoring silence in a man forewarned her of violence.

Yet as Musetta waited patiently for me to speak, I could sense that she feared no harm from me. And how could I explain that her innocent features perfectly resembled those of Saint Clare in the vestibule of a San Francisco orphanage that did not yet exist? I knew damned well I wasn't superimposing recollection on some vague correspondence: This young woman could have been the model for the statue. The likeness went light-years beyond similitude—and it had raised the hair on my neck the instant she glided into the parlor. Her voice was what I had expected Saint Clare's to be—had she ever bothered to answer my prayers.

"You are very beautiful."

"*Merci beaucoup,* monsieur." Her pleasure seemed genuine, but her French had a Scandinavian lilt to it.

Breaking off my long stare, I pretended to give attention to her room, although I found myself listening to her softly breathe as I looked around. The mahogany bedstead was huge, but the bed itself was too short for a man of my height. Beside it glimmered a spitoon, scrupulously clean now—thank God. On a sideboard what I had first dismissed as bric-a-brac was on a second look a neatly arranged collection of fans, the better pieces spread open for viewing. I picked one up. "This lace is quite nice."

"*Ja*, Chantilly, and the sticks are pearl with . . ." Her gaze tumbled to the floor as she realized her faux pas.

I quickly turned to another. It was decorated with scenes of Moorish-looking villages. "Is this one Spanish?"

"*Non*, it was made in Paris. But those are . . . how do you say?—*episodes* . . . from *Barber of Seville*."

"Do you like opera?"

"I have never been." She looked forlorn for a few moments, then brightened. "Has monsieur?"

"Oh, many times. San Francisco has—" I stopped short, trying to recall when the first opera house had been built, afraid of mentioning some production thirty years before it had been written. "Many times," I said, closing the subject by smiling at her. I came close to brushing her cheek with my fingers, but all at once such a gesture seemed, well, too *intimate*; and this setting had an uncanny way of redefining intimacy. "You must have fans from all over the world."

"*Non*, I have need of a . . ." Once again her eyes became quick with trepidation. ". . . *japansk*. . . ." The J had melted on her tongue.

"Japanese?"

"*Oui*," she laughed. "But impossible to find here."

Then, through her open window, over the sound of heavy rain dripping off the eaves, I could hear what seemed like an army of boots pounding across the veranda. Startling Musetta with my abruptness, I cracked the door just as Madame Richelieu said to someone entering the parlor, "*Bonsoir, mon juge!*" And the cultured voice that had seethingly replied to my wish that God rot all copperhead scum, now replied in rapid-fire French to the Creole woman.

I whispered to Musetta, "Who is that man?"

She frowned briefly, but from that I could decipher volumes of revulsion. "*Juge* Terry."

"*Judge* Terry? You mean he's a territorial magistrate?"

"*Non*—not here. He was a *très important* one in California. But he killed a man in a duel—"

"Duel?"

"And now he leads *Le Cause*, our cause, here in Nevada."

I quietly shut the door. "You mean this is a Confederate house?"

"We who live here, monsieur, are southerners," she said, lifting her chin.

"Yes, southern Sweden, I'm sure."

Her eyes blazed at me, but then they softened as she asked, "Does David Terry seek you?"

I nodded.

"That is very bad. He has a great anger. You must go . . . *vite*." She was pulling on my arm with one hand and pointing to the window with the other.

I was halfway through the part in the damask curtains when I stopped and came back inside. She looked at me as if I were mad, and perhaps I was at that moment in which I heard myself say, "You are the most beautiful woman I've ever seen. And I wish to hell I'd never come in here."

She hesitated, then whispered: *"Moi aussi."*

It was an uncanny thing for a prostitute to say, perhaps the perfectly coy thing. But then she prevented me from going by grasping the sleeve of my shirt. "Will monsieur return a better time?"

There was nothing I could answer except: "Be well, Musetta."

Once out on the veranda I began stealing toward the front to retrieve my boots. But the judge had posted a man there, who was leaning on his musket, so I had to backtrack in my stocking feet and slip over the balustrade at the rear of the house. Torture awaited me in the form of a carriage driveway, and I gritted my teeth across the crushed rock, hopping curl-toed, until I reached the sandy soil of the sagelands beyond.

Afar, perhaps as distant as a hundred miles, lightning was throbbing in some amphitheatre of the sky. A milky glow in the clouds showed me where the moon had risen. I struck out across the plain in that direction.

Go east, young man.

9

AN HOUR LATER Horace Greeley was proved correct after all, and I was compelled by the rain-swollen Carson River, which was knocking boulders down its channel like billiard balls, to turn west again, back toward the now darkened city. Like some washout from a fire-walking school, I would limp along on one foot for a while, and then, to show no favoritism, switch with a wince to the other. In addition to blisters, I had slowly raised the conviction that I was here to stay—with no money, not even a pair of boots.

A coyote yowled somewhere out in the black hummocks of brush. Or did Nevada still have wolves in 1861? I filled my pockets with stones.

And now that I was cold, thoroughly exhausted, it came to me with an unhappy certainty: Musetta's moist eyes and inquiry as to when she might see me again had been her expediency for handling a john who tended to wax sentimental. I had been expecting sensibilities of a prostitute I'd not been able to pry out of my own wife. Still, Musetta was beautiful in a guileless way that I had never found arousing before, and as I limped through the night, I was beset by a resentful fantasy in which Judge David Terry played a prominent, if not pornographic role. With a fierce laugh, I gave thanks that I would never see her again. Or would I?

The possibilitity might soon be graduated to a probability—especially if I failed to stumble into the exit opportunity.

The downpour had thinned to a tickling mist, but the sky seemed no less oppressive. The shorter clumps of white sage and bunchgrass were difficult to pick out in this lightfast gloaming, and twice I was pitched face-first against the ground. From a mounting panic I had seized upon the plan of joining up with the sawmill road and entering Carson City once again—but this time not straying off the easterly-vectoring Maxwellian Corridor Rodrigo had described to me, a phenomenon I now sorely wished I had tried to understand.

A bleak moonshine finally escaped the overcast, and my ears had begun to buzz—which they often do when I am very, very tired. The wind had petered out. The unstirred atmosphere seemed dense enough to be sifted through my fingers. And when I blundered at last onto the road, it seemed dimly phosphorescent, paved with fox fire, as it wended and undulated across the desert plain.

Hobbling down Carson Street, past its benighted homes and shops, setting all the dogs to bark, I contemplated ending this trek at Madame Richelieu's. But it was unlikely that I would find Musetta alone, and the pleasure of our second meeting grew stale in my mind before I might savor it. Suddenly, quite viciously, loneliness had enveloped me—not the entwining garden variety, but a great python of loneliness, suffocating me in the slow constriction of its coils. Once again I was seventeen, still weak from my bout with mumps, and having borrowed Brother Tom's Chrysler New Yorker, was wading through the spring mustard beside a highway curve north of Salinas, picking up the shards of a shattered headlight. I had no assurances that these had once been part of my parents' car, but like Helena returning from Jerusalem with pieces of the true cross, I took them back to the orphanage, where they remained in the reliquary of an old shoe box until Rodrigo, intuiting their significance, made me scatter them in the Bay. Only later did I realize his hypocrisy in making me do this. He, too, had been to Jerusalem, many times.

"I've got to sleep!" I wailed against the congested sky. Had a bed with clean sheets awaited me on the far side of a mine field at that moment, I would have risked it at a gallop.

But then I tripped, and the reason why confounded me: Carson Street along this stretch was smooth and sandy. Yet it felt as if my right toe had connected with some kind of abutment. I took three more steps and the same thing happened. And despite being prepared this time, I lost my balance and toppled forward, striking my outstretched hands against—carpet!

"Jesus!" My head throbbed from jangling bells and blinding crimson lights that flashed in dizzying rotation. My fingertips fumbled across the worn fabric and brailled a spot that read suspiciously like dried chewing gum. Rolling onto my back, I was confronted by two files of glass-and-chrome robots facing inward to form a long gauntlet. Their short, black-fisted arms were raised in fascist salutes—perhaps to greet the huge figure who was blearing toward me from some recess of this smokey cavern.

I tried to mutter something, but the absurdity of any explanation I could possibly offer made me mumble drunkenly. I lifted my hand in silent pleading as the figure leaned over me, its face—or lack of one—obscured by a liquidity of light, an orgy of neon, more light than I thought possible after the darkness of the sagelands. The figure creaked metallically at the knees as its talon-hands violated my armpits and jerked me upright. I must have fainted briefly, for when the grayness was flushed from my vision, I was on my knees gaping down at a pinkish, glittering cement.

An automobile horn brayed past me.

I looked up: A traffic signal blinked from yellow to red. Scuttling around on all fours, I squinted through the Coke bottle-green glass door at the security guard, who loomed on its far side, jerking his thumb for me to move on. Above me garish little balls of illumination were alternating spelling: CARSON SILVER NUGGET . . . SLOTS . . . CRAPS . . . PARKING VALIDATED.

"Christ," I croaked.

Despite the rock-bruised soles of my feet (the remnants of my athletic socks hung off my ankles like soiled dickeys), I started running down North Carson Street, which was shiny black from a recent rainfall. On high, the heavens were clear, tacked with loud stars. I passed some poor human derelict, squatting on the curb in clothes even more pitiful than mine. Halting on a sudden idea, I hurried back and stopped beside him. His basset hound eyes watered in greeting.

"What year is—" No, I quickly decided, that was not the way to approach this. "I'm from radio KPTL here in town. For a chance to win a free trip for twelve to Maui—who is president of the United States?"

Tears formed on his lower lids and trembled there like opals.
"They just shot him, son . . . ."

My heart stopped. *"Where?"*

". . . shot him because he was Catholic—like me."

"Christ!"

"No, *He* was Jewish. . . ."

I shot to my feet, scanning the thoroughfare for some glimpse
of a late-model vehicle; but it was apparently an early morning
hour, and other than the northbound taillights of a distant car, I
could see no traffic, no vehicles parked along the street. The
billboards, the barber poles, the neon glass tube signs, the color-
coded curb markings, the parking meters—none of these would
have been out of place in November of 1963.

Rounding the corner at Washington Street at full tilt, arms
pumping furiously, bile worming up my throat, I knew that all my
questions would be answered in the next hundred yards, but was
not sure I could stand the disappointment.

"Good . . . good," I huffed. The psuedo-Victorian Gothic
lettering still read: MARK TWAIN MOTEL. My bare feet slapped the
sidewalk ever faster as I neared the darkened hulks of cars in the
parking lot.

Then it gushed out of me—a breathy torrent of relief. I choked
down a sob.

I danced three laps around my Mercedes, so drunk with delight
I was impervious to the fact that the driver's side fender was caved
in. Splinters of wood had been captured by a buckled spear of
chrome trim. I broke one off: It smelled of creosote. Rodrigo had
bashed a telephone pole, but I could only giggle.

The door to the room was ajar a few inches. Quietly, I slipped
inside. He was slumped over the keyboard of his computer, fast
asleep—as if he had finally passed out in the midst of hysterical
attempts to understand why I had failed to reappear from the Petit
Tour.

I touched his shoulder.

He lurched upright in his chair, then gawked at me a long
moment before crying, "Oh!"

But this single syllable said so much more than that: I can only
liken it to the sound a baby-sat child makes when, at last drowsily
resigned to the fact that he had been deposited with a blue-haired
stranger for all eternity, his parents show up to reclaim him.

"Did it work, Howard?! For the love of Mary, what happened?!"

Dropping the suspenders over my shoulders, I wriggled out of my trousers, the stones I had collected to fend off wolves bouncing on the floor around me.

"Talk to me!"

I heaved my soggy clothing into a corner, then flopped back onto the paradise of a mattress. "It works."

"What about the Cavanaughs' brooch?"

"Lost it someplace on the road—when I started the tour." Through half-shut eyes, I watched Rodrigo cross the room to pick up my clothes.

"Howard!" he said, sharply enough to make me lift my aching, one-ton head. "Look what was in your pocket!" He held the Cavanaughs' heirloom in his fingers.

"But it was *gone* the entire tour."

"I'm sure it was. We might be dealing with opposing contexts of self-reference. I can only venture that the one with the more powerful urges predominated—and resolved the paradox by taking possession of the brooch!"

"Nobody has more powerful urges than Howard Hart," I murmured.

"Don't be so sure. Howard, tell me, please—what was it all like?!"

That question was still reverberating through my mind when I awoke a day and a half later.

"Does any of this look familiar?"

I didn't answer. We continued to stroll down the residential street.

My footsoreness had been aggravated by a morning spent coursing up and down the rows of stone monuments in Carson City's Lone Mountain Cemetery, looking for a name I didn't know, hoping, pathetically, that I would somehow recognize it as being hers. Rodrigo suffered my silence without complaint. But when we came across a nameless headstone with a gloved hand pointing skyward, and I stared up into a wisp of cirrus, he could hold his peace no longer: "Howard, you're putting the experience in the wrong frame of reference. As God is my witness, this kind of thinking is delusional—"

I had walked away from him, on to the next monument.

And now, scrutinizing the houses along Magdalena Street— approximately a quarter mile east of the site of the plaza I had crossed to glimpse inside the hotel I had learned was Ormsby

House—culling the ranch styles, the stucco bungalows, the saltboxes, the duplexes, I focused on the Victorians, even those that had been stripped of their filigree and jacketed with aluminum siding.

"What about that one?" Rodrigo was pointing at a three-story with a witch's hat turret.

I shook my head no: Madame Richelieu's had had no turret or cupola, and besides, there had been the veranda that wrapped completely around the house. "It wasn't quite that rococo . . . the place was more sedate."

"A *sedate* house of ill repute, Howard?"

"Despite what you think, even sin can be in good taste."

He frowned.

We were three houses and a gas station beyond when a delayed image flashed across my weary vision, and I led Rodrigo by the arm back to the early Victorian that had belatedly snagged my attention. *"There!"*

"Are you sure?"

"That's *it*, for Chrissake!"

The veranda had been walled up to create more living space, but I had no doubt that the abandoned derelict had once been the parlor house. The front door and windows were boarded over, so I hurried through clumps of sun-scorched weeds to the side yard, disappointed not to find Musetta's window until I discovered that it was being concealed by an old refrigerator. The back door had been nailed shut, but at some recent time vandals had forced it partly open, and now, favoring my blistered left hand, I finished the job.

My Adidas crunched over broken glass littering the linoleum of a service porch, which connected to the kitchen. There was a circular plate of galvanized metal nailed to the ceiling—to cover the hole left by the wood cookstove pipe, I imagined. Rodrigo, who shuffled in after me, asked, "Do you really think we should be in here? There's a no trespassing sign—"

I walked down a hallway built along the original veranda, turned a corner and found myself inside the parlor—which, with its grease-spotted carpet and Waikiki-motif wallpaper, did not retain the faintest echo of its former elegance. From here I located the corridor that led to Musetta's room—the once carefully polished boards now worn and buckled.

I hesitated before touching the tarnished brass doorknob. It had only been *two nights ago* that I had passed this way. . . .

The door was so warped I had to use my shoulder to open it.

On the facing wall were the spray-painted words: GOD BLESS ELVIS PRESLEY; and below them a magazine photograph of the late singer ejaculating into a microphone. I could fell Rodrigo's eyes on the back of my neck.

"What are you thinking?" he asked softly.

"This thing has fallen into the wrong hands."

"What do you mean?"

"Deep down you and I feel we were dealt some pretty lousy cards. And if we're honest, we'll admit that we're not opposed to shuffling the deck for a new deal—whatever the consequences." I turned when he didn't say anything.

His evasive eyes told me that I was right. As hard as he tried, he couldn't hide his relief. "I was afraid you might not want to go again. You seem so distant, so melancholy."

I grinned for the first time. "Hell, I've *got* to go back. But this time it's going to be in style.

THE GRAND TOUR

10

AURORA WAS ONE death beyond being a ghost town. It was a leveled desolation, a junkyard of burst bubbles: shards of broken bottles, empurpled by a century of ultra violet; square nails, bent and rusted; the shattered heads and bodies of ceramic dolls, crazed and flaked by the moisture of a hundred mountain snows. Not one of the buildings, even those made of brick, had survived to the present, although here and there a few peaked roofs, jettisoned to the ground when their walls decayed out from under them, protruded from the invasive sage like those of a Missouri hamlet flooded by the waters of the Great Muddy. Even under the blithe light of mid-afternoon, with massive cumulus shining in the distance, Aurora could haunt with no solace other than the wind, which shrilled down the ravine that had once harbored the main street. It mussed our hair as if, in being alive, Rodrigo and I were curiosities to be trifled with; it clutched at our clothes like the hands of dead beggar children.

That it was barely spring among these nine thousand foot high peaks of western Nevada was driven home to us while we were backing the Appaloosa mare out of her trailer: A curtain of sleet fell across the sun, and the usually calm horse tried to leap over the hood of my Mercedes. These pills of ice were still glistening in the mud when I snugged the toe of my left boot into the leather-hooded stirrup and swung up onto the McClellan saddle, cooing the mare to serenity once again: "Come on, girl—what's a little weather?"

We had probably paid too much for her at the livestock auction in Carson City. However, inasmuch as she looked rugged and plebeian, she fit my needs perfectly. To show up in May of 1862 with an anachronistic breed was the last thing I wanted. It would almost turn as many heads as appearing with no horse at all between my legs—something unthinkable for a self-respecting Westerner of the nineteenth century.

Rodrigo carefully packed the new magnetometer in one of the saddlebags. Made to his specifications by a precision instrument manufacturer in Reno during the three weeks since the Petit Tour, it was smaller than his prototype and, he promised, much simpler to operate. But I wouldn't have to worry about that until the conclusion of the Grand Tour in late October, when I would use it to find my exit opportunity.

Cinching down the cover strap, he glanced up at me. "Quit posturing, Howard."

Easier suggested than done. The truth of the matter was that my checkered trousers, velvet-collared coat, waffle-patterned vest, red silk four-in-hand tied with affected carelessness, all crowned by a rakish derby—filled me with more self-esteem than any clothes I had ever owned. Within minutes of having donned them I had forgotten that they were the cast-offs of a melodrama troupe in Virginia City, indelibly dusty from years on a collectibles shop rack, and I felt as if I had been born in them. I especially liked slinking my gold watch out by its fob, or patting the Colt nested in the deep pocket of my coat.

A frenzy of research during the past week had confirmed that, indeed, holsters were not the territorial fashion until much later than the spring of 1862; and even a "stinkfoot," or greenhorn, carried a revolver in his coat pocket or in the waistband of his trousers—in addition to the derringer he stashed in his boot. The commonest handgun was the Navy Colt, so named because the cylinder of the 1851 model was engraved with a naval scene, not that it was the preferred sidearm of the U.S. Navy. Overruling Rodrigo's aversion to any kind of weaponry—which I reminded him was stereotypical of physicists since that Manhattan Project business, I had bought both antique firearms because I fully intended to alight in the Comstock Era on equitable terms with the likes of discredited California Supreme Court Justice David S. Terry.

If by happenstance we fell into each other's company again, I intended to give the Tennessee-born attorney and former Texas Ranger a wide berth. In 1856, at the height of the hysteria excited by the San Francisco Committees of Vigilance, he had plunged his bowie knife four inches into a man's neck. The wound did not prove fatal; and inexplicably, public sentiment held the attack to have been "inadvertent." But on a misty seaside dawn three years later, Judge Terry established beyond a reasonable doubt that his rage was of the most deliberate kind. He baited U.S. Senator David Broderick into a duel for having "impugned" his honesty in regards to a patronage matter. Broderick's hasty shot coughed up the sand ten feet shy of Terry's boots; and the judge promptly drilled the good senator through the lapel, then eluded prosecution for murder by taking to the hinterlands of Western Utah Territory, as Nevada was then known. There he mustered around the Stars and Bars a band of secessionist thugs, who organized themselves into the Washoe contingent of the most infamous fifth column on either side during the war, the Knights of the Golden Circle—the selfsame fellows I'd called copperhead scum to their faces.

Fortunately, twenty-six-year-old Samuel Langhorne Clemens did not join their scruffy ranks. Although the Missourian may or may not have served briefly in a Confederate militia outfit—Twain later covered his most telling tracks with a thick layer of hyperbole—his older brother, Orion, was a staunch abolitionist. Orion's mentor, Edward Bates, became the president-elect's choice for attorney general; and after a long line of Republican ward heelers had been rewarded for swinging the third ballot to Lincoln at the nominating convention in Chicago, Clemens was given one of the less plummier sinecures: secretary to the governor of the newly formed territory of Nevada. Samuel, thrown out of employment as a river pilot by the war, stage-coached west with Orion.

Now, as Rodrigo checked on the cloud buildup in the western sky, I gently put my heels to the mare, and she trotted up the gullied trace that had once been Pine Street, Aurora's main thoroughfare, flanked by two and even three-story structures in the early 1860's.

After loafing around Carson City for some months, then trying his luck in a few widely scattered silver camps, Samuel Clemens had wound up here.

I reined the Appaloosa to a halt before a flat place cobbed out of the rocky side of the ravine. At this spot, according to several accounts, Clemens had shared a tiny cabin with Calvin Higbie, a more experienced miner than the young idler who insisted on referring to Aurora by the more poetic name of the surrounding mining district, *Esmeralda*, Spanish for emerald, the gorgeous color of the region's pinion forests. It was in this hovel that Associate Professor Treacher's tale of lost wealth was played out to a bitter conclusion for Clemens and Higbie.

And now, at the coherence of a ray of stark sunlight and the blearing of my mind's eye, a kind of vaporous hologram appeared, wavered into the shape of a slope-shouldered young man with unruly red hair. I smiled at him. "I'm sorry, Sam, but my partner and I have worked too hard these past weeks *not* to strike pay dirt. I'll make sure you'll be compensated . . . *trust me*. . . ."

An empty wallet has no conscience. And a man who dreams of wealth knows no bounds. Twain himself would have been the first to agree, for when he stood poised to take control of the Wide West Mine in Aurora, he could think of nothing but a mansion on Russian Hill, a billiard room off the dining room, a landau and "a coachman with a bug on his hat!" Of all men, Mark Twain, born to poverty, would have understood what I was about to arrange in his behalf—and mine.

In regards to these plans, Rodrigo was not culpable. I told him little, although he watched in stony silence as I sewed a paperback copy of Twain's *Roughing It* into the lining of my coat. And as we prepared to leave the motel in Carson City, he asked, "Are you absolutely sure it was an injustice that Mark Twain received greater fame than your ancestor, Bret Harte?"

Being no litterateur, I was prepared to answer yes, but at that moment—as we were pulling out onto a side street—a white Dodge Monaco veered into the lot from Carson Street. Two men in business suits rushed into the office, and I put the pedal to the floor, scaring the mare and Rodrigo half to death until I felt it safe to slow down.

Driving a hundred miles south along the California-Nevada border to a small, white clapboard town called Bridgeport—the closet outpost with food and hot water to Aurora—we set up a base of operations in a nondescript motel, where I waited until dark before swapping plates with another Mercedes in the lot.

After unloading his computer and peripherals with manic care,

Rodrigo threw himself heart and soul into preparations for my Grand Tour. Years before in Sunnyvale, one of his many employers had done a study for the CIA. Rodrigo had held on to a copy of the software, which surprised me—especially since it was probably punishable by two lifetimes in federal prison, if not outright assassination by the Company. But he must have envisioned this very use for *A Logistical Matrix for the Insertion of Operatives into COMBLOCK or Potentially Hostile Destinations*, and planning for my excursion became almost as simple as painting by the numbers:

COVER. A credible cover must explain or at least excuse gaffes committed by the operative, unless he is totally familiar with the environment. During the Petit Tour, I had endangered myself with my ignorance of Civil War–era politics, so we really put our heads together on a watertight story. Rodrigo suggested that I try passing myself off as a London speculator, but this idea was laid to rest when, in the course of poring over a Nevada history in the Bridgeport public library, I discovered an early census: More than half of the territory's citizens were recent emigrants from the British Isles. So my English accent, which sounded like Alfred Hitchcock on amphetamines anyway, would invite suspicion, not deflect it.

Then inspiration struck, and I asked Rodrigo what was wrong with telling everyone I was an errant Saint from Salt Lake City. Everything I had read noted the strong anti-Mormon prejudice in Nevada, if not the entire nation—largely due to the sect's practice of "spiritual wifery," which Gentiles, or non-Mormons, tended to imagine as some kind of Oriental seraglio, marked by a perpetual state of male post-honeymoon exhaustion, rather than the rather staid arrangement it actually was. But nothing is more useful to a schemer than some rampant prejudice, and as mentioned, I had hinted before at being Mormon in some of my business dealings. Besides, there should be a speck of truth at the center of every lustrous prevarication, and I *was* related to Joseph Smith via Ina Coolbrith.

A *nom de temp* was probably no more than an embellishment; but in arriving at Belmont Howard Rettie for me, Rodrigo and I expended more argument than many couples do in naming their firstborn. Ignoring his suggestion of Ignatius, I chose Belmont because it was in the best motel of that Bay Area town that I had first made love to Eleanor. He then insisted on Rettie—after Father Rettie, his favorite physics professor at the University of

San Francisco; I finally caved in, although it sounded too Irish to me. But strangely enough, this synergism of a name described me better than the one my parents had given me. And afterwards, it seemed as if Rodrigo and I hadn't coined it, but recalled it.

LANGUAGE AND SOCIAL CUSTOMS. Unless the operative's faculties for idiomatic speech and social intercourse are flawless within the given ethnocultural context, he is advised to devote greater emphasis to COVER than this category in his preparation for insertion. Nevertheless, I learned to play faro, the most popular form of gaming in the era, and memorized the limited amount of Comstock argot available in the historical sources. I would rely on my Mormon lack of worldliness to bridge any gaps in knowledge.

MEDICAL FACTORS. Not even FINANCIAL SUPPORT FAC-TORS can inhibit the effectiveness of an operative as severely as injury or disease. Of course, there was nothing in the matrix about a visitation to the Far West of the nineteenth century; but by extracting information from the obituaries in frail copies of Aurora's *Esmeralda Star* on file at the county museum, we determined the state of health in Nevada of 1862 to have been slightly better than that along the modern Gold Coast of Africa. From the matrix, we selected the list of antigens and vaccinations recommended for steerage-class travel to Nigeria. The rural physician who, without batting an eye, filled both my arms with prophylactics against cholera, diptheria, hepatitis, rabies, tetanus, typhoid fever, and typhus, snorted through his nose when Rodrigo, who had kicked himself for not having remembered these measures before my Petit Tour, explained that I'd had no smallpox revaccination since my late youth.

"Listen, *compadre*," the country G.P. drawled, "t'aint no such animal as smallpox anymore."

"There's been a case reported where my friend here is going."

"Where's that?"

"Upper Volta. Please, if only for our peace of mind."

He shrugged. "Well, I'll have to order the vaccine. It might take a couple of days."

"Thanks, Doc," I said. "Say, they haven't come up with a preventative for syphilis lately, have they?"

"Sure," he cackled, "it's called keeping your wick dry."

Rodrigo turned away, mortified.

FINANCIAL SUPPORT. The operative must carry sufficient currency to meet his needs for sustenance and mobility without drawing undue attention to himself by overstepping the local standard of living. This turned out to be the biggest can of worms in the whole matrix, and Rodrigo had to write a new program to arrive at a solution. The long and short of it was—it would be far more profitable to take gold coin out of the nineteenth century than into it. For instance, a thousand dollars worth of gold double eagles at modern prices would have a face value of only sixty dollars in 1862—and during that especially severe winter, flour went for one hundred dollars a sack in Aurora! And that was one hundred dollars *gold*, for newly issued paper greenbacks were not considered worthy tender in Nevada. Even in the rest of the country an informal system of discounting currency was developed, and in this we found an answer, although not a completely satisfying one.

Greenbacks were acceptable to some San Francisco brokers—although at an exchange rate that varied from day to day. In May of 1862 the rate was quite favorable: about ninety-six dollars gold for each one hundred dollars of greenbacks. Soon after this, as the economic and human cost of the war became apparent, the value of the notes plummeted. But if I could make it to San Francisco sometime during that month (and I had another reason for making this trip which Rodrigo knew nothing about), I could convert twenty dollar greenbacks into a substantial grubstake of gold. The problem was surviving until I could make that journey, and for this the only answer was to take what remained of Rodrigo's cash on hand and purchase fifteen 1857 double eagles from a Bridgeport collector—only three hundred dollars face value in territorial times, but hopefully enough to get me by.

Greenbacks we found more difficult to find than double eagles, especially in quantity. Finally we contacted a mail-order numismatic house in Manhattan that offered the amount we required—but with a twenty thousand dollar price tag. Without complaint Rodrigo wired to Sunnyvale branch of the Bank of California for the last of his savings. A week later, we received a sheaf of worn, faded greenbacks from New York.

While Rodrigo rode a Greyhound to Reno to pick up the magnetometer I would take with me on the tour, I used the opportunity to phone Marguerite on the sly, assuring her that Rodrigo and I were both fine before asking: "Do you know where the Cultural and Trade Center is in Japan Town?"

"Of course, my feminist group meets there for sushi every so often."

"Good, I'm sending you some cash—most of it to get you through the summer." I didn't tell her that this was Treacher's down payment on the historical documents. "But with some of the money, I want you to buy me an antique Japanese fan."

"Anything special?" She was trying hard not to sound confused.

"Yes, it has to be appealing, delicate, feminine—you know what I mean. . . ."

She sighed in protest.

"And it absolutely must be older than the 1860's."

"Is that *all*?"

"No. How long would it take you to transcribe a book of, say, three hundred pages?"

"Into calligraphy?"

"Right, and on foolscap parchment, the fancy kind you put those sayings by Saint Teresa on."

"Oh, my Lord, I don't know—a month . . . two."

"I need it done in six days."

"When will I sleep?" She paused. "Very well, I'll try. What is the—"

"The Adventures of Huckleberry Finn."

"Para Marco Twain?"

"Si—but that's the rub. I want no mention of Twain *anywhere* in the manuscript."

She now sounded close to tears. "What am I to do with it when I'm finished?"

"Mail it express to Mr. Belmont H. Rettie, General Delivery, Bridgeport—"

"Belmont. . . ? Who is Belmont? What are you guys up to?"

"Don't worry, everything's okay—better than okay. I'm on the verge of having the best time in my entire life. Rodrigo sends his love."

"Does he really. . . ?

The answer caught in my throat.

Rodrigo accompanied me to the post office to claim Marguerite's package when it arrived, and while I identified myself to the clerk with a library card in name of Belmont Howard Rettie, Rodrigo began riffling absently through the wanted posters. All at once, as I was signing for the parcel, he snapped his fingers for my attention. "Howard!" he whispered.

"What?"

"Come here!"

There I was, staring back at myself from the corkboard of the Bridgeport post office, eyes misty, youthfully pudgy face flushed from too much champagne. And what made me seethe as we strode back to the motel under a lead-colored sky was this: The photograph had been taken at my wedding reception; no doubt it had been slipped into the hands of the feds by my ex-wife.

I was still sitting astride my mare before the site of Mark Twain's cabin, smarting over this betrayal, when Rodrigo began laying on the Mercedes's horn down in the ravine, which was now dark with cloud shadow. "Come on, girl . . ."

I found him cross as hell and didn't know why. He motioned for me to dismount and unhitch the trailer, which I did, as always, without benefit of his assistance. Then, before I could get back in the saddle, he roared off in the car, splattering me with mud.

The afternoon's plan was for him to drive and me to ride west out of the ghost town, turn around as soon as the thunderstorm became fully formed, and then vector east and overtake the entry opportunity somewhere along the road. If not successful, we would load the horse into her trailer and try again tomorrow or the day after.

Rodrigo, after his initial show of temper, was driving with typical preoccupation. The Mercedes weaved from berm to berm, lurched over boulders as big as watermelons, slewed around each mountain curve to a speed less than the mare's leisurely trot. After a quarter mile or so of this—which nearly drove me crazy wondering how he would ever make it back to Sunnyvale alive— he parked in the only puddle within sight and slogged up to me, his wings tips making sucking sounds in the ooze. "As soon as you pass through the corridor, hide the magnetometer over there." He crooked his finger toward a spire of mauve-colored rock. "That landmark hasn't changed in half an aeon. I packed the instrument in Cosmoline. And the batteries are stored separately in the waterproof case."

"What happens if the batteries go dead?"

He frowned. "That's why I protected them too. If they go bad, you'll have to wait around half a century until Edison comes up with an open-circuit cell compatible with your magnetometer."

"No thanks."

"Then for once pay attention to details, Howard. . . ." He started grilling me about the operation of the device, and I responded listlessly to his questions while the mare began nibbling

at some bunchgrass, her mane being dithered by the rising wind.
"Now, tell me—when does the exit opportunity occur?"

"October thirty-first, 1861." I said this only to rile him.

"No—1862! I'm delivering you to Aurora on the evening of
Sunday, the eighteenth of May, 1862! And you'll complete the
tour on the thirty-first of October—five and one half months
later!"

His brusqueness had finally turned me surly: "How the hell can
you be sure the dates were the same back then? What about leap
year and all that?"

"Don't be absurd—our calendar hasn't changed since 1582.
That's when Pope Gregory XIII authorized the adjustments we
now live by. Just *you* keep track of what day it is. *The Territorial
Enterprise* reported a violent electrical episode to have occurred
on the thirty-first of October—so don't miss it."

"What happens if I do?"

"Then book passage to France and wait around thirty-nine
years for Miss Jourdain and Miss Moberly to show up. *They* can
lead you back."

"You mean *1901* will be the next opportunity?"

"Yes, if you're lucky—and I qualify that because I don't know
how the introduction of your mass might affect the headmistresses' Petit Tour. Not to mention how you're going to get a horse
past the guards at the main gate to Versailles."

He was referring to some conjecture he had gleaned from the
data of my recent experience: Insofar as I would enter the Grand
Tour in combination with the mare, I might well have to depart
atop eleven hundred pounds of horseflesh. The postulate was
paradoxical in light of other things he believed; but as that had
never stopped him before, he insisted on this: Should I acquire a
different beast for transportation, gain or lose weight myself, buy
a new suit of clothes, squander all my coins or win more at
cards—I was to weigh in at a freight-wagon scale reported to have
existed in Carson City. Before I struck out for my point of
departure, which, as the periodic tendency would have it, was the
sawmill road—my entry for the Petit Tour—I was to make certain
that my total poundage was 1352, even if I had to fill my pockets
with cannon balls to do it.

At last Rodrigo tramped back to the Mercedes, only to realize
that it had slowly mired itself in the puddle. He plopped down on
the front seat and proceeded to spin the back tires deeper into the

muck by another six inches. "Damn!" he shouted—it seemed as shocking as when Rhet Butler had first said it on the silver screen.

"Turn the engine off!" I yelled over the howl of another pointless acceleration.

He jerked his thumb toward the rear bumper. "Push!"

"Bullshit!"

"Come on, Howard!"

"I'm not going to ruin these clothes!"

He flicked the key to off and quietly slumped over the wheel, his eyes pressed against the backs of his hands. I wondered if he was crying; but when I gently called his name, he glanced up and I saw that he wasn't. Still, he looked inconsolable, and my anger softened in the same instant he said, "You must forgive me my anger. It's something you really don't know about me. It's in my blood, I suppose. I don't know."

Dismounting, I offered him a nip of brandy from my flask, but he waved it off. "Howard, I'm relying on you to be circumspect on this tour."

"Oh, hell, everything was so simple then, how can I mess it up?"

"I mean it. Promise me you'll exercise moral judgment."

"I promise, Brother Tom—if you'll pray for me."

"This is *not* funny."

"It's ridiculously funny—you asking me to exercise moral judgment in the one of the most rapacious eras on the books."

"You are incorrigible!"

"And fucking proud of it!"

He rolled up his window.

Taking my time about it, I closed the running noose of my lariat around the already damaged front bumper of the car, then—with difficulty owing to the lack of a saddle horn—looped the other end of the rope around the pommel several times. "All right, girl," I said to the mare, "let's see if you've ever worked a day in your life."

Rodrigo gunned the engine.

"Easy!" I clenched the reins and started pulling.

Then, for a reason I'll never understand, he shifted into reverse just as the Mercedes began lumbering out of the puddle, and the horse reared backwards, off-balance, jerking her weight against the line.

The bumper popped off the chassis and sank into the mud.

Rodrigo stepped out. He eyed my boots and trousers, which were coated with a Hershey mess: "Sorry, Howard—"

"Don't say anything. Just drive."

A two-toned thunderhead—its dome white and its belly slate-colored—reared up over a barren ridge to the west. The promise of rain in the air had become palpable in the last twenty minutes; and while Rodrigo parked to take another magnetometer reading, I broke out an oilskin poncho and saddlebagged my derby for the duration of the storm.

Impatiently he motioned for me to follow him again.

I gave him the finger.

He started to return the salute, but then changed his mind.

An hour later, in the midst of a squall, he at last decided that it was time to turn around and begin our eastward strike toward Aurora. For the next two miles he drove even more abominably than before, and would have pitched the Mercedes down into a gully churning brown with runoff had I not fumbled for my Navy Colt and fired off a round—just as the front front tire was slushing toward the brink. Charging up to the car, I growled through gritted teeth when I saw him peer up innocently from the clipboard on which he's been scribbling notes. He rolled down his window a few inches, and blinking against the slanting drops of rain, asked, "What?"

I wheeled and continued on toward Aurora before I might say something. I could arrive in 1862 none too soon.

I slipped my hand under the poncho and patted my vest pockets. One safekept my watch, the other the Cavanaughs' brooch. Both were still there.

"Shit . . ."

In the past two hours I'd seen my high expectations crumble into disappointment. The electrical storm had roared overhead without incident, although once I had mistaken overlapping peals of thunder for the rumble and chatter of a freight wagon. And in the last minutes of daylight the now anvil-shaped cloud could be seen squandering its rain on an alkalai flat far to the desert east. A rainbow bent down out of the mists into the ravine that hid Aurora's ruins. And ruins they would remain.

We had failed. This evening I'd miss a surefire test of the accuracy of written history, a real bunk-buster. Yet as I gave the mare a short rest, my thoughts were already turning to the fifth of brandy I'd left in the motel.

Like most vintage McClellans, my saddle had split along a rawhide seam, and the crack now made another grab at my buttocks.

"Damn!" I reared up in the stirrups.

Rodrigo was standing against the skyline, witching for anomalies with his magnetometer. He gave it a quick smack—exactly how Brother Tom had fixed the vertical hold on the orphanage television set.

I wrestled out of the poncho, folded and strapped it behind the cantle.

Languidly he signaled for me to push on.

"Bullshit." I slumped across the mare's back.

She became restless for a few seconds, rocking sideways beneath me, then quieted herself again.

My cheek pressing against her damp mane, I gazed down at the ground. Its pebbly composition—as sharply defined as mosaic tiles only moments before—had grown murky.

And, all at once, I could taste the fillings in my teeth; they vibrated to the sudden hissing in the air.

"Don't look back, girl," I whispered. Gently, I jabbed my heels into her hind flanks. She began clopping through the silent, shadowless, unnatural evening. She didn't have to be coaxed; she knew as well as I that Aurora was no longer empty—perhaps the sweet scent of hay was on the breeze that now picked up around us.

Without turning, I lofted my hand in farewell, although I knew that Rodrigo was no longer there.

I began to reach for my ex-wife's brooch, but then trusted that it, too, was gone.

The night closed behind me.

11

I MANEUVERED MY legs over the side of the cot and slumped there for a long while with my elbows digging into my knees. Cradling my head in my hands, I wrestled with the urge to flop down again on the stiff canvas, which was a foot too short for a man of my height—my feet had lost all feeling as they dangled over the end of this miserable pallet. A band of dusty sunlight was slanting past my face, and I began sifting it between my sore fingers as if expecting the texture to be different from the stuff shining down a century and a quarter later.

"We assayed you for dead yesterday." If light was the same, sound was remarkably different. This male voice of 1862 lacked resonance.

Shading my eyes against the glare, I squinted down the long aisle that divided the dormitory and tried to bring the hazy figure into focus. The woodsmoke hanging in the air didn't help, but I could see that he was sitting up on his cot, back propped against the wall. His features were lost in shadow. I was on the point of asking him where I was, when it came back to me.

Finding a decent hotel room had been impossible last night. An old man had directed me to this boardinghouse, which, as promised, was adjoined by a livery stable. And in the last frail

114

light before moonset, I had led my mare up a lane paved with crushed waste rock to this drafty barracks, thunderous with snoring. Using my saddlebags for a pillow, I'd bedded down in my clothes, too spent to shuck off my boots.

But now my boots were on the floor beside a battered spittoon. My hand shot to the saddlebags—and I was reassured by the clink of gold coins. My Navy Colt was still in my coat pocket; I could feel the bruise it had printed on my hip during the night.

"It's all there," the voice said. "The derringer's in your boot—latest foot fashion, I see. And you got cheek to fancy us thieves."

"I beg your pardon?"

"I say you got uncommon gall to suspect us all like you just done—like Adam counting ribs. Nobody steals here, pilgrim. They say California drew the best of the world and Nevada the best of California . . . *if* this is Nevada, mind you."

"I'm sorry. . . ?"

"I say—if this is Nevada. Some say Aurora's in Nevada, some in California. Nobody'll really know until they survey the line. Now, what the hades made you sleep so hard?"

"I don't. . . ?"

"I kept tally—thirty-two hours from lay down to get up. And you never rolled. Never twitched. Never did nothing."

"I've come a long way."

"From the coast?"

"No . . ." Suddenly I realized that the clanging I had mistaken for a headache was *outside* my skull. "What's that racket?"

"My Lord, man, ain't you never been in these parts before?"

Now was as good a time as any to find out how well my Mormon cover would wear: "No . . . never."

"Why, that's the batteries of stamps crushing the ore—the music silver plays. Where *are* you from, pilgrim?"

"Salt Lake."

"U-tah?"

I nodded without comment.

"Are you one of them Zionites?"

"Used to be."

"What happened?"

"Whiskey." I gave up and sank back down onto the cot. Never had I felt so pummeled in body and spirit. My eyelids were nearly swollen shut, the glands in my neck so puffed out I imagined myself to look like a king cobra. Each joint was painfully arthritic.

Obviously, on this entry I had crawled through time on my hands
and knees.

"No cheek intended, friend—but did you have yourself a
goodly number of womenfolk?"

"What do you think hooked me on whiskey?"

"Bully news!" He clapped his hands together. "Just *how* many
is we talking about?"

"I don't rightly remember."

"You don't remember?!"

"Well, I started out with twenty or thirty when we left Illinois in
'46. The Sioux got a dozen—"

"A *dozen*?!"

"Now wait—the Sioux got eight and the Utes got four. That's
how it was. Or maybe it was the other way around. Anyways,
when Brigham got us to Salt Lake, he made me take on another
score and two of them—"

"Was they purdy?"

"Not a slattern in the bushel. And that last covey—every one of
them was under seventeen. A real melon patch, if you know what
I mean."

"Oh, I do! But if they was so fair, what're you doing here in
Esmeralda? I mean, why in the name of Great Herod would—"
He stopped short. I could feel his gaze passing over my listless,
prostrate form. "By grab, no wonder you look like you've just
come down the flume on a log! You must be here to get your
health back!"

"Precisely. Is there someplace I can wash up?"

"Basin and pitcher at the end of the hall. Rag bin nearby if you
want to dry. Refill the pitcher out back when you're done."

The basin full of tepid water did little to refresh me. Half
blinded by the flat morning rays, I shuffled outside through an
open door, skirted a pile of broken earthenware and shiny tin cans,
and stepped up to the well. Windlassing the bucket down into the
musty darkness, I found myself cranking in tempo with the
pounding of the stamps. Across the ravine I could see the
Stradivarii responsible for this cacophany in ache-minor: huge
iron-shod pistons that were shattering rock with Sisyphean
monotony, and would relentlessly go on doing so until midnight
Saturday, I recalled vaguely. Yes, someone yet faceless in my
mind's eye had mentioned to me last evening, or the evening
before, if I could believe the man inside. On Saturday night the
infernal clamor died away and Aurora's overworked millwrights

joined their mining brethren in her saloons, faro houses, and brothels. I had arrived on Sunday, and that accounted for my delay in acquaintanceship with this acoustical torture that made all Aurorans converse much too loudly, even when the batteries were silent.

I looked completely around: tiered quartz mills clung to both slopes of the ravine, and from their stacks steam hiccupped into the clear blue sky.

The well water was shockingly cold. My hands fell away from my face and I whispered: "My God, I'm *here*."

Everything I had felt upon entering Aurora came back to me in gooseflesh as the ice water dribbled off my chin. My first view of the lamplit town, festively bleared by its own wood smoke, had been like once again beholding the strung colored lights of the Holy Name Society's carnival winking at Rodrigo and me from the parochial school playground—with Brother Tom trying to control ninety-five boys twitching and caterwauling to answer the siren song of a calliope.

I had no sooner worked up the nerve to ride down Pine Street than a column of horse soldiers wheeled around a corner and came trotting my way, almost forcing me to backstep the mare into the crowded lobby of a hotel. Saint Francis forgive me, but what a thing of beauty—a troop of cavalry in full panoply. And what men-at-arms they were: not the anonymous proles of my own time, impressed into shapeless khaki. These were stiff-backed grandees with mustachios and goatees, each decked out in a midnight-blue coat with enough gold piping to hobble an elephant. I asked the man who was helping me constrain my mare by grasping her bridle, "What unit is this?"

"The Esmeralda Rangers!" he shouted over the rattling of silvered harness and scabbarded sabers.

"Union or Confederate?"

"*Union* militia." He eyed me carefully. "Where you from?"

"Utah."

"Oh." Satisfied with my answer, he turned back to watch the parading of the Rangers.

I knew better than to come right out and inquire as to the whereabouts of a Mr. Samuel Langhorne Clemens. During this spring the future honorary don of Oxford University was cutting a rather disreputable swath through the goodwill and generosity of the territory. So far the droop-shouldered redhead was famous only to his many creditors. Anyone seeking information about him would be avoided—I could certainly sympathize with that. So instead of continuing up Pine Street toward the cabin he shared with Calvin Higbie, I decided to hold off any snooping on the Missourian until daylight.

Besides, I had a more immediate matter to settle on this night. "The time, sir, if you please."

The Auroran produced his timepiece by its fob chain with a flourish equal to mine. "Eight and thirty, my man."

"Good." I corrected my own watch. "Would you be so kind as to direct me to Frank Schoonmaker's Bank Exchange Saloon?"

"Certainly, you can see it from here. . . ."

A block later I left the rain-washed coolness of the evening for the body-heated interior of the watering hole. Gingerly picking my step across the floor—the sawdust had been curdled here and there by a spitter missing his spittoon—I found a gap in the throng lining the mahogany bar two deep. I thirsted for a good brandy, but seeing the wisdom in remaining unobtrusive, ordered whiskey. I was given a dirty tumbler and a corked bottle. "Do I pay now?" I was forced to ask when the barkeep said nothing.

He studied me for a moment. Then, tweaking one of his heavily waxed mustaches, he smirked at the saddlebags I was still clutching in distrust. "No—before you go. You're charged by the drink. Four fingers for two bits in this house."

"Thank you." I elbowed my way toward the billiards room in the back. Once inside that den of comparative serenity, where dense cigar smoke wafted among the globes of the chandelier, I positioned myself behind one of the piers that partitioned the chamber off from the saloon proper. This timber was a foot square, and if this was indeed the Sunday evening of 19 May 1862 and what was reported in tomorrow's *Esmeralda Star* was essentially accurate, I would rely on the thickness of the wood to protect me from the stray particles of fate that might be glancing around this establishment sometime before midnight.

From here I had a view of the poker and faro tables. The whiskey was vile, but I worked steadily away at the bottle as I waited.

The same issue of the *Star* had given three inches of space to a dispute over the Monitor claim that pitted representatives of the Saline Company against Misters *Clements* and Phillips, Twain's partner prior to Calvin Higbie: "In the last month, the litigation has been resolved out of district court because there is no district court in this venue." I recalled that Clemens had complained bitterly about this unpunished act of claim jumping in a letter to Orion, which corroborated the same event. In short, I was trying to build a circumstantial case in my own mind that the historical record, while often fanciful and slipshod, could also be reliable on occasion. All my plans for the coming months depended on this being true.

The sound of a slap brought me out of my woolgathering.

I clicked open my watch. It was 9:23.

Everyone inside the Bank Exchange was on his feet. Through the press of shouting men, I could not see who had struck whom, but I had a fleeting glimpse of two figures quick-marching down a lane the onlookers had cleared for them. They went outside. Some customers followed them through the doors, but the majority went back to their cards and bottles. Ten minutes passed, and no gunplay was heard.

A homesick Iowan showed me a daguerreotype of his homely family, then moved on when I could come up with no flattering lie.

A billiard ball softly thudded as it rebounded from the rubber cushion.

Even after an hour no one rushed back inside the saloon to report a murder. This, obviously, had not been the event I was waiting to witness. I began resisting a fierce drowsiness.

At five past eleven a miner decided to forsake the poker table. He did this without comment, even by dint of facial expression, and was replaced within seconds by a blond seaman who had the weathered and roguish good looks of a roustabout. He wore a red canvas jacket tied together at the front along a row of green brass eyelets, which suggested that the material had once been a sail. His naval cap looked Limey to me, although it bore no insignia. He won the first hand dealt to him, and then the next. Time and again his calloused hands glided across the felt to his winnings, which were gold coins, not chips.

Over the next hour, while I became quietly drunk and desperately sleepy, the roustabout's stacks of coins grew so tall they eventually toppled over into a jumbled pile. It occurred to me that his good fortune had not attracted the expected lady with an ostrich plume jutting out of her coiffure. In fact, there were no women to be seen inside the Bank Exchange, just men who continued to drink and gamble with undivided attention.

I began to suspect that the *Star* had printed a hoax—or that I should be keeping a closer eye on the faro table, where a youth with a cherubic face was stabbing the dealer's cards with an angry forefinger. Even at this late hour it was too noisy in the saloon to hear what was being said, and I was trying to lip-read this heated discussion when, from the poker table, came an outraged cry: "You son of a bitch!" Just as I glanced back at the sailor, a bright flash grayed out my vision. Cringing behind the stout post, I realized that the sudden stench hanging in the air was expended gunpowder, although nothing in the world could have persuaded me to reach into my pocket for my revolver, as several patrons had boldly done.

The poker game was over. An old man with a bald spot like a tonsure had doubled over, face first, into his glittering nest of coins. Directly across from him sat the roustabout, still upright. While I watched, his lips parted into a smile that might have seemed defiant had it not also been twitching with confusion. His eyes drifted from face to face as if he were on the verge of asking something momentous. When they met mine, a chill galloped down my spine, making me hunch my shoulders involuntarily. My reaction seemed to amuse him, and he tried to laugh—but then his gaze dropped to the table, which he tried to examine, although his pupils kept wanting to roll back up into his head.

From the direction of his dead opponent a gash of splinters rose up through the soft pine like a gopher's burrow. The sailor's eyes traced the cant of this bore right into his own breastbone. Still smiling, he carefully laid his Colt Dragoon beside his winnings and touched his fingers to his red canvas jacket. For the first time I saw that blood was twining down the legs of his chair and pooling in the sawdust at his feet.

It took no great powers of deduction to see that at the onset of violence, the roustabout had drawn and fired above board, so to speak—while his opponent, perhaps having less time in which to respond, had discharged his weapon up through the table. Their two poker hands were fanned out across the felt in proximity to a pot of considerable size.

The old man had held a royal flush in spades; the sailor four aces. That added up to one more ace in the deck than Emily Post allows.

In the moments it took me to reel this all in, the seaman's ruddy features had paled horribly. Damn him, but he looked to me again—as if asking me to help him come up with something appropriate to say. But then his chin slowly rose like the stern of a sinking ship, and all the animation of his being froze just at the instant it looked like he would totter over, chair and all.

"Gentlemen," the barkeep announced with a wondrous lack of gravity, holding a pencil to the margin of a newspaper, "names for the coroner's inquest please."

Voices began to pipe up around the room: "Donovan, Paddy . . . Rogers, Isaiah . . . Higbie, C. H. . . . Werner, Josef . . ."

Finally a silence told me it was my turn. I swallowed my heart back down and muttered, "Rettie, Belmont . . ."

"What? Speak up."

"Rettie, Belmont Howard." I kept my eyes downcast as everyone seemed to scrutinize me. The silence that ensued was ended, most disgustingly, when one of the dead men let go of his bowels. There followed loud laughter all around.

When everyone had identified himself, the bodies were dragged through the back door, leaving long streaks of blood on the floor. I paid for my bottle and hurried out the front to stand in the middle of Pine Street under a thin crescent of a moon, trying to make sense of what I'd just seen.

Yet I soon came to the conclusion that however gut-wrenching this episode, it had more logic to it than what had happened near the Palace of Fine Arts in my own time: a middle-aged housewife aiming her hood ornament down a sidewalk teeming with pedestrians. Here, at least, one could say that the violence was not senseless.

The cards were always laid on the table.

But more importantly, the *Star* had been vindicated. Its story was accurate:

Last night before the hour of twelve, Alfred Morely, of Liverpool, and Philastus Kane, reported to be from the Humboldt Mining District, shot each other to death over cards in Frank Schoon-maker's Bank Exchange Saloon. The coroner's jury has already rendered a verdict of mutual and warranted homicide. . . .

I looked down into my hands at the sailor's cap. On my way out through the confusion following the removal of the corpses, I had scooped it up off the floor. This theft mystified me; it seemed to go beyond my usual problem. And I could only justify it with the feeling that the dying roustabout had wanted me to have it—so someone might remember what had happened to him.

After trying all the hotels and finding them full, I received directions to the Goddess of the Dawn Boardinghouse and led my weary mare up Winnemucca Street, music from a melodeon sifting over the town. I suddenly halted. She nuzzled her cold nose against my nape, tipping my derby down over my eyes.

The roll call for benefit of the coroner—it had fetched a response from someone named Higbie . . . C. H. Higbie! I had let Sam Clemens's partner slip out of my fingers because I had programmed myself to be on the lookout for *Calvin* Higbie. "Damn it," I groaned, then consoled myself with: "Tomorrow . . . tomorrow."

Now, lingering at the well behind the boardinghouse, I poured a second bucket of water over my head. The ceaseless pounding of the stamps was so concussive I almost failed to pick out the faint whoofing of the melodeon.

And then snatches of a tune, dimly familiar, came my way on the morning breeze: "No, it can't be. . . ."

I hobbled back inside and made for the man lounging at the far end of the room. I wasn't prepared for what I saw—and must have gasped or otherwise showed revulsion, for he began chortling good-naturedly.

"Ain't a good idea to come up on me at a gallop first time. Not that it was anything dear to me. No sir, it was the damndest grog-blossom you ever did see."

Until that moment I had never fully appreciated the contribution a nose makes to the topography of a human face.

"Happened last year," he went on tonelessly, "and I'd be back working underground but for the rock dust—got no sure way to keep it out of my lungs now. I tried, but I just got too blamed sick. So I hang around here, sweep up—that sort of truck."

A few words finally broke free of my shock. "How'd it happen?"

"Oh, my fool meerschaum."

I tried not to stare at the twin apertures poised above his grin. "You mean like a *pipe*?"

"Of course I mean like a pipe. Had it in my shirt pocket. You plan to do any mining?"

"Well, I don't think—"

"If you do, don't put none of your smoking equipment in your pocket."

"Why?"

"Because sooner or later you'll be daydreaming on the job and slip a detonating cap or two in that pocket for safekeeping. I did that while driving a drift, then quit and skedaddled down the hill to McMahan's Del Monte Exchange, where I treated myself to three gills of Virginia Mountain Dew. I was in the middle of some dandy conversation with McMahan hisself when I took out my meerschaum and touched a match to the bowl." He paused significantly.

"Good Lord, it's a miracle you weren't blinded."

"Oh, I was—for six weeks. But that weren't the worst of it."

"What could be worse than—"

"McMahan won't let me on the premises no more."

"Why not?"

"Well, the management loses confidence in a customer what comes in and blasts off his own nose. Wouldn't you? I bear no grudge. I'd do the same if it was my establishment. It's a question of clientele. Why, if you was to be lax on a thing like this, a certain class of folks would be coming in and a'blowing parts and pieces off themselfs all the time."

The murmuring of the melodeon floated in through an open window, reminding me why I had rushed back inside. "There!"

"What?"

"That music—where's it coming from?"

"Purdy, ain't it? So's the player. She denies it, but she used to be a hurdy girl in Virginiatown. Worked in all the melodeon pavilions. These very eyes saw her playing there—naked as a worm, I tell you. Of course, now she's come up in the world. She's a French lady of fashion now that the nigger woman Richelieu took her in—"

"But Madame Richelieu is in Carson City!"

He winked. "I see you get around. Well, she *was* in Carson, but got run out of there last fall. Now she's set up here on Bullion Street. Be careful, pilgrim, she's Chiv as Jeff Davis hisself—"

"She's what?"

"Chivalrous, they call themselfs. But I don't care how much copperhead trash we got strutting round here in Esmeralda—her day's coming. All these rapscallions'll jig on a rope. The Rangers'll see to that." His eyes mellowed again. "Name's Granville, though some folks call me Bloodhound or Sniffles—out of spite, I'm sure."

"Mine's Rettie."

"Honored."

"Now where is—"

"I was up for corporal in the militia when I popped off my nose. Colonel had to let me go on account of the kerchief I wear outsides. You see, when we was afield and passing a stagecoach, why the jehu would take one look at my kerchief and assume the worst, he would. He'd throw down his express box and raise his hands before I could explain—"

"Granville, how do I get to Bullion Street?!"

"You seem almighty eager to get there—for a man on holiday from his harem."

12

I WAS NOT so foolish as to call on Madame Richelieu again without having some explanation for my hasty retreat from her Carson City parlor house. After all, I had been in such a hurry to get away from her good friend and fellow copperhead, Judge David S. Terry, I'd abandoned my boots on her veranda. Yet I was so cocksure of my fabrication, so eager to test this Mormon incognito in the most elegant of surroundings, I was somewhat disappointed when I found the Bullion Street dwelling Granville had described to me. Nevertheless, I patted my coat pocket to make sure the vellum-wrapped Japanese fan was still there, then hurried up the steps.

Madame had come down a notch in the past year. Her new place of business was no more than a brick cabin, all of fifteen feet square, its only claim to pretension a wrought-iron porch railing in the New Orleans style. I could not imagine how this small structure could be further divided into private rooms. And when the music stopped mid-measure for the player, Michelle, to answer my knocking at the door with her gap-toothed smile, I was no closer to an answer: The whole of the interior was given over to a drawing room crammed with the familiar settees and melodeon, plus a woodstove with isinglass panels through which orange flames now flickered. I saw that the long chemise curtains had also survived the hasty move from Carson.

"Bonjour, monsieur." Michelle relieved me of my derby.

"Good morning. Is Mademoiselle . . ." I hesitated. All at once it seemed humiliating to be this desperate to find out Musetta's whereabouts. And perhaps I was more than a little afraid of disappointment. "Is Madame Richelieu in?"

"Behind you, monsieur," the robust voice answered before Michelle could open her mouth.

Madame was sitting in a chair directly behind the door, peering up at me over the tops of bifocals. She snapped shut a book: Flaubert's *Madame Bovary*.

She smiled, but then it quickly faded. She had *recalled*, as I had felt certain she would. A woman surviving on her wits forgets nothing. Then a new smile, a disingenuous one, came to her lips. "A lovely surprise, monsieur. . . ?"

"Rettie—Belmont Howard Rettie."

"Yes, well, sit—*s'il vous plaît*."

Instead of making myself comfortable, I grandly went down on one knee beside her chair, a gesture she pretended to disdain, but secretly delighted in, I'm sure. "I must broach a topic of great delicacy with madame." I glanced back at Michelle, who excused herself and stepped out the back door into what appeared to be an alley.

Madame was sitting ramrod straight as she waited for me to continue.

"It has been revealed to me in strictest confidence," I whispered, "that you count the Honorable David S. Terry among your friends. . . ."

She said nothing, her face a mask.

"That night a year ago, when I came to your *maison* in Carson City, I was the victim of an unfortunate misunderstanding. And what I now say places my safety entirely in your hands."

Her large, caramel-colored eyes widened a little.

"Should I go on?"

She shrugged, which was good enough for me.

At that moment, in a stuffy little room filled with perfume, I couldn't imagine how I might put myself in future jeopardy by saying, "To your ears alone, I will confess that I was on business that night which President Davis himself would not frown upon."

She came close to gasping. "Did *he* send you here?"

"No, another did—an equally famous name I cannot divulge.

But I assure you that this personage has no affection for the striped banner."

"If dis is so, Monsieur Rettie, why did you insult *le juge* and his brave friends?"

"Once already that night I'd been accosted by Unionist bullies—and forced to bear allegiance to a flag I despise. When Judge Terry confronted me, I had no idea he was a man to whom I might divulge my truest sentiments." Manfully, I lowered my eyes. "Now, as then, to say anything more is to put loyal comrades in peril. No, wait—I will say this: The men and women of my persuasion are mostly northerners. But we agree with that sacred ideal of the Confederacy that says each state should do as it sees fit. Particularly in regards to marriage practices." And as if this wasn't a broad enough hint, I then said: "Five years ago James Buchanan sent an army of occupation like a second plague of crickets into our homeland—and earned our perpetual enmity. The first shot of the Great Rebellion was *not* fired at Fort Sumter, madam. I am proud to say it was fired in Utah."

She studied me for a moment so long she almost ravened my self-confidence. But then I saw the smile in her eyes before it relaxed her lips.

"Michelle!"

The young prostitute scurried back inside. "Madame?"

"Café *brulot* for monsieur and myself—*vite!*" But Michelle had just turned for the back door again when madame stayed her and touched my hand in the same instant. "Forgive my manners, *mon ami*—café au lait for Monsieur Rettie, Michelle, if he does not mind goat's milk."

"Of course not."

"De winter took our cow. *Atroce!*"

"I see . . ." In deference to my Mormon faith, which she'd obviously swallowed, my coffee would not be laced with brandy. Well, a price for everything.

She insisted that I make myself comfortable in a settee, and when I politely dallied, she used her Herculean strength to deposit me in it. And before my first cup of café au lait was gone, the woman had acquainted me with each and every woe she had suffered during the past year—she told me everything except the one thing I was starving to know.

The pale whore who had languished at the curtains in Carson City, savoring the only sensual joy left to her, the scents of a rainy evening, had died. "I'm distressed to hear of Mimi's passing," I murmured, although I was relieved that it hadn't been Musetta.

"She lay down and died on dat very divan—de one you sit on."

I tried not to squirm. "Just like that?"

"*Non, non*, she was a fiend, dat poor girl."

"You mean she was difficult?"

"What are you suggesting, Monsieur Rettie?" She glared at me, then dabbed at the corner of her eye with a lace hankie. "Mimi was an angel. A daughter to me. A sister to my girls. *Une grande horizontale* who would still be in Paris but for de trickery of Louis Napoleon." Noticing my complete confusion, she asked, "Does monsieur know de word *fiend*?"

"I must not."

She cupped her fingers near her mouth and inhaled from them as if they formed a pipe. Her eyes became dreamy, intoxicated.

"Oh—an *opium* smoker!"

"*Oui.*" She tucked the hankie in her sleeve. "Dem rascal Celestials! I say to *Juge* Terry—why don't you and your boys close de dens? Dat way, my girls will get in no trouble."

"What did the good judge answer?"

"De power is not his yet. And he is so busy with de war, you know."

"Yes, I can imagine the urgency of his affairs." I tried to sound offhand as I asked, "Is he in town at present?"

Madame brought a finger up to her grin. "*Non,*" she whispered, "in de south of California. Raising an army for *Le Cause.*"

"Say no more." I sat back and breathed easier. There followed a quiet moment in which I wondered why this woman, who was at least a quadroon, supported the Confederacy. But things were going so well with her, I decided to hold my peace. And I was here to take advantage of attitudes, not change them. "It's a shame Lincoln took it upon himself to appoint such a rabid abolitionist governor of this territory." I had no idea if Nye, the former New York Metropolitan Police commissioner, was an abolitionist or not, but it sounded like good press, and as it turned out, every loyal Unionist on the Comstock swore he or his immediate family had harbored runaway slaves on pain of death.

"James Nye is a fool . . . and we all know what fate fools must suffer, *oui*?"

"*Oui,*" I heard myself repeating, although there had been enough menace in her tone of voice to bring the chickory-flavored coffee halfway up my throat. "And . . . and what of his secretary?"

"Orion Clemens? A fool, perhaps, but not dangerous. His brother often calls here—"

"*Samuel* Clemens?" I asked a bit too anxiously, for her eyes once again glinted with suspicion.

"Monsieur knows him?"

"Only by reputation."

"Ah, of course . . ." She smiled. "His exploits as *capitaine* of the Marion Rangers must be well known."

"Marion Rangers?" If she was referring to Clemens's ragtag company of Confederate militia that had disbanded before ever "seeing the elephant," the young drifter had sold her a bill of goods. Mark Twain later foisted an account of his military days on the public, *Private History of a Campaign that Failed*, which quite apocryphally described the shooting of a Yankee scout, a horror sufficient to make him forever renounce war. "No, I hadn't heard of his gallantry," I said at last. "But I'm relieved to know that at least one Clemens has his heart in the right place. I've heard a rumor that he is the mysterious 'Josh' who writes those hilarious pieces for the newspapers."

"Dat, Monsieur Rettie," she said with utmost confidentiality, "is no rumor."

"Does Sam still reside on Wide West Street?"

"*Non, non*, he and his partner Calvin live on Pine Street. A little walk from here." This reminded her of something, and she whispered to Michelle, who rushed out through the back and returned less than a minute later with what I thought to be an elaborately beaded sock that clinked with the coins it held. While Madame was counting out a hundred dollars in double eagles, it occurred to me that this was like the small miser's purse Eleanor had purchased at an antique auction the autumn before our divorce—except that that one had been sequined with jet buttons. "Here, Monsieur Rettie." She pressed the five coins into my hands. "The man gave me one hundred twenty. But twenty I keep for my own trouble in dis affair."

Needless to say, I was flabbergasted. "Who gave—"

"*Le chausseur* . . ." At a momentary loss, she squinted at Michelle: "*Oh, aidez-moi—vite!*"

"A cobbler, sir," the young woman said. "The morning after you jumped out of Musetta's window—"

"I didn't exactly jump."

"Yessir. The morning after, the town cobbler was arriving for his usual when he seen your boots on the porch. Well, goodness, he bust in on us and wanted to know who they belonged to. He'd never seen such boots. He tried 'em on, walked around the parlor for half an hour. Said it felt near as good as . . ." She paused, then giggled suggestively. "The short of it, sir—he offered madame a century-twenty if he could have 'em for a pattern."

"I still don't understand why they're so special."

"Show Monsieur Rettie," Madame said.

Michelle sat beside me, hiked her skirts up to her shins, and after considerable inconvenience with the batteries of buttons, unlaced her shoes. Then she put the right shoe on her left foot and the left on her right, before lacing up and letting her skirts fall around her ankles again. "Don't you see, sir? I still have the old kind, but my next pair'll be like yours. The cobbler said there's a fortune in the idea of fitting each foot special. Not only is it more comfortable, but folks won't be coming to him no more to have just one new shoe made. When one wears out, the whole pair'll have to go."

"Oh, that," I chuckled, wondering for the first time what consequences my slightest act might have on these people. But then I put this unpleasant concern out of mind when madame took what seemed a one-pound gold watch off a circular table, and, checking it, said to Michelle, "*Temps pour Musetta*—go knock."

The young woman had risen and was looking out the front window. "She comes now, madame."

Despite myself, I shot to my feet and peered through the distorted pane of glass. Across the muddy street a row of four shanties leaned against one another in weathered dilapidation. What I saw next cut like a boning knife: A dapper man of perhaps fifty years was chatting to Musetta on the boardwalk as he snugged his pasty hands into his kid gloves. He buttoned his coat over his vest, then reached for his cane, which he had hung by its crook on his wrist, and finally swaggered down Bullion Street.

"It will please Musetta to meet again de roughneck who goes to *l'opéra*," Madame said from behind me.

"You mean she's mentioned me after that one meeting?" As soon as I'd said it, I knew it had sounded ridiculously hopeful.

"You have been a mystery to us all, Monsieur Rettie."

"Yes . . . *vive* the mystery." The last thing I had expected to feel at this moment was *devastated*. Mormon temperance be damned, I was close to asking for a healthy splash of brandy in my café when these unexpected emotions quietly gave way to relief, the stronger pleasure of seeing her alive and well again.

Her eyes, vivacious even at this distance, essayed the sky, reveled briefly in its clarity of blue. Then, a bit wearily, she smoothed back her hair. Only in the appearance of her hands could I discern that another year, a hard and often unpleasant year, had passed for her. Not that they were wrinkled or chafed or anything like that—they just seemed older by that many days. Momentarily, I shut my eyes on the thought of what a decade of this life would do to her.

Lifting her skirts so they wouldn't trail in the mud, she crossed over to the stoop and entered the parlor.

"Musetta?"

Obediently, her eyes darted to the Creole woman. "*Oui, madame?*"

"You have a guest."

She turned and automatically smiled at me. Then, slowly, recognition made her flush—and the cursory smile vanished. She remembered herself only with considerable effort. "Monsieur has prospered since we last met, *oui?*"

Madame Richelieu snorted. "A man like Monsieur Rettie always finds a way to prosper."

"Rettie." Musetta tested the name on her tongue. Although her Scandinavian accent was less pronounced than a year ago, her French one was no more convincing. Nevertheless, she seemed far better acquainted with English.

"Belmont Howard Rettie—please call me Howard."

She sank onto a settee and began twirling the gold fringe of a cushion between her fingers. "Have you been to the opera since we. . . ?" Her voice trailed off. I kept expecting her to smile, but her expression remained distracted, almost severe.

"No, I'm afraid there was no time for opera. Musetta . . . I would like to talk to you."

"As monsieur wishes."

Once again there ensued a transaction with madame, during which Musetta withdrew to the far side of the drawing room and made tinkly noises by toying with the crystal prisms hanging off the bowl of a lamp. Price was only one more piece of evidence that the house's fortunes were on the wane: madame required only ten dollars gold of me, half of what I had forked over in Carson City. I would be Musetta's second customer within the hour.

Apparently, this was no longer an establishment of companionship in which the monsieurs were expected to stay for breakfast.

Then we took our leave of madame and braved a sudden gust that was roaring down the street, making Musetta take shelter in the lee of my chest—*lovely* just isn't word enough to describe how she looked as she smiled up at me.

The shanty, which she referred to as a crib, was depressingly small and dark. My foot nearly knocked over the spittoon, as the only source of daylight was a high window through which rusted stacks could be seen disgorging dirty smoke into the sky.

She sat on the bed, watching me, waiting.

"I have thought of you," I said. "Often."

She started to say something, but then held her tongue.

Instead of the sideboard I had seen in Carson City, there was only a small table in a corner of the cubicle. "Where are your fans?" I asked, afraid that she might have lost interest in collecting them.

"This is not really my room, monsieur."

"Howard . . ."

"*Howard.* Soon madame will build a fine new house for us. But as for now, we must make do."

"Then you still have your collection?"

"Of course."

"Then please . . ." Sitting beside her, I removed the fan from its vellum wrapping. ". . . accept this from me."

Her muffled cry of delight made me grin. But as she dreamily ran the lacquered ebony matrices across her cheek and then carefully unfolded the scene of pearl divers and cloud-piercing volcanic peaks, I began feeling like the damndest fool to ever set foot in a whorehouse. Next I'd be bringing roses and reciting Byron to her; and as soon as I was gone, she and her sisters would huddle together and shriek with laughter about Monsieur Boots.

Musetta must have sensed the change in my mood, for she said very gently, and with eyes I believed were on the verge of moistening: "This is much too fine for me."

I was ready to say the obvious—but it stuck in my throat.

That brief hesitation made her look down, and suddenly her eyes were indeed glistening.

All at once I had to get out of there. I stood up. Looking terribly confused, she set the fan aside and laid her hand on my coat sleeve, lightly. I felt angry and ashamed—which was incomprehensible to a sport who only minutes before had been anticipating the best tussling of his shameless life in this squalid little chamber.

"Let's go back to the parlor for a while."

"If you please." Her voice was barely audible.

My hand was on the door latch when I suddenly turned: "How would you like to go——" I stopped short, amazed at my own stupidity. I'd been on the brink of inviting her to an opera in San Francisco. "Let's go," I finished hollowly.

Madame Richelieu looked surprised when we swept back into her drawing room after so brief an interlude. But then she shrugged, and with a flourish of her stout arm, indicated a man in his late twenties with whom she'd been conversing. He had a mass of chestnut-colored hair and even redder muttonchops. He simpered at me from a settee, one knee cocked over the arm and the other precariously balancing a small snifter of cognac. His face was too soft with baby fat to seem aquiline; but, clearly, his pronounced nose and eaglelike eyes would soon dominate the countenance, give it the gruff, penetrative aspect that would one day be instantly recognizable to the world. Even without the famous mustache framing his mouth, I had no doubt as to the identity of the young slouch.

"Monsieur Belmont Rettie," madame said, "it is my pleasure to introduce Monsieur Sam Clemens."

Clemens deftly caught his glass with his left hand and extended his right for me to shake. I seized it, trying not to let my fingers tremble. His hand was surprisingly delicate, and I realized that his oversized head made one forget his slight frame.

"Charmed, I'm sure, Mr. Rettie."

His drawl was irresistible in the sense that, if I had heard it drifting in from another room, I would have forsaken a comfortable chair just to find out who this satirical but genial tone of voice belonged to.

"A pleasure, Mr. Clemens." I found myself faintly echoing his Missouri accent—a symptom of my nervousness.

An awkward moment, in which no one spoke and Clemens sought refuge in his drink, was broken by madame: "You had no sooner retired with Musetta dan I saw Monsieur Higbie walking past. I mentioned dat you were eager to meet his partner——"

"So I hurried up from the Bank Exchange Saloon without delay," Clemens said with a broad wink. "One does not dally when invited by madame. Fortunately, I was already attired in

Christian costume when the summons reached me." The desired
effect of his swallow-tailed coat and beige trousers was dandyism,
I felt sure—but they were too threadbare to pull it off.

"Forgive me, Monsieur Rettie, but I told Monsieur Clemens of
your admiration for his poetics. I trusted dat you would not
mind."

"Not in the least." At last I had found my voice, although it
was somewhat shaky. "It's an honor to finally meet the man of
letters behind the nom de plume of Josh."

Clemens smiled shyly, even withdrew into a bronchial cough,
but I knew that I had struck a wide and glittering vein of vanity. He
was powerless to hide it. "Madame is too kind to call my coarse
prose poetical. But if I might be so bold as to ask, Mr. Rettie—
which of my lame children did you find the most amusing?"

"Why . . . all of them."

"Come now, generous sir, I'm too lazy to be prolific."

"Was it 'Professeur Personal Pronoun'?" madame asked.

"No . . . although I thoroughly enjoyed that piece."

"Ah, *bon*, den it was 'The Great American Eagle'—*mon
favorite aussi*."

"Yes, that's the one. Now how did it begin?"

"Please, Sam," Michelle said, "do it for us!"

Clemens was already on his feet, hands having gravitated to his
expansive lapels. "Well, if none will be too bored—"

"*Non, non*—you always delight us, Monsieur Clemens!"

He nodded in Madame's direction, then smiled at Musetta, who
had sat quietly beside him. "I was sired by the Great American
Eagle and foaled by a continental dam. . . !" And so he
launched into his burlesque of a Fourth of July oration. My head
was too busy for me to follow along, for it had occurred to me that
my schedule for the coming weeks depended on his. Discreetly if I
could, baldly if I must, I had to discover his plans—if such a
careless young raconteur was capable of them. Then and only then
would I be free to pursue my own ends.

After several minutes in which my grin grew sore, I realized
that Clemens was playing mostly to Musetta and Michelle, who
were stifling their giggles behind their hands. Nodding fervidly,
madame appeared to be taking Clemens's irony as unabashed
southern sympathies. At any rate, I was caught unawares when the
women suddenly began clapping.

"Bravo!" I joined in a moment too late, hoping no one had
noticed.

Clemens beamed, then nestled down into the settee again to blush into his snifter.

I had to find out precisely when Higbie and he would take possession of the Wide West Mine. *Roughing It* failed to mention the date; but from Twain's account I knew that prior to the Wide West misadventure, Higbie and he would visit Mono Lake, the so-called "Dead Sea of California," and fish the tarns of the nearby Sierra Nevada during the height of summer. In late August, having lost title to the rich mine, Clemens would accept a reporting job with the *Territorial Enterprise* in Virginia City, having come to the attention of that newspaper's editor by virtue of his "Josh" articles written here in Aurora. So when he asked me my immediate plans, I swiftly turned the tables: "Well, Mr. Clemens, I'd like to tour this marvelous country a bit—perhaps venture out to Mono Lake. Have you been there?"

"Briefly, but I intend to return for a longer sojourn."

"When will that be?"

"When the weather is less cantankerous, Mr. Rettie, and the snows melt in the Sierra. I'd like to try my luck at fishing on the same trip. So at least a month."

My sigh was almost audible. Now I could depart for San Francisco assured that the little drama at the Wide West Mine would not unfold without me.

"Madame, I seem to be a twist chagrined this afternoon," Clemens said, although he didn't sound chagrined in the least. He did everything but turn his empty pockets inside out.

Madame's affection for him vanished instantly. She took a shawl off the back of her chair and snugged it around her shoulders. The light streaming through the windows had faded, and—incredibly—it was sleeting outside!

"Good God, where did this weather come from?!"

"Welcome to Esmeralda, Mr. Rettie—where a lady who goes a'calling can't hope to feel prepared for all emergencies unless she takes a fan under one arm and her snowshoes under the other."

The Creole woman's boisterous guffawing had not died away before Clemens's pleading voice was again chipping away at her: "My circumstance today, albeit temporary, is *most* distressing."

"Non," she snapped, then went on chuckling.

He sat back, looking miffed until I leaned over and deposited a gold eagle in his palm. "Permit me, Mr. Clemens."

"Why, you are a saint, Mr. Rettie!"

"In more ways than one."

"I shall repay you before the sun sets on Sunday next, I assure you."

"Please, I won't hear of such a thing—it's nothing."

Then, while I was still glowing with my own philanthropy, Clemens sidestepped my knees, took Musetta by the hand and brought her gently to her feet. "Mademoiselle?"

"Whoa . . ." Now I was on my feet.

Still smiling, Clemens inclined his head toward me. *"Whoa?"*

"I'm sorry, but I neglected to mention that Miss Musetta has kindly consented to accompany me to San Francisco. We came in just to inform madame that we will be out the rest of the morning shopping for mademoiselle's wardrobe—"

"Non! Absolument!"

And before I could utter another syllable, madame seized me by the collar and jostled me out the door. When not fending off her breathtaking blows with my elbows, I tried to dig some double eagles out of my pockets. "A deposit—I'll leave a deposit with you!"

This stayed her fist in midair. "How much?"

I promised her two hundred dollars gold, which proved to be a mistake, for her reply to my offer was to bodily dump me over the railing onto a pile of split wood.

"Madame—*Le Cause!*"

She blinked at me, silent for the moment. Snowflakes were swirling down around us, melting on the light brown skin of her upper breast. "What are you saying, you damn rake?"

"Only that I depart for the coast with the noblest of purposes. That Musetta can be of great service to me on this journey—as I will be of equally valuable service to *Le Cause!*"

Madame lowered the stick of firewood she had been winding up to hurl at me. "If you lie—"

"I do not lie. On my honor as a Christian gentleman."

"How long?"

"A fortnight—no more."

A smile threatened the corner of her mouth. She licked the wet snowflakes off her lower lip as she sized me in this new light, then bellowed through the open door, "Musetta, pack—*vite!* You are going to San Francisco!"

Laughing to himself, Samuel Clemens doffed his hat at madame, then at me as he descended the stoop and shambled toward the main saloon district.

Only later did I realize how recklessly I had behaved for the times: What I had done to Clemens would have earned me a lead pill from any other Colt-toting man in Aurora. It had been an invitation to gunplay no self-respecting man could refuse, but fortunately I had issued it to a man too intelligent to put much stock in self-respect, an ambitious young dandy who would later flee from Virginia City rather than consummate a duel he himself had proposed.

Halfway down the block, Clemens began singing:

> "There was an old horse,
> And his name was Jerusalem.
> And he came from Jerusalem,
> And he went to Jerusalem . . ."

He looked back once—and there was no mirth in his eyes. Musetta was quite pleased by my rashness.

13

AT OUTSET I wasn't intimidated by the the prospect of crossing the Sierra Nevada by an Abbot, Downing, and Company–built Concord. Reportedly, this six-horse coach offered a more comfortable ride than the Mud Wagon, or economy model made by the same firm, that Musetta and I had suffered on the nineteen-hour trip from Aurora to Carson City. We'd nearly had our molars shaken out of our jaws, and I honestly believed that I could not withstand the four days of unmitigated jostling that lay ahead of us— especially over one of the most precipitous mountain ranges in the world. So it was a relief to find, upon stepping up into the Concord, that it bobbed and rolled somewhat like a canoe in light swells. Gritting my dusty teeth, I eased my rump onto the thinly padded cushion, then smiled at Musetta who, less than a week away from enjoying her first opera, seemed frightened to death I wasn't enjoying myself.

At that moment our driver tore himself away from the bar inside Ormsby House and ambled toward the coach, discovering potholes in the tough brown mud of the plaza I myself couldn't see. I lost sight of his pinched eyes and otherwise vapid expression as he climbed up into his seat, then—if sound can be any judge—fell down against his footboards. For what seemed several minutes I heard nothing from him, and was on the verge of checking to see if he'd knocked himself out—when someone cried from the front of the hotel: "Hank! Hey Monk—over here! You forgot this!" The Good Samaritan began trotting toward us with a long whip trailing behind him.

Meanwhile, I had to come to the decision to wait for the next stage.

Henry "Hank" Monk's recklessness as a driver was legendary. His most famous victim had been Horace Greeley who, on his western tour of 1859, had made the mistake of telling Monk he absolutely could not be late for a speaking engagement in Placerville. Twain later described what followed: *The coach bounced up and down in such a terrific way that it jolted the buttons all off of Horace's coat, and finally shot his head clean through the roof of the stage, and then he yelled at Hank Monk and begged him to go easier—said he wasn't in as much of a hurry as he was a while ago. But Hank Monk said, "Keep your seat, Horace, and I'll get you there on time"—and you bet he did too, what was left of him.*

I had just taken hold of Musetta's hand and was preparing to drag her out the door, when the most massively ugly woman ever inflicted on me at close quarters blocked our way. Before we could make our exit, Monk had cracked his whip, the horses had jumped, and the stage was lurching forward. In my estimation, the Aurora-to-Carson Mud Wagon had never gone faster than five miles an hour, but we were doing twice, if not thrice that—before we had even cleared the plaza. I slumped back down to face certain death along a road—no, more accurately a trail only an inch or two wider than the axles—chipped out of sheer cliffs whose shadows we soon entered.

My only distraction was the woman passenger—never had I seen such a dire need for facial electrolysis. Musetta caught me gawking and whispered in my ear. "Do not stare so, Howard."

"But Jesus—look at her!" I said out of the corner of my mouth.

Musetta started to giggle, but stopped only by dint of great self-control. "*She* is not a she."

"*What?*"

Then, quietly, so as not to offend the object of our discussion, Musetta explained that the husky woman was a Wells Fargo "shotgun messenger" with a sawed-off fowling piece strapped to his leg, which he had stretched out and propped on our bench, most unladylike—especially the size fifteen boot. This Concord, then, was transporting Nevada bullion, and the express company was hoping to shock some "road agents" into submission. To see this hideous woman bursting from the interior of the coach with both barrels flaming would certainly make me consider a different career, although Musetta suggested that this ruse was common knowledge in the territory and only the most dim-witted of highwaymen would fall for it.

But the realization that I was accompanying a fortune in silver bars gave me a whole new rash of worries, which over the next several tortuous miles coalesced into a vision of me squatting in the road, nursing a goose egg atop my head and lamenting the loss of my double eagles and greenbacks, as my calligraphic pages of *Huckleberry Finn* scattered on the wind. I had no intention of arriving in San Francisco flat busted, so my hand crept deep into my pocket and grasped my Navy Colt.

Musetta pressed the backs of her fingers to my cheek—exactly as my mother had done to check me for fever. "Do not fret, Howard."

"What makes you think I'm fretting?" Then, putting on a show of nonchalance, I peered out my side—and froze. For more than a thousand feet my eye fell away—to a jumble of timbers at the bottom of the chasm I briefly imagined to be a graveyard of smashed Concords. Braving the dust, I thrust my head through the opening in the door, ducked back inside as a roadside ponderosa pine threatened to lop it off, then leaned out again to make sure none of the horses was lame or on the point of fainting—as I was. I have never considered myself to be timid, and in truth I have a reputation for the contrary qualities, but it seemed to me that the trees were flashing past too swiftly and the top-heavy coach was taking the unbanked curves with a bit too much yawing for my taste. Everyone else seemed to be unaffected by these trifles, none more so than Hank—who chucked an empty bottle over the precipice in the same instant we went up on two wheels before crashing down again. I assuaged my smarting pride by imagining how they might react to being in bumper-to-bumper traffic on the Bayshore Freeway, flouncing along at speeds they would believe impossible.

Musetta caught her wicker basket by the handle as it slid under our legs and perched it on her lap. Rousing himself, our friend in drag tried to peek inside as she cracked the lid. "Would you like an apple?" she asked him, so much the genial country girl, rosy with good cheer, I had to smile.

Nodding yes, the guard loosened the chin strings of his calico bonnet with a surly tug.

"And you, Howard?"

"No, thank you." The lurching had gotten to my stomach.

"Something to drink them?"

"All right."

Deftly compensating for the rocking of the Concord, she poured from a flask into two metal cups, which I held for her. The beverage tasted like a wine cooler, elderberry perhaps, that has gone flat. It had a somewhat bitter aftertaste, but the stuff was decidedly alcoholic, and I polished off the first serving in short order, then asked for another.

"You must wait a while."

Then she turned to the shotgun messenger: "Would monsieur care. . . ?"

He showed that he had his own bottle, but grunted his appreciation at being asked.

The road had finally zigzagged up off the sheer canyon wall, and was now safely enclosed in a thick stand of firs, whose fallen needles softened the clatter of the iron-banded wheels. After thirty minutes or so, she allowed me another draught of her cocktail, and I sat back, relaxed for the first time in hours. She glanced at me with such tenderness, which I hoped was not imagined, I softly said, "Musetta?"

"Oui?"

"May I ask you something?"

She waited, the warmth almost deserting her eyes.

"Where are you from?"

The shadows sifting across her face, she stared out at the forest for a long time before saying, "Gotland."

"Where is that?" I knew, but wanted to keep her talking.

"An island near Sweden."

"Is it beautiful?"

"Ja . . . it was *himmel* . . . heaven. But I had nothing to eat." Her inflection as she whispered this was drastically different from that of Eleanor whenever she groused, "I have nothing to wear, *Howard*."

For the moment, I decided to press Musetta no further. I was dying to know her real name, but sensed that this was the only part of her that remained inviolate to male curiosity. I honored her little mystery with a kiss.

She smiled, gratefully.

I had been looking forward to seeing Lake Tahoe sans high-rise casinos, but when Hank rattled us through a cleft in a dirty snowbank at the summit—and I was given a view of "the fairest picture the whole earth affords," according to Twain—my otherwise buoyant spirits dimmed. Much of the eastern slope had been denuded of its trees all the way down to the emerald waters. Even as I watched, the sky over the mountain basin was being smirched by the smoke of a dozen lumber mills, which were undoubtedly charged with feeding the Comstock mines enough lumber to shore up an ever-expanding network of tunnels, hundreds of miles of them by now.

It surprised me to realize that Lake Bigler, as it was currently called, would look much better in my own time. "I hadn't imagined there'd be so much *activity* here." My tone, needless to say, was ironical.

"Ja," Musetta said proudly, confirming what I had already gleaned from conversations with other territorials: The average person here took enormous personal pride in industrial enterprises that in my own age would be considered rapacious. One millwright had come right out and said it: "We're living in the best times a *confusticated* soul can be born to!" The future seemed to mean little to them, and posterity was a word I never heard even in the most grandiloquent of discussions. The age in which they toiled was the capstone to Creation.

Fortunately, the meadowlands surrounding Friday's Station were still ringed with stately pines, and I finished the last of Musetta's cocktail in a better mood, eager to recreate the night away in relative comfort after so much unremitting motion. Long caravans of freight wagons were standing teamless before the tavern, and Musetta had to reassure me that as stage passengers, we were guaranteed a room.

Alighting from the Concord first, intending to assist Musetta down, and then the shotgun messenger—but only in jest—I was seized by this ridiculous urgency that made me clutch Musetta's gloved hand and declare as if they were my last words, "I am familiar with women—and have no prejudices against them!"

I don't have the slightest idea of what I meant by this, but she accepted it with an amused look. And as we floated off toward the inn, I tried to fathom how I could gave gotten so drunk on three dainty cups of wine.

A rampant sense of well-being made me smile warmly at a clutch of Mexican teamsters, who rose from around their cooking fire to doff their sombreros at Musetta's passing. And I saw what I was feeling reflected in their dark eyes: not lust, but adoration, the fearful love of children for something ethereal. Damn, but she carried herself like a saint, and they apprehended that more clearly than the Anglos drinking and feasting inside the station, who merely lowered their guilt-ridden gazes and muttered "m'am" when she shone within their sight.

Drowsily I started up the stairs behind her, but the next few hours did not exist.

"Far . . . Far . . . nej shalla . . . nej . . . nej . . ."
I arose from the bed without waking her and crept in my bare feet over to the dormered window, opening it on an evening that roared with chirping, despite its chilliness. The lake was on fire, or so it seemed until I saw the troika of small steamboats slicing across the jet waters, their coroneted stacks throwing up showers of sparks, a frenzy of electrons. Behind the boats flowed a raft of logs so massive it propagated a wave in all directions, forward and backwards, furthering and recanting, mirroring its own motion in symmetries complex beyond reckoning. And I rode that liquid undulation as it struck the opposing shores of the cove then turned back on itself in a chaos of reverberation—until it was not hosted by Lake Bigler, or even Lake Tahoe, but by some cat's-pawed plane in a bottomless calm that could move anywhere, anytime. God, I felt as calm as a stone.

"Nei, Far . . . nej shalla," she whimpered in the darkness.

I awoke to the warm press of her lips on my forehead. "Jesus—what dreams . . ."

"We should eat something,"

"I suppose."

The table downstairs had been set for the evening's final shift of diners, among whom—the harried-looking innkeeper told us—we were lucky to be included. Although the baked trout, glazed sage hen, and plum duff all appealed to the eye, Musetta and I could force nothing down our gullets. Even the fresh fruit revolted on my tongue. But this didn't matter, for everything the people sitting around the feast said seemed significant, if not momentous.

And when someone inquired as to the time, I heard myself pontificating—after smacking the table with my fist to make sure all were listening to me, "Quite simply, it's the medium for love. Other than that, it's a worthless riddle. And a man's a goddamned fool to think otherwise!"

I was well pleased with myself until it slowly dawned on me that the other guests had become as silent as cabbages. They looked to each other for an explanation to my outburst. It was only then that I caught the guilt in Musetta's eyes.

Bursting into tears, she rushed out of the dining room and through the front door. A ghastly quiet followed at the table.

"Please pardon us," I said to the others, adding with a chuckle: "Newlyweds."

A white-haired matron, who looked like she had been around the Horn several times—tied to the mast—curled her upper lip at me, but said nothing.

"Yours, madam," I found myself shouting, "is the very pretense, the abominable *myth* that has half convinced the Victorian woman she doesn't need a good fuck as much as her man does!"

There were gasps all around the table—except from the old woman. She had fainted dead away into her aspic.

"Now, if everyone will excuse me . . ."

Outside, Musetta was leaning against the trunk of a Jeffrey pine, her shoulders trembling.

"What the hell was in that drink of yours?!" I demanded, more frightened now than angry. But collapsing against me, she wept with such bitterness, I could only say: "Come on, let's walk."

"I am so unworthy, I will have no good memories—not even of this trip."

"Don't talk that way . . . we're going to have a great time."

A torch-lined path invited us to follow it deeper into the forest, and when a gentleman in a stovepipe hat came sauntering toward us from the opposite direction, I asked. "Excuse me, sir—why is this way lit?"

"For 'Nick of the Woods,' my man."

"Who?"

"Just follow the torches." He continued on his way, quite chipper about keeping the secret to himself.

Except for a few quiet snuffles, Musetta had recovered by the time we approached an immense and gnarled incense cedar. In the tree's lowest crotch was a burl, a startling deformity that resembled a hoary-headed Jehovah come raging to earth to exact retribution. No doubt the effect of this chimera was magnified by the guttering light of the torches, but I sensed that even in daylight the tree could cast an eerie spell. "Amazing," I joked, "just the fellow to keep little Lutherans in line." But when I turned, expecting her gentle laugh to follow, I saw that her face was horror-stricken. "What is it?"

"I must go." And before I could argue, she had yanked her hand out of mine and was running back toward the inn as well as she could in her confining clothes.

"Musetta? Stop, dammit! What's wrong?!"

I caught up with her just as she decided to halt and face me. The words gushed out of her: "It was port wine and sarsparilla and—" She cringed as if she actually expected me to strike her.

"Go on."

"—and tincture of opium."

"Oh, no . . ." I backed away from her. ". . . laudanum." After a few moments of looking into her mournful eyes, I stuffed my hands into my trouser pockets and gazed up through a natural atrium in the forest at some nameless constellation. "Are you a *fiend*, Musetta?"

"No . . . not like the others."

"You mean like Mimi—who destroyed herself?"

"How dare you!"

I astonished to see the fury in her eyes. "What do you mean—"

"How dare you say such a thing! You who did not know her!"

"I was only pointing out—"

"Mimi did not destroy herself. Louis Bonaparte did so to her—what with his trick, his *loterie* that gave her passage to America. This country did so to her with its insults—she, who was honored in her homeland. Men like *you*, with your false kindness, murdered her!" And yet just when I thought I'd lost her affection for good, Musetta sealed her lips with her shaking fingers and rushed into my arms. "I do not wish to die . . . I do not wish to die."

"Then you mustn't use opium."

"Sometimes I have such pain."

"I know—but all the more reason to leave it alone. There are better ways to have your revenge on the world. No more laudanum, Musetta."

"Yes, of course," she said, brightening with a pathetic desperation, "whenever I am with you, I will not touch it."

"No, I mean *never*."

Once again her eyes flashed at me. "How can you demand such a thing!"

The answer was obvious, but I couldn't say it—not even when she grasped my face in her chilled hands and repeated the question.

14

MUSETTA GAVE ME a kiss for luck, and I started across a Commercial Street paved with boards—so absorbed by the ghostly sight five blocks distant, I failed to see the portly man careening around the corner from Grant Avenue in a sulky, wearing the light two-wheeled carriage like a hoopskirt cage.

"Howard!" Musetta cried.

I leaped for the sidewalk two feet ahead of the gelding's thudding hooves. But this perilous moment was no sooner past than I was once again captivated by the fog-shrouded thicket of sailing ship masts at the end of the lane—docklands along Front Street, whereas the waterfront in my own time would be a half mile farther out into the bay, resting on a century's accumulation of refuse and dredged silt.

"Howard!"

I turned, asking with a shrug what could possibly be wrong this time.

She drew her hand out of her sealskin muff and pointed at a spot in front of me. Only then did I see that I had come within three steps of tripping over a knee-high water trough. If not these, I had been bumping into hitching posts ever since our arrival yesterday evening in a San Francisco only vaguely familiar to me—thanks to

147

the earthquake of 1906. The sole intimacy my city still shared with me was her fog, which came sifting between the hills as always, although the rolling mounts themselves were more pronounced for being sparsely built upon.

This morning's first order of business had been to convert my wad of greenbacks into gold, which a dour broker did for me, commenting on their sorry condition by asking, "Did you jump ship with these on your person, sir?" But the exchange rate was favorable, as anticipated, and I was relieved to have heavy pockets once again, forestalling the financial embarrassment I had been only three double eagles away from.

This, my second order of business, was no less urgent, although it would not pay me dividends until I returned to the late twentieth century.

Now, hesitating outside the narrow, three-story rooming house, I glanced back at Musetta for encouragement. Her smile was radiant. Surely Madame Richelieu must have said something to her, for while I had told her nothing about my reasons for this trip, Musetta was glowing with the impression that I had been charged with some noble—if not dangerous—mission for *Le Cause*: She had even insisted on coming as far as Commerical Street with me. Giving me one last wave, she began quickstepping back toward Lick House and our sumptuous lodgings, as we had agreed. I watched her until the fog suddenly dissolved her. For some reason her vanishing in this way gave me a chill—she had seemed so ephemeral.

Then I rapped on the door.

A man in his stocking feet answered, holding a newspaper at his side. "What?"

"I'm here to call on Mr. Frank B. Harte."

"Third floor—second room past the landing."

"Is Mr. Harte in this morning?"

"Dunno. The missus would know, but she's out. I stevedore nights, just got home meself. Frank goes to work when he feels like it. And mostly he don't feel like it."

I felt sure that the landlord was disparaging the sinecure Jessie Benton Fremont, the wife of the general and former senator, had secured for my great-great-great-grandfather with the surveyor-general's office—so he might support himself while writing.

"Thank you." I slipped past the landlord and hastened down a darkened corridor bracketed with unlit gas lamps. I started up the first flight. The stairs groaned underfoot.

Midway an *oeil-de-boeuf* admitted some daylight. Pausing there, I wiped the misted-over circular pane of glass then peered out. I found myself wondering where, in the silent, dripping city, Ina Coolbrith might be this morning. By most accounts she had arrived here some months ago, although it would be two years before Harte and she would become involved.

And all at once I had second thoughts about barging in on any of my ancestors. What ghastly consequences might follow this brief encounter? What underpinnings of fate, what future meetings and fathering unions might collapse under the deceptively light touch of my curiosity?

I pondered this for as long as a minute, but then couldn't help thinking about the wantonly lucrative results that instead might spring from calling on Mr. Bret Harte. To assuage my conscience, I promised not to visit Ina Coolbrith.

I bounded up the stairs, two at a time.

The third and final floor. Taking a deep breath, I knocked.

No answer. I tried again, and then again, but even after sixty seconds no one answered the door. I exhaled loudly. "Of all the goddamned times for you to go to—"

The brass latch rattled and the door creaked open.

"—work."

"I beg your pardon?"

His eyes fastened on me. They were large, dolorous, on the brink of excessive moisture. But his drooping mustaches were outlandish enough to offset those haunted dark brown irises. A decade my junior, he nevertheless seemed far too serious for his twenty-six years, although my inane grin, I'm sure, did little to loosen him up.

"Are you in need of something, sir?"

For the first time in my life I drew a blank down to my toes.

"Sir?"

At ten-thirty in the morning, alone in his room, he was dressed to the nines: topcoat, brocaded vest, even a maroon cravat.

"Mr. Harte?" I finally mumbled.

"Yes?"

"Forgive my lack of grace—it's just such an honor to finally meet you."

He accepted this with a nod I found conceited. This glimmer of his twenty-four-carat vanity gave me the impetus to go on in the same vein: "I've read just about everything you've published. . . ."

"Indeed?" His smile was reserved, but not self-effacing.

"Yes, and I'm trying your patience this morning only because many of my friends have encouraged me to do so—to impose upon the good offices of the famous F. B. Harte."

"Please, please, come in, Mister . . . ?"

"Hemingway. Ernest Hemingway."

"A pleasure—kindly be seated there." He indicated a rose-wood-and-velvet chair across from the Byzantine altar of a writing desk where he'd apparently been working when interrupted by me. In later years he may have recalled these days as his Bohemian halcyon, but I saw at once that this natty fop was *bijoux bourgeois* down to the obligatory Persian carpet. He brightened. "Now, Mr. Hemingway, in what way do your friends think I might be of service to you?"

"Well, I, too, am a writer."

He couldn't quite muster a smile for this news. "How . . . nice."

"I should say an *aspiring* writer. I'm unpublished," I confessed desolately—beginning to warm up to my role. "But the editor of the *Golden Era*—"

"Colonel Lawrence?"

"Yes, the good colonel wrote me an encouraging letter . . . when he declined to publish one of my short stories."

"Please don't be overly disappointed, Mr. Hemingway. It's enough of a plaudit to earn such a letter from him." Now that the literary pecking order had been firmly established in his mind, Harte couldn't have become more magnanimous. "Colonel Lawrence has an infallible eye for talent. He's from New York, you know."

"New York!" I gasped.

"Indeed . . . indeed."

At this point I feigned an awkward silence.

"Mr. Hemingway." He chuckled at last. "Do you wish to show me some of your work—so I might render a judgment on it?"

"Oh, Mr. Harte, do I dare ask?!"

"It would be my pleasure."

As if fearful he might suddenly change his mind, I took from my coat pocket the manuscript Marguerite had prepared for me in her meticulous calligraphic hand. I made sure the sheaf of parchment trembled as I extended it to him. "Oh, thank you, Mr. Harte. I don't know what to say except . . ."

He glanced up from the title page. "Yes?"

"I've already dallied here in the Far West too long. I must sail for home in three days."

"Which is?"

"Missouri. I appreciate how busy you must be and would not beg for such a favor—"

He waved off my apologies. "Consider it done by the time of your departure, Mr. Hemingway." He consulted the title page again. "I'm sure *The Adventures of Huckleberry Finn* will prove to be a delight. Please call for it on Sunday morning—evenings find me at the Fremont residence at Fort Mason."

"*General* John Fremont's house?" I asked with just the perfect tone of awe.

"Quite." He rose as a signal of dismissal, then led me toward the door. "It was chilly this morning, wasn't it? I was almost tempted to have the concierge bring up a scuttle of coal for my stove. . . ."

"Awfully chilly . . . yes." What I did next I know to be inexcusable, but his back was turned to me, and as we skirted his imposing desk, I snatched several pages off the slanted writing board and stuffed them in my coat pocket in the same instant I covered the sounds of my theft with a racking cough.

He turned. "Are you well?"

"Oh, yes—it's just this city's vaporous atmosphere."

"I seem to thrive in it. Well . . ." He offered his soft hand. ". . . until Sunday, Mr. Hemingway."

"Until Sunday, Mr. Harte."

I had no idea what I had pilfered from him until I returned to Lick House and read it while lying across the short but comfortable bed. I had taken the first chapter to *Fantine*, a novel in which Harte burlesqued Victor Hugo, a work all but forgotten by the twentieth century. Well, my great-great-great-grandfather had just gotten *Huckleberry Finn* in return—a pretty fair trade, I thought with a chuckle.

Stripped down to a deshabille of linen blouse and pantalettes, Musetta glanced at me through the French mirror above the dressing table. "What is it?"

"Nothing, my lovely." But I lifted my champagne glass at her.

Smiling, she swiveled around on the stool, absently knocking over her *nécessaire de toilette* with her dimpled elbow. "Did your business go well?"

"Yes, I'm sure of it."

Then I saw it on the table among her spilled scissors, tweezers, and tin compacts: a five-pointed copper star.

"What's that?"

She knew at once what I meant—she quickly slipped it back inside the bag. "My things."

The star was exactly like the one the Cavanaughs had framed and hung in their Edwardian parlor, but I had a more voluptuous mystery to delve into at that moment. "Come here," I said, like a fool.

The days in which Bret Harte would read and jealously admire Mark Twain's classic became a holiday for Musetta and me.

That first free morning we hiked to the summit of Russian Hill. And I mean *hiked*, for it involved assisting Musetta over a fence (no barbed wire yet, thankfully) and shooing bony cattle out of our path. We paused near the grassy top while I pivoted in a complete circle, searching for some landmark on the slopes. But it was no good: In the next one hundred twenty-five years these heights would be gouged and reshaped a dozen times; the future site of Our Lady Clare's Orphan Asylum would have to remain unknown.

"What is wrong, Howard?"

The breeze, which was sweeping the Bay clear of fog had also folded back the rose-garnished brim of her bonnet. Smiling, I righted it for her. "Everything's so *changed*."

"Since you were last here?"

I nodded, perhaps somewhat bleakly, for she kissed my cheek.

The most obvious difference was the absence of the bridges, especially the Golden Gate; and undominated by a vermilion span vaulting its brick battlements, Fort Winfield Scott looked far more imposing than how I had seen it heretofore—a barnacle growing off the bridge's southern anchorage. But even more unexpected was to gaze northwest and see a huge sand dune humped between the foot of Russian Hill and the officers' residences at Fort Mason—covering the district where my office would one day be. I had an suffocating image of sand piled against my bay windows as I slumped behind my rolltop, waiting for release from this dusky tomb; yet already a machine something like a dredger was chipping away at the dune's eastern extremity—Musetta watched it in fascination; machinery, even the simplest kind, seemed to mesmerize her.

Turning toward the heart of the city, I found familiarity only in the spire of St. Mary's Cathedral, whose warning under its clock was illegible at this distance, although Brother Tom had tried to brand it on the lizard skin of my soul: *Son, observe the time and fly from evil*. And even this was not the same structure in which Rodrigo would marry Marguerite: St. Mary's would be twice rebuilt to the original plans, once in 1906 and again after a fire in 1969.

Standing there, clutching Musetta under my arm, I did not feel devastated, forsaken, as a person might returning to his home after it has been bombed to rubble. But all the fragile buttresses had fallen away—those unchallenged conceits that life, out of respect, does not go on before and after us. "It's all so real," I said quietly, "*without* me. . . ."

The next day dawned to a drizzle that ruled out sightseeing. Musetta was so listless it soon occurred to me that she was deeply depressed. She said she didn't feel like joining the four hundred other guests to be found at any mealtime in the dining hall, a noisy replica of the one at Versailles, so I pulled the sash to the service bell and ordered champagne and oysters brought to the room. Yet she ignored these bribes and sat at the window, water rippling down the glass, reflecting on her face. Making the best of things, I got quietly drunk. For this reason I was too blunted to think of a suitable white lie when she whispered, her eyes still fixed on an empty and dampened Sutton Street, "I have not been good for you."

I don't know what I had expected from her. And in Musetta's defense, these fanciful expectations might have been the reason for the problem she so accurately sensed. I appreciated how much she had tried to please me, although I was surprised at her lack of inventiveness, which made me suspect that Victorian inhibitions were so pervasive they infected even demimondaines. But then again, perhaps she had not wanted to seem *too* inventive, especially if her affection for me was genuine. We both made love as if all the men who had ever used her were lined up outside the door with their hats in their hands. If I found anything jealousy-provoking, and as a natural consequence, erotic about that image, the feeling inevitably dissipated during our first few minutes into the act—and I probably seemed distant to her.

"No, you haven't been good," I said at last, visibly wounding her until I went on: "Nor I for you. We must stop pretending it's the first time for either of us. There is no new way to please us—

especially me. You would understand that, Musetta, if you traveled to . . . to where I come from.''

"Salt Lake City?"

"Well . . . yes." Taking the magnum of champagne, I went over to her, sat at her feet. "We are very, very fond of each other. That's all we must try to prove."

She rested her chin on the crown of my head, then kissed my forehead. . . .

What followed was not the most exotic bit of lovemaking I have ever experienced. But it was tender, and we both promptly fell asleep afterwards—as if a burden had been lifted.

"Musetta," I asked when I felt her stir beside me, having awakened a half hour before her, "does Madame Richelieu realize she has some Negro blood?"

She pulled away from me. *"Certainement."*

"Then why is she a Chiv? *Le Cause* advocates slavery—although I myself have no objection to the institution."

"Her father was a great Creole gentleman."

"White, you mean?"

"Oui. But more than that—madame is a woman of . . . of *principer* . . . oh!" She clenched her fists.

"You mean *principles*?"

"Ja!"

By now she had flown from the bed and stood naked at its foot, glaring at me.

"I'm sorry, Musetta. I didn't mean to pry."

Then, as swiftly as it had gathered, her anger vanished. She looked ashamed for a terrible moment in which I expected her to cry. But then she said, "I must dress," and turned away from me.

Most likely my ignorance had amused Sam Clemens when I told him I intended to purchase a wardrobe for Musetta in Aurora prior to departing for San Francisco. Not only was no women's wear to be had, the available media for fashions were limited to denim and rag wool—sold by the yard. And the Esmeralda Mercantile was out of thread.

After our scene concerning Madame Richelieu's convictions, I found our embarrassed calm so unpleasant, I suggested a shopping spree, and Musetta jumped at the offer—despite the light rain.

At a dress shop near the corner of Pine and Kearny streets, I doled out one hundred dollars gold for a light blue gown with puffed sleeves and a neckline that dipped tastefully toward the parting of her breasts. She looked magnificent, even in the lackluster afternoon light filtering in through the front window.

As we were leaving, I asked the seamstress-clerk, "What opera's playing in town?"

She was occupied with another customer, some demanding old crone with ridiculous-looking Shirley Temple curls, so her reply was curt: "You'll have to learn that from Maguire's Opera house, sir."

"Is it open now?"

"The ticket office—yes, I'm sure."

I was momentarily stumped. I had no idea where Maguire's was. Smiling, Musetta awaited my next move.

Quickly I hit upon the idea of walking the few blocks to Portsmouth Square, where yesterday I had seen a queue of hackney coaches in front of city hall.

The drizzle had slackened to a mist by the time we passed St. Mary's. Musetta held my free arm with just enough pressure to make the gesture seem possessive. "Thank you, Howard."

"For what?"

"The gown—it is lovely."

"Oh . . . my pleasure."

We had our choice of elegant cabs, so I helped her into the second brougham in line—its white horses were perfectly matched in size and color. "Maguire's Opera House," I said to the driver, who smartly cracked his whip.

Easing back against the quilted cushions, my arm around Musetta, I grinned as I looked out the rain-pearled glass of the windows.

But after only a few moments my confidence began to ebb: We were headed down Kearney Street—the way we had just come. This was not lost on Musetta, whose eyes had narrowed slightly. My humiliation was complete when the horses wheeled onto Pine Street, past St. Mary's spire, and the driver reined them to a halt. "Maguire's, sir."

The opera house was three doors down from the dress shop—on the same side of the street. It was also only two blocks from our hotel.

Musetta struggled to keep a blank expression, but lost the effort as she stepped down onto the damp boardwalk. "Howard," she asked very gravely, "the truth, please—have you ever been to this city before?"

"Oh, *Maguire's*!" I slapped my forehead. "I don't know what I was thinking."

She didn't look convinced; but now the lines were drawn—we both had secrets we preferred not sharing.

I was approaching the ticket window when I spotted the playbill—and halted, almost groaning. She drifted to my side. "What is wrong?"

"Perhaps we should wait."

"Why?"

"I can't think of a worse opera to be a person's first."

Then she, too, saw the playbill. Her lips parted as she exhaled. And when she turned back toward me, I realized that my suggestion had hurt her. But she said with a hint of stubbornness in her voice, "No, I would like very much to see *La Traviata*."

"Musetta," I said as gently as I could, "the story's about—"

"I know what it is about," she snapped. "I have read the novel by Monsieur Alexandre Dumas."

I shrugged, then bought the tickets.

So, as we took our seats in front of the red velvet drop curtain that evening, I could not fully enjoy the sensation Musetta was creating, especially among the male aficionados, as she primly cooled herself with her Japanese fan.

"Pardon me, sir," said some old poop with woolly dundrearies and a monacle as he leaned over my shoulder, "but I am compelled by the Muses to remark—your wife is as lovely as a Venus."

Shifting around, I saw that his own wife was grotesquely fat. "Why, thank you, sir. And seeing the comeliness of your own Aphrodite, I can understand why you're such an excellent judge of goddesses."

They were still merrily twittering to each other when the overture was struck up, and I was gloating to myself that I could cut a silken swath through these hobnobs right to the Money Tree—if only I had more time.

I don't think I watched more than five minutes of the entire performance. For one thing, the limelight was painfully glaring and made the members of the Milano touring company look like ghouls. But mostly I was waiting for some reaction from Musetta as a forty-year-old youth named Alfredo wooed his *fille de joie* away from her life of sin, only to lose her to the streets again because of the secret intervention of his father, who, tragically, glimpsed the sincerity of Violetta's love for his son but persisted in turning her away from him for fear word of the ménage would jeopardize his daughter's impending marriage to a man of excellent family. And during the final meeting between the lovers, at the height of the *cri de coeur* when Violetta wailed, *"Amami, Alfredo!"*—love me, Alfredo!—even I felt a little down at the mouth for these unfortunate but well-fed Italians. Yet Musetta watched dry-eyed, scarcely blinking, so as not to miss a thing. And as the stage was littered with roses and the curtain fell for the last time, she stood even before I did. *"Bon,"* she said, avoiding my eyes. There was absolutely no inflection to the word.

"Bon," I echoed.

A naval officer—Russian, by his accent—insisted that we take the taxi he had hailed for himself, although I tried to explain that it was only a short walk to our lodgings. He kissed Musetta's hand and murmured something in French as he assisted her into the carriage, but she seemed oblivious to his attentions. Then, with an envious smile, he bowed in my direction.

I'm not certain why, but we seemed to affect San Francisco's upper crust in this way—as if we were appealing children of the haut monde, that we had just enough tasteful glamour to remind them of their own delusions about themselves.

As the coach pulled away from Maguire's, I was on the verge of joking about this to Musetta when I felt her sobbing against my chest.

"You see?" I whispered, holding her. "It really isn't a good first opera."

15

SUNDAY MORNING I purposely failed to keep my appointment with Bret Harte. And the next afternoon I visited the offices of *The San Francisco Morning Call.*

Piled behind the oaken counter were mounds of wastepaper through which men thrashed as if they were snowdrifts. Finally, after I had cleared my throat several times, a clerk with garters around his sleeves came rustling through the mess to accept my contribution to the death notices column:

> An Ernest Hemingway of Hannibal, Missouri, died Saturday evening at his boardinghouse on Montgomery Street after a long illness.

The man read it back to me, then asked, "For tomorrow's paper, sir?"

"Yes, and then each day until Friday—how much will that be?"

"Two dollars—don't you want to announce the location of the funeral?"

"There will be no funeral."

"Then name the executor who will be handling the estate?"

"There is no estate."

"Then why not save yourself eight bits?"

"It was the deceased's wish that this be done. And as he himself would say if he could: 'Never send to know for whom the bell tolls . . .'"

"I beg your pardon?"

I slipped a fifty-cent piece in the pocket of his ink-mottled apron.

"Oh . . . very good, sir."

When not abed in Lick House, Musetta and I spent the remainder of the week day-tripping, the highlight of which was a tour of the Bay by schooner. For the first hour we slipped through a gray cloudland. Silvery droplets collected on the sails, then began dripping onto the deck like rain; there was nothing to see, so we sought refuge in the clammy cabin, where the skipper of the five-man crew served us coffee and asked the paler passengers if they felt any snakes in their boots yet. Everyone laughed at his little joke—everyone except one sullen fellow who was sitting apart from us on the second rung of a ladder, hands resting atop his cane. I felt certain he had been stealing long glances at Musetta and me ever since we had boarded the small sailing ship. He avoided my eyes whenever I looked his way, and I have never liked a man who averts a friendly gaze or wipes his lips with the back of his hand after saying something. A man should be able to lie with absolute sincerity, or realize his limitations and stick to the truth. However, he was soon forgotten when the breeze rose by several knots and ferried the fog up against the hills that one day would be thoroughly encrusted by the cities of Berkeley and Oakland. Standing beside me at the gunwale, steadying herself by clasping two tholes, Musetta looked across the Bay. All at once she gasped happily—but didn't explain why. I'm sure it had everything to do with the bright chaos of whitecaps, the mist and green shoreline—perhaps, for an instant, she had glimpsed Gotland again. But I didn't question her.

Thursday evening I returned to Lick House, having been out all afternoon, and smiled secretly at her as I laid a half-dozen shaving brushes and a pot of glue on the dressing table. In the mirror I saw her approach me from behind, eyes inquisitive. I began cutting the bristles off one of the wooden handles with my pocket knife.

"Howard, what are you doing?"

"Hang on a moment and I'll let you judge my handiwork. Here, cut them all off for me."

Cringing from the awful sensation, I applied glue to my cheeks and chin with my fingers. She grimaced as I dipped into the pile of bristles, which were almost the same light brown as my own hair, and began affixing them to my sticky face. Shaking her head, she returned to bed, where she had been reading a year-old copy of *Harper's*.

Ten minutes later I swiveled around on the stool and cried triumphantly, *"Voilà!"*

Musetta made a little sound like a moan, then held her knuckles against her lips before bursting into laughter.

"Stop it."

"Is this meant to be a *déguisement*?"

"Of course it's meant to be a disguise!"

"*Bon*—then you look exactly like a man with the mange." Then she laughed so hard she gave herself the hiccups.

"All right . . . we'll see . . ." I gave the velvet sash a yank, and a few minutes later the bellboy knocked, then stood at the threshold, expressionless, as I said, "A bottle of Lac d'Or champagne, please—iced. And are today's oysters genuinely *today's* oysters?"

"Oh yes, sir. Harvested from south Bay this very morning."

"Two dozen on the half shell then."

Leaving the door ajar, I listened to his retreating footfalls and was on the verge of tossing off a self-satisfied *There!* at Musetta when the bellboy loosed the most asinine giggle I've ever heard.

This pitched Musetta back into the gales.

"Oh, damn you!" I leaped on the bed and began sharing my whiskers with her in a frenzy of Eskimo kisses. Shrieking, she rolled away from me and felt for the thin mustache and tuft of bristles on her chin that I'd given her. "Oh, no!" she cried. "Look what have you done to me!"

"Yes, I've made a proper gentleman of you!"

But then her eyes grew damp, and it was a long, tender time before she said, "Let me help you."

"No, it's too—"

"Please, Howard—I need to help you."

Musetta had no sooner stepped inside the rooming house on Commercial Street than I suffered a lapse in confidence—although in the course of our rehearsal, which had lasted until the early morning hours, she had revealed a talent for dissembling that bordered on a thespian brilliance. And as to the reason behind this little playact: She was content to believe that somehow, in some joyfully mysterious way, it served *Le Cause*. Her enthusiasm made me feel guiltier than hell. But how could I ever hope to explain?

Despite my admiration for her abilities, I knew I didn't have what it takes to remain patiently on the street below as she mounted the stairs to Bret Harte's third-story room. So I ran around the corner and approached the rooming house from the alley. The back door was unlocked, and I slipped inside. Down the main corridor I could hear sizzling and clattering sounds suggestive of a busy kitchen. Fortunately, a back set of stairs saved me from passing that way; and mincing my stride so the wooden stairs wouldn't groan beneath my weight, I reached the top floor and gingerly pressed my ear to Harte's door, which I quickly determined was inferior to the lath and muslin wall as a sounding board.

Musetta was in the midst of explaining that she was the wife of Ernest Hemingway. Her voice grew nicely tremulous as she said, "I arrived here Monday morning, Mr. Harte, on the steamer *Cincinnatus*, only . . . only to find my dear husband . . ."

"There, there, Mary," Harte crooned. "May I call you by your Christian name?"

"Please do, Mr. Harte."

"And you must call me Frank."

"Oh, Frank—what am I to do now?"

The floor inside the room groaned, and I frowned, realizing that Harte had just crossed the Persian carpet, probably to sit beside her. "You must rely on your friends, Mary. And I insist that you count me among your friends."

"Oh, thank you . . . you are so very kind."

"One thing confuses me . . ."

"Yes?"

"How did you learn of my meeting with your husband? After all, even had he written you prior to his death, you were at sea."

"His diary. It was in his room with his other things."

"A diary you say?" For the first time Harte sounded a bit uncomfortable.

"Yes, despite his condition, Ernest wrote fondly of you, your offer to help him."

"And I can only confess my own sorrow upon reading in *The Call* of his passing." There followed a long silence, which left me wondering, distrustfully, but then Harte asked, "Is something the matter, Mary?"

"No . . . it's just that your eyes . . . they are like someone else's I know."

"Someone close to your heart, I hope."

"Yes, I am afraid so. But none of this has anything to do with why I have called upon you, Frank."

"Oh?"—a cool one, Bret Harte, if indeed he was playing dumb. But I felt sure of it: Not only had he read *Huckleberry Finn*, he had recognized it to be the masterwork it was, and coveted the opportunity to publish it under his own name. "And how might I be of service to you, Mary?"

"Poor Ernest's condition—"

"Which was, if I may ask?"

Her hesitation was perfectly timed. "Dementia."

"I see. How did it manifest itself? I found his company to be quite agreeable. Although now and again he seemed at a loss for words."

"Oh yes, there were times when his company was lovely," she said fondly enough to touch even me. "But there were others . . ." She began weeping. "Oh, to go home—that is the only tonic for grief, Frank. When the *Cincinnatus* sails again, for China, and then Europe . . ."

"Are you bound for Scandinavia then?"

"Yes . . . to remain."

"It must be handsome country."

"It is heaven . . . but first there is an important matter to close here. A literary matter."

"Oh?"

I wanted to shout and dance in the hallway: Harte wasn't about to admit that he had received the manuscript from poor old Ernest Hemingway. What more did I need to be assured that *The Adventures of Huckleberry Finn* would soon burst into print under the name of Bret Harte? But Musetta had been instructed to abandon the issue only when Harte flatly denied ever having taken possession of it.

"In his condition, Ernest imagined himself to be a great writer," she went on. "But his works were very crude. Stories about low men and women—of *Negroes* even. One day years ago he just disappeared from our home in Missouri. I had no idea where he had gone—until a letter arrived from a Mr. Washington Irving in New York State. Another writer—do you know of him?"

"Indeed," Harte was finally confessing *something*, at least.

"My husband had given Mr. Irving a manuscript called *The

Adventures of Huckleberry Finn. The late Mr. Irving, in the kindness of his heart, read it. But the words, they were madness, and when he said to Ernest that he should go home for a long rest . . ." She succumbed briefly to a sob. ". . . he punched Mr. Irving on the nose."

"I see. And now you're concerned that your husband gave this opus to me?"

Again silence, but I gathered that she had nodded yes.

"I see," Harte repeated himself—I liked that. "And now you want this manuscript returned to you . . . before it might embarrass you?"

"Please, Frank—if you have it."

The tips of my bow tie began quivering in tempo with my heart—after all, seventy-five million dollars might be riding on his answer.

"Well, I must disappoint you in that regard, Mary. I saw *Huckleberry Finn* in the same light the late Mr. Irving did. It was unabashedly rustic, and the language belongs in a Barbary Coast saloon, not a work of literature. When I read that Mr. Hemingway had fallen to his illness, and expecting no one as responsible as yourself to show up to take charge of the manuscript, I burned it in that very stove. . . ." And to corroborate his statement, Harte could be heard opening the iron door with a grating noise. "Here, Mary, is a portion of an unburned page. The rest, as you can plainly see, has been purified to ashes. Take this last dismal shred—destroy it in private."

I bit my hand to keep from pounding the wall.

"I don't know how to thank you, Frank," she said uncertainly.

"You can thank me by dining with me at General Fremont's residence at Black Point on the morrow's evening."

The bastard—he was to marry in only a few short weeks. But then it occurred to me that my own propensitites in this area might be congenital.

"Frank, you are too kind," Musetta said, "but it would not look seemly."

"Perhaps not in Denmark, Mary—"

"Sweden."

"Yes, well, things are different here. And I can think of nothing better for you at present than bright company. Mrs. Fremont is the very soul of understanding."

"Again, thank you—no."

"Well, should you change your mind—here is one of Mrs.

Fremont's calling cards. The guard at the Fort Mason sentry house
will direct you to the residence. Dinner at eight. Just present this
to the valet.''

"You have been so very kind."

There was the moist sound of a kiss, and I hoped it had been
planted on her hand.

Musetta swept out into the hallway just as I ducked down the
back stairs. But she must have glimpsed my skulking retreat, for
when we were reunited on Commercial Street, she thrust the
charred remnant of the page and Mrs. Fremont's card into my
hand and hurried on ahead of me.

"Musetta—"

"You . . . you spy!"

"I didn't mean to," I said wretchedly. I had been intimate with
her for days now, but never in that time had I imagined that she
might crave trust more than anything else. "Please slow down.
Musetta?"

We were barely on speaking terms when it came time to endure
another five days of being jostled over hill and dale by various
types of coaches. Arriving at last in Aurora, we stepped down
onto a dirt street that seemed to rock and pitch beneath our feet.
Her hand sought my arm for steadiness, but quickly released it.
We walked in silence up to Bullion Street. Then, her eyes large
and anxious as, if to say, *I've come this far before, only to be
disappointed*, she waited for me to say something. But there was
nothing more I could offer: Mine was a sojourn here, not a life
replete with promises and commitments. So after enough seconds
had ached away to the clanging of the quartz stamps, she slowly
turned, lifted the hem of her dress, and rushed up the steps to
Madame Richelieu's drawing room.

I strolled downtown to the Bank Exchange Saloon. Despite my
great-great-great-grandfather's mule-headed insistence on remaining a second-rate author, despite Musetta's return to the web of
intimacies spun by her Creole mistress, I had not lost everything.
There was still much to do on my Grand Tour. But I had lost just
enough to make getting knee-crawling drunk a savage pleasure.

Not until the next morning did I realize that Aurora was nearly
deserted.

16

I HAD NO sooner sobered up than I again subjected myself to torture by horse-drawn coach—this time in an infamous Mud Wagon which, in registering every jolt, no matter how slight, was more seismograph than transportation.

By three o'clock the night before I had drunk more than enough brandy to forget Musetta, but had to wait another two hours until Pine Street, in keeping with the rotation of the earth, reeled past the front doors of the Bank Exchange Saloon again. Only then did I burst out into the first blush of morning and stagger up the rocky lanes before they could start tilting the other way.

I had expected dozens of men to be turning out of their cots at the Goddess of the Dawn Boardinghouse, but the dormitory was empty except for Granville, who, without benefit of a nose, was producing a hog snore he cut short as I hopped past him, trying to pull off a boot that seemed glued to my foot.

"How do, Mr. Rettie? It's been a spell."

"Where's everybody?"

"Cleared out. Gone daft—the whole town."

"What do you mean?"

"Well, Whiteman hisself come through Esmeralda two nights

ago. I'd be gone after him myself, but the white sage is in bloom. . . ."

I slumped onto my cot, trying to decide whether or not I had the energy to put my boots back on so I could go outside and throw up. Then I saw that my boots were still on, but the wave of nausea had passed. *"Whiteman,"* I whispered, sensing some dim significance in the name but unable to put my finger on it.

"You ask me, though," Granville said, "the Lost Cement is a wild-goose chase."

"Aha!" I cried.

"You all right, Mr. Rettie?"

Shoving my fist through the lining of my coat pocket, I fished around until I found my paperback copy of *Roughing It.* I had already dog-eared the first page in the chapter, but had to shut one eye to read it:

It was somewhere in the neighborhood of Mono Lake that the marvelous Whiteman cement mine was supposed to lie. Every now and then it would be reported that Mr. W. had passed stealthily through Esmeralda at the dead of night, in disguise, and then we would have a wild excitement—because he must be steering for his secret mine, and now was the time to follow him. In less than three hours after daylight all the horses and mules and donkeys in the vicinity would be bought, hired or stolen, and half the community would be off for the mountains, following in the wake of Whiteman. But W. would drift about through the mountain gorges for days together, in a purposeless sort of way, until the provisions of the miners ran out, and they would have to go back home. . . .

Mark Twain went on to explain how Calvin Higbie and he had rushed out of Aurora with the others in search of the Lost Cement Mine—not a vein of concrete, like it sounds, but "lumps of virgin gold" embedded in a natural volcanic cement "as thick as raisins in a slice of fruit cake." This lost ledge was still an object of feverish treasure hunting in my own time, but it excited me only for one reason at the present: Although sooner than I had expected, Clemens and Higbie had nevertheless pulled out on their ten-day holiday, leaving me free to conduct some very personal business on the Comstock, one hundred thirty miles to the north—that is, to check on the whereabouts of a certain silver brooch I'd lost along the way.

"Granville—when's the next stage for Virginia City?"

"Night coach departs at five this afternoon."

"Nothing sooner?"

"Not unless you want to ride your horse. But that'll only turn a fourteen-hour trip into a four-dayer."

"Do you know Sam Clemens?"

"Who, old Sam Clemens?" He chuckled. "Why . . ." Then the brightness trickled out of his eyes. ". . . no, I don't believe I do."

"What about his partner, Calvin Higbie?"

"Who, old Higbie?" He slapped his knees. "Why, old Cal?"

"Jesus . . ."

"Calvin I do know . . . yes, indeed, Calvin I do know. We shifted together at the Lady Jane. That was before Cal quit the mine and joined up with some worthless redheaded stinkfoot who lasted one day at the mill before being ordered off the premises—"

"*That* is Sam Clemens." I showed him a double eagle, which flashed in the first rays to stream in through the dirty windows. "May I ask a favor—in strictest confidence?

Granville shrugged.

"Without alerting Mr. Higbie or Mr. Clemens to my interest in them, would you mind posting me a message when they arrive back here in Esmeralda?"

"As long as you intend them no harm, Mr. Rettie," he said with great conviction, although he was still eyeing the twenty-dollar gold piece.

"Oh, nothing like that, believe me. I'm an old friend of Sam's, and want to surprise him."

"Very well. But to what establishment do I address this message?"

I flipped him the coin. "What's the best hotel on the Comstock?"

"The International, without a doubt."

"Then the International it is."

He was now staring at my copy of *Roughing It*. "What's that, Mr. Rettie? I never seen one all soft like that."

"Ah . . . it's my *Book of Mormon*."

"You mean like a Bible or something?"

"Much more than that. I can glimpse the future in the prophet's words."

"Dod-rot it! Tell me what's in store for me!"

"Well . . . all right." Assuming a grave expression, I closed my eyes, then opened the book with a snap. Assiduously I studied the page before me as if it were aswirl with visions instead of half-blurred words. "I see a theatre in the fog . . . yes, a theatre in a foggy city on a bay."

"Hot glory—that's San Francisco, for sure! I can use a change of scenery!"

"I see you, Granville, on a brightly lit stage . . . you, a famous actor."

"Great Herod, that's dandy! What's the play?"

"A moment . . . yes . . . yes . . . I'm quite sure it's *Cyrano de Bergerac*."

He frowned. "Never heard of it. You sure it ain't *Mazeppa*?"

"No, I don't think—"

"If it ain't *Mazeppa*, I just won't do it. What's yours about?"

"Well, *Cyrano* is a wonderful story about appearances and love and—"

"No, no—that just won't do. Once you've seen little Adah Menken in *Mazeppa*, you're spoiled for anything else." His eyes shone with recollection. "Why, when she gets tied naked to the Wild Horse of Tartary to die out on the Roossian prairie—that's poetry! You sure you ain't seen Miss Adah?"

"I must have missed her debut in Salt Lake."

"Don't miss it twice—for your own edification." He paused, then smirked as I flopped down: "No offense, Mr. Rettie, but I never seen a Saint as pitiful tore down as you look this morning. . . ."

At ten minutes after five that afternoon I was drowsily sandwiched between two passengers in a Mud Wagon, scarcely able to keep my eyes open. Exhausted and hung over, I was half asleep by the time the horses started up the hill to north of Aurora, so I had no idea where I was when the driver hollered, "Whoa!" and the coach jounced to a halt.

"Wellington?" I muttered, wondering if we'd already reached our first rest stop.

"Unscheduled," the man on my right whispered, taking his Navy Colt from his coat pocket and tucking it under his leg. "What bloody cheek—we're not a quarter mile out of town."

"Driver!" a voice growled upslope of us. "Let go of the lines and raise your hands—till I s'plain myself!"

I gave a loud groan. We were being robbed—and me with a

fortune in gold coin on my person! Yet in spite of the threat of financial ruin, I could not force my hand down into the pocket that concealed my revolver. My hand knew better.

"Everybody out on this side!" the same voice bawled. "And let me see your palms! Now!"

There was some gentlemanly disagreement among us as to who should be first to get out of the Mud Wagon. However, my good manners prevailed. Turning my ankle on a pile of discarded handguns, I followed the others out to stand facing the harsh and level light of the declining sun. Against this golden fire were the silhouettes of a half-dozen horsemen. I sensed that they were masked, but their faces were awash in glare.

Sighing heavily, the driver threw the express box to the ground, which made the riders laugh, unexpectedly.

"We don't want that, suh. We're soldiers, not road agents. We just want *him*. . . ."

I realized with a start that the horseman was aiming his Colt at me.

None of my fellow travelers argued with him. They left it for me to rasp that some terrible mistake had been made, and that as a stinkfoot of the highest order, I hadn't had the time to offend anybody in the territory. In fact, it had been on my mind to leave Nevada, and now seemed an opportune time to do so. But the next thing I knew, two of the riders had dismounted and were tethering my arms behind me. Darkness rustled down around my head, and I found my ears itching inside a sack that smelled sweetly of grain. Relieved of both my Navy Colt and derringer, I was jostled up into a saddle and we were off at a gallop, shod hooves clattering over stony ground—only God knew in what direction. I didn't care at that moment: It was enough of a trick to stay on the unfamiliar horse, what with my hands unable to reach the pommel and my equilibrium distorted by being blind.

And, of course, I was much too terrified to ask what this was all about.

We had not gone far when the leader called a halt and the sack was yanked off my head, leaving me to blink at another mounted figure, also advantageously positioned with his back to the sun. "Tyler, gentlemen . . ." He gave them a flick of his goatee, and my escort withdrew some distance after my bindings were cut.

"Good evening, Mr. Rettie," the man said quietly, his light gray duster making rustling noises in the breeze.

Behind him the marble headstones in Aurora's wooded cemetery glistened like ice sculpture. Demurely, a cherub was looking over her winged shoulder to see how I might possibly mollify Judge David S. Terry.

"Good evening, Your Honor."

"A friend has acquainted me with an interesting rumor. . . ." His weary tone of voice suggested grief—although he seemed no less fulminating for being sorrowful. Recently, at Shiloh, he had lost a second brother to the war; I recalled this as I looked at the notorious bowie knife sheathed on his belt. "This rumor I find difficult if not impossible to corroborate—without your kind assistance, Mr. Rettie."

I might have plunged for the reins, which had been left dangling free, and ventured an escape then and there—except that several of his henchmen were holding their rifles at the ready. "How might I help you, sir?"

"Well . . ." He paused. The breeze began rocking the pine boughs, moaning around the sharp edges of the tombstones. ". . . I have an idea or two."

I tried to make out his eyes. Then I realized this to be the last thing I wanted to do. "May I ask what ideas, sir?"

"Nothing would please me more than if Mr. Brigham Young chose to actuate his contempt for his Union occupiers. He and his followers have suffered far too long at the hands of the United States."

"I can assure you—"

"Yes, you *can*, Mr. Rettie. But not with words. I don't wish to denigrate the quality of your honor. Yet if all men were perfectly honorable, there would have been no war in the first place."

"I swear—"

"Do not do so," he said ominously. "You have raised more questions than you could possibly answer with a simple oath. To wit, where did you receive thousands of dollars in federal notes, more greenbacks than any reasonable man would care to possess?" From this, I realized that I had been shadowed in San Francisco—Musetta had not known about my errand to the gold broker. "And why did you pass along a lengthy and spurious communication to a Mr. Frank Harte, who is widely known for his Unionist sentiments?"

"I have explanations—"

"I'm sure you do. But no, you will have to evince your sincerity before I can be satisfied you are who you say you are."

"What will this involve?"

"Nothing contemptible, if you are indeed in Mr. Young's service."

"But I have urgent business in Virginia City."

"I'm aware of that. And it is there you shall be contacted."

"By whom?"

But he had spurred his horse away from me. "You shall be contacted, Mr. Rettie."

"But I've missed my stage!"

Judge Terry melted into the shaggy pinions, followed at a canter by his men, who loosed a rebel yell that almost undid my bowels. But one rider remained behind and now trotted up to me.

"Come on," Tyler said, leering at me in his fetching Neander-thal way as he returned my weapons and handed me the reins. "Trail's shorter than the wagon road. You can catch your stage again at Wellington."

My fellow passengers were so pleasantly surprised to find me waiting for them at the way station, and with no bruises or bullet wounds to show for my adventure, they declared a party of thanksgiving that began as soon as the driver had a fresh team of horses to punish—and lasted until first light showed behind the violet-colored echelons of mountains to the east. I had prepared an explanation for them—that my brief kidnapping had arisen because of a misunderstanding over ownership to a claim, a common enough cause for discord in the territory. But this proved unnecessary: The five men, excellent drinking companions one and all, celebrated my release without pestering me for details.

Lord, I thought, *what friendly country for someone with a secret*! And then, lifting my flask, I toasted Nevada, where a man's past could remain inviolate. Then I thought about a woman's secrets too—specifically Musetta's; but that threatened to ebb my rising tide of cheer. So, if I risked contemplating women at all, it was to look forward to the introduction that awaited me in Virginia City. "Gentlemen—to ladies! God bless them!" I cried, my voice warbling from a road like a washboard.

Watching an elipse of desert flicker past under the oil-burning coach lamps, I resolved to keep myself scarce while on the Comstock—and not frequent any of the public watering holes, or even the shameless melodeon pavilion Granville had recommended. I doubted that any of the judge's ex-sharecroppers enjoyed entree to the social circle dominated by the Beauchamp family.

Devastated by the night's revels (and those of the night before!), I nearly dozed through my arrival in that slanting hodgepodge of buildings on the flank of a sage-frosted mountain. But fortunately one of my newfound comrades roused me from an hour's numbness that passed for sleep; and through poached eyes I watched the facades of the C Street structures jiggle past. The boardwalks of this, the main thoroughfare, were teeming with miners, speculators, draymen, and Chinese—all cloaked in fuzzy morning light.

Then, catching the other passengers unawares, I chuckled to myself.

"What is it, Howard?" someone asked.

But I shook my head no. How could I explain that I had just seen a Paiute warrior sauntering down C Street, closely followed by his stout squaw? That of itself was not unusual: Scores of Indians were loitering around town, especially in the vicinity of the outdoor fruit stands. What was noteworthy was that this particular brave was proudly wearing the faded regulation cap of a U.S. Postal Service which did not yet exist—and his squaw was nibbling pine nuts she kept scooping out of an equally worn mailbag. Rodrigo had been right: I was not the first to surmount this Everest—but the view, the extraordinary view, quickly trivialized any disappointment I imagined I felt.

"International Hotel! City of Virginia!" the driver cried over the tintinnabulation of a thousand sparkling harness bells as a sixteen-mule freight wagon rattled in the opposite direction.

I had heard that nothing was on the level in Washoe, but this was proved beyond a doubt when I alighted from the coach and found the hotel portico to be listing acutely. Helplessly, I pitched back into something that splashed and oozed suspiciously like a wallow.

"Are you hurt, Howard?" the only concerned voice of a dozen convulsed ones asked.

"I'm just bully. Help me find my boots. Then let's get a drink."

And we all giggled like school had been let out forever.

17

THERE CAME ANOTHER spate of thumping—although this time it seemed to originate at the door and failed to well up through the flooring to jostle my bed.

"Mr. Belmont Rettie?"

I raised myself on an elbow. And winced. My head was fit only for guillotining, although it was a minor blessing now to be sufficiently acclimated to the stamp mills to be able to tune out their interminable rat-a-tat-a-tating. Then yet another mysterious temblor shook International Hotel to its foundation. Seemingly there had been a dozen of these to the hour ever since I had tumbled into the suffocatingly soft mattress.

All at once it dawned on me: These rumblings were from blasting in the labyrinth of tunnels that corrupted the ground even beneath the main street.

"Mr. Rettie?"

"What is it?"

"A message for you, sir. May I come in?"

"Come . . ." I spied a water pitcher across the room on a tripod table, but realized I could never survive the distance over that rippling wadi of a Brussels carpet to taste the sweet coolness.

I wondered if Granville might be reporting Sam Clemens's

unexpectedly early return to Aurora, but as soon as I saw the pink, tricornered note on the bellboy's silver platter, I remembered: My last act before winking out had been to ring for him. Then, clasping a hand to my left eye to reduce the multiples of vision afflicting me, I had scratched out a note to Miss Eleanor Louise Beauchamp, explaining my eagerness to make her acquaintance after a "revered friend of mine" had spoken so highly of her family. To assure my entree to the Beauchamp mansion, I had included in the envelope Mrs. Jessie Benton Fremont's calling card, which Musetta had received from Bret Harte.

And this, now, was Eleanor Louise's reply. Surprisingly, her hand was not feminine at all: It was big and reckless and cared nothing for margins:

My Dearest Mr. Rettie—

   This evening, beginning at 7:00, my aunt and uncle are
   hosting a most worthy social to benefit the United States
Sanitary Commission. My pleasure can be complete only if
   you attend. Our guests are requested to congregate on F
between Union and Mill Streets. We shall provide you with
appropriate attire.

                                        Eleanor Louise Beauchamp

The Sanitary Commission I knew to be the precursor of the Red Cross, but mention of "appropriate attire" meant nothing to me. When I showed the bellboy the note and asked him about it, he said, pronouncing her last name in some semblance of the French manner, "Oh, Eleanor Beauchamp . . ." Then he simpered.

"What do you mean by that?"

"Nothing, sir." His eyes glazed over as he held out his palm in that timeless gesture of supplication.

"Get a dollar out of my pocket. I hung my coat in the armoire."

"Pardon me, sir, but *I* hung your coat in the armoire. You did so on the floor—along with your muddy trousers. Both of these I took the liberty of having laundered by a Celestial who does not, I assure you, use the spit method. Ah, and the clerk has asked me to remind you that your money is in the hotel safe. *Yesterday afternoon*, when you retired for this lengthy nap, you dropped your receipt on your second try up the stairs."

"Smart ass."

"Sir?"

*   *   *

I hiked up the gravelly, twilit lane toward the highest tier of Virginia City—in terms of both elevation and social status: A Street, whose frilly Victorian manors were little more than a retinue to the queen of the hill, the Beauchamp mansion. The sun had set behind Mount Davidson while I had been dressing for the evening, and now the sky was blushed with variegations of purple. Three snifters of brandy during a long bath had mellowed out the consequences of the carousal with my fellow stage passengers and half persuaded me to stop wondering what Musetta was doing at this or that moment; but even without the booze, I would have soon felt splendid—summer evening in Virginia City!

Then, as I rounded the corner onto A Street, it loomed above me—the Anglican entrance to heaven, a discreet miscegenation of Gothic, Norman chateau and Georgian styles that was, in actuality, not half as grand as Linden Towers; however, here, in a wilderness of sagebrush and mine tailings, it beckoned like a dream.

I had just surmounted the first flight of marble-balustraded stairs in the high retaining wall, when a boy sprang up from a stone bench and asked, "By invitation, sir?"

"Yes." And I began to take Eleanor Louise's note from my vest pocket.

"No need, sir. Mr. Beauchamp . . ." Again the French pronunciation. ". . . wants me to remind anybody what comes here by mistake that the social's on F Street tween Union and Mill."

"Of course," I said lamely, blaming the brandies and a fixation that when I finally met the Cavanaughs' vaunted ancestress, it would be in the grand parlor of this residence, which until this moment had existed for me only in a lithograph hung on my office wall. "Here." I tossed him a quarter. "My mistake—and our secret."

"Yessir!"

Trotting down the slope I had just climbed, I felt no less eager to meet the debutante of whom Cletus Cavanaugh had said, ". . . her arrival in San Francisco from the Comstock marked the goddamned advent of Christian gentility in this city"; and my wife had gushed: ". . . Eleanor Louise was five, maybe six generations ahead of her time!" Fascination at seeing a reportedly beautiful young woman notwithstanding, I wanted to have a little fun at the expense of the twentieth century Cavanaughs. Nothing vicious or disastrous to their lineage, of course. But as I rushed past soft-lit windows and then wended my way through the almost permanent traffic jam of freight wagons on C Street, I relished the notion of a future conversation with my former father-in-law and wife in which I might let slip some telling skeleton about Eleanor Louise *Bo-shamp*, some less than flattering report about her behavior or breeding that the Cavanaughs had conveniently neglected to share with their polo club, which had admitted me only as a "guest of Mr. Cavanaugh" because my own peerage was found by the membership committee to be "indeterminate."

Yet when I reached Union Street, which proved to be the heart of the most industrialized quarter of the city, it seemed as if Eleanor Louise had had a little joke on me: The only structure on that block between Sutton and Mill was the hoisting works of the Madonna Consolidated Mine, the slice of the Comstock vein owned by her family. I had halfway expected to find a church hall or some other meeting place the Beauchamps had rented for the night. But there was no evidence of a gathering anywhere around me.

I was standing there, trying to decide whether or not to feel insulted, when a prim figure marched out of a building that was belching smoke from three chimneys into the rapidly dimming sky. He came directly at me, down a path between tall stacks of shoring timbers, and extended his hand, unsmiling. "Mr. Cropley, sir—superintendent of the Madonna Consolidated."

"Mr. Belmont Rettie . . . a pleasure."

"You are early, Mr. Rettie. The social willna begin till half past the hour." He opened his watch with a sharp click and read its face by the ruddy last light. Then he returned the piece to the pocket of his immaculate white coat. "But I canna thank you enough for it. I told Mrs. Beauchamp that I canna accommodate everbody at once. It's a matter of space in the dry shack and on the cages, you see. Come now, if you will."

I didn't have the faintest idea what he meant by shacks and cages, but I followed without a word, not wanting to appear the bumbling stinkfoot once again. Besides, at that point I fully expected everything to become self-evident within a few minutes.

"This here is the boiler room, Mr. Rettie—the great chugging heart of our Madonna. Watch your head on the pipe there." I could now recognize Mr. Cropley's accent as being Cornish, one which sometimes sounded like Welsh to me, especially if I wasn't listening carefully. Tin and copper miners from Cornwall were prized by their Comstock employers, although the bosses referred to them as "Cousin Jacks," regardless of given name, because upon being hired, a Cornishman usually inquired if there might be work for his Cousin Jack still languishing in poverty on that stony peninsula of England. With my brown hair and somewhat square face, I was often assumed to be one of the cousins—until I opened my mouth.

"This way, now, Mr. Rettie—"

We whisked through shop after shop: blacksmith's, machine, carpentry, and assaying; with Mr. Cropley comporting himself all the while as if he were the captain of a luxury liner, returning the respectul nods of his subordinates by giving the brim of his felt hat a light squeeze. Hurrying across floors that were cleaner than those of my boardinghouse in Aurora, we emerged at last into a cavernous chamber with forty-foot high ceilings. Desert flowers were garlanded off the roof joists, their delicate scents lost under a wilting miasma of sulphur and spent powder. "Main shaft, Mr. Rettie." Steam was roiling up through three adjoining square openings in the floor. This issue looked hot and deadly noxious, and I wondered if it was safe to breathe; but when Mr. Cropley glimpsed my face, he gave me as much of a smile as his austere nature would permit. "All the mines of the Comstock are connecta by tunnels underground. Some shafts, like the Ophir north of us, are downcast—they inhale. The Madonna is upcast— she exhales. What you see here canna harm you—just the warm breath of Our Lady meeting the cool air of the surface. This way to dress, if you will. . . ."

And as he directed me into "the dry shack," which was much like the gymnasium locker room at the orphanage, I tried to pry some answers out of him: ";I wasn't quite sure what the Beauchamps expected me to wear this evening. The invitation did not specify the theme of the social."

"Aye." Then Mr. Cropley withdrew, leaving me to grin after him.

"Sir?" A boy of no more than ten years was waiting to take my coat.

"Ah, thank you . . ."

While he assisted me into a pair of blue flannel pantaloons, a light woolen shirt of the same color, and a felt hat like Mr. Cropley's, I queried him. But all of his answers came tightly wrapped in yesses and noes; obviously he'd been instructed not to bore the guests with any juvenile chatter. He was pulling off my boots when I noticed that he was missing two fingers of his left hand. "Done playing with detonating caps?" I asked.

He nodded sheepishly, but didn't look up as he outfitted my stocking feet with a pair of sturdy brogans.

At that moment a threesome of nabobs in swallow-tailed coats burst into the dressing room and were quickly attended by two other small lads, who set aside the pipes they had been smoking with no apparent fear of censure.

"Of course, it's germane to our suit . . ." one of the men said in a commanding voice, as if picking up the threads of an ongoing argument—and resolutely treating me as if I were one of the wooden stools, although other than his own party, I was the only adult in sight. He was in his mid-twenties, with sandy-colored hair and blond wisps for mustaches. It was obvious: He fancied that he stood apart—from me, his friends, the muddle-headed universe that begged at each and every turn his wisdom. ". . . and so the murder of a chap defending his employer's property is certainly *res gestae*—"

"Come now," one of his friends half whined, "how can you say that when—"

"Have you forgotten I did my clerking for a *justice* of the California Supreme Court?"

"Oh, not this again," the third man chuckled.

"Say what you will—I know what is *res gestae* and what isn't. Excuse me a moment. . . ." And with that he abruptly strode toward me, his right hand outstretched. He would have been the perfect picture of a politician—except that, up close, his smile seemed bent into a perpetual slur. "I don't believe I've had the pleasure."

"Belmont Howard Rettie."

"Oh, yes—you must be Mrs. Fremont's friend. Eleanor Louise is looking forward to meeting you." He had an incisive stare, and I sensed that despite the polite mien, he would challenge everything I said. "How is the good lady? I made her acquaintance some years ago when I lived in San Francisco."

"She's most excellent." That he claimed to know Jessie Fremont immediately put me on guard. "But then again, when isn't she most excellent?"

"Quite." His gaze continued to butt up against mine. "She and I attended Reverend Thomas Starr King's church. Is that where you met her?"

Deciding to take the plunge, I quietly laughed.

He hiked an eyebrow. "Forgive me, I did not mean to pry into your religious affiliation, Mr. Rettie."

"Please call me Howard. And I don't take offense. But no, I am not a Methodist, Mister . . .?"

"Cavanaugh. Hamilcar Ames Cavanaugh."

He finally looked aside—but only because one of the boys was trying to hand him his pair of pantaloons. This was fortunate, because I knew that the color had dropped out of my face. I slumped down onto my stool.

He trotted out his sneer of a smile once again. "Neither am I."

"Sir?"

"A Methodist. At least not any longer. I recently converted to Roman Catholicism."

"Yes, well," I sputtered, trying to regain my composure, "I can appreciate the torment in making such a decision."

"Can you?"

Damn, I despised that smile: It had survived the generations to twist my father-in-law's haughty countenance, and occasionally it had even flashed across Eleanor's lips—whenever I slid into bed and she looked at me as if I had come to fix the plumbing, not make love to her.

"Of late, I've had difficulties with my own faith," I said.

"Which is?"

"I am a Latter-day Saint."

"A *Mormon*? Well, bully for that, I say. You *shall* be stimulating company this evening." He winked over his shoulder at his friends, then turned back to me. "May I venture a personal question?"

"By all means."

He touched his small hand to my wrist. Perhaps it was only my imagination, but his fingers seemed sticky. "Did you suddenly cease to believe in God?"

"No . . . I still believe." I struggled to look appropriately devout. "I believe so intensely, I must have a little holiday from Him now and again."

Hamilcar burst into laughter, then sobering himself without effort, brought his face inches from mine. He smelled of bay rum. Tapping his silk cravat with his fingertips, he whispered, "I believe in the Almighty as much as I believe in this."

"It isn't seemly to compare God to a cravat, Mr. Cavanaugh."

"Why not?" The smile was now gone. "We wear both ties and gods only because it's expected of us." Then, with a self-satisfied

shrug, he motioned for me to follow him over to his friends.
"Gentlemen, may I present Mr. Belmont Howard Rettie. Mr.
Depugh is an officer of the Bank of California operations in the
Nevada Territory . . ."

"Delighted, Mr. Rettie."

"And Mr. Tombaugh is my associate here at the Madonna
Consolidated. Together, he and I keep our good employer, Mr.
Beauchamp, out of legal embroilments."

"Or in failing to do that," Tombaugh said congenially, "we
make sure the judgment is invariably in his favor. A delight to
make your acquantance, Mr. Rettie—especially should you ever
be summoned for jury duty."

"Come, come, gentlemen . . ." Cavanaugh smirked at everyone's clean but decidedly working-class costumes; he seemed
oblivious to the fact that he was dressed in the same lumpen
manner. "I was assured by Mr. Cropley himself," he went on,
"that an availability of refreshment is imminent—and I've learned
that Mr. Cropley is seldom wrong about *anything*."

We filed back out into the main shaft room just as four
millwrights scuttled a long table into place before a group of
Comstock barons and their matrons. The workers gingerly rested
it on the floor because its white chemise spread was aglitter with
hundreds of upturned champagne glasses, which a red-jacketed
steward began righting and filling with robotic precision. Hamilcar graciously offered to get me a drink, then proceeded to take so
long joking with some of the ladies who were attired in protective
garb like ours and quite giddy about it—I got my own glass and
strolled across the polished hardwood decking to a serious-looking
sort who was looming stiffly above me on a three-foot-high dais.
Catching his eye, I asked, "How are you this evening?"

He pointed at the placard I had leaned against:

NO PERSON IS ALLOWED ON THE PLATFORM,
OR TO SPEAK TO THE ENGINEER WHILE ON DUTY!

I jumped away from the sign as if it had burned me and
muttered, "Terribly sorry."

The engineer went back to watching a needle move counter-
clockwise on a dial that indicated what I suspected to be depth in
hundreds of feet. His hands were gripping a helm like that on a
sailing ship, and it took only a few seconds for me to see that his
precise movements were related to those of a huge reel that was

hauling in flat cable. My gaze traced this steel ribbon up to a frame like a gallows poised over the steaming shaft; the cable then plunged downward into the darkness. A bell on the platform was sounded by some mechanical means I didn't understand, and then a kind of open elevator car shot up into view and a half dozen miners emerged from it.

"It's called the cage," Hamilcar said at my side, frowning because he was holding two glasses—and I already had mine. Quickly downing one and setting it on the engineer's platform, he pointed at the miners who, stripped to the waist, were baring pallid but muscular torsoes—the men resembled Greek marbles. "It's miserably hot at the lower levels," he said, his voice a shade higher than before. "But they really should cover themselves before coming topside. Wouldn't you say?"

I didn't know what to say—not after being taken aback by the giddy tone in which he'd posed the question. I was rescued when, unexpectedly for me at least, the cage rose another seven feet, revealing a second level also loaded with sweaty miners. "Ah," I exclaimed, "a double-decker!"

"Wrong." Hamilcar was then proved correct: A third deck was elevated by the engineer to offload another crew. One man wore a camellia behind his ear, and looked quite pleased with himself for it. Noiselessly, the cage whisked below again.

"Remarkable," I said without much conviction, for it occurred to me that I might be asked to ride on the perilous-looking contraption—I, who had no faith in the safety of nineteenth century mechanization. There were not even any rails to prevent an accidental fall into the shaft.

Mr. Cropley took notice of Hamilcar and crossed the increasingly crowded room to say, "Good evening, Mr. Cavanaugh. I hope you find all in order."

"Quite, Mr. Cropley—except for one matter." Hamilcar appeared to be counting heads. "I don't find Governor Nye in attendance so far."

"He canna make it, sir."

"Oh?"

"There's a rumor . . ." The superintendent hesitated.

"Yes?"

"Well, word has it some secesh here in Virginia mean the governor harm."

"Ridiculous." Gravely, Hamilcar checked his watch, then put it away, stone-faced. "Absolutely ridiculous."

"I canna disagree, sir, but his secretary, Mr. Clemens, came in advance this morning. He rode the cage and then said it was too risky for the governor, given the circumstances."

"Is Mr. Clemens here now?" I inquired.

Hamilcar turned toward me. "Do you know Orion?"

"No, but I've met his brother Samuel, and would consider it polite to make his acqaintance as well."

"No, Mr. Rettie," Mr. Cropley said, "I'm afraid the secretary returned to Carson City. Ah, grand, here come Mr. and Mrs. Beauchamp now. . . ."

And in they swept like royalty, to restrained but sincere clapping. There was no pretense in the hauteur of the obese middle-aged couple: They took the applause only as their due, gravitated toward their social peers and benignly ignored those who had not yet achieved a place on their unwritten but exacting registry. But even after a few minutes of nodding and smiling and shaking hands, neither of them had uttered as much as a word.

"Gracious-looking people," I lied—they really looked like gluttons. "But they seem a bit reticent, don't they?"

Quietly, Hamilcar humphed. "Between us, they're dreadfully embarrassed by their French-Canadian accents. I expect they will retire shortly."

"But they just arrived!"

But then, as Hamilcar had predicated, Mr. and Mrs. Beauchamp promendaded out of the chamber, pausing only to whisper to a young brunette I could scarcely see through the throng of hats and bonnets. Although I was a head taller than anyone at the gathering, I had to stand on my toes to get a decent glimpse of the woman.

"Christ!" I gasped.

Hamilcar glared at me a moment. "Yes, she really is a peach, isn't she?"

He didn't say the half of it. She was not the very picture of my ex-wife, and her effect on me arose from something more an enhancement over resemblance: Eleanor Louise Beauchamp was to Eleanor Cavanaugh what object is to image. And whatever her great-great-great-grandaughter would one day hold in hearts, this woman hoarded it in spades. She flashed a smile at an acquaintance, and I found myself trumped right out of my breath. "*That* is a ten . . . a bona fide ten."

"Come," Cavanaugh said with a geniality I should have been

suspicious of, particularly when he added, "let me introduce you to my fiancée."

Eleanor Louise was nearly to the door behind which the women were dressing when Cavanaugh stayed her with a glancing peck on the cheek. Then he said something in her ear, a longer explanation than I might have expected. At last she pivoted toward me with a fetching look of anticipation, and hovered her hand in front of my lips. I kissed it, but I would have rather eaten it like a piece of vanilla fudge.

"Thank you for attending this evening, Mr. Rettie." Pure music—without the bored quality that had set my ex-wife's voice in a minor key. "Hamilcar tells me you hail from Utah."

"Yes."

"Well, as soon as I dress, you must tell me everything about life among the Saints. There is so much I want to learn. So much Sir Richard Burton's book leaves unanswered." Then she was gone inside the forbidden bower that exuded a gust of blended perfumes and gossipy voices as the door swung shut behind her.

My heart sank as if I might never see her again.

Perhaps Hamilcar had been piqued, after all, by the way I'd taken to his fiancée. Without a word, he left me alone to cool my ardor with sips of champagne while he traded forced laughter with a huddle of well-heeled men that opened to admit him, then tightly closed ranks again. I consoled myself by reflecting on this evening's confirmation that Beauchamp-Cavanaughs had sprung from a long line of French Catholics, obviously the peasant variety—despite Cletus's inference that his family had been Episcopalian longer than the Tudors.

Yet I enjoyed a complete revenge several minutes later when Eleanor Louise reemerged in pantaloons and woolen shirt, which in contrast to her flawless and smooth skin, made her seem all the more feminine. To my surprise, she made straightaway for me, and before Hamilcar could take a step to intercede, laced her arm through mine. "Let's be first down, Mr. Rettie. What do you say?"

What could I say but yes? And yes a thousand times! She could have been suggesting that we clasp hands and plunge into the open shaft of the Madonna Consolidated, and I wouldn't have argued in the least. I was so captivated by her slightest expression, the conversations surrounding us blurred to white noise—and it was either a microsecond or an eternity before I noticed the brooch affixed to a black ribbon around her throat, its silver untarnished, scintillant.

"Why, your smile is positively mysterious, Mr. Rettie. Will you share your secret with me?"

Before I might answer, the cage reared up from the depths behind her. I assisted her onto the lowermost platform of the triple-decker, which rocked beneath the shuffling of those who followed us aboard. I was on the verge of murmuring a compliment in her ear when I glimpsed Hamilcar elbowing his way toward us.

Mr. Cropley, who had been supervising the loading of passengers, said with reluctance to the heir apparent of the Madonna Consolidated, "Sorry, Mr. Cavanaugh, but I canna allow it. It's the rule—no more than six on a deck."

"What does it matter how many are on each platform, as long as the total on the cage doesn't exceed eighteen?"

"It's the *rule*," the superintendent repeated pathetically.

Hamilcar was eyeing me with abject contempt when I piped up, "Then allow me to give Mr. Cavanaugh my place."

Hamilcar said, "I won't hear of it, old sport," in the same instant Eleanor Louise restrained me with a firm yank on my upper arm—which I hoped her fiancé hadn't noticed. It wasn't lost on me that *old sport* was a Comstock euphemism for pimp, but there was no use in aggravating an already tense moment.

"See you all below," Hamilcar now said cheerfully.

She ignored the kiss he blew her.

"Thank you, Mr. Cavanaugh, sir," Mr. Cropley sighed, and the bell dinged as the cage lowered seven feet for the loading of the center platform, a grill onto which Hamilcar now stepped. Briefly he looked down between his toes and locked gazes with me—before a woman latched onto him, a buxom one who had disdained changing into "appropriate attire." I found myself looking up her petticoats. There was nothing to be seen, really: It was like peering into a chrysanthemum, but Eleanor Louise had caught me, and my face grew warm.

"Forgive me, I had no idea—"

"There's no need, Mr. Rettie," she said, tightening her grasp on my arm and making sure I could see her smile in the gloaming by drawing closer to my face.

The cage eased down another seven feet for the final load of six, then the bell clanged three times in rapid succession, and to the shrieks of several female voices, we plummeted into the near darkness of the shaft. Timbers bracing our compartment flitted upward in the momentary illusion that they, and not the cage underfoot, were in motion. Then there was a flaring of light, gone so swiftly I had to consult my memory for what my eyes had frozen in passing: a tableau of miners waiting with lanterns in their hands; and to their backs a long tunnel, lined with candles that twinkled like stars. I felt as if I were descending into a vast termitarium, of which the city on the surface was only the thin glazing.

"The station at the one hundred foot level," Eleanor Louise said knowledgeably. "And here's the one at two hundred feet."

"You know, that's just what this is like—speeding past a railroad station in the night."

"Three hundred feet. Do you have a railroad in Utah, Mr. Rettie?"

"Why, no," I admitted. "I was speaking of my experience in the east. Recently I had some business in Washington."

"I see. Four hundred. Don't tell me you plan to offer your services to the war?"

"Oh no—I'm afraid I can't do that, Miss Beauchamp."

"Why not?"

"Well, I have a condition . . ." I paused, trying to think of something, anything.

"May I ask what?"

"Surely, it's called . . . kleptomania." Then I chuckled, expecting her to join me. When she didn't, I let the matter drop, deciding that I had used an anachronistic term.

Suddenly, just as the cage was promising to slow, I experienced a frightful twinge that originated in my groin and promptly shot up my spine to electrify the hair on my nape. I was more sure than otherwise that the cable was going to snap, and a woman's scream from an upper deck did little to reassure me.

"It's nothing," Eleanor Louise said brightly. "The cable always stretches a bit when the cage stops this far below."

"A bit?" My heart was still jammed in my throat.

"Yes, just like an India rubber string."

"Do you come down here often?"

"As often as uncle permits. And occasionally when he doesn't."

Light was shining up around the edges of the platform beneath me.

"Welcome to the five hundred foot level, Mr. Rettie. Why you poor child—your hand is trembling!"

18

THE STATION AT the five hundred foot level was tended by a red-faced German foreman whose threadbare English was draped over a handful of mining terms. Nevertheless, he stood proudly behind a glass case of mineral specimens and explained everything to no one's satisfaction, for nearly all of the eighteen passengers had Celtic brogues, either Irish, Scottish, Welsh, or Cornish, and suffered his lecture in polite silence.

"Sir, a question—if you will," said a notorious stock speculator, according to Eleanor Louise. His dandyism prevailing, he had retained his buff-colored stovepipe hat and now reached inside the woolen shirt to take a pad and stubby pencil from his vest pocket. "The rumor's all over town, but what can you tell us about the new ore development here in the Madonna Con? Are we standing close to this fabulous stope?"

"*Ach*—ore, *ja!*" the German cried, opening the case and waving what appeared to be a clod of dark earth in our attentive faces. "*Der* ore *ist* black sulpheret of *silber!*"

The stock sharp shook his head, but persisted: "Are you telling us it's black sulpheret, like all the other ore on this bloody hill?"

"*Ja—Virginiastadt* ore!"

"Well," the sharp chuckled helplessly, glancing over his

186

shoulder for moral support—when he found none, I surmised that men of his occupation were not far above pimps on the social ladder—"how much silver or gold or both to the ton, my man?"

"*Ja!* Black sulpheret of *silber!*"

"I know bloody damned well what the stuff is—"

"Please—we have ladies present." Smoothly, Hamilcar Cavanaugh stepped in front of the German and gave us his indelibly ironic smile. "Honored company, fellow Unionists, if you will look behind you . . ."

The table blazed like a centenarian's birthday cake, with the gilt flames of a hundred candles—it had been the first thing to catch my eye upon entering the lumber-lined chamber. "Kindly take one and proceed down the drift toward a most marvelous surprise. Each candle holder was fashioned from Madonna Consolidated ore by a Parisian silversmith. Mr. and Mrs. Beauchamp would be delighted if you keep one as a memento of this occasion."

There was a spate of oohing and aahing. Everyone but Eleanor Louise and I rushed for the table.

Furtively, Cavanaugh and the foreman smirked at each other. In my time, this Teuton could be gainfully employed conducting tours through nuclear power plants—not that I didn't admire this bit of subterfuge. It seemed possible to me that the Beauchamps didn't want to drive up the price of their mine's stock at present, perhaps to give their shills and cronies the chance to do some bargain hunting before a newly discovered ore body was announced to the public. Or maybe the opposite was true and they wanted to encourage this suspicion of a fresh strike, although no new ore had been found. Either way, the Beauchamps would win. With a little manipulation, the silver game could be won whether the mine itself was in bonanza or in *borrasca*; the possibilities for profitable deception made my head swim.

"Eleanor Louise," Hamilcar said to her, although his eyes were fixed on mine. "Your uncle has begged me to greet his guests here at the station. May I rely on Mr. Rettie to entertain you for the next twenty minutes or so?"

"Of course, it'd be my pleasure to escort your—"

"I was asking my fiancée, Mr. Rettie," he said coolly.

She shot him a killing glance, which I thoroughly enjoyed, then spun me around by the arm and led me past the table, where we each scooped up a candle then joined the rest of the party in venturing down a seemingly endless tunnel. Keeping single-file to the boards laid athwart the trestles of the ore-car rails, we walked

in silence, ever deeper into this imperturbable world of stone—
until I said, voice hushed, "I didn't mean to be a source of friction
between you and your future husband, Miss Beauchamp."

"You did nothing wrong, Mr. Rettie. And Hamilcar takes
undue liberty when he calls me his fiancée. I have other suitors as
well." She abruptly halted and faced me, her eyes all the more
beautiful for being candlelit. "Are you married?"

I hesitated, wondering if any of the stories I had told in Aurora
had caught up with me. I was ready to deny any attachments
when, call it adulterer's intuition, I sensed that her question was
not an accusation: She preferred my being married. "Yes," I said
with a gallant sadness, "I am lawfully wedded."

"In plurality, Mr. Rettie?"

That nearly took me for a tumble, but I confessed Mormon
polygamy with a slight nod.

"How enchanting!" she whispered. "But I would think it
impossible for you to keep each of your wives . . ." She bit her
lower lip. ". . . secure in your affections."

"It's difficult—but never impossible."

"Oh?"

"Sensitivity toward a woman is an art. It requires patience, so
most men never master it. They would rather face grapeshot than
exercise a bit of patience."

"How nicely put." She ran her tongue along her lower lip,
leaving it to glisten. "Come, we don't want to miss anything."

A hundred or so feet later she stumbled at a joint between two
of the planks, and my hands caught her at the midriff to steady her.
Under the bulky shirt and pantaloons, her waist was tiny. Eleanor
Louise had apparently discarded her corset, which even a woman
as slender as Musetta habitually wore, for I could feel her
lowermost ribs as she turned back to thank me with a smile. On a
hunch I let my hands creep up several inches. She continued to
smile before gently breaking free of me. "I need some champagne, Mr. Rettie," she said huskily.

"Please call me Howard."

"Isn't your first name Belmont?"

"Yes, but I prefer my middle name."

"So do I. But would you mind still calling me Miss Beauchamp? You have such a lovely way with my name. It sounds so
properly British when you say it—*Beechum*."

The tunnel emptied into a capacious gallery, and nothing could
have prepared me for what happened next: From a niche in the

rock wall a small orchestra struck up a waltz—"Come, Dearest, the Daylight Is Gone", the maestro announced. Laughing at my astonishment, Eleanor Louise led me by the hand onto a raised wooden platform that had been covered with canvas and bordered with candles, to which we now added ours. The other guests stepped up to but did not venture out onto this improvised dance floor, and I realized that the Beauchamp debutante was expected to open the festivities with the partner of her choice. I did quite well with the simple waltz; we wheeled around the amber-lit grotto, everything but her face spinning into a warm blur. But my expertise—derived from Catholic Youth Organization sock hops—was not up to the quadrille that followed, and she spared me further embarrassment by suggesting that we find the champagne.

Even after only a few minutes of dancing, our faces were glazed with perspiration. We were experiencing an inkling of the heat that would later torment—and sometimes kill—Comstock miners as they drilled and blasted ever closer to the earth's molten heart. It was perhaps eighty degrees Fahrenheit in that chamber, and the press of reeling bodies was not helping. Fortunately, three ore cars were brimming with crushed ice, two contained magnums of Mumm's, and the third nested a punch bowl with white camellias floating in it like drowned angels. Camellias all the way from Mexico, Eleanor Louise confided in me. There was a welcome coolness near the ice, and we lingered there, even though a well-dressed but red-eyed fellow sidled up to us and insisted on flapping about exorbitant freight rates and crooked assayers, and eventually, the fighting in the east. "Well, my hale and hardy friend," he drawled, scratching his chin in what he probably imagined to be a gesture of great pensiveness, "when are you off to save the Republic?"

"Oh, Howard can't join up," Eleanor Louise said loudly enough for several people to turn their heads. "He's got kleptomania!"

There followed a ghastly silence.

My face burning, I met the eyes of an elderly matron, whose withered lips finally broke into a sympathetic smile.

The man patted me on the shoulder. "I'm sorry to hear that. I hope it don't put you six under no time soon."

"I've been fortunate," I said bravely. "So far, it seems only to affect my hands."

One of which the man now seized. "Well, damned fond to meet you just the same. I'm Sandy Bowers."

I smiled in surprise. "Belmont H. Rettie—but please just call me Howard."

"You bet, *Howie*."

This gave me a start: Momentarily I felt as if I had been stripped of my incognito and he knew as much about me as I had read about him. But Lemuel Sandford Bowers continued to grin stupidly at me without suddenly announcing to the social that I was an interloper from the twentieth century, so my paranoia passed.

He and his Sottish-born wife, Eilley, were the Comstock's first millionaires, although he had been nothing but a mule skinner and part-time placer miner, and she had been running a boarding-house—when Fortuna intervened in their behalf. Sandy owned ten linear feet of the Comstock vein, and Eilley had accepted the adjoining ten feet in lieu of a cash settlement on a boarder's delinquent bill. They consolidated their claims by marriage, and the ·Bowerses' mine went on to produce a hundred thousand dollars a month for half a decade. Two or three years from now, after being snubbed by one European royal court after another, Sandy and Eilley would sail home and construct a granite mansion in a grassy valley west of Virginia City, appoint it with gold and silver doorknobs, accrue an immense library with volumes neither of them could understand, get drunk and dance with Paiutes on the front lawn—in short, they'd do their part to put glitzy American patina on the term *nouveau riche*.

"Well, as long as you ain't going to get shot in the near future . . ." Sandy laid an arm across my shoulders and hugged me with embarrassingly facile affection. ". . . you got to have Eilley do a *peep* for you tonight."

"A what?"

"A look in her crystal."

"Yes, well—after a few more dances," I said none too eagerly. By all accounts Eilley was an intimidating if not bizarre woman. Recruited by a Mormon missionary beating the Scottish heath for converts, she had been dispatched to Nauvoo, Illinois—where she survived the persecution in which my distant relative through Ina Coolbrith, Joseph Smith, had lost his life. Eilley then joined the exodus westward, but divorced her first husband, a bishop, in newly founded Salt Lake City when she discovered that two of his young nieces were in fact his wives. Her second Mormon spouse took her even farther west—to Carson County in western Utah, the first white settlement in what later would become the Territory of Nevada. But in 1857, anticipating hostilities with the U.S. Army expedition sent by President Buchanan to assert federal authority over the Saints, Brigham Young recalled his colonists from the distant corners of his Empire of Deseret. Weary of Mormonism and her unimaginative husband, Eilley remained behind in Washoe, taking boarders, and for a little extra cash, reading their fortunes.

I really didn't want anyone to take a *peep* at my future, although I was confident that Mrs. Bowers could not penetrate my cover story with her powers, but Eleanor was tugging at my arm with both hands. "Oh, please, Howard—let's have her do it. We'll never get another chance."

"Why not?"

"Well, this *is* a special occasion."

From this I deduced that renegade Mormons—like Mrs. Bowers and Belmont Rettie—were not welcome at the more formal entertainments convened by the Beauchamps. But I caved in when Eleanor Louise began massaging the back of my hand with her small, white thumbs, which oddly enough were quite cold, although her face was rosy from the heat. "Very well, Miss Beauchamp, let's look up Mrs. Bowers. It's been a pleasure, Sandy—"

But Mr. Bowers couldn't hear me over his own loud gulping. He had dug a magnum out of the ice and was drinking straight from the jade-green bottle.

Eleanor Louise pulled me by the shirt-sleeve through the ever thickening crowd, almost past a glum-looking Mr. Cropley, who stayed us for a moment. "Are you enjoying yourself, Mr. Rettie?" he asked, implying with the same question that he was having a dreadful time—what with all this confusion threatening the orderly operation of his precious Madonna Consolidated.

"I'm having a better time than I could've ever imagined, sir."

"We're off to a peep by Mrs. Bowers," she said evenly.

"I see—a go at the Washoe Seeress. I dunna believe in such truck myself." Then, after glaring at Eleanor for a long moment that failed to perturb her, he strolled away with hands clasped behind him, repeating as if we had not heard the first time, "I dunna hold with such truck."

I asked her as we hastened on toward a dimly-lit side tunnel: "What's wrong with him?"

"Why, nothing. Mr. Cropley is simply being himself. I mean, he's a most excellent superintendent, and I really don't know how uncle could do without him. But he's a horrid nuisance sometimes."

Perhaps it was only my imagination (although the walls were clearly tapering in on us), but the heat seemed worse than ever, and I was tempted to strip off the woollen shirt and make do with just the top of my linen long underwear, as some men had already done. By the glow of miner's candles, stuck by their spiked iron holders into cracks in the stone above our heads, I could see that a butterfly-shaped pattern of moisture was slowly spreading across the back of her shirt. But this didn't seem to discompose her in the least; on the contrary, she appeared to be invigorated by the increasingly torrid atmosphere—and pushed on with a look of relish.

"Miss Beauchamp, where—"

Holding a finger to her lips, she stopped before a black velvet curtain. Listening for voices behind it, hearing none, she asked softly, "Mrs. Bowers?"

"Aye, lassie . . ." It was a voice from beyond the pale of human misery, although its unearthliness was mitigated by a cranky Scots burr.

"May we enter?"

"Only if you are willing to abandon hope—and embrace the truth, which is no respecter of mortals."

"Oh, I am, Mrs. Bowers."

"Then come in, child."

The space beyond the curtain was cramped, but it vaulted up into a more spacious rotunda glittering with candles. I had to suppress a smile as my gaze lowered from this semblance of the starlit heavens to a tiny woman perched on a thronelike wooden chair that was richly carved with what appeared to be retching demons. Before her on a small table was a crystal ball, brightly flecked with candlelight—as were her black eyes, which were a bit too inquisitive for comfort.

"Good evening, Miss Beauchamp. . . ." Mrs. Bowers's voice was brittle with resentment. I had no idea why. Was it because Eleanor Louise was so beautiful, and she so plain? Whatever the reason, there obviously was no love lost between the Beauchamps and the Bowers. The stout woman then regarded me—but without expression. "Be seated, both of you."

"How nice to see you, Mrs. Bowers," Eleanor said, seemingly

unconcerned that the seeress didn't care for her. "How have you been?"

"I do yet *dree* in mourning, Miss Beauchamp. But so many people asked me to bring my peepstone tonight. There are so many in need of my gifts. I cannot refuse them, even in my grief."

"Yes, I was terribly sorry to hear of the passing of your baby son."

"There will be others," Mrs. Bowers said quietly, but the flash of pain in her eyes said otherwise.

"Oh, forgive me—how rude! Allow me to introduce Mr. Belmont Howard Rettie, a friend of Mrs. Jessie Fremont's." Then she gushed: "Howard's a Mormon—like you used to be, Mrs. Bowers!"

The woman's eyes hardened. Then, for an instant, they seemed hunted, before shining defiantly again. "I see. Do I know you, Mr. Rettie?"

"No, I believe not. But it's an honor to finally meet someone I've heard so much about."

"From whom, sir?"

"Why, everyone of substance here in Washoe."

She knew at once this was a specious lie, but she let it pass with a nod. "In whose behalf am I to look into my peepstone?"

"Oh, for Howard's—I'm dying to see what will become of him!"

"Yes," Mrs. Bowers murmured, lowering her gaze into the shimmering translucence of the crystal, "let us see what becomes of Mr. Rettie."

Eleanor Louise squeezed my hand under the table.

Mrs. Bowers studied the canteloupe-sized ball for longer than what I thought necessary to convice us that she had lapsed into a proper mystical concentration. But eventually she sighed, then laid heavy on her vowels as she half moaned: "I see someone afar . . . aye, much afar . . ." Suddenly she winced so acutely, I decided to recommend an appendectomy if she did it again. Luckily, it passed. "Across the years . . . across the burning distance . . . he pulls the puppet's strings . . . aye, he controls all . . . he who has shaped an unholy science from his own arrogance—"

I laughed softly with surprise; but she cut me short with a glower. Had she honestly glimpsed Rodrigo's hand in this? I was nearly persuaded that she was on the verge of revealing my Grand

Tour when she abolished such an absurd expectation with: "I can see into the black heart of this King of the Sea Gulls . . . he who keeps many women as in a brothel—but dares to call them wives! He who claims to free dead souls from purgatory by calling nubile harlots to the dungeon of his bed!"

"Oh dear!" Eleanor Louise flattened her hand against her upper breast.

"And now he reaches out across the years and distance to punish those who have prospered in the Gentile Republic of Ophir! How he hates all who have prospered despite him!"

In short, Mrs. Bowers had it in mind that I had been sent to Nevada by Brigham Young to castigate her. Perhaps she even believed that I was a Danite—an alledged Mormon hit man tasked with either bringing an apostate back into the fold, or failing that, excommunicating him in the most final sense of the word. How I wished Eleanor Louise had kept her mouth shut; mending a cover story was nothing but hard work, and all my purposes tonight were inclined toward pleasure. I exhaled loudly. "Mrs. Bowers, if I were on temple business, would I visit you with a lovely young woman on my arm? Would I come merry with champagne?"

Eyes no less suspicious, she reached down for a bottle of Scots whiskey and set it on the table with an angry thunk. The liquor was half gone—she had been working on it between peeps, I surmised. "Drink, Mr. Rettie."

I gulped down three hefty swallows, then offered her back a snort, which she took, seeming none the more convinced that I wasn't going to strangle or shoot her at any moment. Undoubtedly she knew that many respectable Saints enjoyed a home brew called *valley tan* on the sly. Wiping her mouth—and smearing her rouge with the back of her plump hand—she smirked at me. "Will you curse the memory of that Prophet of Adultery, that junkman of lost Bibles?"

"You speak of Joseph Smith, I presume?"

"Aye!"

"Well, Mrs. Bowers, firstly, the prophet is a distant relative of mine," I told the truth—for the first time in days, I realized. "And I will not speak unkindly of my kin, living or martyred. But more importantly, I'm here in Washoe on holiday—not on a vendetta against the Church."

"What's that?"

"Madam?"

"That Spanisho word you use."

"Oh—it's Italian for revenge."

She eased back on her throne, but still kept watch on me as if I were a coiled snake. "Aye . . . *revenge*, Mr. Rettie. God keep it pure."

But slowly—in the unfisting of her hand, the widening of her eyes—I could see my words taking effect, and I congratulated myself for having made the perfect rebuttal to her accusations. Had I recanted my Mormonism, she would have felt certain in a blinking that I was indeed Brigham Young's agent come to the Lost Territories with a dispensation excusing any un-Saintly behavior I might find expedient to my mission. Now she didn't know what to think—and both of us could live with that as long as the evening lasted. We sealed the truce with wary smiles.

"Oh, please, Mrs. Bowers," Eleanor Louise said. "I can vouch for Mr. Rettie's intentions."

"I'm sure you can, lassie," she snapped, then leaned into her crystal ball again.

The young woman's reaction—or complete lack of it—to these barbs, confused me. Certainly she was intelligent enough to catch the drift of these insinuations.

All at once it soughed out of Mrs. Bowers: *"No!"*

I must have startled at her outcry, for she whispered, "Be still, Mr. Rettie—for the love of God, be still."

Eleanor Louise and I traded uneasy glances.

Then, just as unexpectedly, Mrs. Bowers chuckled. "The spirits are cutting didoes with me. The bloody pranksters—aye, that's it." She covered the ball with a black scarf, then reached down for her whiskey bottle. "Enough."

"Please," Eleanor Louise begged, "tell us what you saw."

"An impossible thing."

"What thing?" Eleanor Louise brushed off my hand when I attempted to make her come to her feet: I was more than ready to go. "If it's impossible, what harm can there be in telling us?"

Swishing Scotch from the inside of one cheek to the other as she considered Eleanor's argument, Mrs. Bowers finally shrugged and went through the melodramatic motions of washing her hands. "So be it . . ." Then her eyelids attenuated to slits. "In many many years Mr. Rettie shall die—"

"Why, that's splendid! Howard shall enjoy a long life. What's so impossible—"

"But then, in fewer years than what he first lived, he shall become a naked babe again."

Eleanor Louise seized my hand. "Oh, Howard, you're going to be reincarnated! How thrilling!"

"No, lassie," the woman said. "To be reincarnated one passes from one life into another. Mr. Rettie shall take up the same *body* when he is born again."

We were all lapsing into so deep a silence, I rose to my feet on a meaningless laugh: "Well, how discouraging—I was hoping for a different tune on the flip side."

Eleanor Louise's smile was confused. "Whatever do you mean, Howard?"

Instantly I realized my gaffe—but knew better than to try to explain. "Mrs. Bowers," I said, "it's been interesting."

The Washoe Seeress nodded serenely. "Indeed it has, Mr. Rettie. Do give my regards to President Young. And tell him I hope the maggots will soon have a taste of him."

When Eleanor Louise began leading me down the darkened portion of the tunnel, I halted and asked, "Isn't the party back the other way?"

"Quite," she said, irritably almost.

Sheltering my candle with my hand to keep it from guttering out, I fell in behind her. "Are you sure this is safe?"

"What do you mean?"

"The ceiling to this tunnel looks rather . . . cracked."

"It's not a tunnel, Howard—that sounds so awfully *green*, you know." She skirted a boulder in our path; overhead I could see the large pock from which it had dislodged. "We are in what is properly called a drift," she went on, unconcerned by a pile of stone rubble which sometime recent had crumbled off the walls and now forced us to scrabble for some yards bent low. "A drift follows the course of the vein."

"You mean we're actually inside the Comstock Lode?"

"Yes."

"Then how come this stuff doesn't look like silver?"

"Oh, Howard," she sighed. "Nothing looks like what it really is. Are you honestly this innocent?"

"I suppose." This conversation would have been a lot more fun had it not been taking place in tenth of a mile underground. Her heart-shaped bottom was only inches from my face, but I could think of nothing but cave-ins and slow suffocation. "Jesus!"

From what seemed directly above us came at least ten stunning reports, one explosion on the heels of another. I felt more than heard them as they rocked the stone beneath my feet. While they died away in reverberation, she giggled at me. "Oh, come now, Howard. . . ."

Without realizing it, I had clasped my arms around my knees.

"It's nothing." She relit my candle with hers. "Just some blasting next door at the Ophir Mine."

"How *close* next door?" There was a humiliating quaver in my voice.

Like my own, her protective clothes were now sweat-soaked. They clung to her, disclosing the voluptuousness of her figure for the first time. There was a deep flush in the skin of her throat, and her perspiration lay on the brooch like a dew. I saw that her nostrils were dilated—although she was breathing through her mouth.

"I didn't like the way Mrs. Bowers treated you," I said on a rush of desire that left me light-headed.

"What, that poor washwoman?" She laughed, and it flowed out of her with such cavalier ease, I realized why she hadn't taken offense earlier: A queen isn't insulted by what a chambermaid says of her; she can only be wounded by the words of another queen. This was my first glimpse into the social strata that was slowly and surely calcifying; heretofore, the frontier classes had appeared to mingle without much ado, but the seeds of the Cavanaugh oligarchy I knew all too intimately were already germinating in the disdainful eyes of this beautiful young woman. In time, myth would triumph over truth, and the Beauchamps-Cavanaughs would fancy themselves the offspring of New England patriarchs, or European royalty, or perhaps even the Sun God—it really didn't matter as long as their tracks meandering back to serfdom were obliterated. American was less the land of the future than the one in which a humble family might reinvent its past.

Eleanor Louise traced my lips with a cool fingertip. "I would like you to do what you did before."

"Miss Beauchamp?"

She used her free hand to draw mine up to her breast. I took it from there, and her eyes became heavy-lidded. Whenever I wasn't covering her mouth with mine, her breath came out in exquisite little gasps that soon got me panting in the same rhythm. "You're so lovely . . ." I repeated again and again while our coupled shadow danced around us on the walls.

But my pleasure was not absolute: I had been thrown off balance by how easy this was going to be. Musetta's accessibility I could understand: For all her sensibilities, she was still a prostitute. But here stood the quintessence of Victorian woman-hood, that ethereal creature incapable of base desires, groaning as she kneaded one of my buttocks with her hand. The mild form of vengeance I had anticipated enjoying at my former wife's and father-in-law's expense was dissolving under Eleanor Louise's ardor, which was far more domineering than my own.

"What's that?" I asked, drawing my face back a few inches from hers.

"What's what?"

"That smell. Like scorched wool. Its—oh, Jesus!" It had come to me on a stab of pain that my elbow was on fire.

"Howard, what is it?" she asked a bit too placidly.

"You burned me with your candle!"

"Oh! I'm so very sorry." She then insisted on kissing my elbow through the hole in the woollen shirt, which did mollify me somewhat—although I was left with the nagging suspicion that it had not been an accident. "Come, Howard . . . let's hurry. We don't want to be absent too long, do we now?"

And that was enough to douse my fears as we continued deeper into the darkness. She ignored several tunnels that branched off the drift—*crosscuts* into the ore body, she explained officiously, adding: "Really, Howard, if you expect to be treated with respect on the Comstock, you simply must learn more about mining." It required no great powers of deduction to realize that she had sashayed down these drifts many times before. "Now here we find an incline. . . ."

I peered into the dank opening: It sloped away at a dizzying angle. "You intend to go down *this*?"

"Of course—so do you. It's awfully fun. Do you have any phosphorous matches on your person?"

"Yes, I believe so." I was reaching inside my woollen shirt for the matchsticks I usually carried in my watch pocket for lighting cigars—when, in a single, swift motion, Eleanor Louise lined the soles of her shoes up on the descending pair of mine rails, braced herself in a crouch, extended her arms to the sides for balance, and then skidded down the incline. Her candle flickered out, and through the pitchy darkness her squeal of delight echoed up to me before dying away to a frightening quiet.

"Miss Beauchamp . . . are you all right?"

Silence.

"Eleanor Louise?"

Nothing.

"Oh, shit."

But then from below came a throaty laugh. "Please stop your cursing—and come down, Howard."

"These works looked neglected to me."

"Yes, splendidly neglected . . . hurry."

A rustling sound made me hold my breath: "What's that?" I visualized the bottom of the incline to be crawling with rodents or its ceiling to be paved with bats now unfurling their hairy little wings. "Miss Beauchamp, what's going on down there?"

"It's too hot for all these clothes."

As each man has his breaking point, each has his secret fountainhead of courage that, miraculously, gives him daring in spite of his better judgment. I found mine in the visualization of Eleanor Louis Beauchamp awaiting me below, stark naked. Straddling the smooth iron rails with my brogans, I loosed the last of my cowardliness in a great bellow and hurtled down into oblivion. I kept expecting an end to materialize; and when it didn't, I turned my toes inward, trying to snowplow to a stop as I would with snow skis. "What the—" But then I was pitched face first into a pile of dust as fine as talcum powder. "Miss Beauchamp?" I choked.

Her voice came from perhaps fifty feet forward of where I lay: "Do you still have your candle?"

"Yes, I think so."

"Then light it." She giggled.

I couldn't do so fast enough, but by the time the passageway was throbbing with pale yellow light, Eleanor Louise had gone on ahead of me, a retreating phantom in white and flesh tones at the farthest reach of the flame. Holding her shirt and pantaloons in her right hand, she was wearing only a chemisette kind of blouse and drawers; her arms and legs were bare.

"Hey, how are we going to get back up?!"

"There's a ladder!"—a distant echo.

"Why didn't we come down on it?!"

"What fun in that, Howard. . . ?" Her voice trailed off, and I was left alone to contemplate the badly buckled drift, whose rotting wooden supports were overgrown with slimy curtains of what I could only imagine to be ectoplasm, although the vile stuff proved spongy in my fingers, suggesting that is was some form of fungus perfectly adapted to this moist night everlasting. Even with no knowledge of mining, I could immediately grasp how the ponderous weight of the lode above was pressing down on these tunnels in which the effort was no longer being made by the company to shore up the ceiling against an inexorable superincumbency. Timbers a foot square had been mashed down to half their former lengths and were so fuzzily splintered they resembled porcupines rearing up from the ground on twisted haunches. It was a self-closing world that might well slam shut on Eleanor Louise and me in the most blatant case of coitus interruptus on record. Still, I tore after her, for only one thing has the power over fear, and this was it.

I had to duck my head, then double over as the drift pinched ever smaller. The crosscuts gave off a disturbing exhalation of decay, and the rock walls became too warm to touch for more than a few seconds. *Well, Brother Tom always insisted I'd wind up in a place like this.*

"Eleanor Louise!" I shouted—and then jumped straight up in the air when she answered from only a few feet behind me.

"Oh, no—my last name, the British way."

"Very well, Miss Beauchamp." I found her lips already parted; and whatever her admiration for the British, she had obviously learned a thing or two from the French.

"Howard?"

"Hmm?"

"You don't think me *unseemly,* do you?"

"My God, what a word. Whoever told you that?"

For the first time her eyes were soft with remorse, and despite a sudden panic that she might be entertaining second thoughts, I felt sorry for her. "Do you, Howard?"

"Of course not. It's just that you're so . . ."

"Yes?"

"Well, extraordinarily alive . . . so *modern.*"

She laughed happily, but then snatched my candle and disengaged herself from me before I could close my arms around her. She darted down a crosscut. I would have immediately followed had not the boys *next door* at the Ophir let loose at that instant with another string of explosions, freezing me in my tracks, leaving me a trembling mess of Chicken Little expecting the sky to fall. This allowed Eleanor to get far enough ahead with the candle for the unnerving blackness to ooze down around me. I was actually muttering through the rosary, hands wildly grabbling the fetid air before me—when a faint glow bent around a curve in the tortuous corridor.

"It's time to stop running, Miss Beauchamp."

"Who's running, Mr. Rettie?" She had formed a nest from pieces of canvas I had seen used elsewhere in the mine to splice together ventilation pipes, and she now looked up at me, grinning. "Treat me no different than all your others."

Kneeling beside her, I had just taken ahold of her blouse when she moistened her fingertips with her tongue and extinguished the candle. The loveliest sight imaginable faded, but when I groaned in disappointment, she said, "I love the darkness."

I lifted the blouse over her head, then embraced her. While kissing her throat, my cheek brushed against the brooch—making me smile. "I want you, Miss Beauchamp."

"And you shall have me," she whispered.

At that moment, bewilderingly, a match sputtered to life behind me. It seemed to flare like the sun after such an intense blackness, and I might have wheeled angrily to see what fool had intruded on us—had not I heard what sounded very much like a Colt revolver being thumb-cocked.

19

"IT IS 8:33, Miss Beauchamp." Mr. Cropley closed his watch with a resounding click identical to the one that had just plunged my heart into fibrillation. He began to lift his freshly lit candle lantern to have a better look at us where we lay—but then thought better of it. "You canna be gone any longer without young Mr. Cavanaugh being the wiser." The prim little Cornishman looked humiliated by the stodgy duties this moment required of him, and his gaze took refuge in the dusty toes of his boots. "I heard voices. I was much afeared it was some stock sharps. Nosing their way through *La Derrotada*."

"The what, sir?" I mumbled—just to say anything: his wounded pauses were driving me mad.

"The abandoned works, Mr. Rettie." He brightened at the chance to get back on familiar turf. "The lode dips eastward from where we stand. The vein pinches out here—so the Spanishos, who really started this business of silver mining, call it *La Derrotada*, the place of abandonment. Miss Beauchamp has been warned before. It's far too dangerous for . . ." Briefly his eyes met hers, which remained steadfastly unapologetic. ". . . for exploration."

"Well, now," Eleanor huffed, her movements almost dilatory

as she put her shirt and pantaloons back on, "I suppose I must suffer the inconvenience of making an appointment with you in Salt Lake, *Doctor* Rettie."

The fabrication was so patently absurd I could only gape at her.

Mr. Cropley then revealed an instinct for survival even keener than mine. "Are you a physician, sir?"

"Oh, yes . . . a specialist in women's complaints."

"I dunna recall you introducing yourself as a physican, Dr. Rettie."

"Well, I'm on holiday—other than in Miss Beauchamp's case . . . which she wrote me about this spring."

"Then I must beg your pardon," he said tonelessly. "Nevertheless, *La Derrotada* is no place to tarry. Mother Earth shall soon reclaim what is hers, and it would be any man's misfortune to be here when that happens. Kindly follow me now."

On that long, wordless march back to the social, I nearly beat myself black and blue with the felt cap—but still, as Eleanor Louise and I traipsed behind Mr. Cropley into the swell of music and conversation, I looked like I had been doing precisely what I had been doing: rolling around in a midden of dusty canvas with my hostess, who now, without so much as fare-thee-well, sought out her long-faced fiancé and cajoled him onto the dance floor. So much for revenge on the Beauchamp-Cavanaughs.

Three fat little biddies corraled me before I could make my way to the ore cars of iced champagne, my last stop before fleeing from this disaster of an encounter.

"Oh, young man!" one of them squealed, fanning herself with a sheaf of documents. "Have you received your certificate yet?!"

"No, I don't believe so." then, when I saw them eyeing my filthy clothes, I said lamely, "I lost my bearings in one of the drifts and fell down. Twice." I felt certain they were fully aware that I had come within the striking of a match of squiring Miss Beauchamp. My embarrassment made me an easy mark, and not until the scroll of parchment was rustling in my hands did I realize what I had done in a state of numbness:

This Certifies that

Mr. Belmont Howard Rettie

is a Member of the Nevada Branch

of the United States Sanitary Commission

and has contributed
100 Dollars in Gold Coin
for the Benefit of the Sick and Wounded
of the American Army and Navy in the
War for the Suppression
of the Great Revolt
commencing in 1861.

Rodrigo would have had a fit had he known: He had warned me on pain of death to stay within my budget. If I ran out of money, how could I earn more? I most assuredly didn't have the guts to become a highwayman.

I glanced at Eleanor Louise. She was merrily chatting to a covey of dandies—and resolutely ignoring me. Her eyes darted right past me several times without pausing to acknowledge my existence. I was glowing with hatred for her and her future husband, who was no sooner called to mind when he materialized at my side, standing very straight, his hands fisted.

"Mr. Rettie. . . ?"

I could feel the blood leave my face. "The social seems quite a success—"

"I demand satisfaction," Hamilcar said, so only I could hear.

"Satisfaction, sir?" I struggled to sound indignant, but my voice was tinny with fear.

"Yes. Will you take the air with me?"

Trying to turn my greater height to advantage, I stood taller and gestured for him to lead on toward the station. "I would consider it a privilege, Mr. Cavanaugh."

"Thank you, Mr. Rettie."

He stormed ahead, for which I was thankful—I was busy with a gagging reflex, which I fought down with intense concentration. My first thought was to seek Eleanor Louise's help to flee through one of the connective tunnels to the neighboring Ophir Mine. But I suspected that now, after our mise-en-scène before Mr. Cropley in the lower depths of the Madonna Consolidated, she wouldn't deign to speak to me—at least until the next time we were alone. My Navy Colt was in my coat pocket, and my derringer snugged in the toe of one of my boots—all of which were in the dressing room above. I had not anticipated the need for firearms in socializing with the Comstock's gentility. But these accessories I would gladly abandon along with my suit of clothes if presented with an opportunity for flight. Most of my money was in the safe at the International Hotel, thank God. So I lit upon a desperate plan: to bowl over Hamilcar as soon as we reached the top—and then sprint into the night. I was not about to give anybody other than Eleanor Louise *satisfaction*.

As the attorney and I stepped onto the lowermost cage platform, the German handed him a candle lantern. Then, receiving a terse nod from his superior, the foreman tugged on a bell rope three times and the triple-decker began ascending with only Hamilcar and me aboard. We had not gone far when it slowed, then stopped completely, rocking woozily on its cable.

"What is it?" I demanded, trying to sound cross at being kept from pistols at twenty paces.

Hamilcar was boldly leaning over the edge of the railingless deck and peering below. This compelled me to do the same: Far down in the depths was a silvery glimmer of water. With a spiteful swig, he polished off the last of his Mumm's and let the glass slip from his fingers. I had almost counted to five by the time there was a soundless splash on the distant surface—around four hundred feet, I estimated.

"That's the sump you see, Mr. Rettie. The waters from all the works collect down there before being pumped out." He was smiling—but I took no comfort from it. "This winter a poor miner tripped at the two hundred foot level. Seven hundred to the bottom—from there, witnesses say his body made a humming noise as it fell past each station. Mr. Cropley had to use grappling hooks to recover the remains. A forearm had been pulled off at the elbow, a foot at the ankle. That foot was found dangling by its tendons on a timber two hundred feet below where the poor fellow lost his balance. Rumor has it that this is the fate Governor James Nye might have suffered tonight—had he attended."

All at once pistols at twenty paces didn't seem so bad. I inched away from the precipice toward the center of the deck.

With a jolt, the cage resumed its climb.

"Mr. Nye is very fond of champagne, I'm told," Hamilcar went on. "So we can imagine that he would have left the five hundred foot level quite late. Just for the sake of speculation, let me suggest that as he took his leave from the dance, he would have been separated from his aides at the station we just left. Forced by a mass of well-wishers to share this very platform with a select group of men—one of whom would have been his murderer." Hamilcar pointed at the bracing that separated our shaft compartment from the adjoining one. The lights of a station flashed across his pallid features as he quietly said, "About now the assassin would have begun watching the cross beams, timing the interval of their passing—so he might seize the perfect moment in which to nudge the governor over the side, through one of these openings and into the next shaft compartment." He sighed deeply. "But Nye caught drift of this plot—only God knows how. Men are indeed feckless, aren't they, Mr. Rettie? So the assassin never got his chance. He had to occupy his evening with more frivolous pursuits."

"You mean this man was at the ball?"

"Except for one indiscreet absence, yes indeed."

When I recoiled, expecting the worst, Hamilcar laughed. "Yes, indeed, *you* would have been uniquely qualified for this task. A stranger who, after the deed, could have melted back into the Mormon nation, from whence he sprang just as mysteriously."

"No—"

"Come, now, old sport, didn't Governor Terry promise you an opportunity to prove your sincerity?"

My head was spinning. "*Governor* Terry? Do you know what you're saying?"

"Exactly. David Terry holds an appointment signed by President Jefferson Davis—effective as soon as this territory is wrested from Union oppression."

"Jesus Christ! *You* are Terry's man in Virginia City!"

"Quite—and proudly so. Although I'd appreciate it if you will not repeat that amazed cry on the surface."

"The Beauchamps . . . Miss Eleanor—"

"Nominal Unionists. But given the right circumstances, they could be persuaded to see the Confederate point of view—like most everyone else in Nevada."

"But *you*—"

"Born in Kentucky. My half brother is already serving with the Army of Virginia."

"This . . . this pretense—"

"What are you suggesting, Mr. Rettie?"

Again seeing pistols and twenty paces in my mind's eye, I said no more.

"It's common knowledge I clerked for David Terry when he served on the California Supreme Court. My affinity for the Chivalrous Cause is presumed by many." The arrogant smile appeared again. "It's also widely presumed that I'm too pudding-headed to have views. Even a *pious* man like yourself must admit that we sad mortals are punished only for being caught. Secret acts that remain secret also remain blameless. So I have every intention of remaining blameless—until the Confederacy triumphs here."

"That might be easier said than done, especially if you keep trying to blow away the territorial governor."

He hoisted an eyebrow. "Blow away?"

I shook my head in frustration. *"Assassinate."*

"Oh, come now, Mr. Rettie—you don't honestly believe that unmannered ploy of yours to meet Eleanor Louise actually did the trick, do you? Even if Mrs. Fremont were acquainted with the Beauchamps, which she's not, she would have given you a proper letter of introduction—not one of her visiting cards to fob off on them like a laundry ticket. I was at the Beauchamp's home when your message arrived. Their butler handed it to me to pass on to Eleanor Louise. *I* wrote the invitation. And what happened later—well, she has a fascination for oddities such as yourself." The light of the hoisting works house was now spilling down around the edges of the cage, catching the coppery glints in his otherwise blond mustaches as he craned his neck and looked up. "What I demand to know is this: What is your interest in the Beauchamps? Are you a fortune hunter, Mr. Rettie? Certainly you can't be interested in yet another wife."

I was spared making a reply—we had arrived at the top. I strode directly for the dressing room, having decided that this new turn of events was not best addressed by knocking Hamilcar Cavanaugh down and then bolting into the darkened streets of the nearby Chinese quarter. Grinning, he took a stool across from me as a boy scurried out of hiding with our coats and boots. Relieved to be in possession of my weapons again, I ventured, "Why are you trusting me with all this information?"

"Oh, don't flatter yourself, Mr. Rettie—if that is indeed your name. I have no reason to trust you in any regard. But I do have the means."

"Means?" I grunted, the boy helping me squeeze into my boots.

"To kill you—or have others kill you. Here in Virginia City. In Aurora. Even in San Francisco." He chuckled, gutturally—and the hair on my neck bristled. Heretofore I had not dreamed that such an apparent affectation could be passed on genetically; but the essence of Cletus Cavanaugh was encoded in that smug laugh. "Well, Mr. Rettie, will you take some refreshment with me?"

We had no sooner stepped out into the cool, mountain night, its air almost sinfully sweet, than Hamilcar stopped short and drew my rattled attention to an unnatural glow that was throbbing over the roofline of the hoisting works. "Come—hurry . . ." For the first time all evening his voice was tinged with excitement, and he broke into a trot across the yard, clambering atop one of the stacks of timbers and then helping me up with a surprisingly strong grip.

Above the lamplit windows of Virginia City, on the otherwise darkened flank of Mount Davidson, a fountain of white heat was shooting up out of a divot in the ground. It was if some ancient specter, perhaps Fortuna herself, had wriggled up out of the Comstock Lode and was dancing in ethereal skirts with the same wavering undulations of the aurora borealis. It all appeared too insubstantial to be fire as I knew it. I looked to Hamilcar.

"Firedamp, old sport," he answered before I could ask. "Carbureted hydrogen gas—at least that's what Mr. Cropley says it is. Comes from decaying wood in the oldest mines. That shaft's beside the site of the first discovery." His face made deathly white by the ethereal stuff, he grinned at me. "I've never witnessed an episode this pronounced." It was plain enough to see in his eyes: He considered this chimera to be some kind of auspicious omen; while I in my confusion and dread, saw it as the funeral pyre of an uncomplicated past that had existed only in my yearning.

Then he touched my arm. The gesture was unsettling for its apparent tenderness. "It really won't be necessary to kill you, will it?"

My mouth too dry to form words, I shook my head no.

"Good." He squeezed my arm again. "Because the stakes at issue are enormous, old sport. It could mean the outcome of the war itself." He leaped down off the pile, and I waved off his offer of a helping hand. "You see, Nevada silver might well decide the economic battle being waged behind the smoke of cannon and muskets. What we rebels do here in the territory is no backwater affair. No, sir. Instead of enriching Washington's coffers, this wealth could be used by the Confederacy to buy munitions and materiel from the English. It might even be used to induce Great Britain to enter the war in our behalf—or, if not that, at the very least to seize the Oregon Territory, which the queen continues to claim as her own. Even Old Father Abraham appreciates the superiority of our military leadership, the elan of our fighting men. I think he'd sue for peace if he faced a logistical disadvantage as well. And I'm absolutely positive that President Davis could come to an accommodation with your Mr. Young— especially if you Saints promise to harry the Union forces here in the West, as you did so capably five years ago. Were you involved in that?"

I shrugged. "A bit."

"Why so glum, old sharp?"

"I prefer not to discuss actions that some still consider worthy of punishment."

"Well said, well said," he chirped, guiding me onto what I recognized to be infamous D Street, two rows of whitewashed cribs. The small porches were jammed with whores in various states of undress, lured outside to enjoy the firedamp display. Through the open door of one cubicle I could see a man in long johns, propped up on an elbow in bed, frowning at the bare-chested woman who was begging him to join her on the narrow veranda.

Hamilcar had turned so affable in the last few minutes, I decided to venture a complete but civil break with him and his fellow secessionists. "Well, I would now hope that my trust-worthiness can be taken for granted—"

"Not quite yet." He halted and smiled faintly, as if he had been anticipating my very words. His hand slithered into the inner pocket of his swallow tail coat, then came out with a tiny apothecary vial, which he laid across my palm. He was no longer smiling. "Tomorrow morning at ten you shall depart for Aurora."

"But my business here isn't concluded."

"Consider it concluded, Mr. Rettie. Be on the ten o'clock Mud Wagon," he said, ignoring the scene unfolding to his back: One blowsy whore had dragged another off her porch by the hair, and the twosome were now groveling in the street, pummeling each other with their fists. "Aboard your coach will be a garrulous old fool. If he does not bore you to death before reaching Wellington station, you are to administer the contents of this vial to him. It will not be terribly difficult—Captain John Nye will drink anything put before him that is not frozen solid."

"Governor Nye's brother?!"

"The selfsame."

"Damn you, Cavanaugh! I won't murder him!"

"Keep your voice down!" he hissed, closing my hand around

the vial as I tried to thrust it back on him. "You will murder no one. Captain Nye will become ill for as long as a fortnight—and then recover. But in that time a message will be sent to the governor that his brother is dying in Aurora. The loving brother that he is, James Nye will at last be induced to leave his citadel of Carson City for Esmeralda, where we southern patriots enjoy something of a parity with the Unionists. There the good governor will join John Brown in abolitionist martyrdom."

"You don't expect me to—"

"No, this momentous a thing calls for military force. But you shall remain handy at all hours—in case your services are required." He took another object from his pocket and gave it to me: a five-pointed copper star at which I stared, wondering if this was the very one that hung in Cletus's parlor, as Hamilcar continued in a low voice, "Should you need to contact us, this will suffice as a safe-conduct. Please do not brandish it among those who mean us ill."

I knew all my arguments would prove useless, but I was desperate: "Won't something this . . . this *outrageous* bring the army from Fort Churchill down on your heads?"

"I should hope so."

"*What*?"

"We look forward to such a persecution. It will inflame the hearts of Democrats and southerners who thus far have been content to sit on the fence. Yes, a heavy Union hand will only swell the ranks of our militia. And once we have sufficient strength, we shall engage the United States Army openly on the field of battle." His eyes darted toward the firedamp as it roiled up into an even more blinding fountain that bleached the city of its colors and made the buildings look as if they'd been fashioned from plaster of paris. He smoothed down his mustaches with a finger. "I would consider it a singular courtesy," he said after this pause, "if you would refrain from disappearing with my fiancée for periods of time that compromise your good judgment and her honor." He raised his hand before I could object. "Please spare me the obvious, Mr. Rettie. I have no illusions about Eleanor Louise, believe me. But I prefer that my peers keep *theirs* about her."

I nodded, gravely. "Very well, Hamilcar."

His forefinger struck me like a fire poker in the neck. "Mr. Cavanaugh. *Always* Mr. Cavanaugh—as long as we are compelled by mutual interest to have any dealings with each other." Then a vicious joy came into his eyes as he surveyed the block-long gauntlet of cribs, raucous with drunks and laughing prostitutes. "Before us lies almost anything a man might desire. But only almost, old sport." He threw his arm around my shoulders. "Nevertheless, I intend to have my satisfaction."

20

CAPTAIN JOHN NYE had an indefatigable cheerfulness that quickly exhausted all who blundered into his society. He spent most of that jouncing Mud Wagon ride blandishing my fellow passengers into revealing the names of all their relatives so he might claim to know one or two—and immediately strike up a one-sided conversation about this alleged acquaintance. "Great Jehoshaphat!" he would cry upon hitting cognominal pay dirt. "I know your Uncle Enoch as well as I know my own brother!" Then a warm flood of recollection would gush out of his mouth, and his beard would wag merrily, or a tear would threaten his eye, as he recounted things that were as true of Trotsky as they might have been of Tutankhamen.

But in Belmont Howard Rettie he met his challenge.

My head was still reeling from the profligate hours spent in the company of Hamilcar Cavanaugh, and even the thinnest conversation tasted like gruel on my tongue.

Never had I known a more listless intoxication than last night's. The revels had ended at dawn, with me secretly wanting to throttle my ex-wife's illustrious ancestor to cut short that comtemptuous laugh—and wondering what he could have required of a prostitute that cost three times the prosaic thing I had done to her sister in dejected silence.

"But surely, Mr. Rettie," Captain John nagged me out of my stupor, "you can't originally be from Utah. Mr. Young's westward migration began but fifteen years ago."

"Correct, sir," I muttered. "I'm not originally from Utah." I avoided his keen eye by pretending to study the inland sea of sagebrush on all sides of us. I was afraid he might glimpse the harm I would soon inflict on him—and indirectly, his brother.

"Then where exactly *are* you from, Mr. Rettie?" he persisted some minutes later.

"State of New York."

"The fair village of Palymra?"

I gave up. "Yes."

"I knew it! Then you must be related to Joseph Smith!"

"Yes."

"Great Jehoshaphat! We barged together years ago on the Erie Canal! Of course, back then he was a Presbyterian. . . ."

And so it continued with only one interruption—the Mud Wagon became mired in a creek and Captain John, overcome by commiseration for the driver and his schedule, pressed the passengers into a gang to push and pull the wheels free. Hours and hours later, under the rose quartz sky of a Nevada dusk, we alighted, ooze-splattered and bench-sore, at Wellington way station for supper.

Due to the delay caused me by Judge Terry on my trip to Virginia City, I had not stepped inside the station. And for that I now thanked him.

A snow-flecked comb was tied by a string to the common washstand and mirror. The fact that our host did not change the basin water after each washing finally proved too much for one fastidious fellow. He protested, which only made the stationmaster's face tremble with indignation: "Why, twenty men's used that today—and you're the first to complain!"

Nudging a large dog off the bench, I took my place across the table from Captain John, who regarded me so warmly whenever I glanced up at him, I finally kept my eyes on my meal and ate without uttering a sound—which wasn't easy, inasmuch as the menu consisted of salt pork adrift in rancid bacon grease and a side lump of something akin to shortcake. It all went down like clay as the apothecary vial grew heavier and heavier in my vest pocket.

A sudden thought made me lower my fork: *What if the dose proved lethal?* Hamilcar had promised me that this tincture of belladonna would do nothing more than make the old man ill; however, wasn't the plant from which this poison was extracted also called *deadly nightshade*?

"Great Jehoshaphat!" Captain John was exclaiming to the stationmaster. "If your name is Jones, I met your father aboard the *Star of Majorca* on my first trip around the Horn in '49!"

I tossed down my handkerchief, which had to double as a napkin, then slipped the vial out of my pocket. I held it under the table, hesitating, trying to assure myself that the result of this act might dovetail perfectly with my own plans.

My scheme to turn Samuel Clemens away from writing, making him a silver baron in the process, hinged on John Nye becoming ill: This was the juncture at which I had planned to step in and tinker with the cogs and wheels of history. But never had I dreamed that *I* would be the agency to land the governor's brother in his sickbed.

That sometime in the coming weeks the old man would become indisposed, regardless of what I did, was confirmed by Twain in *Roughing It*: *I met a Mr. Gardiner, who told me that Capt. John Nye was lying dangerously ill at his place ("Nine-Mile Ranch") and that he and his wife were not able to give him nearly as much care and attention as his case demanded. . . .* When Clemens rushed from Aurora to nurse Captain John at this nearby ranch house, he would inadvertently forfeit the ownership of the mine Calvin Higbie and he had just acquired by a fluke in the mining laws.

I believed these to be facts—but didn't know precisely how or when they would unfold during this summer. By going on holiday to Virginia City—all to toy with a woman who wound up doing all the toying—had I forever altered some dim causality? The consequences of running afoul of David S. Terry and his unexpected minion, Hamilcar Cavanaugh, began mushrooming in my mind. Was it even remotely possible that Hamilcar's suggestion was true—that the diverting of Nevada silver could affect the outcome of the war? Unwittingly, had I knocked Captain John's otherwise mundane illness out of some grand but abstruse synchronization—and now only God knew what would happen? *Oh no*, I bemoaned to myself, using my knife to skid a piece of pork around the tin plate full of grease as I wondered how I could ever explain to Rodrigo why I had "adventitiously" let the Confederacy win the Civil War. Of course, a weakened Union might tempt Mexico to reclaim the Southwest, and I would return to find Rodrigo the *alcalde* of San Francisco. But I then admitted to myself that this kind of thinking was overly optimistic: I might go back only to discover that he had been branded a heretic by some latter-day Inquisition and burned at the stake. Each new possibility I entertained suggested a dozen more I was neglecting. I might well have to poison poor old John Nye just to get the universe back on an even keel.

I was trapped. What was worse, I wasn't entirely sure how it had happened. "Time . . . wherever you land, it's a sheet of goddamned flypaper," I reflected, not realizing that it had been aloud.

"Why's that, Mr. Rettie?" Captain John asked.

"Sir?"

"Why is time like a sheet of flypaper?"

"I don't know."

"Quite." And he turned to continue shaking the limbs of a Mexican teamster's family tree: "You know, amigo, I knew some Gomezes in Sacramento . . ." He had set down his stoneware mug of ale perilously close to mine.

I shifted the vial from hand to hand. In that moment, with a swarm of moths popping dustily against the glass chimney of the hurricane lamp, I was a hairbreadth away from drawing Captain John aside and confessing what I had been charged to do to him by a closet secessionist so some misguided Democrats could lure the territorial governor to a violent death. All at once it made perfect sense to denounce Cavanaugh to the federal authorities—if only to spare my own neck from the gallows should Judge Terry and his irregulars actually succeed in gunning down James Nye. It was my duty as a Republican. And I was growing quite cozy with the idea of doing Hamilcar some first-rate dirt when it hit me.

Although saving the Union was no doubt laudable—and every good Republican should do it every chance he gets—the same sterling act might inaugurate something I had never imagined possible before embarking on this Grand Tour: I could be editing my former wife right out of the twentieth century.

Rodrigo had mentioned something about misadventures of this sort being "absorbed rather than actuated"—whatever that meant; but in this dismal moment as I clenched the vial, I had no doubt that if I informed on Hamilcar Cavanaugh, his great-great-great-grandaughter would no longer exist when Rodrigo picked me up in late October. Even if Hamilcar were fortunate enough to escape the noose, he would certainly be sent to some pestilent prisoner of war camp from which even the hardiest emerged broken in spirit and body; and should he beat the odds and survive, the Beauchamps would never consent to marry off their darling ward to a convicted traitor.

As I mulled over these cheery prospects, struggling to make things easier on myself, I tried to think of my ex-wife as the glacial shrew who had locked me out of Linden Towers. But it was no good. I could only recall her as the remote but beautiful girl who had tilted her head then smiled as she first noticed me crossing a frat-house carpet with my pride cupped in my hands.

There was but one thing for me to do, although my intended victim kept beaming at me as if I were his own son.

Fingers trembling, I pried the cork out of the vial and waited for Captain John's light brown eyes to quit pouring over me like me like honey. Finally he looked away to examine a daguerreotype one of the passengers, a shy young Belgian, handed to him: "*Mon Capitaine*, this was my mother—"

"Great Jehoshaphat!"

And then, although I can offer no reason why—for I had been perfectly willing to poison him at that instant—I poured the tincture of belladonna out onto the earthen floor beneath the table.

I thought no one had heard the trickling noise, but the stationmaster summoned his cowering dog and kicked the poor beast.

Arriving in Aurora shortly after midnight under a moonlit sky sheeted with high clouds, I made straightway for Clemens's and Higbie's cabin on Pine Street. It was darkened, but given the lateness of the hour, I decided that this was no proof the partners were still away on their junket to Mono Lake. I clicked a pebble off the stovepipe. Then another. When no one responded, I kicked the sidewall and ran quickly for the shadows—should either Clemens or Higbie decide to answer me with buckshot. I felt reasonably sure they were yet gone, but couldn't rest easy until I knew for certain. The barkeeps at a half-dozen saloons had not seen either of them for days; and the faro dealer at the Bank

Exchange mentioned that in the interests of collecting a long due loan, he was looking for Clemens himself.

Paying for a bottle of Sezerac brandy (and thus declaring my determination to finish it on the spot), I took a table near the back. An Englishman who claimed to be the San Francisco correspondent to the *London Times* struck up a conversation with me, but so pointedly asked for my assessment of the Esmeralda political situation, I soon suspected that either Terry or Cavanaugh had hired him to check up on me. Excusing myself, I scooped up the bottle and wandered out into the night. I had no desire to return to the Goddess of the Dawn Boardinghouse and swap yarns with Granville until first light, so my restlessness left me at a loss what to do next.

A cold wind was skirling down the ravine.

I hiked up through the sage to a rocky spur and stood above the steam-driven town, which chugged and puffed like some elaborate plaything a child had neglected to turn off before retiring. I found myself trying to pick out Madame Richelieu's blue lamplit window on Bullion Street, imagining the warmth and laughter and melodeon music that might await me within her drawing room. But then I thought of other things awaiting me there, and all at once the brandy seemed solace enough.

I have been confused before in my life, but have always made the best of it, realizing that the brightest of us—like Rodrigo—are as inept as the least of us when it comes to sizing up our own emotions. But there seemed no way out of the pit I was digging for myself tonight; I had never felt more strongly about something— or understood it less. I had anticipated a glorious time in seducing Miss Beauchamp, probably because she was reputed by the modern Cavanaughs to be the most worthy young woman on the Comstock. But that fantasy had collapsed within a half hour of meeting her. And while traipsing around the intestines of the Madonna Consolidated in the sultry wake of Eleanor Louise's appetites, I had found myself thinking about something Musetta had said during our tour of San Francisco Bay.

I believed then that it had been her way of letting me know why Madame Richelieu, a mulatto, was a copperhead, but now I saw much more in her unhappy words aboard the schooner: "In our own eyes we are always more what we want to be, and less than what we are. Everybody but me, I think. I am less than nothing. I expect nothing more. . . ."

To Eleanor Louise life was Saturday night with a purse full of gold. To Musetta it was Sunday morning—with hell to pay for sins that didn't even stack up as sins because they weren't her fault. And her purse, no matter how conscientiously she degraded herself, never got full—that was the real injustice of her occupation, she couldn't even afford the decadent comforts everybody imputed to her. As her looks faded, she had nothing but starvation or the vilest forms of prostitution to look forward to. Yet she persisted. She chose to live, when Mimi's way would have been so much easier. And I should have argued when she said that she was less than nothing. To be able to admire her kind of courage, a man must be truly helpless at least once in his life. I should have gently shaken her by the shoulders and *argued*, for it was now clear to me, despite all my inner denials: I admired Musetta and not Eleanor Louise, who like my ex-wife was alluring only because she was spoiled and unfeeling and ravishingly contemptible. For the first time in my life I admired a woman for her better qualities—and still desired to make love to her. And as if that was not bewildering enough, she was a prostitute who wanted the Confederacy to win the Civil War.

Taking shelter alee a boulder, I pulled my coat collar up around my throat. I drank. I missed Rodrigo and Marguerite, badly. A little while later I finally slept.

Dawn scarcely penetrated the slate-colored canopy of clouds anchored to all four horizons. The wind had not slackened; and when I stood on my tiptoes to stretch the kinks out of my back, it licked through the seams in my clothes like tongues of fire.

I strained to see if Clemens's stovepipe, like the others in town below, was leaking its own blue thread into the gale—but still, the partners had not returned. Behind me on the reddish hillside loomed a canvas sail configured like the baggy lateen on a dhow. This contrivance, I had learned, was rigged to feed fresh air down into a mine shaft. The diggings here in Esmeralda were more primitively worked than those on the Comstock, which were the most modern in the world. But that meant only one thing to me: In humble Aurora, the path to the silver tree had not yet been completely covered up by those who had first stumbled across it, and a clever fellow could still wrest his fortune from these forlorn hills—if he were so inclined. And had the time.

The graveyard shift at the Wide West and a few adjoining mines had just let out, and files of miners were winding down the slopes toward Pine Street. Some branched off toward the Chinese

brothels at the lower end of town. Most ducked inside the saloons.
But a handful made their eager way up to Madame Richelieu's.

I dulled my hangover with sips of brandy, although my stomach
came close to revolting.

An hour later a blond woman made the traipse across Bullion
Street from the drawing room to one of the cribs—on the arm of a
miner. I burrowed deeper into my coat and filled my mouth with
brandy.

The woman had been Musetta, of course.

Before she could emerge some time later, I quit my post on the
spur and hurried downtown to the Bank Exchange Saloon, where I
breakfasted alone—although the Englishman was still there and
kept watch on me from his own table. When I was finished eating,
he invited me to play billiards with him, which I accepted, if only
because I needed a little diversion—ruminating about Musetta was
going to drive me out of my mind.

Things went along pleasantly enough for a few hours, but then
Mr. Wickham, as he called himself, steered our chitchat back to
politics. I waved off any opinion about the secessionists on the
grounds that I was a Mormon, news that appeared to delight him.
That he wanted to know if Brigham Young considered the Oregon
Territory to be part of his Empire of Deseret, convinced me that
my newfound friend was more than a newspaperman, although his
line of questioning also suggested that he had no links to the local
copperheads. No, Mr. Wickham was obviously on crown business
in Nevada. Instead of answering him directly, I said, "Listen,
Wickie, do you speak German?"

"Say what? German? Why no, I don't believe so."

"Well, learn it."

"But why?"

"So you can pass it on to your grandchildren and great-
grandchildren—*if* and when Washington loses this war. Not that it
matters one way or another to me what happens to the English-
speaking *Gentile* world at the hands of the Prussians."

No dummy, he caught my drift at once: "Bismarck?"

"Otto's a pussycat compared to those who will follow in his
bootsteps."

"How do you know this, Mr. Rettie?"—all business now.

"I don't. It's just my considered opinion."

"Ah, well then." He chuckled. "It's your turn to bank for the
lead."

At four o'clock a hard rain mixed with sleet began pelting

Aurora. The barkeep shut the front doors and built a fire in the wood stove. "June!" he grumbled.

Staring through the back window, I watched the big drops twinkle on a silt pond. The wind was shrilling through the crack in a broken pane with the authority of having come that way before. I couldn't recall having ever been in a deeper funk, and I knew damned well only one thing would relieve it.

"Of course, I've read Sir Richard's recent book on your cult," Mr. Wickham said, "but if you don't mind a question or two about your practice of—"

"For Chrissake, Wickie, do you honestly think a sane man would willingly take a dozen wives for his own, when just one woman is enough to fill his head with snakes?!"

"Sorry, old man," he said, as taken aback by my outburst as I was.

"Forgive me—and good afternoon. I must go." I hung up my cue and strode outside, an icy gust tossing pilled snow at my feet like pearls. I was completely baffled by what had just seized me. One moment I had been considering going back to the boarding-house to rest, the next I was filled with a mindless urgency that told me I was only seconds away from being irrevocably too late. Up the glistening, stony surface of Winnemucca Street I tramped, breaking into a run as I rounded onto Bullion Street.

She was stepping out onto the porch at the moment I splashed up to Madame Richelieu's. The young sharp clutching her hand regarded me with a faint smile—as if he thought congratulations were in order for having procured her company.

"Buzz off," I said to him, almost not recognizing the grim voice to be my own.

"I beg your pardon, sir?"

"Let go of her."

"There seems to be some mistake."

"There's no mistake. Let go."

Carefully, he did so. Then with his left hand he wiped a drop of rain off the end of his pug nose. His right hand was hovering outside the fur-lined flap to his coat pocket.

Well, Howie, it occurred to me, almost abstractly, *the son of a bitch is going for his revolver. He's right-handed, you're a southpaw—the fatal instant will be symmetrical.*

Of its own accord, my hand was flowing down toward my Navy Colt when he said, sounding quite wounded, "I don't think you understand, sir. I've made arrangements for the entire night."

"Then it's incumbent upon you to make other arrangements." Whoever this maniac was who had taken possession of me—he sounded utterly fearless. Musetta had backed up against the railing. From the corner of my eye I saw her bite the webbing between her thumb and forefinger to keep from screaming.

"The bloody cheek!" he cried.

"Quite," I said.

In his outraged eyes I could see myself tumbling backwards, an explosion of red covering my upper breast. But then, unexpectedly, the man let his arms hang limply at his sides, and he said with a tongue so dry it softly crackled, "Madame will hear of this!" Yet instead of storming back inside the drawing room, he tore down the steps and disappeared around the corner without looking back.

"Howard, quickly!" Musetta grasped me by the coat sleeve and led me down a narrow alley. She hesitated before plunging across the next street we come to, and I slumped against an outhouse, trying to fortify my legs against the rubbery weakness that had begun to undermine them. I began swallowing with an ominous rhythm—and then felt the blood leave my face.

"Howard, are you well?"

"Of course," I said with a weak smile, fully appreciating how, once again, I had just courted the surest way of getting shot in territorial Nevada: I had insulted a man's honor. Now, if he chose, he could gun me down—with or without advance notice, even in the back, and it would be held to be justifiable homicide. This sharp might not prove to be as reasonable, or craven, as Sam Clemens. Taking several huge breaths that helped me hang on to a day's load of brandy, I said miserably, "No, I'm not well. Nor have I been well."

She clasped my face in her warm hands—God, it felt lovely.

"I've missed you, Musetta."

Her eyes softened, but she wouldn't let us linger there. Instead she checked the street for pedestrians, then pulled me behind her in a dash for a lean-to that had sprouted like a burl off the brick wall of a brewery. We slipped through an unlocked entrance and down a hallway that run the length of the clapboard structure. This passageway failed to open onto a parlor, although a wood stove stood in a shadowy alcove at its far end. Passing up two doors, both securely shut, we stole through a third, and Musetta lit a lamp, for the stormy twilight gave a scant light through the small window.

"Where are—"

She covered my mouth with her hand, then smiled when I kissed her palm. "Whisper only. This is my room. Michelle is sleeping next door."

"What about the . . .?" Lowering my eyes, I didn't finished.

"The cribs are for business. They are too small for living. Someday soon, when things get better for madame, everything will be under one roof again for us—as it was in Carson. Oh!" Mention of the Creole woman reminded her of something: "Please make no noise—it is madame's habit to sleep in *petit* naps. And one never knows when she goes to rest in her room down the hall." Frowning, she lowered the brightness of the flame. "Madame does not trust you."

"Why not?"

"She says you are a scoundrel with a dozen wives pining for you in Utah. Is that so?"

"No, not in the least."

Her eyes became tender again. "I believe you. I think you have no one right now." She cracked the door a few inches and made sure no one was in the hallway. "Stay here."

"Where are you going?"

"To ask madame for the night off."

"Will she let you, just like this?"

"*Certainement*—I will tell her my monthly has come early." Then Musetta was gone.

I drifted to the window: It was snowing, huge flakes shattering against the glass—but I could no longer be surprised by Esmeralda's surrealistic weather. I wrestled out of my wet coat and hung it on a brass hook that had been polished to a gleaming. The room was more than tidy, its appointments genteel and tasteful. Once again she had found a bureau on which to display her fan collection. It made me wince with guilt to see, of all the others, the Japanese one spread open and featured on a wire rack she must have fashioned herself. I shouldn't have, but I riffled through the perfume bottles, scarves, and whalebone combs inside the topmost drawers—and resisted the urge to pocket a scented lace hankie that seemed as much a part of her as her hands or eyes. Tucked in a Swedish Bible I discovered her programme for *La Traviata*.

Howard Hart, I groaned inwardly, *what the hell is wrong with you?!*

Footfalls in approach made me quickly cover up any evidence of my snooping. She came through the door beaming, but her face became grave as soon as she glimpsed mine. "Howard, what is it?"

Only then did I realize what I had been searching for. I sank onto her bed. "How do you make sure not to have a child?"

She started to turn away from me, but then sighed: "I cannot have a baby. I was married once, so I know." Then she watched me closely.

At dawn I had seen her escorting a man to his pleasure, but that sight was nothing compared to the hammer blow of those few words: *I was married once*. I remained silent, staring through the window until the snow shot down through the evening sky in black flecks. Finally I said, "I must sleep."

"Yes . . . you should rest."

Sometime in the night I awakened and knew by her shallow breaths that she wasn't asleep either. "Howard?" she asked in a hush. "Are you ill?"

"No. The stamp mills must've disturbed me"—which was only partly true. I had been dreaming of Rodrigo's Sunnyvale condominium: Rising from the beanbag chair, I padded in my bare feet through an oppressive nocturnal stillness into his bedroom— and there glimpsed Marguerite ensconced in his skinny arms. I smiled upon their reunion, although I had no idea what miracle had made it possible. But then a dream-voice warned me that something was suddenly missing from my own life, perhaps the now familiar cadence of the batteries of stamps. And on that thought I found myself back with Musetta, sighing in her sleeping ear, "I, too, can have no children. We are children enough, you and I." Then I awoke.

"Howard?"

"I'm sorry."

"For what?"

"I'm too tired to make love. It was a rough trip from Virginia City. And last night I had virtually no—"

She shushed me by pressing a finger to my lips. "Often it is more just to be held."

21

SUNLIGHT POURED THROUGH my half-shut eyelids. There was pressure and then slight movement at the foot of the bed. Comfortably nude, I smiled, visualizing Musetta donning her white stockings, then held my arms out to her and whispered, "Come here. . . ."

"I *have* come here, Mr. Rettie. All the way from Virginia City last night in an abominable Mud Wagon."

Hamilcar Cavanaugh sat sneering at me. Musetta was nowhere to be seen.

"How'd you know where to find me?" I said before I could think better of it.

"We're all being watched. The stakes in this affair make it necessary. As I watch you, someone watches me . . ." Clenching a fingertip of his right glove between his front teeth, he yanked his forearm out of the kidskin gauntlet. ". . . so don't be offended. What I know to be true about human nature recommended my departure from the Comstock even before I had seen the outcome of your efforts."

I considered diving for the Navy Colt in my coat on the cane chair, or the derringer in my boot beneath the bed—but catching the ugly light in Hamilcar's eyes, dismissed these notions as delusional thinking of the highest order. Instead I stalled: "Madame Richelieu won't be pleased to find you in here."

"On the contrary, I'm here with her consent. It's your intrusion that displeases her—but you may thank me that you've been permitted to slumber late. Feel free to make use of these accommodations—and the wench, Musetta, until I say otherwise. She *is* the most delectable of madame's crop, don't you agree?" Then he chuckled when the heat rose in my face. "Well now, how did things go at Wellington station?"

"Fine."

"I see. Then perhaps you can tell me why, not twenty minutes ago, I observed Captain John Nye at his breakfast in the Bank Exchange Saloon?"

"Eating?" I asked, incredulously.

"Oh, that's not the half of it. He was feasting—a dozen Mono Lake sea-gull eggs, three rainbow trout, two large venison steaks." His eyebrows became chevrons. "Need I continue?"

I shook my head no. "The old man must have a remarkable constitution."

"Or you have absolutely none at all. Which is it, Mr. Rettie?"

"How dare you insinuate such a thing!"

But it proved an ill-chosen moment in which to bluff, for as I watched, frozen with disbelief, Hamilcar produced a revolver from his waistband and pressed the cold, octagonal muzzle against my bare chest. "A Pettingill .44 caliber taken off a captured Yankee captain—a gift from my brother, Mr. Rettie. It's hammerless. No need for thumb-clocking." And to confirm this he slowly squeezed the trigger, turning the next cartridge in the cyclinder toward its appointment with the firing pin.

"Please—there could be an accident!"

"Oh, it will be no accident. Now, tell me what occurred at the way station!"

"I don't know. I poured the vial in his ale—"

"Tell me what happened!"

Then it came to me that continued denials would only earn me a bullet in the heart. "All right, I'll tell you. Just lower the gun. Please lower the gun."

He did so.

Close to blubbering, I took a deep breath. "I did not think it honorable to poison an unsuspecting man. Now, had you asked me to engage him in a fair contest—gunplay, let us say, I would have—" I stopped because Hamilcar was convulsed with laughter.

Wiping his moist eyes with the back of his hand that still clutched the revolver, he said, "My God, but you can peddle the rot, can't you?" Rising off the bed, he went to the tin basin Musetta had probably filled for me. He dipped the fingers of one hand in the water, then sprinkled his pale face with the drops. "You are as poorly acquainted with honor as I am. It smacks of hypocrisy on both our tongues. So spare me any further mirth." From his coat pocket he took an apothecary vial, one three times bigger than the first. "Do you know what this is?"

"Tincture of belladonna. . . ?"

He ignored my reply. "*This* is your reprieve. Accept it, take it down to the Bank Exchange Saloon, pour it in Captain John's gin punch. Do so cheerfully—and you absent yourself from a summary execution. *Yours*, Mr. Rettie. Do you accept my generous offer?"

"Just tell me, please, why one of your people can't do this?"

"In the coming days the Knights of the Golden Circle must make themselves scarce. In fact, you can help us by passing along the rumor that Governor Terry and the faithful are en route to the Confederacy by way of Old Mexico. No one associates you with the Cause, and for that reason you are invaluable to our plans. No quibbling now, do you accept?"

"You have to understand that I have business of my own to handle in the coming weeks."

He studied me for a moment. "Of what nature?"

"Personal—a mining venture, if you must know."

"I had thought Brigham Young excommunicates his followers who dabble in the mines."

"He does, but—"

"Oh, spare me another of your canards, old sport. I have no objection to your affairs as long as they don't jeopardize our mutual enterprise." He hefted the vial in the air, then caught it smartly in his fist. "For the last time, Mr. Rettie, do you want your reprieve?"

I held out my palm.

"No," Hamilcar Cavanaugh said, leering at me, "you must come and get it."

The first thing I heard after shutting the double doors of the Bank Exchange behind me was Captain John's voice, soaring above the hum of conversation: "Higbie?! Why, Great Jeho-shaphat! I knew a Higbie in the Downieville Digs!"

I didn't want to believe it.

At the center of the overheated saloon the old man was holding court with none other than Sam Clemens and a stolid-looking plowboy I presumed to be Calvin H. Higbie—the last two people I wanted to meet at this moment. Thanks to my copy of *Roughing It*, I knew pretty much what these future millionaires would be doing in the coming days—and didn't want to prematurely alter an iota of this scenario. But too late: Captain John had bolted up from his chair and was flagging his arm for my attention. "Mr. Rettie! My boy! Haloo!"

I might have run—but for thoughts of Hamilcar Cavanaugh. So, sighing, I shuffled over to the table and allowed Nye to confiscate my right hand for at least three minutes of vigorous pumping.

"I'd like you to meet my most excellent friend, Mr. Sam Clemens of Missouri—"

"Oh, Mr. Rettie is an admirer of mine," Clemens said drolly, letting me know by not rising that he hadn't quite yet forgiven me for denying him Musetta's favors. "This is my partner, Cal Higbie."

"Pleasure." Higbie's eyes flickered up from the table only briefly before focusing again on a fragment of black and crumbly rock he was methodically pulverizing with the wooden handle of his steak knife. "Lookee this, Red," he said to Clemens, who leaned over to closely inspect the grit.

Clemens verdict came in a growl: "Damn!"

"You must forgive the low spirits in which you find these gentlemen this morning," Captain John said. "They've returned from a fruitless search for the Lost Cement Mine, only to have their noses rubbed in news that the owners of the Wide West Mine have struck a fabulous bonanza. Mr. Higbie here got himself a specimen of the new rock."

"Ain't like no Wide West ore I've ever seen before," he muttered out of his profound absorption with the stuff.

Suddenly I found myself hemmed in by two concerns at once:

Immediately I had to devise some way of slipping Captain John his tincture of belladonna Mickey Finn—without anyone becom-ing the wiser. The three men had been helping themselves to an ironstone china pitcher, from which Nye now poured me the last draught of gin punch, then failed to order a refill, although his own tumbler was empty. As chance would have it, the vacant chair had been the one directly across from my Captain John. I would have to reach across both Clemens's and Higbie's fields of vision in order to doctor the old man's glass. The vial grew sweaty as I turned it in my hand beneath the table.

Secondly, Calvin Higbie's suspicion about this specimen from the Wide West was my long awaited signal that things were going to start happening for the partners and that it was time to back off from their company.

"I just don't get it." Higbie rubbed a flake of the ore between his fingers until it was reduced to a powder that glittered with what even I recognized to be specks of native gold and silver. "Just lookee at it!"

"The lucky wretches have followed their pittance of a vein right down into the Heart of Ophir!"

"No, Red," Higbie said adamantly. "A stream of water don't turn into whiskey, no matter how far down you follow it." With that he stood, upsetting his chair behind him. "I'm going back to the cabin and wash out a pan full." He rushed out of the saloon without saying good-bye.

"What do you make of all this, Mr. Rettie?" Clemens asked, more worshiping his cigar than smoking it.

I hesitated, but then decided there was no real harm in helping things along their predetermined course. "I really don't know, except . . ."

"Yes?"

"Well, when I looked up at the Wide West on my way here this morning, armed guards were posted around the shaft."

Clemens plucked the cigar out of his mouth. His smile was more stunned than quizzical, but he quickly put on a show of nonchalance by yawning.

"If you ask me," Captain John said, "the more durable fortune to be made in this country will be found in—"

"Cattle," Clemens interrupted, winking at me.

"Don't scoff, my young friend. And that's why I must be on my way now. Gardiner is finally letting go of some breeding stock out at his Nine-Mile Ranch. So I'm off as soon as I can get my flask filled."

My only chance was trickling through my fingers like sand. "Before you go, sir, let me stand for a round."

"Thank you, Mr. Rettie, but I never have more than a pint before noon."

"Then let me see that your flask is topped off."

Captain John seemed surprised at my offer, but nevertheless handed over the handsome silver vessel: "Very well, thank you. Old Tom Holland's my weakness."

Meanwhile, Clemens was going through the now familiar ritual of plumbing his pockets for that elusive gold eagle he never seemed to find in time to help with the tab.

"Forget it, Sam," Captain John muttered—as if he had been through this pretense once too often.

"A bottle of Sezerac please," I said to the barkeep, who sidestepped down the ornate buffet to locate the brandies.

Steeling my hands against quivering, I uncorked the vial and dumped the liquid down the spout of the flask, pocketed the empty receptacle, then breathed again. The barkeep returned with bottle, tilting it so I could read the label.

"Oh, I'm terribly sorry. Did I say brandy? I meant gin. Old Tom Holland will do nicely. . . ."

Clemens wasted no time in taking his leave of me as soon as Captain John had farewelled everyone in the saloon and ridden off toward Nine-Mile Ranch. "Always a delight, Mr. Rettie," he said carelessly, then hurried through the doors as quickly as his rambling gait would permit. I followed him out, but remained on the snowy boardwalk as his boots shattered a thin film of ice that had formed over a large puddle during the night. He halted on the hump in the middle of Pine Street and gazed up toward the comb of reddish quartz on which stood the works of the Wide West Mine. Then it seemed as if an invisible hand pushed him back a pace—his astonishment to espy rifle-toting guards ringing the distant shaft was that strong. I could actually see the question take form in his gray-eyed squint: *What secret are the mine owners protecting with such unremitting attention?* Reaching into his vest pocket for a fresh cigar, which he then neglected to light, Clemens started off at a trot toward his cabin and Calvin Higbie, who by now, I suspected, had washed out a pan full of the ore—and discovered its residue to be spangling with precious metals.

Wasting no time myself, I scrabbled up onto my rocky spur once again and peered over the crown of the boulder at the cabin just as Higbie seized Clemens by the sleeve and dragged him inside.

From within, a blanket was hung over the broken window facing me.

Chuckling to myself, I reached through the torn lining of my coat pocket to retrieve my trusty copy of *Roughing It*. I had referred to Chapter XL so many times, an accommodating poltergeist dwelling in the book now cleaved the pages to the very place:

I now come to a curious episode—the most curious, I think that had yet accented my slothful, valueless, heedless career. Out of a hillside toward the upper end of the town, projected a wall of reddish looking quartz-croppings, the exposed comb of a silver-bearing ledge that extended deep down into the earth, of course. It was owned by a company entitled the "Wide West." There was a shaft sixty or seventy feet deep on the under side of the croppings, and everybody was acquainted with the rock that came from it—and tolerably rich rock it was, too, but nothing extraordinary. I will remark here, that although to the inexperienced stranger all the quartz of a particular "district" looks about alike, an old resident of the camp can take a glance at a mixed pile of rock, separate the fragments and tell you which mine each came from, as easily as a confectioner can separate and classify the various kinds of candy in a mixed heap of the article. . . .

Twain went on to describe how Higbie had brought a handful of the new ore to the cabin.

. . . and when he washed it out his amazement was beyond description. . . . He puzzled over the rock, examined it with a glass, inspected it in different lights and from different points of view, and after each experiment delivered himself, in soliloquy, of one and the same unvarying opinion in the same unvarying formula: "It is not Wide West rock!". . . He said once or twice that he meant to have a look into the Wide West shaft if he got shot for it.

That, I concluded, snapping shut the paperback, was where things stood at the present moment.

By nine o'clock, under a sun white like molten lead, the night's snowfall had receded to the blue shadows beside the shanties or to the deeper crannies in the hillsides. I shed my coat and kept vigil in my shirt, eventually removing my garters and rolling up my sleeves. By noon it was impossible to believe that only twelve hours before this flawless sky had been choked with snowflakes. Once, I began to turn my head to look for any activity on Bullion Street—but then appreciated the wisdom in not doing so.

At four movement on a plateau to the west of Aurora brought me to my feet out of a warm drowsiness: A double column of horsemen galloped through the pines before descending into a vale beyond. They rode with the bearing of cavalrymen on some urgent mission—and there had been no mistaking the distinctive panama hat of Judge David S. Terry in the van. What mischief did they have planned for tonight? But then, Calvin Higbie rescued me from any profitless worries about the local copperheads.

He slipped out the back of the cabin and dashed up the barren slope to a line of pinions, which he worked stealthily up the ravine until I lost him in the shadow of the jagged projection of the lode being worked by the Wide West. The operation here was nothing as fancy as that of Madonna Consolidated; and instead of a hoisting-works house sprawling over the shaft, there was only a gallowslike headframe from which an iron bucket was lowered and raised on a rope.

Nothing happened for over an hour, and then a single rifle report cracked over the ravine and rippled away in echo. A terrible silence followed. Higbie could not be seen coming down from the outcropping, even after ten interminable minutes. Finally my hope petered out.

"Mother of God!" I staggered up out of concealment. "They've shot Higbie!"

Clemens must have heard the report, too, for he had tiptoed out of the cabin and was standing behind a wagon, peering up at the Wide West. He started jogging toward the mine, but soon slowed and halted with arms akimbo, then started running again only to stop once more, rub his chin with his fingers, and finally slink back inside the cabin. So much for *Calvin H. Higbie, of California, an Honest Man, a Genial Comrade, and a Steadfast Friend*. Deep down, a man with literary ambitions knows he is ten times more valuable than his worthiest friend.

I had no idea what to do. And recrimination was prodding me with a sharp stick: Somehow, with one of my seemingly insignificant misadventures here in Aurora, had I set into motion a cause and effect that had now cost poor Cal Higbie his life? A dim but scrupulous voice was commanding me to go up there and recover his body for Christian burial, but I had no desire to give Aurora's boot hill its most peculiar tombstone:

Belmont Howard Rettie
born March 22nd, 1953
killed June 12th, 1862 while
claim-jumping.

I had just lit upon the idea of informing the town constable of Higbie's unfortunate end, when heavy footfalls clattered in the talus above me. Hugging the far side of the boulder, I laughed softly with relief as the resurrected Higbie came busting down the slope, sweaty and panting—but by all indications, unpunctured by the Wide West's marksman. He had doubled around the mine, probably because a search had been organized to find him, and was scampering down my side of the ravine. Within minutes he was safely inside the cabin, and the window began glowing cheerily with lamplight.

In *Roughing It*, Twain, true to form, omitted mention of his lapse in courage and said only of Higbie's brush with death: *He failed that day, and tried again at night; failed again; got up at dawn and tried and failed again.* . . .

Reasonably assured by this that I would miss nothing essential by retiring from the spur for the night, I headed for Musetta's room—the expectation of a pleasant evening ahead making my boots feel as light as slippers.

"But why must you return to work tonight?" I asked a second time.

And once again averting her eyes, Musetta said she was worried that her monthly would soon begin to flow in earnest and then she would be caught in a lie to Madame Richelieu.

"Is that so unpardonable?"

"Oui!" But then sat beside me on the bed. "Please, Howard . . ." Smiling unhappily, she unfisted one of my hands and kissed it.

"Christ." I went to the bureau and poured myself another slug of brandy. At last I beheld the depths of Musetta's servitude. Madame Richelieu didn't give a damn if she took another night off—I was sure of it. Nor would the Creole woman believe her fib that last night's malady had been a "false start." Madame was in cahoots with Judge Terry and would honor his wishes as conveyed to her by Hamilcar Cavanaugh. But I didn't argue. Musetta rose and turned to her isinglass mirror, where she primped her hair with a meticulousness that nearly drove me through the ceiling.

Then she went out. I took the brandy bottle back to bed with me.

Three hours later she swept back into the room and asked me on her way to the bureau, "Would you care for something to eat?"

I shook my head no.

She glanced back at me through the mirror. "Howard?"

"No, thank you."

With a nonchalance that was just a bit too studied, she removed something from the bottom drawer, half concealed it in the folds of her skirt, and went out into the hallway again. After an absence of several minutes, she returned it to the drawer, then excused herself by promising, "Midnight, Howard—if not sooner."

"Sure, good hunting."

Noiselessly, she shut the door.

Going to the bureau, I felt no compunction in examining what she had tried to keep me from noticing:

It was a small, round-cornered leather case, like one for a manicure set—except that it was fastened shut with brass clasps instead of a zipper. The first thing within to catch my eye was a vial labeled by a precise hand in ink that had browned: *Corrosive Sublimate*. It was tucked in a jumble of implements that were a mystery to me until I began reading the inside lid:

THE DAVIDSON RUBBER COMPANY
Patented March 31, 1857
DIRECTIONS for Using the Syringe,
Before inserting the Injection Pipe, immerse
the Suction Pipe, and compress the Bulb a few times,
until the air is expelled and the fluid flows freely . . .

I realized the irrationality of the act as soon as I had done it—but done is done, and the contents of the kit were strewn across the floor, the vial crushed underfoot. I slammed both of the doors that impeded my rush out of Madame Richelieu's dormitory.

Outside, the mountain winds were icy, inhumanely clean.

Damned if it wasn't like having the libretto to an opera the next morning when Calvin Higbie sneaked up the hillside behind the cabin once more and skulked toward the Wide West, concealing himself from the guards' view behind the towering comb of quartz that hosted the fortune he was zeroing in on. Twain, for once, told it like it happened without embellishment, perhaps because he remained snug in the cabin during the entire episode:

Then [Higbie] lay in ambush in the sagebrush hour after hour, waiting for the two or three hands to adjourn to the shade of a boulder for dinner; made a start once, but was premature—one of the men came back for something; tried it again, but when almost at the mouth of the shaft, another of the men rose up from behind the boulder as if to reconnoitre, and he dropped on the ground and lay quiet; presently he crawled on his hands and knees to the mouth of the shaft, gave a quick glance around, then seized the rope and slid down the shaft. He disappeared in the gloom of a "side drift" just as a head appeared in the mouth of the shaft and somebody shouted "Hello!"—which he did not answer. He was not disturbed any more. . . .

Reconnaissance complete, Higbie wended his way back down through the twilight, and I abandoned my breezy vantage in order to retrace my steps and then approach their cabin via Pine Street like any other pedestrian. I waited behind a rick of firewood in the yard of the adjoining shack until I saw Higbie steal into his own abode as if he were a burglar.

An hour later he entered the cabin, hot, red, and ready to burst with smothered excitement, and exclaimed in a stage whisper: "I knew it! We are rich! It's A BLIND LEAD!"

"Say it again!"

"It's a blind lead!"

"Cal, let's—let's burn the house—or kill somebody! Let's get out where there's room to hurrah! But what's the use? It's a hundred times too good to be true."

"It's a blind lead, for a million!—hanging wall—foot wall— clay casings—everything complete!" He swung his hand and gave three cheers, and I cast doubt to the winds and chimed in with a will. For I was worth a million dollars, and did not care "whether school kept or not!"

But perhaps I ought to explain. A "blind lead" is a lead or ledge that does not "crop out" above the surface. A miner does not know where to look for such leads, but they are often stumbled upon by accident in the course of driving a tunnel or sinking a shaft. Higbie knew the Wide West rock perfectly well, and the more he had examined the new developments the more he was satisfied that the ore could not have come from the Wide West vein. And so it occurred to him alone, of all the camp, that there was a blind lead down in the shaft. When he went down the shaft, he found that the blind lead held its independent way through the Wide West vein, cutting it diagonally, and that it was enclosed in its own well-defined casing-rocks and clay. Hence it was public property. Both leads being perfectly well defined, it was easy for

*any miner to see which one belonged to the Wide West and which
did not.*

Higbie said:

*"We are going to take possession of this blind lead, record it
and establish ownership, and then forbid the Wide West company
to take out any more of the rock!"*

Then out trooped Sam Clemens and Calvin Higbie, arm in arm,
forcing me to flatten myself against the cabin wall. They flew
down the muddy lane to seek the mining district recorder in any
one of twenty-five saloons—so they might legitimize their claim
before retiring to a sleepless night, frenzied by visions of Nob Hill
mansions and steamship cruises around the world: a dream they
would soon forfeit through abysmal negligence—but for the
intervention of Howard Hart, a name that, strangely enough, no
longer seemed like my own.

I let them go on their spree.

Aurora, the blue and red lanterns of her many brothels winking
on against the sunset, seemed too garish for my mood, so I ambled
up the stage road onto a bluff fragrant with sage blossoms and tiny
wildflowers which looked like they'd been painted on the rocky
earth. I rounded a bend through the trees—and the imposing
silhouette of a man astride a horse stood directly in my path, as
immovable as statuary.

My first fear was robbery. However, that concern became a
trifle when the man drawled, "Where you headed, Rettie?"

"I'm just on a stroll . . . enjoying the air."

"There's plenty of air back in town." And when I failed to spin
on my heels fast enough, Tyler drew his saber and hollered, "Git,
or I'll cut you down!"

22

THE NEWS WAS all over town . . .

I found abundant enjoyment in being rich. A man offered me a
three-hundred-dollar horse, and wanted to take my simple,
unendorsed note for it. That brought the most realizing sense I
had yet had that I was actually rich, beyond shadow of doubt. It
was followed by numerous other evidences of a similar nature—
among which I may mention the fact of the butcher leaving us a
double supply of meat and saying nothing about money.

By the laws of the district, the "locators" or claimants of a
ledge were obliged to do a fair and reasonable amount of work on
their new property within ten days after the date of the location, or
the property was forfeited, and anybody could go and seize it that
chose. So we determined to go to work the next day. About the
middle of the afternoon, as I was coming out of the post office, I
met a Mr. Gardiner, who told me that Capt. John Nye was lying
dangerously ill at his place (the "Nine-Mile Ranch"), and that he
and his wife were not able to give him nearly as much care and
attention as his case demanded. I said if he would wait for me a
moment, I would go down and help in the sick room. I ran to the
cabin to tell Higbie. He was not there, but I left a note on the table

for him, and few minutes later I left town in Gardiner's wagon. . . .

And so I looked up from my copy of *Roughing It* to catch a final glimpse of Sam Clemens riding off in a hay wagon toward one of the grossest failures ever chalked up to simple negligence. The reason for this dereliction was simple enough: While Clemens would be nursing the governor's brother back from a bout of "spasmodic rheumatism," confident all the while that his industrious partner was taking care of the assessment work required of them to hang on to the Wide West, Calvin Higbie would once again fall prey to the siren song of the the Lost Cement Mine.

Mr. Whiteman had passed through Aurora earlier this morning, and Higbie—believing himself to be on a boundless roll of good luck—had accepted the enigmatic prospector's invitation to go after a second fortune in the space of a few days, trusting that Clemens would take care of the assessment labors. At best this was a shaky trust, given the Missourian's proven abhorrence of physical labor.

While I watched on high from the spur, Higbie galloped up to the cabin on a borrowed horse, and impatient to be off, tossed a note through the broken pane in the front window, not realizing that Clemens, having left his own message on the table, was already gone and would not read Higbie's crumpled warning until millions of dollars in Wide West silver had forever slipped through their grasp. I had only to open *Roughing It* to read Higbie's words to "Red": *Don't fail to do the work before the ten days expire. W. has passed through and given me notice. I am to join him at Mono Lake, and we shall go on from there tonight. He says he will find it this time, sure. CAL.*

Now there remained little for me to do until that fateful night nine days hence.

I kicked around town, played billiards for drinks with other members of Aurora's considerable leisure class, watched a badger whip six mongrels into cowering submission in the orchestra pit of a melodeon hall that passed itself off as an opera house (I lost a fifty dollar bet on the hounds), but mostly stood treat for Granville at a Chinese-run gin mill that accepted patrons in the habit of blowing off their noses with detonating caps—the owner probably thought all Caucasian noses could be improved in this manner.

Still, even when punctuated by these amusements, the days of waiting seemed as long as a stint in a lifeboat, and I found it increasingly difficult to ward off a growing sense of loneliness, especially when the evening shadows first lit upon town in faint-hearted blues and purples.

One dusk I sought to assuage these feelings by visiting my Appaloosa mare at the corral of the livery stable, to let her nuzzle my throat. But it was no good. I knew what I really needed. Nevertheless, I vowed never again to call upon Musetta, and then toasted my vow with big quaffs of brandy—which only eroded my resolve, and as soon as it was dark, I sneaked inside Madame Richelieu's dormitory.

Musetta answered my muffled knock on the door. She just stood there for what seemed an eternity.

Later I blamed the brandy, or my failure to rehearse an explanation for my sudden appearance, but when it flew out of my mouth, it seemed as boyishly solemn as the Hail Mary I had recited at my confirmation: *"I love you . . . dammit."*

Her eyes moistened and her lips half parted. But she said nothing as she opened her arms to me.

An hour later, my loneliness banished, I cheerfully sent her off to work, then reclined on her short bed to enjoy a cheroot and marvel at how completely I had liberalized my attitudes in so brief a time, and what dividends of pleasure this change was already paying me. It was all sham, of course. I felt like hell. And as the wind rattled the window, it was all I could do to keep from leaving again, forever. I turned to the distraction of *Roughing It* and my plans with a vengeance:

When I had been nursing the Captain nine days he was somewhat better. So much so, indeed, that I determined to go back to Esmeralda. I took supper, and as soon as the moon rose, began my nine-mile journey, on foot. Even millionaires needed no horses, in those days, for a mere nine-mile jaunt without baggage.

As I "raised the hill" overlooking the town, it lacked fifteen minutes of twelve. I glanced at the hill over beyond the canyon, and in the bright moonlight saw what appeared to be about half the population of the village massed on and around the Wide West croppings. My heart gave an exulting bound, and I said to myself, "They have made a new strike to-night—and struck it richer than ever, no doubt." I started over there, but gave it up. I said the "strike" would keep, and I had climbed enough hills for one night.

As I entered the cabin door, tired but jolly, the dingy light of a tallow candle revealed Higbie, sitting by the pine table gazing stupidly at my note, which he held in his fingers, and looking pale, old, and haggard. I halted, and looked at him. He looked at me, stolidly. I said:

"Higbie, what—what is it?"

"We're ruined—we didn't do the work—THE BLIND LEAD'S RELOCATED!"

A few weeks after the disaster, Clemens would abandon his dreams of silver wealth and accept a job offer from the editor of *The Territorial Enterprise*, the first step in an ever-lengthening stride that would eventually overtake Bret Harte and make Mark Twain the most prosperous man of letters of his day. This would become history, and as a bitter but minor footnote to it, Harte would die in arrears to a dozen creditors—unless I could step in at the precise moment on which my future would pivot and totter toward one of two very different conclusions: the first, which I knew all too well, leaving me indigent, at the mercy of the Cavanaughs, my wedding mug shot in post offices all over the country; the second guaranteeing me the advantages of heirship to the estate of the Literary Colossus of the Nineteenth Century— Francis Bret Harte!

Then early one afternoon I awoke groggily, having wiled away the night in a faro parlor, and realized that tomorrow this crucial moment would make its brief appearance, then vanish forever. Throwing off the covers that were still sweetened by Musetta's perfume, although her side of the bed was empty, I dressed and hurried downtown to a mercantile to once again sort through a bin of camel-hair brushes until I found several with the light brown tone I required. After paying for these and a bottle of glue, I stepped briskly from the store—and right into a lanky ruffian with an overbite.

I was on the verge of begging the stranger's pardon when I recognized him—Tyler! His lips curled back as he prepared to either grin or speak, but I didn't wait around to find out which it was.

I sprinted across Pine Street and down into a drainage ditch that coursed the center of town. Behind me I could hear his boots slap the hard, wet sand in pursuit, and he nearly caught me as I slogged across the knee-deep ooze of a silt pond, and then again as I pounded up a flight of wooded stairs into a quartz mill—but I was able to kick away his purchase on my trouser leg and then thread my way among the huge amalgamating pans with greater agility than he. I might have given him the slip in the clutter of pipes and hissing machinery had he not suddenly shouted above the thunderous batteries, "Stop—or I'll shoot!"

My own Navy Colt was inside my coat pocket, beating against my thigh for my attention as I ran, but I then suffered a demoralizing mental picture of me groping for a revolver as slippery as a pollywog in the same instant a piece of my skull popped free and skittered across the floor of the mill—my last sight.

I halted, and he closed on me.

"What do you want?" I rasped.

Tyler shoved me along the narrow side street of Chinatown, through what seemed to be the entire expatriate population of Canton, past a chockablock assortment of brothels, mah-jongg palaces, and joss houses, and finally down a dozen earthen steps into a gloaming pungent with incense and malodorous humanity.

All was silent in this basement, but not with the insensate calm I had experienced in the depths of the Madonna Consolidated Mine; the oblivion here was artificial, conjured up to shut out the world of pain above.

A red lantern was hung from the timbered ceiling. It was surrounded by a bright nimbus that gradually faded as my eyes grew accustomed to the dimness. Ignoring the taciturn old Chinese who tried to give us each a pipe and horn-shaped box, Tyler pushed me toward the far wall, which came slowly into focus as I passed through the strange, gelid light. A tier of shabby bunks materialized out of the acrid smoke, and cadaverous figures could be seen haunting these slots, their faces bluish as if from putrefaction—but I then noticed that each occupant was equipped with a small alcohol lamp that issued a sickly blue flame from which he kindled his pipe before inhaling deeply. Surprisingly, all of the smokers in this den were Caucasians, mining types I would have never imagined to find prostrated here, gazes stupefied. But this was nothing compared to my shock at discovering Hamilcar Ames Cavanaugh to be reclining in a bottommost bunk, a pipe clenched in his pale hand and his habitual sneer softened by a look of dreaminess. "Good evening, Mr. Rettie."

I did not correct him that it was yet afternoon. "What's the meaning of this?"

"A diversion of a few hours . . . a few short hours is all I have before . . ." His whisper trailed off into a pointless chuckle. "Ah, yes," he reminded himself, his languid hand reaching down under the blanket for a thick roll of currency, which he then pressed upon me.

They were Confederate treasury notes, all big denominations. "What's this for?" I asked.

"Ten thousand's there—keep it on your person. Thieves everywhere."

"But *why* are you giving me this?"

He stared at me for a long moment, his pupils so dilated they seemed entirely black. Then, gesturing for me to lean closer to his mouth, he spoke so low only I could hear: "Governor Terry asks that you serve as our eyes and ears in the next forty-eight hours. Tell Madame Richelieu if you overhear anything *unseemly*— especially concerning the Esmeralda Rangers. We must know at once if the Rangers muster." He smiled. "You did well in the matter concering Captain John, Mr. Rettie. Governor Terry was . . . pleased . . . wants to express his appreciation to . . ." Then he faded into some tantalizing vision.

I hesitated a moment, but then pocketed the wad. The notes were probably worthless—unless I could work out an exchange for greenbacks, or even gold, with some Dixie-bound Comstocker. But having been going through my savings as wantonly as Sherman would ravage Georgia in a few years, I was in no position to toss away funds, regardless of their credibility as legal tender.

"I have just been abroad in the future," Hamilcar said without warning.

My hand froze as it came out of my coat pocket. He was staring at me as if he knew *everything*, and I was suddenly gripped by an unreasonable fear that he might. "What do you mean?"

His voice became even softer, although I was convinced that no one else in the den could make out his words—or cared to. "I saw on the morrow's dawn a certain gentleman in Carson City receiving a message. Ostensibly, it came from Monoville, south- west of here: 'Your brother John desperately ill, come at once.' There was no time in which this usually cautious gentlemen might request a cavalry escort from Fort Churchill. After all, the garrison is more than thirty miles from the territorial capital. So headlong for Monoville he hied in his private coach, bypassing

Aurora to save time. And what is time but gold . . . when a dear brother is dying? Don't you agree, Mr. Rettie?"

I said nothing. Had Tyler not posted himself on the steps, I would have run for daylight right then and there.

"Between Monoville and Aurora," Hamilcar went on, "a steep and forested defile clamps down upon the road. A stage driver must duck low not to be slapped in the face by branches. And *there*, Mr. Rettie, the Knights of the Golden Circle shall strike their blow for freedom."

My hand was trembling more from fear than outrage, but nevertheless I tossed the Confederate notes back on his chest. "I'll have no part in that."

"And so shall you have no part, old sport. But you can be of service to us in the way I have suggested—become our eyes and ears. That's all."

"How am I to do this?"

"Simply frequent the public houses—and listen. It's no secret that there's a Judas in our camp. How else did James Nye get wind of our plans for him at the Madonna Consolidated? The very idea of treachery enrages Governor Terry. And God, what anger can do to that otherwise courtly man. But I'm better acquainted with human nature than he. It's hard to disappoint me." After a moment's fumbling, he successfully tucked the notes back in my coat pocket; I suppose I pretended not to notice. "If there is a rumor of our plans, find out the dastard who spoke so promiscuously among our enemies, Mr. Rettie. Tell madame of your findings—before the morrow's adventure becomes a . . . misadventure. Just keep . . . your copper star on your person . . . should you need it. . . ." Then, smiling lazily, he rolled over, showing me his back; and Tyler snapped his fingers that I might leave.

Her unbound hair was splayed golden across her pillow.

For a moment I thought that the shaft of moonlight, now streaming in through the window, or perhaps more racket from the graveyard shift in the adjoining brewery, had awakened me. But then I realized that it had not been the moon or the lack of zoning laws.

As long as I stayed awake it was a simple matter to recall that James Warren Nye had not been assassinated in 1862. He had gone on from the first territorial governorship to serve as a U.S. senator before eventually dying in the mid-1870's as pacifically and champagne-ridden as he had lived. In my time there existed no account of an attempt being made on his life; and certainly, with as much excitement as secessionist activities stirred in the territory, an attack on the governor's coach would have been given a prominent place in Nevada history.

But as soon as I dozed off, the nocturnal demons were free to weave their hallucinations—the worst of which was Governor Nye slumped against the roof of an overturned Concord, his corpse riddled with copperhead bullets. And from this gory vision, more than my lean and addled powers of reckoning, I saw that my Grand Tour had tripped off a string of events I would never be able to rectify.

I heard Musetta stir, then she pulled me down to her. "Tell me what bothers you so. . . ."

But, smiling, I could only sigh, "I'm glad you're with me tonight." Her monthly had genuinely arrived, and never before had I been delighted for the woman with whom I was sleeping to be so accursed. At least it kept her out of the cribs.

"Please, darling . . . what are you thinking?"

I was thinking that there was still time to sneak word to the Esmeralda Rangers. Hamilcar Cavanaugh, in the midst of his smug intoxication, had carelessly divulged the location of the ambush. But I could divine no way to blow the whistle on Judge Terry and his minions without ensnaring Cavanaugh in the process. And that, without a doubt, would affect my ex-wife, who I continued to recall with an affection she didn't deserve. I reminded myself that Eleanor was no Mother Teresa, that she despised me with the holy disdain of the rich for the unrepentant poor, that she had tried to land me in prison; but these mantras to revive my hatred for her collapsed under a single truth—she didn't warrant preemptive extinction simply because Howie Hart, in his eagerness to finish out the twentieth century in the lap of luxury, had screwed up the nineteenth.

"Howard, did you hear me . . . ?"

But suppose that I kept mum, and James Nye was indeed murdered and supplanted by David S. Terry. And Nevada, as a slave state began channeling its mineral wealth into Richmond's war chest. And the Union—outgeneraled on the battlefield by the likes of Lee and Jackson, threatened by a Great Britain that still resented a rift that was less than a century old—was compelled to sue for peace. If that actually happened, how could a triumphant Hamilcar Cavanaugh fail to win Eleanor Louise Beauchamp's hand? And wouldn't that assure a life for their great-great-great-granddaughter?

Yes, but my ex-wife would regain that unborn life, which was rightfully hers, only at the expense of the United States of America. And that might not do. If on the outside chance we would meet again at some country club in the beyond, I could explain that this had been my impossible choice—it had been either her or the Union. Of course, it might not hold water with her: I had always suspected that the latter-day Cavanaughs cared no more for foolishness like abolition than their antecedents did.

I slumped into Musetta's arms. "Jesus . . ." Everything that had so neatly crystallized in my mind shifted again into a fresh set of paradoxes; I could see no way out of these kaleidoscopic conundrums, which according to Rodrigo, even Einstein had found worthy of a nervous breakdown. "There's got to be a way out."

"Of what, Howard?"

And then I sensed that Eleanor might not be the true reason I was taking no action. I sat up. "Tell me something, Musetta. . . ."

She frowned, but didn't turn away as she sometimes did when I became too inquisitive.

"What does *Le Cause* mean to you?"

"Why, it means Madame Richelieu," she said peevishly, "and *mes amies*!"

"Is that all?"

"What more can there be?!"

"Good." I surprised her with a kiss. She was as much a secessionist as Abe Lincoln, and that removed a formidable obstacle from my path. But now, although I had finally made my choice, there followed no lessening of tensions.

She must have felt this in my body, for she whispered, "Would you like me to do the *other thing* to you?" Apparently she believed that a man might explode if inflated with too much sexual desire between releases. "Howard?"

"Yes?"

"What would you like me to do?"

Perhaps it was my fault for saying it half jokingly: "You can tell me you love me."

She stared at me in horror—as if I had just taken a swipe at her with a knife. Then, as tears filled her eyes, she looked away.

"Musetta, I'm sorry—"

"I cannot say such a thing now. I will explain another time. But not now. Please go."

"It's four in the morning, for Chrissake!"

"Go!" she sobbed.

I tried to comfort her, but she recoiled at my touch.

So, dressing while she wept, I then wandered out into the last light before the moonset, chilled, confused, ashamed, alone. I sensed that I had violated her—and more viciously than any man before me; but I didn't understand the nature of my offense in the least, which only got me angry.

"Good-bye, Musetta," I said, looking back at her window, which was darkened by her silhouette.

The stamping of the batteries set my cadence as I made for the Goddess of the Dawn Boardinghouse. There, I would awaken Granville and ask him to carry a secret message to his former comrades in the Esmeralda Rangers: They could become eternal heroes in the War Between the States if only they might slip out of Aurora in unobtrusive twos or threes—and wearing their workaday clothes, not looking like Shriners on a toot.

I was going to save the Union, after all.

But I didn't feel a bit heroic, for I knew that as soon as tonight's business was concluded, I would flee from Aurora and never set eyes on Musetta again.

23

"THIS AIN'T EXACTLY provided for in the Esmeralda Mining District laws," the recorder said. He was enthroned on a stool behind a plank set upon two sawhorses—his alfresco office on the brink of the Wide West shaft ever since Clemens and Higbie had laid lawful claim to the blind lead. He had successfully halted any further activity on the site until this moment, when I had arrived from downtown with a pick over one shoulder and a shovel over the other. "I even kept the old owners from going underground to get their equipment," he went on. "You got to understand my position, Colonel Higbie—"

"*Cap'n*, laddie—it's Cap'n Herman Higbie of the good packet *Betty Grable*. Come to do me baby brother Calvin's assessment work on the hold of this here mountain." My impersonation probably fell somewhere in between Yosemite Sam and Popeye. But it was important only that I sound authoritative, especially in the presence of the hopeful "relocaters" who had grown more numerous—and restless—each day that neither Clemens nor Higbie had materialized to do their reasonable amount of labor on the ledge. Now, as the midnight deadline came ever closer, they could scarcely contain themselves from rushing the gaping hole in the ground, and like lemmings, hurling themselves down toward the faint melodies of wealth that had been beckoning them without pause. I played more to these hangers-on than to the flustered recorder: "Now are you telling me it jibes for me brother's mine to be jumped for nonwork because him and his partner's got Christian business in yonder parts of the territory?"

"No, sir. But I reckon we should let the district officers—" His voice thinned to a whine as I strode away from him, "Captain Higbie. . . ?!"

I swept along the circle of waiting miners. Scrutinizing them down to the yellow calluses on their fingers, I scratched my grizzled beard—but not too roughly, for fear it might flake off in my hand. This growth with gray highlights plucked from my own temples was more convincing, I felt sure, than my first disguise in San Francisco, which had made Musetta helpless with laughter. "Who here will work this day for the sugar in his tay?!"

"How much, Cap'n?" someone asked.

"Ten dollars Yankee gold."

A dozen hands shot up against the pearlescent-blue sky.

"That's the spirit, laddies. You there—" I pointed at a Scandinavian altogether too large not to select. "Go below, me lubber, and keelhaul the winzes."

He blinked at me for only an instant before realizing that if he hesitated any longer, someone else would get the ten dollars. "*Ja . . .* sure." He turned to a comrade: "Lower me away in the bucket. I must keyhole the winze."

Meanwhile, the recorder had cracked his officiously water-marked book of records and was reading for the benefit of all Aurorans within a mile's radius, living or otherwise, as if the words formed some incantation that might make me shrivel and vanish: ". . . Whereas, together will all and singular the tenements, hereditaments and appurtenances thereunto belonging . . ."

"Laddie," I said to a boy, doffing the murdered sailor's cap I had swept up off the floor of the Bank Exchange my first night in town, using it now to gesture at the headframe above us, "go aloft and trim the tholes off the mizzen thar."

"Yessir!"

The recorder glanced up from his tome and carped at me, "No one touches any ore!"

"Put me alee of your blow! Me midshipman is just going topside thar to trim the mizzen!"

"Oh . . ." Then, his eyes quick with uncertainty, he went

back to casting his legalese spell: ". . . or in anywise appertaining, and the reversion and reversions . . ."

"You thar—yes, you!—go below and help the Norseman. After you're done keelhauling, report to the boatswain and start shifting the ballast to port. We got a starboard list on this mountain fit to gag a maggot. And you—run to the chandlery for a pint of spar varnish . . ." And so I continued recruiting laborers, who cheerfully threw themselves into these madhouse chores, until I had pledged several hundred dollars in gold coin—nearly all the money I had remaining to my name, other than the Confederate treasury notes Hamilcar Cavanaugh had forced upon me. But what did the cost matter? If I failed, nothing but poverty and imprisonment awaited me in the twentieth century.

While kicking unsightly pinecones off the southern extremity of the claim, I paused and listened, wondering how far volleys of shot could be heard on a still day like this.

At my bidding, the Esmeralda Rangers had indeed trickled out of town this morning. Although Granville had seemed deeply moved by my request to carry the message to his old colonel, he spent an inordinate amount of time making sure I'd gotten it right from my undisclosed source: that the ambush was planned for the South Road and not along the western or northern approaches to Aurora. By now, if all had gone well, the Rangers should be closing their net around Judge Terry and his men—although, hopefully, one Knight of the Golden Circle would not be present at the battle to have his cravat shot off. Before transforming myself into Herman Higbie, I had left a note for Hamilcar Cavanaugh with Madame Richelieu:

My Dear Mr. Cavanaugh—
I have most amazing news. It would please me to meet with you
at the Wide West Mine at eleven tonight. Is it sufficient to say
that I have received word the Saints are now interested in your
endeavors?

Alas,
A Fallen Saint

If this long-awaited promise of Mormon collaboration didn't persuade Judge Terry to excuse Hamilcar from today's engagement, I had no idea what would. Nevertheless, for my ex-wife's sake, I had tried.

* * *

At dusk I ordered myself windlassed below in the rusty ore bucket so I might supervise the varnishing of the fo'c'scle: in actuality, the timbered station (quite rude when compared to those of the Madonna Consolidated) that gave access down a short crosscut to the blind lead, which glittered under candlelight with galaxies of free gold suspended in the black sulpheret of silver. For once, even a neophyte like me could see the richness of this fabulous ledge. It was all I could do to turn away and go topside again.

The cloud bars in the west, which had been underlit with crimson, had gone somberly to gray while I was below, and the crowd had broken out torches. These were kept burning even after the full moon crested Aurora Peak at eleven o'clock. It took all this time for the mining district officers to convene an emergency session at the site. Through the harried recorder, they requested a conference with me; but good-naturedly I hollered over my shoulder, "Got to scull the scuppers before she's shipshape!"

One of my laborers flagged me down with his sweaty bandana: "Cap'n Higbie, we was wanting to know if you want the bilges pumped."

"Of course, laddie—glad you thought of it!"

Then I noticed a figure working his way through the dense throng, and I sighed with relief.

Hamilcar Ames Cavanaugh was so obviously a man of executive ability, the recorder gave up his stool so he might sit. He regarded the furious but meaningless work on the mine with a smirk, then looked me dead in the eye. Just when I thought he was on the verge of recognizing me, or even denouncing me, he took a long cigar from his pocket and lit it.

The crowd had begun to grumble, and I grew nervous that the district officers might be goaded into some action against me. It was time for a little public relations. So, pasting on a smile, I began introducing myself around the fringe of the mob, explaining that, as Cal Higbie's long-lost brother, I was only fulfilling the requirements of the law in his absence. If there was any resentment that the Wide West would not be up for grabs at midnight as many had expected, I tried to deflect it by hinting that the reorganized company would soon be filling superintendent and foremen positions. "Aye, laddies, there'll be a berth for everybody when this here Wide West gets sailing under full canvas!" Gradually, this kind of talk turned the mood affable once again, and I was offered several bottles as I pumped outstretched hands and promised to remember names when hiring time came.

"Good eve to you, mate. Herman Higbie's me handle. And yours?" Then, recoiling, I let go of this man's big, square hand as if it had gone leprous on me. *Tyler!*—I almost shouted. What was he doing here? And why wasn't he south of town, being peppered with shot by the Rangers at this hour? But then, before my shocked silence could give me away, I realized that a trusting soul like Hamilcar Cavanaugh would go nowhere without a bodyguard or two. "Aye indeed," I recovered myself, "I don't think I've had the honor."

"The hell you ain't." He flicked his receding chin toward the crenellated outcropping—on top of which loomed the silhouette of a man in a panama hat. And to assure me that there was no confusion on his part about who *I* was, Judge Terry touched two fingers to the brim of that hat in a brisk but disparaging salute.

There was now only one thought buzzing in my head: flee!

Spinning around, I had taken less than a stride when I bumped chests with Hamilcar.

"Easy, Mr. Rettie." He chuckled humorlessly. His right hand was thrust deep into his coat pocket, and jutting through the cloth was the protuberance of what I guessed to be a revolver's muzzle. "Your excitability gives me cause for reflection."

"What . . . why are. . . ?" I stammered, in the same instant I dismissed any notion of going for my Colt—I really don't know why I bothered carrying one. "Why aren't you all on the South Road?"

"Yes, Mr. Rettie . . ." His bared teeth were flecked with torchlight as he steered me by the elbow toward the moon shadows of the headframe, where we might enjoy a grim privacy. ". . . that is the question of the hour."

"But Governor Nye could be arriving there any minute—"

"Along with the Esmeralda Rangers?"

He had me cold. We both knew it. But to throw in the towel was to bow my head to the executioneer. My voice was raw with terror: "My purposes tonight have nothing to do with the rebellion, I assure you."

"Thank goodness, Mr. Rettie, for yours is the most wretched incognito ever foisted on the public naiveté." He tried to put me at ease with a smile, but it only intensified my urgency to take to my heels. That smile was altogether too compassionate to be wasted on anyone but a doomed man. "And as to your other activities, Governor Terry and I thank you."

"Thank me?"

"Quite so, old sport. We counted on your duplicity to draw the local militia out of Aurora. Well done."

Hoodwinked. Duped into providing the copperheads with what they required most to murder the territorial governor. All at once, I didn't need to inquire to know that the mise-en-scène in the opium den had been staged for my benefit. Something within me had refused to believe that a man as meticulous as Hamilcar would take the eve of battle off just to blow a little dope; and now it seemed glaringly suspicious that all the dream-bunks had been taken by Caucasians—Terry's men, of course. I was still faulting my own gullibility when another doubt landed on me like a hod of bricks: Had Hamilcar been smoking opium, his pupils should have been constricted, not dilated. I wasn't positive about this, but it now fit in with the rest of my having been manipulated by the secessionists.

Yet despite the numbing weight of these realizations, the voice of survival deep inside me screamed: *Keep talking!*

"Then James Nye isn't coming by way of the South Road?"

"Oh, such alacrity of mind in the service of so craven a heart. But I won't waste another breath by asking the true name inscribed by your parents on that mind and heart. We are on a schedule, you and I. It is enough that you are here, Mr. Rettie, and that you're widely believed to be a follower of Mr. Brigham Young. You have been a boon to our efforts. We were close to despairing that further attempts on Nye's life were futile." My eyes tracked his as they shifted toward the outcropping: Judge Terry had disappeared, but his absence was twice as intimidating as his presence had been. "And yes," Hamilcar went on after eyeing an axe and kicking it out of my reach, "James Nye will not use the South Road. A message was left for him at the Big Meadows way station, informing him that his brother, having taken a turn for the worse, was moved from Monoville to a physician's house here in Aurora. In fact . . ." He peered across the ravine to where the road from Big Meadows, looking chalky in the moonlight, ribboned down off the western ridges into town. "I expect his private coach to appear at any minute."

"Then you're going to murder him?"

"Murder is a criminal term, Mr. Rettie. It has no more meaning in war than trespassing or malicious mischief."

In one part of the crowd hats were being doffed and men began stepping aside to clear a lane. I had learned that this signaled the approach of a lady, but my attention was divided when Hamilcar grasped my upper arm, painfully, and whispered, "Ah, how nice—you're not the only one to come to the ball in costume tonight."

Confused, I looked up again.

It was apparent that the good citizens of Aurora saw Musetta in one light—and that alone. For now as she came to the forefront, not in her ordinarily vivacious clothes but in a somber black dress and with a fall of dark brown ringlets dangling midway down her back, the men seemed not to recognize her, nor her "mammy," who followed at an obsequious distance, her features half hidden by a lace shawl—Madame Richelieu with a slavish aspect she would have never dreamed of assuming without some dire issue being at stake.

Musetta looked bewildered as she kneaded a folded parasol in her hands—and waited. It was clear to me that she had no idea what was coming next—because, when madame whispered in her ear, she listened intently before giving a timorous nod and following the Creole woman back through the breach in the crowd. A few seconds later I could see them walking farther up the ravine, toward no apparent destination. They soon halted in the brush and turned to face the Wide West again.

For the first time I saw how Musetta might wind up in the stockade at Fort Churchill—or worst yet, on the gallows. Momentarily anger overcame fear: "What's she doing here?!"

Hamilcar calmed me by poking me in the ribs with his yet concealed revolver. "I'll be glad to explain, old sport, as long as you keep your voice down . . . there, that's better. As James Nye's coach descends the hill into town, his attention, no doubt, will be drawn to this festive scene. Half the territory's here. And the torches can be seen blazing for miles. Mark my words—he'll instruct his driver to come up the ravine. A moth to his flame, Mr. Rettie."

"*Then* you'll gun him down?"

"Oh, ne'er so simple. Most of these dolts you see before you are for the Union. To assassinate the abolitionist pig in so manifest a way would put us at disadvantage—even with the Rangers far afield. No, we must turn to delicacy if we are to succeed tonight."

"But why is Musetta—"

"I am trying to explain. When Nye steps down from his

Concord, you shall be the one to approach and greet him—as Captain Herman Higbie or Belmont Rettie or the Marquis de Lafayette . . . it makes no difference to me, old sport."

"I'm not going to shoot him."

"Oh, spare me this. You'd cut off his hand and chew it to the bone if we put sufficient pressure on you. But your statement is correct. Quite simply, you shall inform Mr. Nye that it would be a great honor for you to present him to your wife, who waits a little ways outside this rude commotion. She has long been an admirer of his. In fact, her beloved servant was liberated from slavery thanks to one of his former interests—the Underground Railroad. This poor Negress would now like to express her gratitude to him. What politician can resist the slightest morsel of adulation—even with a brother on his deathbed?"

"Bodyguards. Surely his guards will prevent—"

"Our scouts have determined Nye to be accompanied only by his secretary, Mr. Orion Clemens—whose brother I believe is an acquaintance of yours?"

"Yes," I said, too weakened by dread and Hamilcar's ironclad thoroughness to raise any more objections.

"Well, Mr. Clemens will be delayed by another of our party as you lead Nye toward Musetta and madame. Should the secretary attempt to intervene, he, too, will die. But otherwise, we have no irremediable quarrel with him."

I glanced up the ravine once again. Musetta looked small against the night. Unable to keep still, she was taking skittish steps in place. She was also holding her umbrella in an unnatural way—at port arms. Beside her, Madame Richelieu remained as immovable as one of the boulders that lined the rim of the gorge.

Then it struck me that Musetta's parasol might be a trimmed-down rifle or even a foil of some sort. "*She's* not going to kill Nye, is she?"

"Again, keep your voice down. And don't be absurd. The woman's a common hurdy. She's not privy to a thing other than the few instructions madame has given her."

"Then madame will pull the trigger?"

"Wrong again. That honor is reserved for Governor David S. Terry, CSA." Hamilcar then nudged me aside so he might check the stage road for Nye's coach. "Now, Mr. Rettie, kindly tell me of this *amazing* news of which you wrote."

"Oh yes, the news . . ." I looked over each shoulder as if for eavesdroppers. Then I smiled conspiratorially, although my heart was trip-hammering and I wanted only to be gone from this place in the worst way. Pausing, hoping to bait Hamilcar with a moment of suspense, I found myself trying to recall who had defined courage as *glibness under pressure*. I reminded myself that I had made a living—and a pretty decent one, too, until the Cavanaughs had intervened—by convincing people that it was possible to get rich without lifting a finger. And now I had to come up with the best pitch of my life.

In case he had not heard about recent events in Aurora, I began by telling him how Higbie and Clemens had relocated the blind lead; then, still smiling, although my facial muscles ached, I asked, "What do you think of the practice in this mining district of the principal claimant being permitted to declare coclaimants?"

"I think—what does this have to do with a Mormon revolt?"

I kept plowing ahead, although his fingers had begun fidgeting with a mustache. "Do you have any idea of the assayed valuation of the ledge beneath our feet?"

"No," he sighed, "but the Esmeralda mines have never rivaled the richness of those on the Comstock. The best here? Perhaps four hundred dollars to the ton."

"*Three* thousand dollars to the ton, Mr. Cavanaugh. That's the independent assay on the Wide West's new ore."

After a long moment Cavanaugh shook off a perfect stillness— and blinked. "An independent assay?"

"Quite." As an investment counselor I had seen it a thousand times before: how the specter of untold riches steals a man's breath, mesmerizes him with shivarees of ease and luxury, then stampedes all his desires down the path I had laid before his feet. Taking advantage of Hamilcar's momentary pensiveness, I wrapped my arm around his shoulders and led him back out into the torchlight. "Now, I believe that I can prevail upon the owners of this lovely little prospect to include your worthy name in the book of records. Good Lord, man—they've only scratched sixty feet into the ledge!"

His eyes gravitated toward the clutch of boulders above Musetta and Madame Richelieu, then back to my face. "I . . . don't know."

"Don't tell me you're thinking of passing up this opportunity! Oh, I've got it . . ." I steepled my hands together under my chin. "Your overriding concern is *Le Cause*. Of course. Well, let me assure you that Sam Clemens is a decorated veteran of a Confederate militia company from Missouri. I'm absolutely positive he will be well disposed toward the kinds of activities you and Governor Terry envision for Nevada's future."

Hamilcar slowly grinned. "And what is your gain from this swindle, Mr. Rettie?"

I touched my hand to my breast as if he had just wounded me there. *"Swindle?"*

At that instant a cry arose from the throng, and through the milling clusters of townies I could glimpse a group of a half-dozen men barreling up the ravine. My first thought—and Hamilcar's, too, by the way he stiffened—was that here, at last, was James Nye. But this notion was dismissed as soon as one of the district officers shouted, "It's Cal Higbie! Now we can scrape this goddamned thing off the griddle once and for all!"

Too fast, I thought to myself, *it's accelerating too fast. I'm going to crash and burn.* But then a calmer self prevailed: *Take it one step at a time, Howard. You always pined for want of a rough-and-tumble world like this one.*

I unpocketed my watch. Two minutes before midnight. I took a step toward Higbie, who had just muscled a path through the crowd to glare at me, his barrel chest billowing, when Hamilcar snagged me by the coat sleeve. "I'm an accomplished marksman. Is a warning necessary?" In that moment he had Charles Manson eyes. "Mr. Rettie?"

I shook my head no.

"Oh," he said as if it were an afterthought, "do you still have your copper star on your person?"

"Yes."

"And your treasury notes?"

"I do—but a lot of good they'll do me here."

"On the contrary, Mr. Rettie. They will soon prove to be eminently valuable." He let go of my sleeve.

Crouching forward like a wrestler, Higbie stared at this brash poseur who was making himself at home on Clemens's and his claim. The fierceness in his eyes told me that all his instincts were crying *foul play* as he looked me over. But, wisely, he said nothing. This was all I demanded of him: a little horse sense.

"Why, Cal boy! Bless you, laddie!" I tried to pump his hand, which resisted mine. But that didn't stop me from giving him an affectionate hug. "Sam Clemens," I said before he might get a word in edgeways, "ran off to Nine-Mile Ranch what to nurse John Nye, who was down with a most scurvious grippe. And these lubbers was about to haul down your colors and hand the Wide West over to any freebooters what come along!"

Distrust had cocked his lower jaw to the side, but my prayers were answered in that he continued to hold his tongue. Once again Hamilcar was menacing me from behind—but I tried not to be distracted by his presence.

"So, Cal boy," I happily roared, "what with your first mate and you abroad in the land, your big brother Herman here done the assessment work so you can hang on to the Wide West! What do you say?!"

24

GOOD OLD CALVIN H. HIGBIE. *An honest man*, as Twain had written so glowingly of him. With a life fit for an Oriental potentate shimmering in silks and sequins before his bovine gaze, eternally his—this host of luscious pleasures—just for muttering a word of thanks to his long-lost brother, Higbie puffed out his chest and declared, "I never seen this imposter before in my life. I got no brother named Herman."

"Why, it's the grippe! Me baby brother's delirious with that scurvious grippe!" But my bellowing was in vain. The uproar was deafening, and the most insistent voice of all belonged to the recorder. Flanked by his fellow officers, he seized me by the lapels and was trying to shake the truth out of me: "Who are you?"

"A shillaber for Clemens and Higbie, that's who!" an Irish voice howled. "They's too rich and lordy now to blister their hands with a shovel!"

Out of the corner of my eye I watched Hamilcar: His puzzlement was apparent; but it was quickly shoved aside by some idea that gave his eyes an extravagant light. Before I could free myself from the recorder's grasp, Cavanaugh reached over my shoulders and yanked the false whiskers off my chin.

"Damn us all!" someone cried. "It's that Rettie stinkfoot! I played billiards with him just this week!"

"Why, indeed!" Hamilcar cried pointedly. "It's the *Mormon*, Belmont Rettie!"

"Is the Wide West up for grabs then?" an old sourdough demanded.

The officers consulted one another for a moment, then cried in unison, "Yes!"

As Cal Higbie raced off to tell Clemens the ghastly news, an argument of a hundred voices erupted on all sides of me, but soon gave way to a consensus that, as I had enlisted a crew that was laboring away on the claim when it came up for relocation at midnight, the blind lead was now rightfully mine. Rather than contest my newfound status as king of the hill, everyone was toadying up to grab a piece of me, begging to be named a coclaimant.

Everyone except Hamilcar Ames Cavanaugh.

The muzzle of his revolver was still denting his coat, and he almost seemed to be provoking me with a sneer to go for my own gun. He was showing me something in this instant, and it sprang from an immense confidence—perhaps that he had already won and I was too slow to see how I had been checkmated.

Then it came to me. I saw how I had been maneuvered into helplessness.

"You bastard!" I shouted at him—but all my fury was swallowed up by the pandemonium. He hunched his shoulders, although a silent chuckle kept it from being a gesture of apology.

I railed against my own stupidity. I should have put myself in Judge Terry's place, and from that vantage of utter ruthlessness, imagined how things might unfold:

The moment James Nye was lured by me up into the shadowy recess where Musetta waited at madame's side like a staked lamb, the judge would order a rifleman to fell the governor. Nye would no sooner crumple into the dust than the hidden marksman would dispatch me as well. Madame would reach down for the revolver still in my pocket (explaining why Hamilcar had not done so, although he had had every opportunity to disarm me). After expending one round into the earth, she would slip the Navy Colt into my lifeless fingers, then drive Musetta before her into the darkness—to ready horses, perhaps? As to poor Belmont Howard Rettie: The shocked crowd would find the pockets of the Mormon assassin to be brimming with Confederate blood money, in addition to a curious five-pointed star fashioned from copper. One of Terry's agents might come forward to swear that he heard me cry upon pulling the fateful trigger, *"Sic semper tyrannis! Brigham Young is avenged!"* This good citizen would claim he had tried to prevent the assassination—but, alas, answered a second too late with his trusty Sharp's rifle.

The desired result of this would be a renewed hysteria against the Mormons, perhaps even another hotheaded federal campaign against the Saints that would draw Brigham Young into an alliance with the South. But at this point these speculations became too rarified for the time and the place. I had to save my own skin—and promptly too.

I tried to reach into my pocket with the hope of jettisoning the roll of treasury notes and the copperhead star. Yet, with his movements going unnoticed in the tumult by everyone but me, Hamilcar had drawn his Pettingill revolver and now hid it behind his leg. A slight but fierce shake of his head persuaded me to keep my hands out of my pockets.

The claim book was thrust under my nose. I couldn't hear what the recorder was saying, and hollered for him to repeat himself.

"It's agreed, Mr. Rettie, the blind lead is yours!"

"But Twain—"

"Who?"

"I mean Clemens . . . Higbie . . . it *has* to be theirs."

"They've done forfeited. It's the law. Whatever they paid you, Mr. Rettie, it ain't a tenth of what this mine is worth."

"Can I name them as coclaimants?" I asked, grasping at straws.

"No, sir—that'd run agin the forfeiture provision. Just put your signature right behind the big number one."

I paused, glanced at Hamilcar, then asked the recorder, "Can I name a coclaimant other than Clemens or Higbie?"

"Sure."

"Very well." I raised my voice so it was certain to be heard in the boulders above the ravine. "I would like to name a dear comrade of my student days—Hamilcar Ames Cavanaugh—as a co-owner of this vein!"

A laugh escaped him in a snort, but then he sobered as I held the book open to him.

"Here, Hamilcar, you do the honors first."

Forced to switch the revolver to his left hand, he scribbled his signature, then shoved the book back toward me. *I'm warning you!* his eyes shouted.

"Now I will sign," I said ceremoniously, quivering out *Belmont Rettie*. "And I will include a few other trusted acquaintances as coclaimants." Instead, I wrote:

COPPERHEADS TO KILL GOV. NYE HERE TONIGHT! MUSTER ALL ARMS TO STOP THEM! A UNIONIST.

Relieved that the irksome affair was at last resolved, the recorder snapped shut the oversized ledger and tucked it under his arm in order to accept a bottle from a friend. I could not catch the officer's eye before Hamilcar was prodding me with his Pettingill toward the headframe again.

Desperation suggested every sort of improbability to me. Hamilcar had mentioned the existence of a spy in the copperhead camp. Perfidy was to be expected in a fraternal war such as this, but the point was—had Cavanaugh been hinting that he himself was the double agent? It did not seem likely. In fact, it was absurd, and along with feigning an epileptic fit, I tossed the idea on a mounting pile of junked hopes.

At last, revealed through the trees by the flickerings of its lanterns, Governor Nye's Concord came clattering down the western ridge into town. The driver's "Whoa!" drifted thinly to us on the breeze. The coach remained stationary for several seconds while he looked our way. Then the jehu leaned over and consulted with someone inside the Concord. He shrugged, then took the slack out of his driving lines with his left hand and stung the rump of his right lead horse with his whip. As Hamilcar had predicted, and now celebrated with a chuckle, the governor could not resist investigating the torchlit hullabaloo up at the Wide West.

Hamilcar jabbed me hard, almost viciously, in the small of the back with his Pettingill.

"What the—"

"Incentive," he whispered, "to do exactly as you've been told."

"Damn you." I tried to rub the ache away. "I'll need some latitude to convince Nye of my sincerity. I can't just walk up to him like a robot—"

"A what?"

"It doesn't matter," I sighed. "Do you want every Unionist here so suspicious he'll pull out his revolver?"

"It is only my revolver that you must worry about."

"You've got to trust me." I lifted the flap of my coat pocket. "If not, take my gun right now."

"That won't be necessary."

"Good," I lied, for his answer had only confirmed that I was operating under a death sentence. "So let's go greet the governor."

"I will decline that honor." He seized my arm again. "But you may be assured that I am *behind* you in every regard, old sport."

Those fifty paces to where the Concord had come to a creaking rest seemed like a trek across the continent. Not only did I have to throw together some sort of plan, but I had to *believe* in that plan to make it work. Panicky urges to run came close to winning me over—but I fought them down, knowing full well that the Knights of the Golden Circle had me trammeled. Every one of them knew me by sight. I could recognize only a handful of them.

First to step down from the coach was Orion Clemens. Darkly bearded, he nevertheless had his younger brother's aquiline stare. "Secretary Clemens!" I glommed onto his hand before he knew what had hit him. "What a joy to see you again!"

He smiled distantly—trying to place me, no doubt.

James Nye then alighted from the Concord and drummed his fingers on his belly as he tried to make heads or tails of why Aurora's entire voting population was congregated on a hillside under a midnight moon. "Welcome, Your Honor!"

Grinning, he touched the ivory head of his cane to his top hat. "What excitement is keen enough to keep Esmeralda up halfway to dawn?!"

"The Wide West is relocated, sir—to me."

"I see. And you . . . forgive me, I've enjoyed your company a dozen times—"

"Belmont Rettie, Your Honor."

"Yes, of course. Congratulations on your good fortune, Mr. Rettie."

Orion Clemens's face dropped. He had been grubstaking his brother's mining ventures for nearly a year; and undoubtedly, Sam had written to him about the windfall of the blind lead. Now that it was lost to me, he could scarcely speak, so heavy was his disappointment.

Then I felt the muzzle of Hamilcar's revolver as keenly as if it were still being ground into the small of my back. I glanced over my shoulder—and saw that Cavanaugh's eyes were vociferous, hateful. "Your Honor," I turned back to Nye, "my wife waits just outside the confusion. She would be thrilled to see you again. And, no doubt, she'd like to use this occasion to thank you for championing the cause that led to her Negro servant's freedom."

"Indeed? Yes, well, Mr. Rettie, I'd like to visit with all my constituents here. Even those who still believe that the Esmeralda District lies in California!" A few boos were mixed among the laughter. "But I received a message that my brother lies ill somewhere in these environs."

"Do you speak of Captain John, sir?" I asked, my nervousness apparently being mistaken for mournfulness.

Nye steeled himself with a deep breath for bad news. "I do."

"Why, he's at Nine-Mile Ranch—doing nicely."

"What?"

"Oh, he's as weak as a kitten. But Sam Clemens, who nursed him, says he's feeling all kinds of better after his bout with spasmodic rheumatism."

"Glorious tidings!" Nye exulted.

"Sam's here in town?" Orion asked grimly.

"Uh, yes—just arrived back tonight. So, Governor, will you cheer my wife for a moment?"

"Gladly, Mr. Rettie! Lead the way!"

"Mr. Clemens!" A man in a gray duster had stepped out of the crowd. Judge Terry's man, making his move to separate the governor from his secretary. "Can I bend your ear for a spell? It concerns a business proposition I'm sure'll interest you, sir."

"Oh, gentlemen!" I grasped both Nye and Clemens by the elbows and briskly swung them around. "Before we do a thing, you must examine for yourselves the wondrous blind lead uncovered below!"

Hamilcar charged forward a stride, hesitated, then sifted back into the shadows of the headframe. His eyes flared at me, cougarlike, as I led the governor and his secretary toward the shaft.

"Yes," Nye said, "I'd like very much to see an ore body that keeps an entire town out of bed!"

"Take my candle, sir," one of my crew offered.

At my bidding for them to descend first, Nye and Clemens clambered inside the big bucket and stood waiting—looking for all the world like two missionaries about to be boiled by cannibals. This picture might have cajoled me into laughter had I not been close to vomiting from the expectation that at any instant now, Hamilcar would dart out from the far side of the headframe and shoot me right between the eyes. I only hoped that he would be dogged by uncertainty for a few seconds more.

"Men aboard! Lower away!" I ordered the miner standing closest to the windlass.

With a lurch that made both men grasp for the hawser, the bucket began inching down into the darkness. I was watching their slow progress when Hamilcar stormed to my side, his face contorted as he alternated glaring at me and his vanishing prey. Obviously he was torn between blasting either me or the governor on the spot, and while he vacillated, I sneaked my own revolver out of my pocket and held it behind my back. Meanwhile I had tucked my right hand in my coat front, Bonaparte-style; I didn't think Hamilcar knew I was a southpaw.

Finally I saw it flash across his eyes like a meteor: He had come to a decision. But he had just started to swing his barrel in my direction when he felt something press into the soft tissues of his belly.

He startled, then slowly looked down at my Navy Colt. "What in the name of hell are you doing?!"

"Trying to save you, you stupid son of a bitch. Drop it."

"A company of militia surrounds you! This is lunacy—"

I started to thumb-cock my hammer.

Immediately there followed a thud as his revolver struck the ground. I pocketed both his weapon and mine, then checked below: The bucket had stopped, and the governor's candle could be seen bobbing into the side tunnel.

Giving Hamilcar no time in which to think, I dived for the axe he had shunted aside earlier. My first blow glanced off the hawser as if it were made of steel, not hemp. Two more swings started a few of the braids fraying, but my visions of sundering the stout rope with one thwack were quickly frustrated. Hamilcar began shifting his weight as if readying himself for a lunge. But when I hefted the axe in his direction, he showed me his palms and murmured, "Easy, old sport."

I delivered one more attack on the rope and then shielded my eyes with my forearm as the individual cords began pirouetting one by one into a burl of fuzz. The hawser finally gave with a crack, and the empty bucket plummeted away, hitting bottom with a horrendous clang. I threw the axe down the shaft after it.

At that moment a shot whistled overhead. And then another before the first had echoed to silence.

"See!" Hamilcar hissed. "You bloody fool!"

"Wait! Citizens!" Straightening up again, I waved my arms toward that part of the crowd from which the reports had come. I was gambling that they had been fired by Unionists who believed I was trying to harm Governor Nye and his secretary instead of isolating them from copperhead violence. "Friends of the Republic—listen!" No more bullets zinged past, so I decided to go on: "There are traitors and cutthroats among you who mean to assassinate Governor Nye! I am not one of them! That's why I just lowered him and Mr. Clemens to safety! Believe me—I beg you!"

The townies began looking askance at one another. Every man present had drawn either a handgun or a knife, but the battle lines were so muddled, no one could launch the hostilities without endangering his friends. I prayed that this confusion would keep long enough for me to get off the most important lie of my life.

"These same secesh might have already murdered the governor in Virginia City had not my noble friend here . . ." I snaked my arm around his shoulders before he could find the presence of mind to shake off my embrace. "Hamilcar Ames Cavanaugh— whose blood flows federal blue—alerted Fort Churchill to the machinations of these scabrous vermin!"

"Bully for Cavanaugh!" someone shouted.

"Turncoat!" a copperhead screamed from another quarter of the gathering melee.

"What Chiv trash just said that?!"

"You looking for me, Billie?! Well, here I is!"

Men began dropping their torches to the ground, and in seconds only scurrying boots could be seen in their glow.

"And tonight, loyal brothers," I hurriedly went on, because so many weapons were being cocked it sounded like crickets, "the governor might have fallen victim to a second insidious plot had not this true son of the Republic helped me organize an answer to their treachery!"

A figure in a panama hat was plowing through the throng, moving inexorably toward Hamilcar and me, shoving men aside as he came. "Cavanaugh!" he cried, his voice a screech.

When Judge Terry had thrashed completely through the ring of bodies, he halted, his goateed face underlit by the guttering torches, the cords in his neck strained to the point of snapping. *My God*, I thought as I inched away from Hamilcar's side, slipping my hand inside my coat pocket, *eyes that gone with rage belong only in hell*.

Terry was clutching his bowie knife in his right fist, working the flat of the blade with his thumb, and a derringer in his left. He glanced at me—but only fleetingly before his glassy eyes fixed on Hamilcar. "You Judas!" the words boiled out of him. "You unholy Judas!"

For the first time I saw Hamilcar Cavanaugh stripped of his composure, his face glistening with the most pungent kind of sweat. I might have enjoyed his discomfiture—had not I still been dangerously close to Judge Terry's line of fire.

"David," he pled, "don't you see what Rettie's doing?!"

"I see only the ghosts of my two beloved brothers . . ." Terry was almost whispering now. ". . . stiff and cold from Yankee shot. They beckon from the grave for me to avenge them."

Of course, I had no intention of letting this psychopath kill my ex-wife's great-great-great-grandfather, although after Hamilcar had so blithely escorted me to the brink of my own death, could I be blamed now if I wanted to see him squirm a little?

However, Judge Terry then aligned the derringer with his crazed dominant eye, drawing a bead on the fountainhead of the Beauchamp-Cavanaughs, and I brought one of the revolvers out of my pocket, thinking it was Hamilcar's, tossing it between his boots.

In the same split second Hamilcar seized it, I realized my mistake: I had thrown him my Navy Colt, which unlike his Pettingill, required thumb-cocking before it could be fired. Clenching his teeth, he was pulling on the obstinate trigger with both forefingers when a white flash of almost laser brilliance caught the onlookers across the cheekbones, stroboscopically freezing their startled expressions. There followed a second explosion, one from my Navy Colt, but Hamilcar had accounted for the difference in the revolvers ages too late, and he was down on one knee, grasping his shoulder with red-stained fingers, sobbing. "The bastard shot me!"

Judge Terry was limping up the ravine—toward Musetta and Madame Richelieu.

Guns were booming on all sides of me. "Musetta!" I cried, flinching at yet another nearby report. "Run!"

She couldn't hear me over the din.

I suppose I hesitated, briefly. For one thing, at that instant a double line of copperhead horsemen, loosing rebel yells, charged out of the darkness and up a hillside as bold as thunder. But they found nobody handy up there to kill, so they wheeled and came

down with far less trim to their ranks. I had just started to descend
the embankment toward Musetta, ditching the Confederate notes
and copper star as I ran pell-mell over broken rock, stumbling at
every step, when one of these returning cavalrymen forced me to
perform a mélange of humiliating gyrations by whooshing his
saber at me most smartly. I was on the verge of shooting him when
he decided I was small potatoes after all—and rode away to harry
someone with a better sense of humor.

The judge was just hobbling up to the women when I called out,
"Hold it right there, David Terry! Throw down your weapons and
surrender!"

I felt quite bold and manly: His derringer was empty and I had
not seen him reload. My revolver, which I now aimed at Terry's
solar plexus, was very much loaded. It was one of those situations
for which I wished I had composed a speech, prior.

"Surrender?" he asked, his voice now cloyed again with
civility. Madame was tearing a strip off of her shawl to stem the
flow of blood darkening his trouser leg. "On what terms, Mr.
Rettie?"

"None, sir. It must be unconditional."

"Oh, I always insist on terms. In that case—"

His derringer arced up into my face, which I thought to be a
pathetic way of suicide for the judge until, in a horrifying instant,
I saw the *twin* holes in the snout of the squat little gun.

From force of habit I was fumbling to thumb-cock my weapon
when it came to me with the hollowest kind of feeling that I was
clutching Hamilcar's Pettingill—and there was no hammer to be
pulled back. I knew then that my shot would be tardy. Yet during
that instant of consternation in which I began to squeeze the
trigger, Musetta suddenly filled my sight picture, and immediately, I eased off the pressure. She had thrown herself across Terry's
arm, forcing it downward. His shot richocheted harmlessly off the
stony ground.

He hurled her aside, then turned the derringer around in his
hand and wound up a pitch—after that, a gray drizzle formed
inside my head.

When I could see again, I was staring up into a pall of gun
smoke that had turned the moon the color of molasses. Musetta
was weeping over me, touching my forehead precisely where it
throbbed the worse. I struggled up onto my elbow and groped for
the revolver, which was laying in the brush beside me. In my
befuddlement I imagined that Judge Terry's bowie knife had

skidded across my throat, for there was blood all over my neck and shoulders. I was on the point of fainting when I realized that the flow was from the goose egg his derringer had raised on my brow.

Meanwhile, Madame Richelieu was helping Judge Terry make his escape up the slope toward a tableau of horses waiting prickeared on the crest. "Musetta!" she bawled over her shoulder. "Come, *vite*!"

Musetta started to obey, but I grabbed her by the wrist.

"No way."

The hottest fighting, which had been confined to the area around the shaft, now surged toward us, then over us to the drumming of hooves and boots. I threw her down and rolled on top of her.

"Howard," she said, aggrieved, "you are lying on me!"

"You're one to complain."

She began squirming under my weight as her eyes beseeched the Creole woman, who was now helping to lift the judge into his saddle. "Madame! Wait!"

"Let her go, Musetta."

She scratched at my hold on her. "But who else do I have?!"

25

I HELPED MYSELF to another glass of champagne. Pouring was no easy trick, given the jiggling of the Concord coach, and I used my silk handkerchief to wipe any drops of spill off the royal-blue cushions and the rosewood veneered door. The Puget Sound oysters I did not quite trust, even though I had been assured by the grocer that they had been packed in ice ever since leaving Washington. Nevertheless, food poisoning was as rampant a killer as cholera in Washoe, so I parted the brocaded curtains and flung the half shells out into the dusty sage: The coyotes would eat in style tonight. With my head already out the window, I could not resist the satisfaction of one more look at the bright brass letters tacked to the panel running the length of the coach: WIDE WEST CONSOLIDATED; and in small capitals beneath them: A RETTIE-CAVANAUGH COMPANY.

One of the four armed guards topside noticed me leaning outside. He hollered above the pounding of the hooves of the matched white horses, "Is everything all right, Colonel Rettie?"

"Quite." And indeed it was, for the most part. "Just splendid, thank you."

It was now the last week in August, hot but not stifling, owing to the dryness of the desert heat. A month had elapsed since the

Battle of Esmeralda. Hamilcar and I had been given postdated honorary colonelcies in the Esmeralda Rangers as part of Governor Nye's scheme to procure Medals of Honor for us. But we didn't receive these newly authorized decorations, largely because no one was killed during the engagement. In fact, including Judge Terry and Hamilcar, only six combatants had been wounded, none grievously. So the battle was deemed to have been of insufficient gravity, especially when held up against the recent debacle at Shiloh, where thousands had lain dead on a carpet of peach blossoms.

Miffed by this show of Atlantic chauvinism, Nye had sent the Esmeralda Mining District book of records to his old mentor, Secretary of State William Seward, who then took it with him to a cabinet meeting to show to the president. Lincoln's eyes, according to the eastern newspapers, had grown damp behind his bifocals as he read:

COPPERHEADS TO KILL GOV. NYE HERE TONIGHT! MUSTER ALL ARMS TO STOP THEM! A UNIONIST.

In a gushy epistle of patriotism that had just arrived, John Greenleaf Whittier begged me to lend him the words *Muster All Arms* for the title of one poem of many he was putting together about the war. I planned to give my consent, of course, and would save Whittier's letter for Associate Professor Treacher.

Yet all in all, this little firefight had ended the War Between the States in Nevada. Brought back to Aurora at a gallop by the eruption of gunfire that had echoed for miles, the Esmeralda Rangers had rounded up more than thirty secessionists too stupid to flee, and carted them off in irons to Fort Churchill, where the cavalry persuaded them to jog around the parade ground carrying heavy sacks of sand on their backs until each and every Knight of the Golden Circle saw the benefits to his health in taking the oath of allegiance to the United States of America.

Judge Terry and many of his followers, it was rumored, had escaped to the Confederacy through Mexico. Madame Richelieu, the same sources claimed, had gone as far as Tucson with him. The region was temporarily in the control of a pro-Southern faction, and business was good along the Old Butterfield Road when the Apaches weren't chasing the stages, so she had decided to set up shop in Arizona.

No poultice is as soothing as money, and so it was that Hamilcar

and I made our own unfriendly peace. Before he had departed for
Virginia City to handle some important company business for me
there, we had enjoyed a little tête-à-tête in my fine new brick
house on Roman Street.

"I saved your honor, your freedom—and your life," I opened
the sullen proceedings, swirling the brandy in my snifter.

The word came up his throat like a bubble of bile: *"Why?"*

"My reasons will remain my own. You must agree never to ask
again."

He nodded miserably, then winced from some discomfort his
shoulder suddenly gave him.

"And as long as we are associated, you must also agree never to
try to bully me. You must never lie to me. You must never touch
my person except to shake my hand—if we occasion to meet in
public. Otherwise, you may omit the amenities—especially
referring to me as *old sport.*"

He tried to smile sardonically, but failed. "And if you believe
me guilty of one of these trespasses, Mr. Rettie?"

"I'll sing a very different aria to the federal authorities than the
one I first sang to them, Mr. Cavanaugh."

Yet within the hour he had found his claws again, and bared
them—not at me, he knew better than that—but against the former
owners of the Wide West, who I had invited up to the house for a
parley.

Cunningly, Hamilcar batted them this way and that with his
encyclopedic knowledge of mining law, and ultimately brought
them into the fold—with their fixed capital and experienced
labor—as *very* junior partners within the proposed consolidation.
The former superintendent was unable to extricate his good sense
from his resentment, and it was for his replacement that Hamilcar
would travel to Virginia City. With the right offer, we hoped, Mr.
Cropley could be induced to leave the Madonna Consolidated.

At this point seven of us owned so many "feet" of the claim
proportionate to our importance in the firm (I was president and
Hamilcar first vice-president). But this system of ownership
seemed antiquated: After all, linear feet in a vein are finite, while
shares of a public issue can be an infinite source of assessments—
fees the corporate board can charge the shareholders for im-
provements or expansion. And so within three weeks of its first
offering, the stock of Wide West Consolidated, according to the
copy of *The San Francisco News Letter and Pacific Mining
Journal* I was now trying to steady in front of my eyes, was at an

Icarian high, having doubled, trebled, and quadrupled in value. This proved what I had believed since my college days: To accrue an immense fortune, a hardworking, clean-living fellow needs only a medium-sized fortune to begin with. By the sunlit ides of August I owned a million dollars worth of stock in the Wide West alone—and had begun diversifying into other concerns all over the Far West. Shooting fish in a barrel. I almost felt guilty. Almost.

Any success I enjoyed concerning a certain young Swedish lady was not so clear-cut.

Madame Richelieu's flight from Aurora had thrown Musetta into an obdurate depression. She sat on the stoop of a derelict crib like an abandoned kitten for one full day, and the only reason she didn't chase after madame and Judge Terry, I'm sure, was the knowledge that the twosome had nearly implicated her in the murder of the governor—something that didn't hold well with her Lutheran upbringing. Secretly, she possessed a finely honed set of morals; it was her misfortune that life seldom let her use them. The result was that she found herself in a netherworld, and when I attempted to rescue her from it by inviting her to share my house with me, she rewarded me by taking to my camelback sofa for three days, where she wept continuously and refused anything but weak tea from my middle-aged Paiute housewoman.

"What is it?!" I finally exploded.

"You are going to leave. Then I will have no one."

I had no idea how she had sensed this, but I quibbled: "Leave? Where the hell would I go?"

"Wherever you came from, Howard."

"I don't think I could part from you—even if I wanted to."

"Do you want to?"

"Sometimes . . . but never for long."

After this her mood brightened considerably. She started eating. She took long walks in the sharp coolness of the evenings. We even began making love again. But then, after one frenzied bout in the seven-foot bed I had ordered from San Francisco, she clung to me and sobbed, "Do not leave me, Howard! Please, do not go!"

I made no reply, and for this I was sentenced to a week of silence, which I wiled away by riding around Aurora on my Appaloosa mare, admiring the stacks of fresh lumber that were rapidly being assembled into an impressive hoist house over the Wide West shaft.

"Ah, girl," I sighed into one of the horse's downcast ears,

"sixty-six days and we've got to leave all this forever. And even if I intended to make another trip like this, well, no offense, you'd be out of style. . . ." Yes, by 1924, the next Grand Tour opportunity after 1901—Rodrigo had let slip, America would move on rubber tires and not horseshoes—but that is when I had intended to show up out of the tachyonic blue, posing as my own great-grandfather, armed with the patrimonially-incriminating letter Bret Harte had written to Ina Coolbrith. Then, had everything gone according to plan, I would have commandeered my just portion of the family fortune (aggrandized, no doubt, by Bret Harte's runaway success with *Huckleberry Finn*) and invested it in fifteen companies that would pay dividends to their shareholders without interruption for more than a century, plus one fledgling growth stock called International Business Machines—before skipping back to my own time.

But nothing had gone according to plan: Bret Harte had cremated *Huck Finn*, and Samuel Clemens had not become an owner of the Wide West. Only Hamilcar seemed to have benefited from my machinations: Buoyed by Napoleon Beauchamp's hearty consent, Eleanor Louise had at last agreed to marry the hero of the Battle of Esmeralda.

Clemens was now so disgusted with himself in particular and the silver madness in general, he ignored my repeated invitations to discuss "mutually beneficial concerns over dinner." Inexorably, he was headed toward a career in writing; and I began to see that there was nothing I could do to stop him from ruining his future. But then my own problems took precedence.

I owned a fortune I could never haul back into the future with me. Of course, some twentieth century firms had been going concerns in 1862—the Bank of Boston, for example, had been extant since 1784. But if I now invested in like stocks, how could I lay claim to the portfolio a century and a quarter later? That is why I had intended to rely on my Harte lineage in the other scheme—but to span a much shorter period of time. One clerical error, one legal judgment over all those years, could deprive me of my due.

I had considered a more direct method: stashing coin or bullion in the surrounding hills; but was doubtful of ever finding this priceless cache after more than a century of intensive mining, earthquakes, flash floods, and avalanches (the mauve-colored monolith Rodrigo had claimed would last for aeons was "located" along with half of Esmeralda by my own company as part of a vigorous expansion, and I barely had time to recover my buried magnetometer before the spire was blasted to smithereens). Besides, like the skulking Mr. Whiteman, I was now believed to be a diviner of bonanzas—and was watched from the brush most everywhere I went.

I might have decided on cramming my saddlebags with mint condition double eagles—except that Rodrigo had been so worried about the effects of weight on a portage around the uncharted cataracts of time, he had insisted that I weigh my horse and myself before attempting to depart. And I was not about to pack five stone in gold coin up and down that road outside Carson City for however long it took me to stumble back into the present tense: Belmont Rettie was now the district's juiciest target for robbery.

I strolled home from the Bank Exchange Saloon one night to find Musetta gone, her Japanese fan spread neatly across my pillow. I spent a frantic hour searching the town and then three more riding the darkened roads before it came to me with a sad sense of relief that this was for the best. In those moments, with my mare's hooves scuffling along the luminescent gravel, I gave up Musetta.

Yet when I reached home at four, I found her curled up like a small child in my bed, face patinaed with dust, so exhausted she didn't stir when I slid in beside her. I didn't ask her why she had fled, or even why she had returned. All that mattered, I realized, was that it had been ill-advised not to let her follow Madame Richelieu the night of the battle—and that I had to find a way to end this unhappy arrangement before I departed for Carson City and terminated my Grand Tour. Still, I could not find the words to tell her to leave, they died on my tongue each time I tried to say them.

An answer came in the form of a letter from Miss Beauchamp. Her bona fide handwriting—not Hamilcar's forgery—was girlish, almost innocent-looking:

Dearest Mister Rettie,

It would be so wonderful to thank you in person for saving my Hamilcar from those horrid insurrectionists. Please call on me when you can, although my aunt and uncle are in California until September . . .

Probably shopping for a few small counties, I mused.

. . . and Hamilcar has gone with them to see a specialist in San Francisco for the agony his shoulder is still giving him.

With an eternal gratitude,
Eleanor Louise

From any other Victorian young lady, I would have taken the hint to make my visit when her family and fiancé had returned. But from Eleanor Louise this was a green light to come to Virginia City forthwith—before these nuisances might show up and spoil any illicit fun we were rolling around in.

I had been standing in my vestibule as I read this. In the parlor at the end of the hallway Musetta could be seen staring right through a book of librettos. *Yes, this is the only way; we care too much for each other to end it on friendly terms.* I loudly crumpled up Eleanor Louise's letter and deposited it in the bowl of the calling card stand—before hurrying outside to order the company Concord readied for the trip to the Comstock.

When I returned a half hour later to begin packing, the letter was no longer there; Musetta had withdrawn to the small room the builder had intended as a nursery. The door was locked. After testing the silver-plated knob, I had started to knock—but then stayed my hand.

"Colonel Rettie!" One of my guards startled me out of reliving this morning's bleak parting. "Man afoot on the road!"

This anomaly of a human being sans horse twenty miles outside Virginia City might well signal a robbery. Limned in the late afternoon shadow of the coach flittering along the ground, my guards could be seen hoisting their shotguns and rifles as they steeled themselves for ambush. The jehu used his blacksnake to goad the team out of a trot into a livelier two-beat gait that jerked the coach sharply. Knowing all too well that a mining company coach was the choicest game to highwaymen, I dipped into my pocket for my Navy Colt.

The revolver was not there.

As the driver closed distance on the pedestrian, I ran my fingers along the cracks between the velvet cushions and kicked aside the small Persian carpet covering the floorboards. Muttering to myself, I sat back. I no longer carried a derringer, because a man of means did not go around gut-shooting his detractors with a "lady's gun": He hired others to do this kind of work for him.

But as the slope-shouldered figure in slouch hat flashed past my window, I had to scoff at the alarm into which my hirelings had thrown me. The man afoot was armed with nothing more threatening than a bedroll. I pounded the ceiling with the crook of my cane. "Driver, stop! I know this pilgrim!"

"Whoa!"

I stepped outside and waited for Samuel Clemens to amble up.

He had to dig deep into his reserves of good humor to smile. "Good afternoon, Mr. Rettie—or forgive me, it's *colonel* now, isn't it?"

"It's Howard, Sam. May I offer you a ride?" When he hesitated, I added, "There's iced champagne inside."

"I don't suppose you have oysters as well."

"I did, but they went bad on me."

He laughed with the helplessness of exhaustion, then unslung and beat the powdered alkali out of his bedroll before tossing it to a guard. He eyed my heavily armed retinue uneasily, then entered the lavish coach as if embarrassed that his clothes might soil the upholstery. But, jocularly, I pushed him down into the seat opposite me and poured him a glass.

Tentatively at first, he sampled the champagne, then drank thirstily on the realization that this was not a sun-induced dream after all. Giving him a refill even before the coach had lurched forward again, I asked, "You have business on the Comstock?"— although I already knew what his answer would be.

"Indeed. A Mr. Barstow, managing editor of *The Territorial Enterprise*, has—by the grace of cheek—offered me a reporting position with that paradigm of sagebrush literature . . ." He held out his glass again. ". . . at the breathtaking sum of—hold onto your hat now—twenty-five dollars a week or ten cents a squib. My choice."

"I'm sure you'll turn the opportunity to great advantage."

"Perhaps." Then, for an uncomfortably long moment, he held his natural loquaciousness behind tightened lips. But finally the champagne began to work on him: "It will forever serve my mystification why you tried to help my partner and me hang on to the Wide West. And *that*, Mr. Rettie, is precisely what you were doing when thwarted by my guileless friend."

"Well, Sam, my explanation would impose on your good

nature the burden of keeping a confidence. . . ." I waited until he gave me a slight nod. "I've done many things in my time to earn my bread. But there was only one of these occupations that earned my undying affection. It's gone forever now—the war killed it. But whenever I meet someone from that special brotherhood, I see to it he's piloted clear of life's shoals. I like to let him know, if I can, that he's got at least *mark twain* under his keel. I expect that he'd do the same for me—if the need ever arose."

At this mention of two fathoms—safe water, in river jargon—Clemens's eyes sparkled. Then he chuckled. "Apostate from Salt Lake, purveyor of Union espionage, Mississippi pilot—will I or anyone else ever know the absolute truth about you, Mr. Rettie?"

I toasted him with my glass. "There can be no absolute truth in a universe in which the context keeps shifting."

"Is that a Mormon tenet?"

"No, merely the observation of a sojourner."

"You speak then of the itinerancy of this life, I take it."

I shrugged and turned the talk away from metaphysics: "What do you see ahead for yourself, Sam?"

"Well, having failed at everything else, I intend at this point to become a man of letters." His grin was self-effacing.

"Yes, that's probably for the best." Then, after half a magnum of champagne, it slipped out of me: "You caught the spirit and vernacular of these times better than any of your contemporaries."

"I appreciate the compliment—but you speak about my career as if it's already concluded, not in its halting first steps!"

"I'm sorry—it's an idiosyncrasy of mine to jumble my tenses."

"And you, Mr. Rettie, what mountains to conquer from here? A mansion on Nob Hill? A trip around the world? High political office?" He couldn't completely strain the bitterness out of his voice.

"Like I said, it's just a sojourn, Sam. And in the end, each of us has to walk away from it all. I don't really know what a man can take with him. Love maybe. I don't know."

The moment was rescued from excessive solemnity when we both smirked. From that moment on we enjoyed a freer conversation that spirited us all the way to the divide that separates the town of Gold Hill from Virginia City. There, for the first time in miles, he took stock of his surroundings and then begged me to halt as frantically as if he had sniffed smoke inside the coach. He clambered out and waved impatiently for his bedroll to be thrown down to him.

"Sam—what is it?"

The careless drawl returned with a simper: "If I am to become a man of letters, I have appearances to begin thinking about. And it will read much better that I trudged alone through each of the one hundred thirty wilderness miles from Aurora to my new career—and not that I was delivered to the ghat of *The Territorial Enterprise* as pampered and well-watered as a lapdog! Farewell, Mr. Rettie—I do indeed hope we'll meet some other time."

"Always a distinct possibility, Mr. Clemens."

26

ELEANOR LOUISE KEPT me waiting twenty-four hours after my arrival in Virginia City.

If she was teasing me with this delay, I chose not to mind. I accepted her dilatory behavior as an appetizer. One had to appreciate the sensibilities of such a connoisseur of the lascivious; and if she didn't opt to take a man by complete surprise—as she had at our first meeting—she could probably be counted on to nurture an exquisite anticipation right up to the instant of bursting.

I struck up a conversation with an affable enough fellow in the Bucket of Blood Saloon, who happened to be a member in good standing in Virginia Engine Company Number One, which was hosting a stag party that night to celebrate its recent triumph in the competitions of the Annual Firemen's Muster. All of the Comstock volunteer fire companies were stoutly pro-Union, and my name jogged the second assistant hose chief's memory, who rose from his prairie chicken and cranberry sauce to announce that here, sitting modestly among them, was "the Leonidas of the Battle of Esmeralda!" Quite a cheer arose, the red shirt and monogrammed dickey of the company were thrust upon me in honorary membership, and I might have had the occasion to proffer a few aw-shucks to the gathering had not the constable

278

rushed in at that moment to shout, "Hurry, boys! D Street's afire!" That this was the sporting row, and their brave efforts would be witnessed by bevies of half-naked strumpets, made their preparations all the more feverish.

Yet as it turned out, only an abandoned stable was engulfed. The consensus was that the structure could not be saved, so a small cannon was rolled out, and to a chorus of hurrahs, the charred timbers were leveled with a blast of grapeshot that also blew Saint Paul out of a stained glass window in Saint Mary's in the Mountains two hundred yards down the hill. At most of the firemen were Irish, a hat was quickly passed to benefit the restoration. I wrote out a draft for an amount sufficient to re-lead all the church glazing in Nevada, which was considered to be the dandiest bit of charity anyone could recall. But by then the claret had worn off and I didn't feel like returning to the gala and being lionized the rest of the night.

So I slipped away from my newfound friends and began wandering up and down Virginia's steep avenues until I reached the town's outskirts. The moon crested the mountains in the east and lit up the ridge that held the Comstock's dead in its stony arms. The marble monuments glistened bone white as I tread slowly among them. *My God*, I suddenly thought, *she's already lost to me—gone to Tucson and Madame Richelieu's, perhaps, gone to her grave certainly in the instant I depart from this Grand Tour.* I slumped down onto the cold lid of a crypt. Then, after the grimmest possible hour or so, punctuated only by the distant plaints of coyotes, I chuckled to myself, and these anxious feelings subsided: *Howard, the way to forget one woman is to concentrate on another. . . .*

And so, with the utmost resolution, I fixated on Eleanor Louise and her voracious charms until the appointed hour the next day.

The Beauchamps' Chinese butler left me to rock from foot to foot atop a huge parquetry of the Virgin in the foyer. Part of my restiveness arose, no doubt, from the expectation of seeing at any moment Eleanor Louise float down the winding staircase in all her toothsome glory. But there was another reason as well: I was sure that someone had me followed through the twilight from the International Hotel—so positive that I had ducked into a general store to lay down forty dollars gold for a Colt patent revolver and a box of cartridges. My coat pocket reassuringly weighted down once again, I had hurried on toward A Street.

At last Eleanor Louise made her entrance, the brooch scintillant at her throat—but nothing compared to the flashing of her eyes. I didn't have to tell her how gorgeous she was: My light-headed silence did it for me.

"Good evening, Mr. Rettie."

"Good evening, Miss Beauchamp." I kissed her hand.

"How nice to see you again. I've made arrangements with our new superintendent for us to visit the Madonna Consolidated—and shame on you and Hamilcar for stealing Mr. Cropley from us. Not that uncle is really angry. He says Mr. Cropley will still be in the family, so to speak. Now, we must go down in the cage before the day shift starts coming up—"

"Thank you, but no," I said firmly, having forseen this possibility. I had made up my mind not to venture down again into *La Derrotada*—whatever the cost. Once had been more than enough to tempt fate.

She blinked at me in surprise. "I don't understand. I was sure you'd like to go underground."

"Oh, I would. But my claustrophobia prohibits it."

"Is that like kleptomania?"

"Yes, only it's . . . more confining."

She sighed. "Oh, well—"

I pressed a kiss on her. When she didn't resist, I wrapped my arms around her back. She had just started to respond when, down a hallway, footfalls could be heard in approach. I started to back off, but she held me fast, and from that moment on it became a contest of nerves to see who would pull away from the other's mouth first. I conceded at the last possible second before discovery, and she laughed under her breath.

The butler stood in a doorframe, hands folded before him, looking like he had borrowed someone's death mask for the evening. "Missie like brougham hitch up, bring round front?"

"No, Lee, I've decided to entertain at home this evening."

He nodded impassively—I made a mental note never to play poker with this fellow, who also might well be the progenitor of my ex-wife's housemaid. If that was the case, I was a Johnny-come-lately as far as despising the Cavanaughs went.

"Missie like refreshment set out in the parlor?"

"Please, some amontillado would be nice. And then that will be all this evening, Lee. Come, Howard . . ." She led me by the hand to a settee in the parlor. "We wanted an English manservant ever so much. But as you must realize, no worthwhile European person comes to America wanting to be a servant. And as for Irish domestics, well, we've had our share of bad experiences with them, even though auntie begged the new priest, Father Manogue, to help keep them in line. Uncle says—what's the use of having a religion if it won't help you keep the servants in line? Do you think that blaspheming, Howard—''

At that instant the floor lurched slightly and then seemed to sag toward the far corner of the room. "Earthquake?" I asked.

"Oh no," she said, once again with vague contempt for my ignorance, "the ground's subsiding under our house—the Chollar Mine is right below. Hamilcar's going to get an injunction against them to stop digging until they come up with a better method of shoring their works. But there is no such method." She then lowered her voice to a conspiratorial whisper: "This will shut down the Chollar, and when the stock goes low enough—uncle and Hamilcar are going to buy it all up. He says the Chollar is worth fifty mansions. Isn't that frightfully clever?"

"Hamilcar *told* you this?"

"Well, not exactly."

"You mean you were eavesdropping?"

"I most certainly was not! Auntie and I were sitting in their company at the time." She took my hand off her knee. "Any fool realizes a woman can't be expected to understand such matters."

"But you *do* understand, Miss Beauchamp—completely."

Her lips trembled as she resisted the mischievous smile that finally broke free. "Oh, what fun are you? You know women as well as if you were one yourself!"

I proved that this was not entirely true by sliding my hand up her skirts, although the barriers of undergarments proved impenetrable. This was the moment in which Lee entered with the sherry; and as I hastened to compose myself, Eleanor Louise clenched her thighs around my forearm, delaying me long enough for the butler to glimpse what I'd been doing. But again—his was a flawless poker face, while mine was on fire.

"Thank you, Lee. You may retire for the evening now."

As he withdrew, she whined in my ear, punctuating her sentence with a sharp little thrust of her tongue: "Are you absolutely settled we shan't go to the Madonna Consolidated tonight?"

I wavered, but then wisely recalled some particulars of my last descent into the inferno. "Don't you have a dark closet in your room? I mean, isn't half the fun pretending?"

Her eyes brightened. "Oh, how novel! Is that a Mormon practice?"

"No, all of our closets are stuffed with spare children." I rose and reached for her hand.

Once we were upstairs, she immediately went to her nightstand oil lamp and turned it so low her bedchamber seemed infused with a warm, amber mist. But that wasn't good enough to suit her, for she then blew out the flame, and the only light left us was that from the corridor spilling in through the partially open door. She giggled softly.

Somewhere downstairs, the front entry perhaps, a latch clicked shut. I dismissed the sound as Lee doing some last-minute puttering before turning in.

A match sizzled to life, catching Eleanor Louise's tongue as it glided across her front teeth. She lit a candle and handed it to me. "You lead the way."

"Where?"

Her eyes shifted toward a three-quarter-sized door, which I swung back, revealing a long, walk-in closet so dense with clothes it muffled my voice as I asked, "Now, isn't this so much better than some dusty old mine?"

She shrugged as if to say that I wasn't completely forgiven for ruining her plans, but then she slipped past me and down the aisle between the twin banks of rich-looking garments. Slowly she turned and let her shawl slink down off her arm onto the floor. When I offered to help, she smiled but gestured for me to stay where I stood—and just enjoy the show. Thirty pounds of silk dress fell away. Then a woollen petticoat. A crinoline petticoat. A cage of watch-spring steel hoops—and I'd thought as a boy that a training bra was difficult. Even while on holiday in San Francisco, Musetta had worn nothing this elaborate. Perhaps a prostitute could not spare twenty minutes to undress for each customer; time, after all, is money, and in the final view, I had probably been nothing more than a john to her, my illusions not withstanding.

Eleanor Louise shed her whalebone corset and finally a set of linen drawers. She was entirely nude but for the brooch and a pair of high satin boots when she murmured, "*Now* I need your help. Untie them, please."

Setting the candle on a hatbox, I knelt in front of her and tried to steady my fingers in order to attack the laces which were looped around what seemed several hundred mother-of-pearl buttons. "I'm not sure I'm going to like you being married," I said.

"Whatever do you mean?" Her tone was guarded.

"Nothing, really."

"Surely you meant something, Howard. What does a Mormon woman do if she decides not to marry? Work as a domestic?"

"No."

"Barter herself to men—God forbid?"

"Of course not."

"Then what are you talking about? What manner of women do you know?"

"It was an idle remark—please forget I said it." The laces were becoming hopelessly tangled under my ministrations.

"I had a cousin," she said distantly. "She became a school teacher. It cost Sarah her reputation—poor dear."

Gasping, I gave up—her laces formed Gordian knots I would never solve in this lifetime.

Laughing at my frustration, she began massaging my shoulders.

"Keep your boots on," I hyperventilated. "I like boots. All right?"

But Eleanor Louise did not answer. Instead the fingers dug painfully into my neck. And when I glanced up I saw that her candlelit eyes were transfixed—but not on me. I knew then, without turning, that someone had come noiselessly into the room. And that could only be one person. I was too far gone with desire to be ashamed: "Tell Lee to get the hell out of here!"

Her eyes refused to move away from the intruder. She was shocked as she had never been before, and from this I realized that it was not the butler who had interrupted us.

I scuttled around on my knees just as Musetta wiped the tears off her face with her right hand, then joined it to her left to hoist my Navy Colt revolver to eye level.

Twice, she cocked and fired.

Eleanor Louise slumped down among her discarded clothes. She fell an eternity before I could rise, screaming for Musetta to throw down the gun.

27

LEAF BY GOLDEN leaf, the cottonwoods were dissolving on the breeze, dappling Carson City's main street with frail dollars that twinkled across the dust to form piles aweather the barns and fences. To the west, over the Sierra, an already boisterious thunderhead was building, although I waited in sunlight astride my mare for the weigh master to stop tapping the cylinder of iron back and forth across his beam scale with a needlessly moistened finger—and tell me the total poundage so I could depart from the nineteenth century.

"I never weighed just a man and a horse before," he said. "Mostly do cordage and ore. Sometimes hay, if the rancher wants to sell it that way—"

"What's the total?" I interrupted; the mare needed watering and a little rest before we started up the sawmill road.

"One thousand, three hundred and forty-niner, sir."

"Good." The horse would easily take on four pounds of water at the nearest trough. I tossed the weigh master a double eagle and ignored his thanks as I rode across a sandlot to Granville, who was dozing on the bench of the buckboard that had brought us from Aurora with my mare hitched to the tailgate. He had tied a kerchief around his face, bandit-style, to keep the blowing grit out of his nasal orifices. And although he voiced no complaint, I could sense his disappointment that I had left the Concord in an equipment shed on the Wide West property. The luxurious coach would only be like honey on wheels to the swarms of highwaymen (more and more failed miners were finding gainful employment in this manner), and I had no intention of losing the magnetometer to some oaf who would then travel the countryside claiming to cure arthritis with it.

Granville roused himself. "Where to now, Colonel?"

I checked the western sky. My experiences with Rodrigo assured me that the storm would have to brew another hour or so before I might slip across to the modern side of the Great Paradox. "Let's go get a drink."

"Yessir!"

It was strange to think that Rodrigo had *already* driven up the sawmill road in my now battered Mercedes (or some other car, if he had totaled it in the intervening months). Somewhere, up that canyon now disgorging dust in the first inklings of a storm, on the far side of a convoluted artery swelling at this very moment with an invisible flood of cosmic plasma, he was waiting for me in his lank and fretful away.

It would be good to see him, but devastating never to see Musetta again. I had been resisting a vague urge to cry since dawn.

Tying off my reins on a hitching post and retrieving the saddlebags, loaded with the magnetometer and a modest amount of gold coin (at least the Grand Tour wouldn't be a total loss), I led the way inside Ormsby House, through the sleepy midday quiet of the lobby and into the bar, where Granville and I took a table under the light of a window. I broke out the small oilskin packet of papers for the third time that day.

"Colonel, if you don't mind me saying . . ."

"Saying what?"

"Well, you look like the mirth's been sluiced out of you. Is there something I can do?"—another broad hint for me to explain why we had left Aurora just when Mr. Cropley had announced that the blind lead had widened into a Holland tunnel choked with silver and gold ore.

"Give me a minute, Granville, and I'll tell you why. . . ." Then, after our third round, I quietly said, "In a short while I'm going to get up from this table. You are not to follow me."

His eyes skittered back and forth in confusion. "Where you going?"

"I have promises to keep."

"What do I tell Mr. Cavanaugh?"

"Just that." But then I had an inspiration: "And that I might return tomorrow or in twenty years." It was untrue, impossible in light of the periodic tendency Rodrigo had determined; but Hamilcar's uncertainty that I might reappear at any moment to reclaim half of whatever he had accrued in my absence could canker into a nice little ulcer. "And this, my friend, is for you." I laid an envelope on the table in front of him.

He removed the stock certificate from within and stared speechless at it.

Smiling, I asked, "Well, what do you say?"

The portion of his face not concealed by the kerchief had reddened. "Don't know what to say."

"Come on, you slouch."

"Colonel Rettie, sir—I cain't read."

"Oh—well, it entitles you to five hundred shares of the Wide West."

He made a quick mental tabulation, then lifted the kerchief to wash down his astonishment. The value of the stock was around twenty-five thousand dollars. "God rot it, Colonel—I knew right off you'd be lucky for me!"

Then, while he fondled the document and assessed the new possibilities in his life, I unfolded a week-old copy of *The Territorial Enterprise*. The article had a Mark Twain byline, the first to appear—although Clemens was not supposed to adopt this nom de plume until the coming February:

Mademoiselle Musetta, a fille de joie well known to even those in Esmeralda who will not admit so, pleaded guilty yesterday to a yet unspecified act of "extreme incitement" in one of our fair city's better neighborhoods. Mademoiselle could not meet her fine of five thousand dollars, so she instead elected for nine months of incarceration. This hermitage, no doubt, will enable her to acquire the clarity of purpose one must marshal to raise an astronomical sum of money while cut off from any means of support, decorous or otherwise. . . .

It had cost me a small fortune to keep the incident at the Beauchamp mansion this ambiguous in the public apprehension:

two thousand to Barstow, the managing editor of the *Enterprise*, plus four to the judge. And it was not easy to buy a territorial magistrate. He received so many offers of bribes in a working day, he was obliged to retain a broker to discreetly handle the negotiations—and up the price if a counterbribe was received. Unfortunately, the effectiveness of my payoff was mitigated by good old nineteenth century morality—proudly flying all its double standards.

Musetta had done nothing more than punch two thirty-six caliber holes in the backside of the closet door—if one does not count the bruise Eleanor Louise sustained on her chin when she fainted dead away; and the loss of my septuagenarian years through anxiety in the everlasting seconds ended only by Lee surprising Musetta from behind and prying the revolver out of her frozen hands—before she could try out the next two shots on me.

The press and the judiciary duly appreciated the stain the publicizing of this affair would leave on one of the proudest fiefdoms on the Comstock—and Virginia, like most instant cities, was smarting under its coarse affability for want of respectability. Yet despite my bribe and my close friendship with Governor Nye, the judge maintained that the increasingly raucous skin trade had to be admonished, even if the warning came somewhat circuitously. He said to me over toddies in his chambers: "Just last week, Colonel Rettie, a hurdy carved up one of her patrons for pure sport. He was a Frenchman. But still. And now this? Gunplay in one of the finest homes on the hill? No, sir, an example must be made. And trust me that this can be done without embarrassing the Beauchamps. As to the harlot, she must serve time. The court declines your humanitarian offer to pay her fine in her stead. And on your honor as a gentleman, I rely on you not to circumvent my desires in this matter. If her fine is paid, I will know it was you who did so, Colonel—and I shall not be contented. The affair would have an entirely different complexion if she were a relation, or your wife . . . but now we stray into *reductio ad absurdum*."

Despite all my palavering about not wanting to see the Beauchamps shamed, my real concern in these dealings was for Musetta. I had no doubt that Eleanor Louise could handle Lee—and then Hamilcar upon his return from San Francisco. But Musetta, scorned by those who had taken nothing but pleasure from her, was now completely helpless, and she certainly couldn't afford to launder her reputation—not at these prices.

A burst of laughter made me look up: A dozen or so nabobs

were addressing the long bar in Ormsby House, making the
spitoons chime softly with wads of chew—the territorial legisla-
ture had adjourned for the day. An aged black man put away his
polishing cloth, and with a self-amused flourish, addressed the
piano. I expected tinny strains, but the tones that flowed around
me were mellow and warm. Once again I had been misled by
Hollywood: The hammer felts of this instrument had not the time
in which to dry out in the desert air, creating the hackneyed sound
that backgrounds all saloon scenes.

I took out the letter and opened it as carefully as if it were a
Dead Sea scroll:

Virginia City
16 October 1862

Dear Mister Rettie,

Not trusting her written English to convey her deepest
sentiments, Miss Musetta has begged me to take this dictation
for her and arrange it according to what I intuit to be the
essence of her expression. I must admit to you, my unsinkable
pilot, that in the course of the travesty that masqueraded as her
trial, I developed a great fondness for this woman, and were
her own affections not so firmly declared, I might try to leave
you bobbing in my wake of my considerable charm. But alas,

Sam Clemens

I drained my snifter before reading on:

Dearest Howard,

Forgive me. I meant the woman no harm. Nor would I ever
harm you, but I was crazy as only love can make a person. If I
could not have you, I wanted no one to have you. And I
wanted you more than anything, for I loved you ever since I
first saw you at madame's in Carson City. I still want you, but
have always known that such a thing is impossible . . .

It happened every time: I had to press my lips together. This
was heady stuff for a kid who had been orphaned well past the
prime adoptive age. Someone was actually confessing to want me!

You must not think that I am a bad person. I am just a foolish one. All these months I wanted to say that I loved you—but first needed the courage to tell you my real name. In love there can be no lies. And so now I tell you: I love you, Belmont Howard Rettie.

She had affixed her signature to the bottom of Clemens's loping scrawl:

Klara Asplund

As I returned my keepsakes to their pouch, the barkeep was lighting the chandeliers against a sudden gloaming—the storm had begun to thicken most of the sky visible through the window.

"Granville . . ." I offered my hand. "It's been dandy."

"God rot us—ain't it been?!" Then his eyes moistened, taking me my surprise, as displays of affection always seem to do. "Can I walk you outside, Colonel?"

"You bet."

On the boardwalk we were stopped dead in our tracks by a rainbow that arced out of the thunderhead and plummeted away in a triad of red, yellow, and violet behind the snow-dusted ridge that separated us from Virginia City. On the far side of the plaza horses ran tameless across a pasture, their uplifted tails bent by the wind.

"Ain't that the purdiest sight a man can behold?!" Granville cried, his voice puffing against his kerchief, irrepressible with joy. "There's something you cain't turn your back on no how!"

"The Bride of rain . . ." I started to explain that this is what some African tribes call a rainbow, but then fell silent, struck by a connection of ideas triggered by Granville's words.

These past days, in my struggle to turn my back on Musetta, I had taken refuge in a proviso of my own era: that men dare not prevail over women with impunity. In that context my offer of marriage would be patronizing, vaguely demeaning; but in this time, it was the only means by which Klara Asplund might enjoy some dignity, a life beyond drudgery, safe from violence and addiction. That I could command such power in her world was not right, but that did not make it less so. I could not turn my back on her, so I would bury this double-edged gift in trust and affection as soon as it was accepted, and never mention it again as long as we both lived. As much as possible, she would be her own person. And with this promise made, the burden slipped off my shoulders.

"Granville . . ." I began to weep despite my best efforts. "I'm going back inside and sit down."

"Colonel? You all right?"

"I have a note to write to a friend. Do you mind running an errand for me?"

"Hell no!"

I signed a draft on the hitching post and handed it to him. "Take this to the Bank of California branch—let them fill in the amount. I want mint bags of new double eagles."

"How many?"

"Exactly one hundred seventy pounds worth." I consulted my pocket watch. "If we leave Carson by five, can we reach Virginia City by midnight?"

He squinted up into the darkening sky. "If the road don't mud up on us. Can I ask the colonel why he's got to reach the Comstock by then?"

"I must not keep Mrs. Rettie waiting another day."

"Oh . . . you starting to ship your wives out from Utah?"

"No, this will be a new one."

"A *new* one?! Damn but you got cheek!" But then his gaze narrowed. "Does this mean you've decided to stay?"

I nodded yes.

He looked anything but jubilant.

"What's wrong with that, Granville?"

"Well . . . can I still keep the stock?"

An Afterword

FROM *THE VANISHING GEDANKIST*, by Kellogg Norris, with permission of G.P. Putnam's Sons, Yuma, Arizona, Global Copyright 2019:

. . . What Rodrigo Estrada discovered in the saddlebags of that riderless Appaloosa mare remains a mystery, although two pieces of circumstantial evidence offer some hint as to the contents. Within ten days of having returned to Sunnyvale, Estrada, quite plausibly on the basis of a considerable bank transaction, was notified to appear for an Internal Revenue Service special audit, one of several appointments he failed to keep prior to his disappearance on November 16th. And Berkeley Professor Geoffrey Treacher, in the foreword to his *A Harte in Twain*, thanks "R.E. for primary sources beyond value." It might also be presumed that the saddlebags carried a message from Hart to Estrada, a communication that would be of inestimable worth in establishing that the misnamed *Rettie Apocrypha*, taken from the 1915 Panama-Pacific International Exposition time capsule, were genuine eyewitness accounts of early Nevada life and not an ingenious hoax. The assertion that these three packets (allegedly *inserted* into the capsule at some recent time but prior to its accidental unearthing during post-earthquake reconstruction in 2016) are fraudulent, rests entirely on the belief that detonating caps were not in use in Nevada until later than 1862, although there is new evidence that John Ericsson, the Swedish-American designer of the Union ironclad *Monitor*, may have introduced a stable nitroglycerin explosive and mercury fulminate caps seven years before his former student, Alfred Nobel, applied for his patents on dynamite and blasting caps.

Unfortunately, Estrada left no such missive behind in his flat to be dutifully preserved by the police. However, his personal copy of Georgyne Tamberlane's *Golden City Built on Silver: The Comstock Origins of the San Francisco Aristocracy* (1940), found in the bedroom along with his diary, drops tantalizing clues as to what issues, what reflections on time as disparate from present and future, such a message from Hart might have included:

. . . Whereas Hamilcar Cavanaugh was respected as a city father, Belmont Rettie was beloved. And no fete was considered complete unless graced by the lovely and elegant Klara Rettie, the youngest daughter of the jarl of Gotland and niece of the Swedish monarch. Because the gregarious silver baron and his wife tended to be secretive in their philanthrophy, it could only be assumed that their generosity had founded the Franciscan Brothers' Our Lady Clare Orphan Asylum on Russian Hill (Klara, after all, is the Swedish equivalent of Clare; and many swore that none but she could have been the model for the marble of Saint Francis' gentle companion that still graces the institution's vestibule). The Retties, whose conversion to Roman Catholicism was personally blessed by Pope Pius IX on the Italian stopover of their tour to the Holy Land in 1867, politely declined to resolve the question one way or another, as did their frequent houseguest, the archbishop.

However, in later years Rettie defined the limits of his affability by refusing to speak to either Cavanaugh or his handsome wife, the former Eleanor Louise Beauchamp of Virginia City. The Cavanaughs became closemouthed whenever asked to explain their side of the contention that in 1877, severed one of the most successful business alliances in the West. The Retties also refused to shed light on the cause of their devastated relations with the Cavanaughs. Thus, the reasons for the bad blood between the great families remained the property of the antagonists.

That Rettie prospered more than Cavanaugh after the schism is unquestioned. He bought James Flood's Linden Towers in Menlo

Park, an extraordinary mansion whose magnitude and charm can only be imagined—as it was thoughtlessly razed in 1936 by land speculators. His financial and political foresight were so uncanny they eventually attracted the attention of President Arthur, who appointed him railroad commissioner in 1885. His last public appearance was at the Panama-Pacific International Exposition in August of 1915, where, hands trembling with age, he added a portfolio of "historically edifying papers" to a time capsule that will be opened in the year 2015. He died four months later on Christmas Eve, surrounded by orphans from Our Lady Clare's, having attained eighty-nine remarkable years. Klara followed him in death the following autumn, and their ashes were reunited on the waters of Lake Tahoe. . . .

The exhilarating effect of this bit of regional history on Estrada can only be appreciated by recalling his ambiguous standing in his own scientific community. That he was a *gedankist*, or thought experimentalist, was accepted, although reluctantly, by a coterie of theoretical physicists who were all too fond of the anecdote that Einstein had been able to describe the universe on the back of an envelope. Behind his back, Estrada was called Henry, meaning *Henry Ford*; for at Stanford and then at his sundry Silicon Valley employments, it became apparent that Estrada had more interest in mass-producing time phenomena than postulating about them. As Dr. Fratelli suggested to the police, "Rodrigo's obsession struck me as being, well, opportunistic. Don't ask me what he wanted out of it. Acceptance of his ideas meant nothing to him. He had no interest whatsoever in politics, cars, clothes—you name it. But I know he wanted *something*."

The answer to Fratelli's question can be found in the final entry of Estrada's diary, which in light of the forementioned facts and the psychoanalysis of his personality in Chapter 2, cannot be explained away as the preface to a suicide pact he made with his former wife, Marguerite Pico, and then carried out at some remote location yet undiscovered, as the police concluded.

Phoned M. tonight. Told her H, is forever well—and loved at last in the way he needed. Mentioned how money had begun to worry me again, but that he left me enough to do my own work full-time. Then it gushed out of me. Everything. The earliest fears that something monstrous would take over if I ever caved in to joy. Shocked her so badly she couldn't speak for several mins. Crying,

I think. Asked her if she would go with me. Where, she had to know. To confront the ghosts who are keeping us apart. I needed her help to do this. I was afraid to go alone. Her answer: Yes, Mother of God, yes. I explained that it wouldn't be easy on either of us. Could prove dangerous or futile or both. Ibid on her reply, but with more tears. Tomorrow then. At last, after years, I am drowsy. The night promises peace. I shall be fulfilled—in God's good time.

MORE SCIENCE FICTION ADVENTURE!

BESTSELLING
Science Fiction
and
Fantasy